FAIR COMPANY

By the Same Author

FULL FLAVOUR

Fair Company

By
Doris Leslie

New York
The Macmillan Company
1936

Copyright, 1936, by
D O R I S   L E S L I E.

All rights reserved—no part of this book
may be reproduced in any form without
permission in writing from the publisher,
except by a reviewer who wishes to quote brief
passages in connection with a review written
for inclusion in magazine or newspaper.

First Printing.

PRINTED IN THE UNITED STATES OF AMERICA
BY THE STRATFORD PRESS, INC., NEW YORK

823.912
L56f

Feb. 1932

141199

To

Harold S. Latham

AUTHOR'S NOTE

THIS NOVEL, in which I have attempted to describe the social and political changes and development in England during a hundred and thirty years, has naturally necessitated much research in order to obtain an accuracy of fact to aid my fiction. To those authors, therefore, of the past and present, whose works have been of invaluable assistance, I herewith render my deep appreciation and most grateful thanks:

To G. M. Trevelyan for his "British History in the Nineteenth Century"; to E. Beresford Chancellor for his "Life in Regency and Early Victorian Times"; to Captain Gronow (1810–1860) for his "Reminiscences"; to Holbrook Jackson for his "Eighteen Nineties"; to John Gore for "Creevey's Life & Times"; to the proprietors of *Punch;* and to Trevor Blakemore, poet, for his vivid verbal recollections of the pre-war period.

I wish also to emphasise that although I have introduced certain historical personalities and incidents to decorate the background, all characters, letters and excerpts from diaries mentioned in this book are entirely fictitious, and as far as I am aware no parallel can be traced to any living person, nor to any firm of publishers extant.

DORIS LESLIE.

INTRODUCTION
(1933)

I HAVE been told I have a year to live, or to be precise ten months, for it was in June that I received my sentence. So, if I last out my ten months' grace, I shall have had sixty-four years of life. I've lived. And when I die, I shall die without regret and with, I can safely say, an easy conscience. I am no sentimentalist about the change that is called death. At its best it may really be the great Adventure, and at its worst, no worse than sleep.

However, this that I intend to write, although no writer, is not about myself. I am just a little weary of myself. Lying here and following that fellow's grave insistence upon 'rest'—a superfluous precaution, it would seem, since soon I shall be resting through eternity—I have had time enough to think upon myself, and the topic is unfruitful—in more senses than one; for I leave behind no issue, to my knowledge, and die as I have lived, unwed. But once I loved a woman. That, though, is another story, and my own.

Be it understood then, that my appearance in these pages is subsidiary. I am here merely as *compère,* to ring up the curtain on the changes of the scene; to tell, in so far as I have knowledge of what has gone before, the story of these women of my house, to whom, in the shape of Laurencina who follows me hereafter, I bequeath my heritage.

A very comely shape, so I infer, who see it even now reclining here beneath my window in the sun and a state of semi-nudity,

3

clad only in what seems to be a handkerchief. When I venture to suggest that such brevity of costume were more fitted for the footlights of the Moulin Rouge—as I remember it—than the garden of Wroth House, she tells me that I'm 'stuffy.' She says that what I need is an intensive course of 'psyching'—whatever that may mean. She studies all these Freudians and can discuss the ethics of sexology *ad nauseam*. They all do of her age and generation. Are they the worse for it, I wonder, or the better? Too wise in their unwisdom. They know so much—and yet—they know so little!

She then, my Laurencina, is the fifth woman of Wroth House, and God knows what she and that young man of hers will make of it. I'd like to see a male heir installed before I go, and she informed me only yesterday that she intended to 'produce' but added that she would not marry Robin till she'd 'lived' with him. Is this bravado, common-sense, or mere vulgarity? I confess I'm all at sea. I cannot cope with her. She is far beyond me, and all that I had clung to as 'Tradition.' Are they degenerate or regenerate, these youngsters? Only the future race can answer, the race as yet unborn.

My brother Laurence was her father, killed at Neuve-Chapelle. His young wife followed not long after, a victim to the influenza epidemic of '18. They left me Laurencina, then aged three.

Women are predominant at Wroth. Almost one can hear the rustle of their petticoats, the whisper of their sandals on the floor. Or perhaps I like to think so. I know them all; I've learned to know them all from the lives they've left behind them in their letters, diaries, journals—how they wrote! And how damned well they wrote—in those days before the penny-post, when letter writing was a luxury and a form of self-indulgence exploited only by the idle rich. I have learned much from exploration of these fragmentary tokens found in disused chests, in attics, in odd places hereabouts. In particular the diary of one Lady Pinkerton, ex-actress and contemporary of Siddons—she who is no Wrotham but who sponsored one—and from whose lively journal I will serve excerpts.

The Pinkertons have gone. They are extinct. He comes to life in the pages of her journal as a blustering dotard, senile, effete, of no use to himself, his wife, or his descendants.

He had a daughter by his first wife, Anne. She who in 1785 died of the smallpox. Their child Harriet, at sixteen, was first seduced by and then married to Glyn Wrotham, who bought for her Wroth House, and proceeded there forthwith to break her spirit. It didn't take him long.

There are no records here to probe the secrets of that marriage. Nothing to tell, save what one may imagine of a child's suffer-ings, pitifully young, helpless and bewildered by the vagaries of a sadistic brute, and none but a besotted father to turn to for pro-tection. Much he gave her! It is said he sold her to Glyn Wrotham in part payment of a sum lost to him at faro. One can believe it in that age of turbulence, unrest. The century was dying, and the world was tortured with the labour pains of birth, the birth of a new era. Across that strip of water that divided us from France before air-transit joined us to the mainland, the air itself was blood-stained. Europe trembled at the Terror; a dynasty had fallen, and in Corsica a man was marking time.

One knows little of this girl of Pinkerton's. There is a minia-ture that shows her lovely. She escaped that marriage soon enough, in childbirth, and left Glyn Wrotham twins. A boy and girl; the boy for whom they named me, Prior. And Sabrina.

Pinkerton's place, Cheam Royal, marched with ours. Not three miles distant on its site stands one of those road-houses called 'The Yellow Frog.' One of those places with a swimming pool, a dance hall, a jazz-band, and frequented by a motley company in cars.

From my window as I write, I can see the grey ribbon of the by-pass road boring like a tapeworm through fields that once lay all untouched. I can remember—I've lived long enough for that —when on the summit of Cheam Hill I saw the beacons lit for the Queen's first Jubilee. I can remember further still. And that which I cannot remember I will record as faithfully as I can reconstruct, although I say again, I am no writer. What I do now I do partly for my pleasure, to while away these last few months; and partly, too, because I wish to hand to Laurencina the story of our women as I heard it from my sister Charlotte, and from Sabrina, who is first of them. She who lasted out a century or thereupon. So long she lived.

And because life is slipping from me I feel I want to hold it for all time, to imprison in these pages something of the spirit of a nation that has survived a world catastrophe and the weight of a world's penalties. The spirit that survived a Waterloo, and lives on unchanged, although perhaps enfeebled; and which will survive today as in the past, and maybe in the future, whatever yet may threaten to destroy it.

PRIOR J. WROTHAM.

BOOK ONE

SABRINA
Born 1796   *Died* 1891

Chapter One

I

ON JANUARY 23rd in the year 1806 Jess Barrett married Pinkerton. It was the same year and day that marked the death of Pitt, and troublous times for England. Notwithstanding that so recently at Austerlitz Napoleon had struck his giant-blow and doomed the peace of Europe for ten years, Jess Barrett's world—a world which lay between St. James's Street and Drury Lane—was too far removed from that unknown Moravia to make of much account a distant battle, or to heed the trumpet-call of a new conqueror.

It was wise of Jess at forty when she found her charms were waning, to replace her slightly faded laurels with a coronet, and, lawfully protected by her lord on whose bounty she had battened for ten years, to retire from the limelight with as good a grace as she could muster.

He was seventy and dropsical, so fat that he could scarcely see his feet. His jowl hung loose and flabby. He cared no jot about his clothes, cared for nothing but his drink, his food, his women. Jess had marked him as her quarry from the first, unless she might have found another more attractive to her taste with just as good a rent-roll and ancestry.

She could, however, act the part of a devoted wife as excellently off the stage as on it. She played the countess to perfection. Pinkerton had the better of that marriage. Even a coronet, a position in society, the laugh of all her dearest friends and a

9

mansion in Mayfair, could scarcely compensate for Pinkerton. Or so her dearest friends avowed, who spread reports of the most spicy nature; who said she had been forced into retirement from Drury Lane because she made her dressing-room a bawdy-house; said it was she who had given old Pinkerton his illness; said she drank, was vulgar, was the bastard daughter of a circus clown; this last as nearly true as rumour can be.

She was the result of an early indiscretion between a young lady of high rank and a small-part actor of no name at all in Garrick's company. The actor's wife, poor woman, childless, barren, took the unwanted thing and mothered it.

Jess was weaned behind the footlights and made her début at the Lane when she was twelve, at the same time as Siddons' first appearance there as Portia.

She was never a great actress, but she was a homely soul with a great heart and greater bosom. It may have been her rapidly increasing weight that decided her to leave the stage for:

"The new gowns," her journal tells us, "are so flimsy and so strait as to be worn only by a child. How shall I play a Virgin of eighteen with a Bust that measures Fourty and the waist lifted half a dozen inches from its rightful place?" Further we hear:

"I have made me a good Compound for thinning down the Figure recommended by Old Lizzie [her dresser, could this be, at Drury Lane?] who had it from Mary Robinson herself. Take a pint of distilled Water of Green Pine apples likewise the same quantity of Orange Water 1 dram [*sic*] of Borax the juice of 14 to 16 leaves of the dried Senna boyled and left to chill. I shall offer it to Pinkerton, though I doubt if aught will flatten out his Paunch. I go in Terror lest he die of a Seizure when he is to Bed with me, and to keep him from Temptation I . . ."

The remainder of this entry is superfluous.

She took him out of London—not too far out. Cheam Royal

would today have been little more than an hour's run from Marble Arch. The mail-coach took three to four from Tyburn.

She played her part as dutifully as she knew how, and how it must have bored her! She doctored him and purged him (with the concoction of green pineapples and senna?) and drove with him to take the air in a post chariot painted to her taste in purple with a lining of blue cloth, a 'bouge' behind, three lamps in front and panels varnished a rich yellow. Such a performance as never was to hoist him! His man at the rear pushing him up, my Lady pulling him in, she squeezed narrow as the size of her permitted, in her corner, and my Lord damning to hell his valet, his queasy stomach, and his wife.

She had him down there at Cheam Royal a full fortnight before she fell foul of the twins. She knew of the existence of the twins, knew that Pinkerton possessed a grandson but no heir, and that is all she did know of them. Children, she regarded as a nuisance, best kept in their place, which was not with her, or so she had decided, until ennui and perhaps something more inclined her to the part she was to play.

She had met Wrotham once in London at a masquerade given at Vauxhall in honour of the birthday of the King, in which he —Wrotham—appeared as Mephistopheles, and she as Diana. Her journal tells us she amused herself. Also at Brighton at the house of Mrs. Fitzherbert (this after Jess Barrett had been raised to rank of peeress), she renewed acquaintance with him and records it thus:

"Sheridan was there, Warren Hastings and the Creeveys. She gives herself Great Airs since she has been admitted to the confidence of Mrs F—tz—t. She has no *'ton'* [which it appears that Lady Pinkerton is rapidly acquiring], and was dressed most unbecomingly in Yellow which ill-matched her Complexion. Creevey was discussing the proposed raising of the Property Tax to 10 per cent. He seemed violently opposed to it and said that it will make the Devil of an outcry in the Country. I was placed next to Wrotham who in Full Dress looks more like the Devil than when disguised as him. He feigned Ignorance of any former Introduction thinking no doubt 'twere wiser to forget it in such Circumstances and Surroundings. He is a dangerous Brute, but Lord! how he is Fascinating! His dark hair sparsely powdered— though they do say powder is out of Fashion now—and teeth as white as Almonds. He hath as fine a pair of eyes as I have seen on any man, coloured like watered Ink, not blue, not black, but something 'twixt both. It was a joy to see his Legs after too much sight of Pinkerton's. An excellent good Calf he has indeed. Almost as great a Beau as Brummell but his manner is moody, supercilious and affected, with a mouth most viperish cruel. It is said he killed his wife with his Brutalities, that Women are mad for him and that even Mrs F—tz hath cast an eye in his direction. But Pinkie swears his latest Conquest is with Lady J—rs—y. From my Lord I hear also that Wroth House is a Seraglio of Beauty, when he is moved to entertain there, which he does Handsomely. At all other times the place is a Shambles, servantless, or nearly so, and those poor children left to their own devices which I'll warrent, if they be true Wrotham breed, will be to not much Good."

And later, this:

"February 27th, 1806.

"Such a day as never was! My Lord hath a Migraine, and rages like the Deuce. He vows I gave him too much Physick. Mrs Elliot came to me with a long face and longer tale of the stillroom maid who is, she says, with Child by a cow-man. Have they no sense these Wenches that they so ill-manage their Affairs? They get together under a hedge and leave all else to God. It is a monstrous Worry. I cannot turn the fool adrift and will have to send her to old Lizzie when her time comes, for she has I hear no Parents. Then these Brats of Wrotham's. I drove over there to see them. It is a low, solid-built white house standing in some goodly Acres and well wooded, but shamefully neglected, the Curtains dirty and the Drive all weeds.

"Wrotham is in London where I would to Heaven I were! An ancient sour-visaged man opened me the door in livery that would disgrace a Tinker. I asked to see the Twins and was told they were at lessons with the Vicar, Mr Seeley. So Wrotham cares that much to have them tutored three days in the week. For the rest they run as wild as the Gipsies. I left word that they should come to Dinner and ordered a Capon, Mutton-pye and Syllabub. They arrived late. Pinkerton was raving and I never in my life beheld a couple of worse Mudlarks than they looked. Their cloaths are Beggarly, their hair so matted that I was for fetching a fine tooth-comb to curry them before we sat to Table.

"A handsome pair for all that. The boy smaller than the girl, a pale elfin child with the most innocent of looks and the air already of a Cavalier. *She* is a Demon and would be a Beauty were she washed. Brown as a Berry with a skin beneath the tan like milk, hair with some gold dust in it, those Devil's eyes of Wrotham's which will be most Devastating in a woman, and a mouth as red as though it had been painted. They sat as mum as mice, eating quite prettily, speaking only when addressed and gentle-toned until they started fighting. And this over some Sign or other that must have passed between them for not a word was spoke, when she ups and clouts him one across the ear that turned it blue. And this at Table under the noses of the Footmen. He at her then like a small Fury—the candles overturned, my new vase broke, the dogs set barking and Pinkerton roaring out to stop them like a bull gone mad. Such a To-do as gave me Palpitations.

Sabrina with a cut lip from that young Prior's fists, blood on the damask, and my Famille Verte in pieces.

"My Lord gave them first a Hiding for it, and then a Crown Piece each for not crying when he beat them. I sent them home in the Barouche, am still in a flutter, and have twice vomited from Shock. A first night at the Lane was less exhausting.

"*Mem.* Before they come again I must supervise their Wardrobe, and see to it that their heads are cleaned. . . ."

II

To be driven home in a grand carriage all shining paint and silver harness was Adventure.

Sabrina sat up primly, knees together, toes pointed in the First Position, hands folded in her lap. She bowed this way and that to the stunted shapes of thorn-bush in the hedges, glimpsed through the carriage windows as the lamps lighted them in passing. She was a King's daughter, and was dressed in ermine and a velvet gown. All the people cheered as she drove by. There was an ox roasted whole, and feasting in the market-place, for she was to marry the Prince of Wales. Not the present Prince of Wales, he was too fat. Almost as fat as Grandpapa. She had seen a picture of him once, and nothing like a prince was he. No! The prince *she* was to marry had hair as yellow as a field of mustard, had eyes like bluest glass and a fine Manly Bearing. He would wear a suit of mail. He had fought a Dragon, a fire-breathing Dragon with long claws.

"Are there truly dragons?" she asked Prior.

"No, you flumpetty fool, there aren't. There never were and never will be. My ear still hurts." He rubbed it.

"What's flumpetty?"

"It's a word," said Prior carelessly, "that I made up. It means two things. It means flump—to be a flumpet. That is to say to

be a person who is simple in the head, a half-wit like yourself—
and petty as like petticoats— Ouch! You would, would you?
Hell-hound Bitch!"

They were at it again pummelling each other, she making the
best use of her nails.

"Only cats fight scratching," panted Prior, grabbing at her
wrists; for all his smallness he was the stronger of the two. "Now
leave me be or I'll be sick on you. That syllabub is heaving."

The threat sufficed to make her stop her clawing, and they settled down in amity for the remainder of the drive, she with a
palmful of sugar almonds to be halved in equal portions, stolen
from the table at Grandfather's.

"What made you hit me, though?" asked Prior, scrunching.
"These are good. How did you manage to get them? I tried to,
but those men in yellow plush were staring."

"I got them while we fought—when the vase broke and she
was making all that fuss about it. I got another thing as well."
Sabrina eyed him sideways, half mischievous, half doubting to
see how he would take it. "A thing that smells. I found it in her
bedroom. Look." She dived a hand into her pocket and produced
a vinaigrette in silver, jewelled with amethysts and fine turquoise.
She bade him hold it to his nose. "It smells like Christmas pudding when the spices are put in."

"But that's stealing," Prior told her while he sniffed. "And
you'll be hanged for it."

"No!" Sabrina paled, clutching at his arm. "I won't! No, Prior!
Will I? Not if I give it back, I won't. It was so pretty. I never
had a pretty thing before." A new idea leapt up and scattered
the moment's panic. "I know. We'll have a hanging when we
get home. We'll hang Jemima. We haven't had a hanging for a
long time. Let's, Prior, shall we?"

"I don't play at hanging dolls. That's babies' games. Hi! Don't pinch! I've had enough of it—I'm black and blue. What will you buy with your money? I shall buy a book."

"I'll buy— Look! There's a coach outside our door. Can it be Wrotham back again?"

Prior thrust head and shoulders through the window to peer up the bending drive.

"The Deuce it is!" returned he gloomily. "Who else would it be? Dang him!"

The carriage came to a halt before the steps. The children were out and up them before the footman had descended from his seat. There was an air of bustle and excitement; a handing out and carrying of bandboxes, and of more unwieldy luggage. One of the men from the stables led away two saddle horses. In the hall, lit by fire and candlelight, their father, spurred and booted, stood in his caped riding-coat, straddling the hearth. Two gentlemen were with him, and a lady.

Shadows danced on the oak panelling, on antlered heads and pictures on the walls, and hid the dust that lay like a fine gauze on wood and gilt and marble. The lady stood in shadow, too.

Their father, who seemed in high good humour, came forward with a hand to each.

"Well, my chucks!" He kissed Sabrina's mouth, and smelled of brandy. "Come here and be acquainted. My son, my daughter . . ."

The only name Sabrina heard was Mrs. Burnaby. She was all eyes for her—so fine a lady never seen before. She wore a dress of white mull-muslin, and over it a pelerine of purple velvet edged with sable fur. Long ends of yellow ribbon tied her poke bonnet. She had yellow gloves and little scarlet slippers.

One of the gentlemen, very elegant in a suit of bottle-green, was taking snuff from a gold box and offered Prior's nose a pinch and made him sneeze.

The lady, smiling, stooped to him; the candlelight was on her face. Her hair was gold against her pinkish cheeks; her mouth scarlet as her shoes, and all about her was a smell of musk.

"Why, what pets, Wrotham!" Her voice was high-toned, drawling, very sweet. "Although they don't look much alike for twins. You could never play Sebastian to her Viola, my little man." She laid a small gloved hand on Prior's hair. "But I don't suppose you read your Shakespeare yet."

"Yes, I do." His lashes lifted in a quick upward look. "But I read Milton most. I like 'Paradise Regained.'"

"Do you indeed? So do we all!" laughed the lady, and the gentlemen laughed very loudly, too. Prior reddened to his ears, and jerked his head out of the lady's touch.

"I'm named for a person from Milton, Mr. Seeley says," Sabrina put in, glowering. She could not bear that they should laugh at Prior; she must have her share if they would tease him. Nor had anyone the right to tease him but herself. Fiercely she loved him, and hated the whole company—hated, suddenly, the lady most of all.

"Sabrina fair, listen where thou art sitting, under the thing-ummy-bob translucent wave," trilled out the lady. "But good heavens, Wrotham, what a learned pair! They overwhelm me." She moved away with her fingers to her curls under her velvet bonnet, her eyes astray for her reflection in the mirror on the wall.

"A very dirty pair!"

Wrotham's lips stretched tight across his teeth in the smile that Sabrina knew and dreaded—it boded usually a beating.

"I must apologise for my two cubs. They run amuck when I'm away." He rounded sharply on Sabrina where she stood, chin raised and eyes defiant, and none but she and Prior saw his changed threatening face.

"Go to your room," he whispered, "and don't dare to leave it. I'll give you hell for this—disgracing me. You stink of the stable."

"We've been to Grandpapa's," Sabrina piped, though quaking.

"Not in those clothes, I trust." Their father's face relented in one of those sudden twists of mood that were his daughter's, too. "Go! Run along upstairs and get you washed. Be off with you!"

They went.

In the large attic which did service as their nursery, barren of all comfort, and filled with such lumber as could there be stored, they were met by Hannah—she who had tended them from birth, but who in consequence of a slight weakness for the bottle had not been overstrict in her survey. She bathed them once a week, saw to it that their clothes were mended when she thought to, and had given them the only love they'd ever known.

"Such wickedness!" wheezed Hannah. She was old and stout and ugly, with a red pimpled face. "To go visitin' milord in them old rags. I'd laid out your best clothes and scoured the grounds to find you, but you'd gone. What'll milady think of you, God knows! And me, too, for sendin' you to Cheam lookin' like gallows-meat. And the house here full of company and no warnin' from the master to say that he was comin'. He's brought baskets of food along of 'im and not a soul to cook it—excep' me. An' if he thinks that I can do the work of twenty 'ands, then he's mistook, for I can*not* and won't. Did ye come in the back way?"

"No, by the hall—and Wrotham introduced us," Sabrina told her grandly. "One of them's a very pretty lady."

"Ay! Trust him for that," was Hannah's dark rejoinder. "And what will she think you are—your hands—your hair! God's sakes! What have I done to be plagued with two such Satan's imps? Go quick and clean yourselves. The bath is all put ready. Go on now. Must I tell you twice? You, Prior, first, and Sabby can have hers after you. She's dirtiest."

"I want my supper," Prior said. "I'm hungry."

"Bread and water's all the supper that *you'll* get, my lad, and a good hidin' by way of flavour. Be off now, do you hear me?"

Prior wrinkled up his nose and sniffed.

"Pouf! You smell of Hollands, Hannah!"

"Oh, do I! I'll clout your ears for sayin' so—ye devil!" screamed Hannah in a rage, her hand lifted to do it.

Prior dodged. "Indeed you won't! My ear's had all it's going to have today—it's burning still. Come, Hannah—don't be cross." He slid his arms around her waist to hug her. "We're sorry, aren't we, Sab? Can we have currant bread for supper and a glass of cowslip wine? Can we? *Dear* Hannah."

He could coax the heart out of a stone; he had that way with him. Sabrina had not his knack, nor on her lips the art of cajolery; so always where she loved most was she the more restrained. Yet she could love, and deeply.

She stood still and watched this byplay with glum eyes, her red mouth twisted in its crooked smile that held a hint of mockery and of something wistful, too. A hole burned in her pocket —or so she felt. That silver thing! What had made her take it? It must have been the Devil tempting her. Stealing! Thou shalt not—which commandment was it? But—something to have all of one's very own. Something pretty like fine ladies play with. Something belonging just to her—to no one else. Not even Prior. It must be given back or she'd be hanged if they found out—or at the least put in the stocks. She shivered standing there on one foot like a stork, the other rubbing at her ankle, a thoughtful finger to her lip.

"Now then, my lady!" Hannah barked at her. "Will you stand gaping there all night? You get yourself undressed."

"Hannah," Sabrina said, "suppose a person stole a thing—what happens?"

"Stole? What thing?" Hannah's mouth fell open. "Lord's mercy! Don't tell me you've been stealing."

"No! Never!" The lie leapt to her lips before she had time to stop it. Another sin to be accounted for if God were listening.

"I only thought—'cos Prior said—no, Mr. Seeley said," she stammered, floundering, "that it was monstrous wrong to hang a man for stealing money to buy bread when he was hungry. If they'd hang a man for stealing just a *little* money, they might hang a person for—for—anything, maybe."

"Maybe they would," retorted Hannah grimly. "And for plaguing me, like as not. You'll both end on the gibbet, I shouldn't wonder, and then you'll fry and frizzle down below. Yes, you will, unless you say your prayers and sit good and quiet at your books, and mind me when I tell you. Now off to bed. I'll bring the bath in to you. You'll need another bucketful to get you clean."

No comfort there. Sabrina slunk away filled with remorse and the best of resolutions. She would give back the silver thing to-night. This very night. She would write a letter to Grandpapa's new lady asking for forgiveness. Yes, indeed that must be done, and quickly. She would take the letter and the silver thing herself to Cheam and give it to the lady. She would ride over on Butterfly, and Prior would come, too, on Lightning. And on the way back they would play highwayman. That would be the grandest game!

She could hardly eat her supper for excitement, longing to tell Prior of her plan, but dared not till Hannah was out of sight and hearing.

When she undressed she slipped the silver toy beneath her pillow. Not till both were scrubbed and in clean shifts, sitting up in their small curtained beds eating currant bread and quince preserve—for Hannah had relented—with a sip each of cowslip wine to wash it down, did she propound her scheme to Prior. He was more inclined for sleep than for adventure.

"You can give it back to her tomorrow. Why tonight?"

"If you won't come I'll go alone," she said.

"But we can't," Prior demurred, "until they're all abed. And they'll stay late down there drinking and that. Best wait till morning. He'll see us go and stop us, anyway."

"You're a coward, then!" she flashed, "to be so scared of Wrotham."

"Damn you to hell—I'm not!" He aimed a crust at her. It hit her on the nose. She was out of bed and at him in a trice. Seizing his pillow she pressed it on his head and sat on it. "I'll smother you unless you say you'll come!"

He squirmed and squealed and giggled, for she was tickling him in vital parts, till, wearied of the game, she let him be.

Hannah came bustling in to take away the light, rated them roundly for the racket and tucked them up in bed with a sound kiss for each.

"Good-night, my bonnies. Say your prayers and ask the good God to forgive you for your naughtiness lest Something Bad come down the chimney to carry you off."

Unperturbed by this dark warning, Prior was asleep almost before the door had closed on her.

Sabrina lay wide-eyed and wakeful, staring at the window where a shaft of moonlight fell across the floor. A tree-top tossed and nodded in the window pane and through it one star winked, caught in the bare tree-branches. The wind moaned sadly in the chimney. Only Something Bad could moan like that. Her flesh went chill. She cuddled in the blankets and envied Prior's sleep.

For hours it seemed she lay there, turning, twisting, shutting tight her eyes, to see behind their burning lids a galaxy of fireworks, of sparkling pin-points that advanced, retreated, spun

and dazzled her. And hot she felt—and cold! And tried to say
the Lord's Prayer, but the right words would not come. All she
could think of was the letter that must, must, *must* be written.
. . . From below came the sound of revelry, of men's laughter,
and the tinkling flutelike treble of a woman's.

Presently she dozed and must have slept, for when she dreamed
that she was falling through a cloud, and woke with a great
bump, her heart pounding in her chest, the moonlight on the
floor had shifted and lay on Prior's bed. In the window-pane that
one star caught in the tossing tree-top was larger and more clear,
and the moon's face stared down at her askew and grinning.

All was quiet now, and very late it must be with the moon so
high.

Noiselessly she crept from bed. Should she waken Prior? He
lay so still, so pale in the moonlight, she thought in a great sudden fear that he was dead, and went to him, leaned over, heard
him breathe, and herself breathed again. Well, she would not
wake him. She would go to Cheam alone. She would put on
Prior's clothes and ride Butterfly cross-saddle. There was more
charm perhaps in solitary venture.

Tiptoe and very quiet she proceeded then to dress, taking her
brother's trews, his soiled small frilled shirt, his jacket—a trifle
narrow in the chest for her. She slipped what she had stolen into
her pocket, and a pretty boy she looked when she had done. Prior
slept on.

The long corridor below was dark; no sound except the wind,
no light except the moon, and that came sliding through the latticed window on the staircase to make a pool upon the polished
floor for all the world as though white blood had spilled there.
Moon's blood—a horrid thought.

She would go down the servants' staircase, so to the stables—
she would have to climb the wall if the gate were not unfastened

—and with a hand upon the green baize door that led to lower regions, she remembered that the letter was not yet written. That must be done at once. Note-paper. A pen. Where should she find them? In Wrotham's study. Quick!

The carpet was like moss beneath her feet. Softly she sped back again along the way that she had come, paused at a door, ajar; went in. No light again, but the moonshine through three windows gave enough. How still the house! How late—it must be one. A clock struck two. It was later than she thought. She had never been awake so late before.

Then through the silence came to her a sound, the smallest sound as of a whimper, half a moan. . . . Her father's study joined another room divided by a door between. The room in which her mother, so Hannah said, had died. . . . Her heart beat fast, and faster. What was it? A whispering voice, and again, that stifled murmur. She began to shake. Was it the Something Bad threatened by Hannah, come to haunt her? Was it her mother's ghost? the mother she had never known, and seldom heard of? It couldn't be. No mother's ghost was bad. She crossed her fingers. Crossing fingers drove away the Devil. . . . Silence again. But a silence now that seemed to speak.

All the corners of the room were black with shadows. Shadowy faces peered at her from the walls, but they were only pictures. That old man in a ruff, he was a good old man, that Wrotham. He had fought with Drake in the Armada when England beat the Spanish. He would not harm her, for all he looked so pale in the moonlight, and as though his eyes were following her when she moved with a scared glance across her shoulder, to the desk that stood under the middle window. She licked her lips and swallowed. Pooh! A picture. Just a painted face—but another backward glance told her that certainly his eyes were chasing her, and all that she did now was closely watched. She knew that she was terribly afraid and, although she wished with all her heart that she were safely back in bed, her sense of duty warred against indulgence. Always—all her life it would be so.

There was by great good chance note-paper ready there. The inkpot with its cover off, the pen conveniently placed. So, seated at her father's desk and scared out of her wits, all ears for sounds that had no right to be, with infinite labour and the moon for lamp, she managed this:

> "Wroth,
> "Wensday morning,
> "Two o'clock. a.m.

"Dear Madam *

"I appoligize for the misteaking of your Propperty which I am going to put in the Letter Box at Cheam with this Letter for I can not sleep untill I have returned it I can not be hanged if I give it back I have never took a Thing what is not mine before. This is not Monney for which you get Hanged for taking & I only took it because it was pritty. Pray forgive me Madam and exsuse the Blot

> "Beleiving me yr
> humbel
> sarvent
> "Sabrina Harriet Wrotham.

"Post-scrip. Also some Suger armonds from the Table but those we have eat so can not give back. Prior did not take Any Thing."

She finished it, folded it, and was prepared to go when something stayed her. That sound again! A softest, sighing moan and then the sound as of two whispers mingled.

* This, which eventually reached its destination though at the time delayed in consequence of subsequent events, was pasted in Lady Pinkerton's journal, from which I copy it verbatim.—P. J. W.

Her eyes strayed to the door that divided the two rooms. They were behind that door, those sounds, and instinct told her they were human sounds. Her heart narrowed, and now her fear was not of the unnatural but of something else. Something indescribable and fugitive, something that held her rooted to the spot, her lips apart, her breath a little hurried, ears strained to hear again the muted murmur of a voice that, scarcely heard, was yet—she knew—her father's.

Then while she stood there in a moonbeam, eyes wide, nostrils aquiver, and all her slight small body turned to stone, the door that she had left ajar was opened wide, and a man's shape appeared. He held aloft a candle and she saw his face, flushed with late wine, the tassel of his nightcap bobbing on his nose, his dressing gown clutched round him, his naked legs below it. A tall thin stooping man who peered beneath the candlelight like some gigantic bird. And for all that his appearance was ridiculous it was at the same time reassuring. This was no ghost, no Devil. This gentleman she recognised. He was one of those who had accompanied her father, not he who had offered Prior snuff, but the other, whose laugh—as she remembered—was like the clucking of a hen when it is laying. At once all her fears fled. Here was a guest within her father's house, and she her father's daughter.

Undisciplined and untamed though they were, those twins, they had the instincts of good breeding. Politeness now prevailed and, divining as she supposed his need, she had no thought but to help him.

"Were you looking for the closet?" asked Sabrina. "It's the first door at the end."

"God damme!" cried the gentleman, and dropped his candle on the floor.

Sabrina darted forward to retrieve it. "Here it is. And not gone out. Did I frighten you?"

"You did, you little devil," he told her, staring. "Why are you not in bed?"

"I had a thing to do—I had to do." The candle showed her to him in her brother's clothes, an elfish boy.

"The queerest house," he grumbled, "that ever I was in. Do you always take these midnight prowls?"

"Not always. Never," she added in a burst of honesty, "before."

"I have a boy," he said, "about your age. No—older, I think. He's round about fourteen. And he's at school at Eton, and that's where you should be."

"I—" Sabrina was beginning, and then stopped. She grasped the situation, found it droll and giggled. Here was a joke indeed!

"My father went to Eton. P'r'aps I'll go one day. Shall I know your boy there?"

The gentleman made no answer. Rocking a little where he stood—he seemed unsteady on his feet—his eyes had turned towards the door whence those strange sounds had come, all silent once again, like death.

"Here, you!" He took her shoulder in a grip that hurt and wheeled her round. "Did you hear—see—anyone go in that room?"

Her heart began to reassert itself with a cold nameless dread, but she spoke up warily.

"I saw—no one."

He glanced at her, his bony fingers clutching at her arm. "Well, I did. An hour since. And by God! I'll surprise them."

In three strides he was across the room, and had flung open the door, the candle raised above his head and all beyond in shadow.

There followed a confusion.

Sabrina, cowering, saw nothing, for her eyes were closed, her hands pressed to them in a panic. But of what she was afraid she could not tell.

She heard a woman scream, and something heavy fall, accompanied by the crash of broken glass, as though a table had been overturned; heard voices raised, her father's expostulatory, suave, and very calm, but by his tone she guessed his wolfish smile, and her flesh shivered. Then words uttered on a high cracking note: "Caught in the act, you —— whore! You —— filthy slut!"

She knew them for bad words but was not shocked. She had heard such used among the stablemen too often. And then:

"The laws of hospitality carried to the full in your own house, Wrotham—eh? Christ damn you! But you'll answer for it!"

The sound of a blow on flesh with a flat hand, and through the dreadful sobbing of the woman, her father's voice unhurried, very clear.

"We will settle this tomorrow, Burnaby. No, today. It is already morning. Can you find your room? Your candle has gone out—permit me."

The child, trembling in the darkness, crept away. Her letter was forgotten; it lay where she had left it. Unseen, she fled to the safety of her attic and of her sleeping brother, upon whose bed she laid herself, curled close to him for comfort. And there, exhausted, and still dressed in all his clothes, Sabrina slept.

III

The result of that night's doings made some noise in London clubs for a considerable time. The death of Major Burnaby mortally wounded in the lung by his opponent's ball was received with loudest indignation, and rumour was rife about the name of Wrotham. The cause of the duel was not far to seek. Wrotham had made too free of his guest's wife under his own roof, and Burnaby was out for blood. He got more than he had bargained for, poor devil.

His position delicate—there was talk of an enquiry—Wrotham lost no time in quitting England and possible detention at all speed. The affair had leaked as far as Carlton House. The Prince was disapproving. Burnaby had been in Royal favour: also, it seems, the lady.

Jess Barrett gives us further insight to the matter in her diary of March 3rd:

"We have had enough excitement in the neighbourhood to compensate me for the Doldrums of last month. That poor, *poor* Burnaby! Although the greatest Simpleton I always thought him and blind as a Mole over the Peccadilloes of that dolled up Wife of his. To bring her here to Wroth was a case, I think, of Reckoning without his Host. My Lady J—rs—y's Bubble looks like to Burst. And *what* a *Scandale* to have happen at our doors. I had it all from Percy Dallas who was staying in the house and was Burnaby's Second. Joddrell, sent for Post-haste to Barnet in the morning, supported Wrotham. Dallas said that Burnaby, poor Brute, was choke-full of cold Punch as Stand-me-By and had been overcharged the night before. Wrotham's head is as hard as his heart and nothing raddles him. I saw him with my own eyes at Vauxhall put down enough to lay out a Regiment.

"Burnaby won the toss and fired first, but missed. His ball grazed Wrotham's shoulder. Dallas swears that Wrotham meant to kill him. There will be the Devil to pay for this. Wrotham has left the Country which is made too hot for him, but where he has hid himself none knows unless it be the Lady. I would not be in *her* shoes for all the Money in the Mint nor all the Royal Graces.

"In the meantime I am concerned with the Fate of those Poor Brats. I did not bargain for the pair of them when I took over Pinkie. . . ."

And thus it came about that the future of Sabrina was decided, devolving as is the way of life upon the turn of accident.

Their father gone, Wroth House left in charge of stable-boys, a doddering manservant, and Hannah, was no place in Jess Barrett's estimation for the descendants of her lord. Not that he had much say in the matter. Given all that he could drink, more than he could eat, and access to his wife's chamber, he allowed her a free rein. The twins had never been of great account with him. The boy was not his heir; with two wives he had begotten but one daughter, and though he might have hoped to see a son installed at Cheam it was as well in view of past debaucheries and his present state of health, that the hope was not forthcoming.

So, for the next few years Sabrina was transplanted. The weed that had run wild in the gardens of Wroth House, was placed under glass at Cheam and flourished. The service of an excellent Miss Jeans was then secured, and between the two, so strangely ill-assorted, sprang up an unaccountable attachment. Unaccountable to the sensitive, beauty-loving child, when one understands that this good Jeans was thirty-five, gaunt, forbidding, with a face, so Pinkerton avowed, to scare the birds.

"Damme, Jess! Why couldn't ye have found a wench more tender? She has a set of teeth like my old mare's."

Knowing her lord's weakness, Jess may have had her reasons for employing a lady so worthy but untempting, and since after the first shock at sight of her Sabrina seemed not too opposed to her tuition (she had been well grounded by the Vicar, and lessons had never been to her a purgatory) Miss Jeans became an installation at Cheam Royal.

Hannah was retained as housekeeper at Wroth. This at the children's frantic intervention. Indeed, Sabrina threatened, if their dearest Hannah should be sent away, to drown herself. Jess, in a panic—there was a lake at Cheam—thought better of it. Hannah stayed on, and from time to time Sabrina rode to Wroth on Butterfly to see her, to be cosseted with currant wine, wept upon with ginny tears, and loved in Hannah's fashion.

Prior went to school. First to a Mr. Abingdon's at Canterbury, and afterwards to Eton, where a letter to his sister, dated January, 1809, tells her:

"I am Fag this term to a Fellow called Shelley he writes Poitry and looks likes a girl. The fellows bait him but I would rather fag for him than anyone. He does not bullie like some of the Hogs do hear and he does not treat me as a Fag. He read me some of his Poitry and I shewed him one of mine called Hesione which I shewed to you last holidays about the daughter of the King of Troy who was given to a Sea-Monster to be raiped. Shelley said it was a good Theame and that I must coltivate my Talant. A Fellow named Burnaby spoke to me to-day for the first time since I was hear. He is a great Blood. He said one day I will account with you for what your Father did to mine. I asked him what did my Father do to his but he would not say. He is leaving this Term and going in the Army. I have had three Fights this Term when I come home I will shew you the Rules of Boxing."

That early contact with a preternatural intelligence may have been responsible for the moulding of Prior's later life. Subsequent letters to his sister show that the seeds of eloquence had not fallen upon fruitless soil, as witness this precocious effort, dated May 21, 1810:

"I have been reading a book that Shelley has lent me by a man named Godwin. It is called Politicle Justice. It is magnificent. Shelley says there is no God in the sense that we understand God but he did not explain in what sense *he* understands

God. I also am wondering if there is an All Mighty if so Why is
there such suffering of the Opressed and such great Poverty in
our Country and why are there Wars and killing among Men
which is Murder when all is said whatever may be the Cause.
Shelley says that while Rich people feast and revel the Poor are
eating *Snails* and *Pig's Food* left in the Troughs disdained by
the Pigs so great is the Poverty in England. There will be a Revolution like the French had if it contineus and I will throw in
my Lot with the Opressed and against all Tyrantry for the time
will come when the Worm of Opression will Turn.

"I am transalating Horace he is magnificent. What Power!
What Language. If I could only express in Words all that I feel
as Shelley can. I think Shelley will do something Tremendous
one day but not here in this Murdrous Place which Shelley says
is Death to all Spontaeneous Creation and devoyed of any Independence of Thought or Action. They call him 'Mad' Shelley
and make his life Hell mine too for upholding him. He is going
to Oxford next term and I would to God I were I lothe and detest this Degrading life of government of Brutes by Brutes all
caste to one Pattern and living only for their stupid Games which
is meant to be Sport and Manly but which is utterly Primitive
and Barberous. . . ."

IV

While Prior at Eton translated Horace, wrote 'Poitry' and ex-
pounded his Shelley-cum-Godwinian theories of Utopia, Sabrina
under the guardianship of Miss Jeans pressed flowers in the pages
of her Bible, sewed samplers and was forgetting how to swear.

In England in those years between Sabrina's childhood and
adolescence, great events were rising.

Pitt, who had died lamenting, "My country! How I leave my
country!" left her in sorest straits. He left her to that hashed-up

Ministry of All-the-Talents, to the fanatic whimsies of a half-mad King, who in his lucid intervals could still assert authority under power of the Crown. He left her between the deep sea of industrial revolution and the devil. And he left her doomed to war.

The mighty shadow of Napoleon now bestrode the whole of Europe. With no Nelson on the high seas to oppose him, no Pitt to fight him in the Council Chamber, still undeterred by his failure to capture the British Army in the first Peninsular encounter, he prepared to strike his death-blow to the country he both feared and envied.

But he, who in 1812 had set England and America at loggerheads, had silenced every European power except Russia and Great Britain, and who in spite of that disastrous retreat from Moscow saw himself invincible, self-crowned Monarch of the World, had not taken into his account the name of Arthur Wellesley. . . .

In the year 1813 that marked for Bonaparte the beginning of his end, Jess Pinkerton brought Sabrina up to London.

To Jess, and to all those who formed her circle, now limited to St. James's and Mayfair, it mattered nothing that the price of corn rose higher, that men starved and children died for want of bread; that women worked as beasts of burden underground in mines, that their babies, too, worked in the airless dark, in factories, in mills, distorted from all shape of childhood, their little bodies rotted with disease; worked till they dropped, and were replaced by others younger, a pale massacre of innocents. Topic enough for dinner table talk when one remembered Robert Owen on the Clyde agitating to protect the workingman, building new homes for him—for which he'd never thank you—and promoting education among infants!

There might be talk of riots, of the smashing of these newfangled machines, of controversies among the Whigs in the cause of Catholic Emancipation, but all too far afloat for St. James's or Mayfair to get the drift of it. George III now permanently insane, was in retirement at Windsor, and the Regent ruled at Carlton House when Sabrina, at the age of seventeen, first came to Town.

Jess, determined to present her with a flourish when the time for presentation should arise, kept her awhile in the background in a semi-chrysalis condition. It may be she was lonely with none but the good Jeans for company.

They talked and walked and sewed together, or took the air in the Pinkerton barouche with two tall footmen in canary plush behind. And once they visited the Tower and saw:

". . . A number of caged savage beasts [from a letter undated —to Prior, still at Eton], Lions, Tygers, Wolves & great white Bears. Poor Things, they looked so sad & fierce, confined in such a narrow space. I thought how vastly superior they appeared & especially the Lions, to the common gaping crowd of Human Beings who surrounded their cages. From the Tower we went to a Pastrycook's in Cornhill for refreshment. While we sat there we were alarmed by a prodigious uproar & shouting of 'Mad Bull! Mad Bull!' Hardly had we time to recover our surprise when the mob began to rush Pell-Mell round the corner urging forward a poor over-driven Ox that could scarce stand for fatigue and fright! I'll swear not less than five hundred people were in pursuit headed by a band of butchers, labourers & urchins who were goading the wretched animal which was no more mad than I into a Fever. I was for rushing out to stop the Hunt, but Jeansie forbade it and held me firmly by the arm! We took a hackney Coach back to Curzon Street & on the way yet another Adventure. Our Coach was stopped in a Blockade at Holborn where a Crowd was collected to watch a man on a raised plat-

form shouting & gesticulating very violently. We could not pro-
ceed for the Crowd prevented our moving either forward or
back. It was greatly unpleasant because of the inquisitive &
threatening looks of the Populace, indeed more villainous types
of faces I have never seen, pressed close to our Coach window in
a very ill-favoured Manner.

"Miss Jeans said they recognised us as Members of the Upper
Classes & were hostile in consequence. She believed it to be a
meeting of Agitators clamouring for Reform. An unpleasant Incident occurred. Some Wretch in the Crowd aimed a rotten
Apple at our Coach Window, & splintered it but did no other
damage beyond giving us a Scare!

"Your hopes for a happier Existence for the Down-Trodden
is far from realisation. They defeat their own ends, in my
opinion, & lose all Sympathy by the Dastardly manner in which
they make their Appeal."

She was not always so serious-minded. Another letter tells of a
play she witnessed at the Lyceum Theatre, again attended by
Miss Jeans—"who I think was not apprised of the nature of this
Comedy, founded on the Theme of 'The City Madam' by Mas-
singer & entitled 'Riches, or the Wife & Brother,' a revival of the
original Production of three years back. I laughed till my sides
ached, less at the Performance than at poor Jeansie's Countenance
which grew ever longer & more sour, till at length she hustled me
out before the last Act was over, saying it was not fitting to my
years to watch so *Broad* a presentation of the Modes & Manners
of *Society!*"

Most of all her recreations Sabrina enjoyed her promenades in
Hyde Park where cows grazed in rural pastures and where it
was possible to buy a glass of new milk at a farm set among
the trees, near to the Serpentine. And soon she learned to know
the paths and glades not too much frequented by Fashion, where

hawthorn blossomed pink and white and red, just as it might be
in the hedgerows at Wroth. Country-bred, she pined for open
spaces, but on the whole she suffered Curzon Street with tolerance. Though ostensibly still under the guardianship of Jeans,
she was permitted to attend the drawing-room when Lady Pinkerton entertained to tea and gossip, her familiars.

The glimpse these had was of a coltish child, slender, large-
eyed, sulky-mouthed, with a curling crop of fawn-gold hair and
dark brows arched on a white forehead. A pleasing glimpse, but
"something of a gawk." Thus the ladies, for whose verdict Jess
didn't give a fig. "A fine filly," the men called her, modified by
the addition, "a little too long in the leg."

This coming as it did from one qualified to know, gave Jess a
shock. Yes, the girl was tall. Too tall. Bred fine enough but too
straight in the back when fashion bade you droop. Miss Jeans
had drilled her, it would seem, too carefully. Now let her loll.
Jess showed her how in a pose used to advantage as Ophelia.
Then Signor Gambetti must teach her how to waltz. Everyone
was waltzing. There were waltzing parties given in the mornings
at Melbourne House. Caro Lamb had set the fashion, and Jess
was not far behind in following her lead. Sabrina in one of her
weekly letters to her twin tells him that the unrivalled lion of
the season—with the whole of feminine London at his feet and
Childe Harold's first appearance to his credit—called in at
Curzon Street to watch this latest pastime.

Sabrina, it seems, had not succumbed to Byron fever, for: "I
find him *Odious*," she writes, "though I pity him for his poor
crippled foot. He is every bit as handsome as they say he is, like
a Greek Statue with his perfect features & tightly curling hair,
but he has an Insolence of Manner, a studied *Courtesy* and a
general Air of over-bearing Arrogance which is unpleasing. He
actually did deign to look at *me* and to ask Jess who was 'the

pale tall Nymph with the head of an epaecene (or epiecene—I
cannot spell it!) boy!' They say Lady Caroline Lamb is frantic
with love for him. I have seen her too. She is *Adorable* with her
enormous great dark eyes & fairy-like Grace. She has no Beauty
but something *much more*. I have heard she went to Byron's
house tricked out as a Page in silks and laces! I may tell you I
have heard all sorts of talk of other things not meant for *my*
ears for Jess and all her *Satellites* regard me as half-weaned &
possibly half-witted! You would be amused to see the Innocence
of my Bearing! . . . Such *Oddities* as visit here you never saw!
There is one ridiculous old Beau called Sir Rodney Perch who is
—or was I think—enamoured of our Jess! He is sixty if a day
& wears stays so tight he looks like an Hour-glass! Rouge in his
wrinkles, a dyed red wig & the most girlish of giggles! The
speech here in London is the strangest thing you ever heard.
They *Baa* like sheep. It is considered 'tonnish' to speak with an
odd nasal drawl & they indulge in peculiar turns of phrase that
seem meaningless. 'High-honeysuckle' is one. Everything that is
not quite so bad as it might seem to be is called 'High-honeysuckle.' To me however London is 'Low-honeysuckle.' . . ."

Lady Pinkerton might have been a little startled had she known
that while Sabrina retired mouselike to her corner with a docility
that did credit to Miss Jeans, she was keeping a mental register
of all she saw and heard. But no doubt Jess underrated that
caustic, young intelligence.

Despite a past that might have been equivocal, Jess—it will be
seen—had attained a present unimpeached, and an entrée to the
glories of high life. To be sure, she had an earldom to support
her. He, still alive, surprisingly, though thinner, was now nothing
but a childish old man, pitiable in his dotage and unloved. Jess
kept him out of mind and as much out of sight as was compatible with her position as a wife. Sabrina sometimes read to him.

He was not in the least deaf. He would bid her bring a stool near to his chair and there she would read Rabelais till her throat ached. He had, too, a taste for Fielding. She read him portions of *Tom Jones;* and once she read to him the Bible. This at his request.

"That psalm—that what's-its-name—my mother used to read to me when I wore petticoats. 'The Lord is my Shepherd. . . .' "

Sabrina read it and he cried. Sat hunched up in his great carved chair, his chins sunk on his stock and cried. He looked quite dreadful with his wig aslant (on his second marriage he had taken to a blond curled wig in place of the powdered one of former years), his mouth tremulous and mumbling like a baby's, and his bleared eyes drenched with maudlin tears. She thought him drunk, smelled that he wasn't, and for the first time in her life began to love him: loved him for pity, for the marred and wasted life that had been his, for his preposterous three chins; for that terrible blond wig, for all the shocking details of his senility. Loved him because he was so very old and tired, and because there was that in her which must give love where it was needed.

"Poor Grandpapa"—she laid a cool soft hand on each of his— "what is it? What's the matter?" Coaxingly she soothed him. He was her baby then; a nightmare baby, but her own.

He sniffled; a drop came from his nose. She took her handkerchief and wiped it off.

"There! That's better. Aren't you well?"

"No. I have a pa-pain. Where's Jess?"

"I'll find her. Is it a bad pain, my dear?"

His eyes bulged at her, rolled up, stared fixedly at the ceiling.

"One flies. Three," he counted like a child. "Three flies walkin' on the ceilin'. Upside down. Where's that woman? Where in Hell is Jess?"

His blackish tongue came out and licked his lips. They remained open. He went on talking with his eyes uprolled and fixed.

"I think she's give me poison. Dosin' me with physic and puttin' plasters on me arse. She's no good. Always a fly-be-night. Waitin' for me now to die. I've tied it up—the money. All on her. You and the boy don't get a penny till she's gone. And she'll last out the pair of ye. Give me a pen. I'll alter it. I'll sign me name, I'll wri—"

He choked. His lips stiffened and turned blue. His eyes, still fixed, were showing bloodshot whites.

Sabrina was afraid. He looked so strange and awful. She flew to the bell-rope, pulled and pulled again.

His man came, scared and pale.

"My gracious, miss! What's this?"

"He's ill," she panted, "very ill. He was taken badly—of a sudden. Go quickly for a doctor—send for her ladyship. No, I'll tell her. You wait here—"

He did not die. By a miracle he lived, with one side of him completely paralysed, half his wits gone; helpless, bedridden, wearing the blond curled wig that the remainder of his sagging mind insisted on.

Jess took it not too hardly, though she registered concern for three whole weeks; gave up her dinners; was seen never at a rout, nor at the Opera, but often at the herbalist's in Shepherd Market, buying concoctions. She had him bled and dosed and doctored, consulted the physician of the King himself. No woman could do more. When he was pronounced completely out of danger until another seizure should occur, she once more gave attention to Sabrina.

Chapter Two

I

FOR REASONS best known to herself, Jess had decided that Sabrina's first appearance in society should be masked. This may have been in order to allow the girl to feel her feet, not too conspicuously. A Mrs. Heriot at Richmond was to give a masquerade in June. Jess saw to it Sabrina was invited.

Great preparations were afoot in Curzon Street. Modistes and milliners arrived with boxes. Sabrina was to go as Dawn—this, after endless consultation, Lady Pinkerton's decree. Diaphanous and cloudy in palest pink and pearl, layers of gauze spangled with crystal dewdrops ballooning round her feet, stars in her hair, and a rose-shaded mask hiding all of her features but her mouth.

Jess thought the whole effect enticing. "Very apt and virginal," she said. The child's skin was white enough to show it, therefore let the neck be cut round, very low. Sabrina blushed at herself in the mirror at a fitting. Miss Jeans suggested to sew in a fold of gauze. Jess snapped at her smartly for her interference, bade the modiste cut it lower still, and pronounced the effect both elegant and chaste.

For herself she had chosen Boadicea with a helmet on her head, a silver plate upon her chest and pink silk tights upon her legs—still good and shapely—under transparencies of muslin.

"It is modish now," she told Miss Jeans, "to reveal more of the figure both above and below. The gowns are damped this year to make them cling."

Miss Jeans protested it was enough to make the wearer die of chill. She hoped Sabrina would not become a victim to such folly. She strongly disapproved of the costume of Sabrina—of all that it exposed; of the masquerade, of Jess, of the whole business.

To most of us there comes sometime a day—perhaps a moment—of significance that may be set aside in memory as a centrifugal force whence all other points converge. All history is founded upon trifles—a lady's garter, a game of bowls, the blind eye of a hero, a scrap of paper. Trifles such as these have become legendary, and are remembered when the greatest of events, calamities and triumphs are forgotten.

So it may be that had Jess at that ball not sat so long at cards, or had Sir Rodney Perch not been so pressing; or had Sabrina's mask not been of shaded rose—had it been black—had she been dressed as Night instead of Dawn, or as a Columbine, a Gipsy, or in any other costume less appealing to one person in the room, her life might have been woven to a very different pattern. But why speculate?

The fact remains that Jess played cards and Sabrina went as Dawn—in a mask that was of satin, shaded rose.

Richmond was a long ride in the coach, and Jess had ample opportunity on the way to give advice as to behaviour.

"It is not, perhaps," she told Sabrina, "quite *en règle* that you should attend a masquerade at your age, but I think it better you get rid of your first clumsiness where you are not so certain to be recognised. In fact, no one need know who you are. There will be no introductions. You may dance with whom you please. At midnight you remove your mask. It is a house of highest *ton,* therefore I know you are safe to accept as partner any of *her* guests. Don't tell your name even if they ask you—men are more intrigued by mystery—and I'm not anxious for the whole world to know that you are there. Don't wander in the grounds—it may get rowdy. She keeps the finest cellar. I shall play cards."

Sabrina sat in silence.

Her glass had revealed to her a stranger, someone she had never known. Arms, neck and bosom—she blushed at the remembrance of their bareness, and under the folds of her cloak, hugged her arms round her. For her glass had told her she was lovely. . . . . And she loved herself. She was in love with that mirrored image of herself, that white rose-tinted vision whose reflection she had never seen before; had never cared enough to see before that she was red-lipped and starry-eyed, less child than girl and more than half a woman.

Now everything was changed. She seemed to sway in rhythm to the jolting movement of the coach. She felt impalpable and airy as though she, or something of her, were escaping. From what? To whom? She was a bird winging towards the sun, and her heart sang.

And as the coach rolled on its way impressions gained a fleeting new perception. The darkening scene imprinted on the dusk gave fervent glimpses of the turnpike at Piccadilly, the market gardens of the Brompton Road, an orange square of light in a bow window, an outflung spray of blossom in a hedge—and in the air the dewy scent of grass, the smell of cows; above the rapid clip and clop of horses' hoofs, a wood pigeon's sleepy croon.

Jess, upright in her helmet, her silver plate ashine under a flimsy wrap, talked on.

"For you understand, Sabrina, that you *must* marry well. And I'll see to it you shall."

To the detriment of her top-heavy helmet, Jess gave a prophetic nod.

"I am concerned—Confound the thing! It's slidin'. I am concerned about your future. I suppose you realise—perhaps you
don't—that Wrotham has not a penny piece to give you. He dare
not show his face in England. And if he does—"

Jess paused.

"It's seven years," Sabrina said, "since Wrotham went away."
. . . Why mention Wrotham now? Her moment ebbed. "Is he,"
Sabrina asked a little breathlessly, "likely to return?"

"I tell you, girl, he daren't. And if he does it'll be ruination
to your future. He would have to stand a trial. Good God! What
a calamity it would be if he came back just when I'm launching
you! That's why I am so anxious to settle you in *case*—but he'd
be raving mad to risk it. I knew a man called Campbell—an old
flirt of mine—poor brute—was hanged some years ago in Ireland
for killing a Captain Boyd in duel. Hanged! It's true there was
suspicion of foul play; but the law don't blink at bloodshed, I
assure you, and the facts of Wrotham's case will hardly bear
investigation. The Lord send that you'll be married off this
season—it don't do you any good to have a stigma to your name."

There was, then, no forgetting it. Often in the night would
come the memory of that far-off scene at Wroth etched on a
child's consciousness to puzzle it and haunt with sounds and
whispers, to instil into the questing mind of a young girl a secret
curiosity, a latent fear.

But I won't—deep down in her, Sabrina cried. I won't be
'married off'—I won't. I won't! To whom should I be married?
To some giggling old Beau all painted, dyed and wrinkled like
that old Perch? Or to one of those dressed-up dandies who
dance round Jess and flatter her? Why should I? I am a Person
—not a wax doll for sale or for hateful men to paw. . . .

She said, her face pressed to the coach window: "What place is this we're coming to? Is it much farther yet?"

"Not far now," yawned Jess. "There was a highway robbery at Barnes last week. I dread crossing the Common. We may be set upon. Lean back, child, don't show yourself. They are more likely to attack if they see women."

Highwaymen! She was young enough to feel elated at the prospect. Someone bold and handsome might come romantically to rescue. Her heart sank down again. But nothing wonderful would ever happen. Romance belonged to books, not to real people. Always a pendulum of changing moods, she now felt drained and empty. Jess with her worldly chatter perplexed and saddened her. She wished she were not going to this ball—decked out in gauze absurdly with a mask across her face, Jess more absurd than she in gauze and armour. She would be lost and awkward in a crowd. What matter if her glass had called her lovely? She was a gawk. A tall, great clumsy gawk. Signor Gambetti had said "Gawk." Had screamed at her in Latin frenzy, lifting his fiddle high above his head as though to dash it to the floor, and her own brains out with it! So! If she could not learn the waltz, well then, she couldn't. An odious, silly dance that made you giddy. She wished—ah, how she wished that she were back at Wroth with Prior, and with Hannah (dear Hannah and her bottle!), and old Butterfly, and Lightning and the dogs! . . . Supposing Wrotham did return, what then? Would she and Prior have to live with him at Wroth? . . . A stigma to her name. What did Jess mean? Was it a crime to fight a duel? Duels were fought every day. Lord Castlereagh had fought with Mr. Canning. It had been mentioned in the *History of Our Times* that Miss Jeans gave her for her birthday. But to kill in open fight—would that be murder? Something, for sure, was wrong with a name that had a stigma to it. Wrotham. Her father. . . . My father, she said wonderingly, and felt again across the span of years the spell of his attraction. As though a shutter had slid open she saw his face revealed, his insolent, wry smile, his hard lips, his eyes so dark and burning; remembered once again her fear of him that one word could turn to hate—or adoration.

If all things had been different. If I, she thought, had been of different birth. A village girl. A housemaid. Or a boy. . . . Yes, suppose now . . . Yes, suppose that I had been a boy. I might have gone to sea, gone to the wars, made my own life—not had it remade, for me. And *what* a life! This London, Jess, poor half-dead old Grandpapa—all unreal things. A masquerade indeed.

And still Jess talked.

". . . So that if anything happens to poor Pinkie, you, my dear, will get nothing till I go but what I choose to give you. You need not fear, I'll see to it both you and Prior shall be treated fair. And there's a thousand each put by for you with accumulative interest which you can have when you're eighteen. That's from Pinkerton—he made it over to you at your birth and Wrotham can't touch *that*—but God knows if there'll be anything to come to us after Pinkie. We've spent beyond our means. I don't regret it. We've lived well, and we'll go on living well while there's anything to live on. Half the land's sold already, and the other half will follow in due course. I tell you I lie awake o' nights half crazed with worry of it. What do you suppose it costs to keep up two establishments?"

"I don't know," said Sabrina.

"Fifteen thousand pounds a year, my dear, at least. More than we can ever meet. His income is reduced to half with this shocking war taxation. Still, I have me jewels. They'll go to you if I don't sell 'em. Now what's the fool stopping for? God send we're not held up!"

"There's a line of carriages in front of us," said Sabrina with her nose against the glass. "He can't get on."

"We'll not be there till midnight at this rate," grumbled Jess. "What in the devil made me choose this villainous tin helmet! I'll never keep it on me head."

"Why not take it off then?" said Sabrina. It was news to hear that she and Prior would have each a thousand pounds and not much longer now to wait for it. Did Prior know, she wondered. She would tell him. A thousand pounds was a vast deal of money. With such a sum she and Prior might set up house together. Go abroad. See foreign countries. And she might marry whom she pleased. There was no knowing what might come about with money of one's own to spend. . . .

She felt herself important. In the space of a few minutes she had grown a few years older; was already building castles in the air.

Mrs. Heriot's house at Richmond stood in its own grounds on the heights above the river. The windows of the ballroom had been opened wide, and the sound of fiddles could be heard above the rattle of carriage wheels as vehicles deposited their ornamental burdens at the door.

Sabrina, horribly self-conscious in her scanty robes, kept close to Jess. She wished that she had taken Miss Jeans' good advice and worn a scarf. Miss Jeans had told her she might just as well be nude. "What is not flesh," Miss Jeans had said, "is flesh-coloured. You're disgraceful." Was she? Jess did not seem to think so. In the ladies' cloakroom she was reassured.

"You look," Jess told her, "quite delicious, and I'm proud of

you. Wait! Let me pin up this curl. Now! Just a touch of rouge
—yes, I insist—you're too pale with excitement. *I* always turn
scarlet. I never saw such eyes—the pupils are enormous. The
Frenchwomen drop in belladonna to get the same effect. Just a
soupçon here—" Jess dabbed each fresh young cheek with the
hare's foot from her reticule and stood back to admire. "Yes, enchanting! Now the mask—what a sin to hide you! But you can
get rid of it at midnight, or sooner if you want. Let your skirts
trail and take small steps. We must find our hostess. She'll be unmasked to receive."

In a flutter and still chatting, Jess led the way along a pillared
corridor with marbled walls where at intervals stood monumental
flunkeys in cream and scarlet. "Half these men," Jess whispered,
"have been hired. She don't keep a big staff. See—their liveries
don't match. She's all show and no money. There she is in purple.
What a guy! Is she meant to be Nell Gwynne with that red wig
and oranges?"

Sabrina followed in a daze. Her fears were all forgotten. The
brilliantly lit ballroom contrasting with the quiet night beyond
framed in rose curtained windows, presented a fantastic spectacle.
Candles from a myriad crystal lustres shed their radiance on a
revolving medley of clowns and Columbines, knights and jesters,
pages and ploughboys, flower-girls and queens; a mask with a
nose twelve inches long, one with green eyes that glittered—the
most droll assembly ever seen. On all sides was heard the falsetto
squeak of disguised voices mingling with the murmur of vio-
lins screened in an alcoved gallery. Sabrina's feet trembled to
dance. She turned to speak to Jess, to point out to her this costume
or that, a blue-faced Puck—blue hair! A man in an ass's head—
Bottom, for sure! Yes—waltzing with a daisy-crowned Titania
—but Jess had vanished. She was alone in all that colourful mosaic
that whirled around her like a dream.

Alone, but not for long.

Someone touched her on the arm, a voice lisped in her ear: "I know you! Your lips, fair mask, remain unhidden. The sweetest lips in London—tee-hee-hee!"

A figure bowed before her coquettishly attired as a blue and silver Pierrot, his jacket buttoned tight across his chest, a rose behind one ear, and his face as painted as a harlot's. That old fool, Sir Rodney Perch! She knew him for his giggle, for a large wart on his chin, for the way his false teeth wobbled in his shrunken gums. How hideous he looked in those gay trappings. His eyes peered gloatingly behind his mask.

"Will the lovely nymph of Curzon Street deign to dance with a poor Pierrot?"

Before she could refuse him his arm was round her waist, his breath, that smelled too strong of wine and garlic, on her cheek. He held her all too tightly; she was sure that he was drunk. He whirled her round and twittered: "Ringy-ringy-roses! What a white throat you have! Poor Pierrot pines to kiss it!" He thrust a spindle knee between her own.

"No! Let us stop!" Sabrina cried. "I am giddy. I cannot dance the waltz."

"Oh, come! You can. One and two-oo, one and two-oo, one, two, three—"

Couples jostled her. A cowled monk trod on her gauze. Her head swam, her feet were leaden, she was wretched.

"Pray, sir! Indeed, I cannot—"

"Practice only is required. You insist? Then let me take you to the garden. It is cooler there, and I—tee-hee!—am hot. We will sit and watch the moon."

"No—if you please. I am looking for Je—for Lady Pinkerton." With an effort she wriggled herself free. His fingers clutched her arm.

"You shall not so soon escape me, lovely mask. Such a full-grown young lady as she is tonight! A white rose waiting to be plucked. Would that I—tee-hee—might be the plucker!"

This was dreadful. He was walking her away, edging a passage through the maze of dancers towards one of the open windows that led on to the terrace. He gripped her elbow in a vice, there was strength in his thin fingers, and the more she strove to free her arm the tighter did he hold it.

"Oh, please to let me be!" she panted. "I do not care to leave the ballroom."

All unheeding this resistance, Sir Rodney half led, half dragged her to the terrace, deserted now, for the dance was in full swing. But down in the dusk of the garden shadowy figures wandered, and fairy lamps festooned among the trees shone there like glow-worms. The moon, bright as a new shilling, rose up behind a cloud.

Her escort on a high cracked note began to sing:

> *"Au clair de la lune*
> *Mon ami pierrot . . ."*

He is decidedly, Sabrina thought, the worse for drink.

"Sir," she protested, "you are pinching my arm."

"Poor little arm! It shall be kissed." He dived his head.

Not only did he kiss, but he bit into the softness of her arm below the shoulder as though it were ripe fruit. And at that first taste of her, greedy for more, he snatched at her mouth; kissed that.

At this point it is shocking to record—but quite authentic—that Sabrina smacked his face. She may have had excuse for her behaviour. I hold no brief for it. The fact remains that in the space of a few seconds all Miss Jeans' years of training were forgotten. Sabrina smacked Sir Rodney's face and smacked it hard.

"You detestable old man!" she screamed. "You beast!"

It is known she called him 'beast' though never certain if the tale that went the round of clubland the next day were true or not—that his right eye was black. Certain it is, however, that the story of Sir Rodney's teeth became a legend—to this effect: that his plate fell out and was smashed upon the paving-stones, so hard Sabrina hit him. If Jess Pinkerton had seen her!—but she didn't. Jess was at cards and losing.

"Spitfire!" yelped Sir Rodney when sufficiently recovered from surprise and shock to utter. "Damme! What a spitfire! Tee-hee-hee."

He'd giggle in his coffin, thought Sabrina, filled with scarlet shame at what she'd done, when she saw him stiffly stooping to retrieve his damaged property; shame and compunction. For she must have hurt the poor old silly creature to make him lose his teeth. She had behaved like a virago and was utterly disgraced. There was nothing for it left her but to mumble an apology, to gather up her skirts, and run away.

She ran the whole length of the terrace and paused at the end of it for breath, her elbows on the parapet, cold hands to her hot cheeks. The night was still, the music fainter. Beyond dark shapes of trees, below the sloping gardens, lay the river, dark, too, and gleaming. She could smell roses. Stars hid in the heavy warmth. A night bird called; a moth flew against her forehead. No leaf stirred.

She heard a quick step on the terrace and turned in a scare prepared for further flight.

A man stood there beside her, not Sir Rodney. This man was tall, and Sir Rodney short. In the moonlit darkness she saw that he was young, saw his face, unmasked and laughing, his fair uncovered head, an Elizabethan ruff, a cloak slung from his shoulder; doublet, hose, a sword. She blinked at him.

"I followed you," he said, "from the ballroom. I was about to ask you for a dance when he forestalled me. I saw what happened yonder. I was not in time. I would have done it for you."

"Oh!" breathed Sabrina.

He came a little nearer; the moon was in his eyes. "Will you waltz with me, Rose-mask?"

"I cannot waltz, sir," said Sabrina.

"Then will you talk to me?"

His mouth curled upwards at the corners in a smile like a faun's. He said: "I saw you when you first arrived. Saw your rose-mask. The only one that colour in the room. You were standing in the doorway. Who are you? May I know your name? . . . I know that you are lovely."

A hand fluttered to her heart and rested there. She had no words for him, but she was happy. Gloriously happy. He was young.

He laughed a little, underneath his breath.

"I can see your eyes like stars behind your mask. Who are you? *What* are you?"

"I am Dawn," she said.

He echoed it; drew a deep breath.

"I might have guessed you. . . . Dawn."

They stayed together the whole evening. Three times she danced with him. He showed her better how to dance the waltz than old Gambetti. Her feet were winged in tune to the music of the fiddles, to the music in her heart. His head was close to hers, so close he held her, and his hair smelled deliciously of jasmine.

But after those three dances they found their way of one accord back to the garden. He knew that garden well. Their hostess, he had told her, was related, a cousin of his mother.

He led her to a Gothic temple at the end of an alley lined with yews, cut into strange shapes of bird and beast. From there they could see the windows of the house, brilliantly lit, and occasional couples who wandered among the trees, or stood in shadow, bodies locked together, strained each to each, as the dark intensified; for at midnight the music ceased, the fiddlers went to their refreshment, drink flowed more freely, and the company unmasked.

Decorum with the masks was thrown aside; the guests, as Jess had prophesied, were becoming rowdy. The times, one must remember, were licentious. It took near upon three decades and the accession of a Queen to disperse the social cloud of disreputabilities that resulted from the Royal influence at Carlton House.

To Sabrina the scene presented a phantasmal beauty. It shocked her not at all to see more than half the male company advanced in drink. Drunkenness in those days was held in no abhorrence; it was the privilege of gentlemen, a manly failing at its worst.

The gardens and the fairy-lights, the joyous atmosphere of freedom, the whispering couples, the low laughter, the coloured costumes dimly seen under the coloured lamps; the heavy scent of stock and fainter roses; night warmth and sweet night breath; night sounds in stillness—an owl's cry, wild, discordant mingled with a man's far-off guffaw—and the tall youth beside her, no stranger, though she did not know his name—all thrilled her heart with secrets, with such happiness as she had never felt before. He had all to tell her of himself. He was a soldier, a lieutenant in the Fifty-sixth Dragoons, had been to the wars, had served under Lord Wellington at Salamanca. He had been wounded.

She caught her breath. "But—wounded!"

"Shot in the head. Not serious. I've a scar under my hair and a deep one—I'll show you in the daylight—on my forehead."

She saw him lying bleeding, broken, wounded. . . . In the daylight he would show her. Did that mean that they might meet again, or would this night pass into morning here, and then—for ever—separation? Unbearable to think it. How she loved him! Her love leapt up, was born at that moment when she saw him in imagination bleeding from the head in his brave scarlet tunic on the field of Salamanca.

"Do you go back again," she asked him, "—back to the wars?"

"Indeed I hope so, soon."

"How soon?" Her voice was faint.

"My leave expires in two weeks. I shall be sent to Weymouth. From thence, God willing, to join my regiment at Almeida."

"Will you," she questioned fearfully, "be engaged again in battle?"

He smiled. "If I'm lucky."

A little cry escaped her. "Oh! These wars!"

"All's fair in war," he said, "and love. The two march together always. That is the law of life."

"You think—" she murmured foolishly.

"I know."

He found her hand and held it close. A delicious pang passed through her at his touch, and left her breathless. He seemed to think it natural to sit there clasping hands in the shadow of that temple among the black-plumed trees, with the brooding summer night about them. Such happiness to her was almost pain. She did know that the eternal cause had brought him to her side, that this tremulous sweet feeling, this dark witchery sprung from some source as yet untouched, unfathomed, was youth's homage to young Love. She knew only that a miracle had come to pass, a miracle akin to birth—and death.

He said: "It is strange to feel I know you. There is something that is half familiar. I think I've dreamed you. Always."

She had dreamed him for sure. He must be brave and strong

and honest. Just that same strength of jaw, and lips that tilted in a smile at the corners; clear-eyed, and all as she now saw him, so she had dreamed.

His fingers twined in hers.

"Do you believe that our lives are mapped out for us beforehand by some scheme? I am a fatalist. Are you? Do you think this night was planned and that we *had* to meet?"

Yes, yes! We had to meet . . . But the words remained unuttered. She let him talk.

"What is your name?" he whispered. "I do not know it yet. You don't know mine."

She shook her head. What did names matter?

"Tell me," he pleaded, "who you are. Tell me all about you. You're not"—his voice sharpened and he held her hand more tightly—"you're not married?"

"No." She laughed softly for sheer joy. "Not married."

"Where do you live? In London?"

"For a while, yes. My home is in Hertfordshire. And yours?"

"My home is with my regiment. I have none other. My parents are both dead. May I see you often until my leave expires? Time is so short for me. May I call upon you at your father's house? Have you a father?"

"Yes."

"A mother?"

"My mother died when I was born. I have a twin brother. He is at Eton still."

"At Eton? That is my school, too. He is there now? Then you are young—younger than I had thought you."

"How old, then, did you think me?"

"I cannot think. You're ageless."

"I am seventeen."

"So old! Tell me your name."

"Sabrina."

"Is it true? . . . 'Listen where thou art sitting, under the glassy cool translucent wave'—the loveliest words ever written, and they're yours!"

But she had lived before this moment of recurrence. Where had she lived it? When? An involuntary shiver passed across her, an unaccountable chill fear.

"Are you cold? You must have my cloak. But—please."

He unslung his cloak and wrapped it round her, cared for her tenderly. "There! I should have thought of that much sooner. Your gown is thin. Are you quite comfortable now?" He took back her hand in his. "Your hand—so soft and boneless. You're so calm." (Calm did he think her!) "So different to anyone whom I have met before. You speak so little, yet I feel all that you would say. I think we have one mind. Are you unreal? Will you go away from me tonight, and will I never see you any more?"

"No—I hope—" she stammered.

"But of course I am going to see you every day. May I call on you tomorrow? Where do you stay in London?"

She told him where.

"I'll remember it . . . Sabrina. I shall always call you Dawn."

He sighed; drew nearer, his arm was brushing hers. She held her breath for fear; not fear of him, but of her happiness.

"Tell me"—her voice sounded to her own ears like a bleat, so strained, so shaken, but she must speak of casual and ordinary things—or die. "Tell me of your—of your soldiering. Have you met Lord Wellington?"

"I have." His shoulders squared instinctively as though to a salute. "He reviewed us before Salamanca. There is only one man second to Wellington in this world—at the moment."

"And who?"

"Why, Boney!"

"Have you met *him?*" For he might have met the Lord Himself. All things were possible.

"No, not yet. How adorable you are! Have I met Bonaparte! As though we were on speaking terms—"

"I know"—she was blushing to the ears—"I am very foolish."

"You darling!" He laughed in that way of his underneath his breath. "Would you like me to tell you something that I saw, though? If it would interest you."

"Pray do, indeed." As if anything he said could *not* interest her. ('You darling!' He had called her 'darling.')

"This happened during Salamanca. I actually *saw* it happen. I was shot soon afterwards." Her fingers tightened under his; she felt his quick response. "Dear, I was not hurt badly. Do you really care that I was hurt?"

It was as if her unspoken thoughts passed from her to him on tenuous magic wires.

After a pause in which both seemed to probe this bewildering new secret, he went on:

"While the battle was at its height—we were stationed halfway up the hill at that time, I remember—we saw a detachment of thirty or forty French horse galloping over the top of it, just as Wellington was ascending. I doubt if they even knew that it was Wellington. What they were after was a couple of guns that were being escorted by a squadron of light cavalry. They charged, driving our cavalry *through* the guns—you understand? And Lord Wellington and his staff were caught up in the mêlée with them and driven to the bottom of the hill. Gad! It was a mess! Impossible to see which was French or which· was us. It would have been laughable had the odds not been so serious. Our lot rushed forward just in time—for that handful of British was being vastly outnumbered and then it might have been Kingdom Come for Wellington. I can tell you! It was a narrow squeak."

Sabrina shuddered. Yes! A narrow squeak for *him*. She was not concerned with England's hero, only with her own.

"And then?" she murmured when he stopped.

He turned to her. She saw his face, a shadow in the darkness. "Then? I do not know what then. I only know what now." His voice dropped to a whisper. His hand was on her heart.

She yielded unresisting to the sweet surprise of touch, to the tumult in her blood that answered his. "Nothing but you now . . ." His mouth on hers spoke to her parted lips. "Nothing in all the world but you. . . . My Dawn."

II

It was past two when Jess rose from the card table. For her the night had spelled disaster. She had no luck at all. Never in her life had she played a poorer hand, and never had she lost so big a sum. But none to see her would have guessed her agitation.

Bereft of mask and helmet, she beamed upon the company, was full of quips and laughter and cracked a joke or two that made the gentlemen uproarious and the ladies very shocked. Then, having written out an I.O.U. in lieu of payment, she revived her flagging spirits with Madeira.

The first cause of her presence there that evening was forgotten. She had lost sight of Sabrina in view of greater issues. All that now engrossed her was how to meet her losses. What in the Devil had made her play so high? She had overdrawn too heavily on Pinkerton's account to dare present his bankers with a further cheque, signed for him, since he could not sign himself. She would have to sell her diamonds or borrow. But from whom? It was not so easy, Jess decided, to find ready aid at fifty. A glimpse of her hot face in a mirror served only to increase her state of mind. For her paint had run, her nose shone through the pearl powder, and it struck her that her arms looked like a pair of thighs. Too fat by far, and growing fatter though she starved. And nine hundred odd, what's more, to find by morning. . . .

"A delightful ball, dear Mrs. Heriot! I have enjoyed each minute, I assure you. I never knew an evening go as quick. Allow me to compliment you on your costume. Are you not Nell Gwynne? The sweetest taste, and so becoming. Do you attend the opera tomorrow? They say that Catalani has surpassed herself. . . . No, I shall not visit Bath this year. My husband is too poorly to be moved. Oh, better certainly but hopelessly incurable, I fear. . . . *Good*-bye, Lady Sefton. I hope to have the pleasure of meeting you at Lady Castlereagh's rout on Thursday. No? Then perhaps at Almack's. . . . Not tonight, Sir Rodney . . . unlucky at cards *al*ways."

"Perhaps luckier at love, hee-hee!"

"La, sir! One still may hope! Surely it is very late? There seems to be an exodus. Is the dancing over? And— Good gracious! Have you seen Sabrina?"

"Not for some hours. The charming nymph—hee-hee!—has been spirited away. Pray allow me to get your ladyship some refreshment."

"No, but you can help me find my child. This damnable play of mine has driven her clean out of me head which is splitting fit to crack. Deuce take it!" Jess did not trouble to parade her *grande dame* airs for the benefit of so old a friend as Rodney.

He screwed a glass into his eye, and with a glance across his shoulder drew her mysteriously aside.

"A word with you, dear lady, first. Just one little word!"

Jess tapped an impatient foot. The old rake! Prinked up to look eighteen. He must be sixty. But money to burn and none to spend it for him, though all knew that Mrs. J—d—n had tried

her very best. He liked them younger. . . . And what on earth was
this the man was saying?

"Sabrina! 'Tisn't true!"

"I'll vow it is! She—hee!—knocked out my two front teeth, the
hussy!"

" 'Ods me life! She didn't!"

Jess Barrett's sense of humour outweighed her better judgment.
Several ladies turned their heads to see who laughed so loud; saw,
shrugged and smiled, looking down their noses. *That* woman!
How did she worm her way into these houses?

Sir Rodney was aggrieved.

" 'Tis no laughing matter, I assure you. The girl's a demon."

"Yes. She was so as a child, but only when she's roused. You
must have roused her, Rodney!"

"I tried my best. My denture must be mended first thing in the
morning. My man has fixed it up meantime with wire. I always
bring him with me in case—hee-hee—of an emergency."

It was too rich. Jess held her sides. It is possible she may have
had her full share of Madeira. "I see," she spluttered, "that there's
a broken one in front. Oh, mercy! Laugh and grow fat, they say.
I dare not—for fear. So she can care for herself, it seems. What
were you doing to her, for heaven's sake, to make her hit so
hard?"

"Nothing, I swear. She—hee—didn't give me time!"

"You're a sad dog, Perch." Jess mopped her eyes with a handkerchief of gauze and silver lace. "And is that all you have to tell
me?"

"No, indeed. That's but preliminary. Come here."

He took her by the elbow and piloted her to a sofa in the corner upholstered in lavender brocade.

"Now, madam—" Approaching his mouth to her ladyship's ear,
he whispered at some length. At first Jess appeared incredulous,

but presently her eyes narrowed and grew thoughtful. Once or twice she nodded with pursed lips. When he had done, she told him:

"You astound me! What am I to say? You must ask *her,* not me. She's so young. A child."

"So were you, my dear, when first we met. She has a spirit. And by George! But she's a beauty. I want an heir—hee-hee! If I'm not past getting one."

"Pooh!" said Jess. She was thinking rapidly, in some confusion. It would be monstrous. 'Twould be a monstrous sin. Nine hundred pounds to be procured by morning—that was certain. There were half a dozen mothers who would set their caps at *him.* One of the oldest families in England, and nothing like as bad as he was painted—although he tried to be. Neither beggars—nor Sabrina—could afford to pick and choose. She was not all men's fancy. Too much of a stick. Never a sparkle. That Jeans had ground her far too well in book-learning and such. No social flair. None whatsoever. *And* not a penny to her name. . . . Nine hundred pounds was nothing to old Perch.

Jess rose to her feet.

"It's late. Call on me tomorrow morning. We can't discuss it now—my head'll burst." She put a plump hand to it. "You can order me my coach. And for God's sake help me find Sabrina."

III

Miss Jeans each Sunday visited a widowed sister who lived at Chelsea. It was Miss Jeans' custom on fine days to walk through Hyde Park as far as the turnpike gates at Piccadilly, and from there to hire a hackney coach to cover the remaining distance.

On the Sunday following that masquerade at Richmond, Miss Jeans emerged at three o'clock precisely from the house in Curzon Street. The sun was hot, and Miss Jeans paused before proceeding, to unfurl her parasol. At the same moment she was accosted by a blond young man in a cinnamon-coloured suit, who appeared as if from nowhere at her elbow.

When afterwards recounting that incident to Sabrina, Miss Jeans particularly emphasised the colour of his suit, for it appears she had been planning that same instant a summer dress of just that shade. A remarkable coincidence, she thought it.

He was hatless, Miss Jeans said, and she noted that he had a scar upon his forehead. A long, deep scar, and red as though it had been recent. He carried his beaver—too warm for such a day —and bowed in military fashion, heels together.

"Ma-madam—" He was stammering and very nervous. "Pray, Miss Jeans—excuse me. I beg—you will allow—"

He knew her name, it seemed. That was so astonishing. That he should know her name! Had he not said her name Miss Jeans would have walked on without deigning further notice. But that he should know her *name!*

"Sir?" Miss Jeans spoke coldly, but from under the green shadow of her parasol, she eyed the youth with no disfavour. Miss Jeans was neither less nor more impervious to charm than others of her sex. Moreover, she had been associated all her life with Breeding. Had she not taught scions of the aristocracy the use of the globes, the history of England and a smattering of French? Was she not herself the daughter of a Rural Dean? Therefore her judgement in passing him without the briefest hesitation for a Gentleman, was not, she knew, at fault, however unconventional his mode of introduction.

"My name," the young man said, "is Burnaby. John Burnaby."

Miss Jeans frigidly inclined her head. The name was indeed familiar, though for the moment, and in what connection, she could not for the life of her remember.

"Of," he added quickly, "the Fifty-sixth Dragoons."

Miss Jeans' acknowledgement of this information was a thought less chill. Sabrina's predecessor had married recently a Captain of Dragoons. Miss Jeans had been invited to the wedding. (And for a whole week afterwards Sabrina had been surfeited with a description of the bride, the uniforms, the dresses, and the presents. Miss Jeans had never seen such company. "The *highest* society, my dear. The *county*. Not the ultrafashionables at all. Everything exactly as it should be. None of the ladies was even *slightly* painted. I made a note of that.")

Nevertheless, though unimpeachable his status and though Miss Jeans was in a flutter, she was at no loss to make him see that she could not comprehend the reason for such unceremonious intrusion.

"That," he said, emboldened, "is what I will explain. If you will be so immensely kind as to permit me to accompany you upon your walk—if you will only be my—be our—be Sabrina's and my confidante and friend—"

"Sabrina!" cried Miss Jeans, now seriously alarmed. "Are you acquainted with Miss Wrotham, sir?"

"Am I acquainted?" repeated this odd young man with violence. "Of course I am acquainted. Would I be here upon her doorstep regardless of admittance if I were *not* acquainted? Would I know you—and all about you—and that abominable household—"

"Sir!" Miss Jeans interrupted in a tremble. "You must be out of your mind!"

For she began to think so, not without some reason. He had not slept for nights, and had passed most hours of each day since the evening he had met her, on the pavement opposite Sabrina's window—or rather the window which fond imagination told him was her own but was in reality Miss Jeans'.

"We cannot talk," he said impatiently, "in the middle of the street. Do, of your goodness, accompany me yonder. It is not far to the gardens. There we can sit."

Miss Jeans, describing afterwards that extraordinary encounter, said she was swept completely off her feet—figuratively speaking, one presumes—although it is certain that young Burnaby was in such a state and she so utterly bewildered, that he might have conveyed her where he wished her by main force. The opportune arrival of a passing cabriolet solved that present difficulty. He hailed it, and Miss Jeans scarcely knowing how she got there —she must have been infected by his madness—found herself within the space of a few seconds hustled in beside this total stranger and clattering over the cobbles in the direction of Hyde Park.

At the entrance in Park Lane he called a halt, paid off the driver, and, maintaining a firm grasp of Miss Jeans' elbow, hurried her away.

"This," she panted, "is most—is *most* unusual."

"The circumstances of the case," he told her, "are unusual. And I am desperate."

Indeed he looked it. A lock of hair had fallen on his forehead. His eyes were dark-ringed as though with much fatigue; beads of perspiration stood on his upper lip; he certainly was pale.

The Park at that hour was virtually deserted. The lower classes did not dare to trespass on the precincts of their betters, and Fashion was at its Sunday dinner; nor did it promenade till after five.

"I have never," Miss Jeans said, "seen anyone so vehement—so determined. He marched me off as though I were a prisoner, as undoubtedly I was. Short of breaking my arm I never could have freed myself. Such a grip he had! We sat under an oak-tree near the water." There were some cows grazing near by. She feared they might be bulls and was for moving, "—until I saw—I mean—"

The situation, Miss Jeans said, was *most* embarrassing.

Not to young Burnaby, however, who poured into Miss Jeans' ear an incoherent jumble of a rose-mask, Sir Rodney Perch, the name of Wrotham and a duel, told in a flood of such loquacity as would have done more credit, Miss Jeans considered, to a Kemble, than a lieutenant in the Fifty-sixth Dragoons.

"And when she heard that I was Burnaby—you see—she hadn't an idea. Nor had I. We neither of us knew the other's name. All I knew—hers was Sabrina. I wrote to her. Yes, certainly I did. I put 'Sabrina' on the envelope and passed the note through to her by a footman."

"Would you believe it!" gasped Miss Jeans.

"Yes, I bribed him. Waited there outside that house for hours gazing at her window."

"Miss Wrotham's window," Miss Jeans interposed, "is at the back."

"Is it? Never mind. I stared up at *a* window, hoping for a glimpse. All day I never saw her. I stayed there until dark. I saw her at last come out with Lady Pinkerton and that preposterous old— God!" He clenched a fist.

"What preposterous old—hem!" Miss Jeans asked, faintly.

"That Perch. They drove away. But she had dropped a glove. I picked it up. *This* was inside it. Bless her! She was as strategic as I."

'This' was a crumpled note which he produced from his breast pocket.

"The first," he said, "that I received from her. This urges me to leave her in peace—not to be so insistent."

"And very properly," declared Miss Jeans. "Really, sir, I wonder that you—"

"Yes, but wait. All sorts of bees are in her bonnet. You know about the duel in our family—how my father challenged hers. You know what happened—he was killed—"

"Oh, dear me, yes!" exclaimed Miss Jeans. "Too tragic."

So that was where she had heard the name before. Such a scandal, too. And Mr. Wrotham abroad never daring to set foot in England for fear he'd be arrested. Yes, Miss Jeans, like everybody else, knew all the details of *that* affair. And this peculiar, impulsive Mr. Burnaby was none other than the son of—*what* a mother!

She was permitted no time for reflection.

"I was about to tell you," went on the incredible young man. "Where was I? Yes, Sabrina. Well. She has a bee. Takes the whole front of the offending to herself. She feels that this question of the sins of our two fathers— I swear, ma'am, no Quakeress could be as stern. But that by the way. I overcame *that* difficulty with yet another note. It happened, as I told her, seven years ago, and is forgotten now. And in any case where two men meet with pistols, the odds are even. Death may come to either. I am satisfied the fight was fair, although I grant my father had just grievance for a challenge. What's done is done. We can't recall it. And good heavens! Must our lives be ruined in our parents' cause?"

With an effort Miss Jeans collected her errant forces.

"Nevertheless, sir, I fail to fathom why, instead of resorting to these complicated methods of communication, you did not call upon Miss Wrotham at the house like a Christian, instead of parading the streets—if you will pardon me for saying so—like a lunatic."

"Because, ma'am, although I do not think I am a Christian, it is quite possible I am a lunatic—or if not now I shall become one if that door remains shut in my face. And secondly because

I was not *permitted* to call at the house. Don't you suppose I *did* call at the house—the very day after the ball—only to be told that neither her ladyship nor Miss Wrotham were at home? I called again later in the afternoon and received the selfsame message, which was repeated every time I rang the bell. Lady Pinkerton no doubt has her reasons for thus putting me beyond the pale. I am ineligible. I have no rank, no title, and very little money beyond my pay. I admit I am no fitting suitor for Sabrina. Nevertheless, Miss Jeans, I persevere."

"I am truly amazed, sir," Miss Jeans protested with some warmth, "that you have the effrontery to press upon Miss Wrotham your attentions in direct defiance of her wishes and Lady Pinkerton's command."

"Effrontery, you call it! I tell you it was a matter of our lives —Sabrina's life and mine."

"This is fantastic, Mr. Burnaby."

"No, it's not. It's love. Have you ever been in love, Miss Jeans?"

"Sir! Such a question I consider an impertinence."

"It is not always thought so. May I go on?"

There was, of course, no stopping him, so on he went.

"All this while, you understand—you see I am quite frank with you—I was aching for a sight of her. I implored her to meet me—"

"Really, sir!" Although bewitched, Miss Jeans was truly scandalised. "How you can sit there with the face to tell me—"

"That's the whole point—I *am* telling you. There's no deception."

He turned upon the startled lady so irresistible a smile that her sails went into immediate collapse. As she put it afterwards, he had a way with him. (It is presumed Sabrina also had discovered that.) Although one was not *certain*, Miss Jeans said, if he were sincere or joking. For he talked so very quickly, and had such answers ready, and altogether it was the most ridiculous, extraordinary interview that, in Miss Jeans' experience, had ever taken place . . .

"I implored her," he was saying, "to meet me early in the morning in Shepherd Market, before the household was astir. More bribery. I've spent pounds on those damned footmen—"

Miss Jeans closed her eyes.

"Sabrina's maid—now this is confidential. You're not to take advantage of it and get the girl dismissed. Promise me?"

It is astonishing to relate that Miss Jeans promised. That is to say, a resigned nod of her head spoke for her; she had no chance to utter.

"I knew you would be kind. You love Sabrina. Who could not? Well then—we met. She has risen every morning of this week at six o'clock. Her maid was in her confidence. Do, ma'am, compose yourself. We paraded the empty streets from end to end—I vow we both know Mayfair better than our beds. Ah! don't be shocked! Sabrina tells me you are tolerant." His eyes, the bluest that Miss Jeans had ever seen, were very bright and earnest. He spoke solemnly. "Imagine, ma'am, my horror, when I heard only this morning that she is to be forced into a marriage with Sir Rodney Perch."

"Mr. Burnaby!" The shock of this announcement caused Miss Jeans to drop her parasol. He picked it up. "Can this be true?"

"I am not a liar. Did you not know of it?"

"She has spoke no word of it to me, but I fancied— Oh, thank you, Mr. Burnaby. I really am so put about—I hardly know—I *fancied* she looked worried these last few days. And Sir Rodney Perch *has* been a constant visitor since—"

"God damn him!"

"Pray, sir, control your tongue!"

"I can't. I'd strangle him for tuppence." He leaned forward

and took Miss Jeans' hand in both of his. Yes, actually! But what is the more surprising, Miss Jeans did not withdraw it.

"Listen, my dear Miss Jeans. It is at Sabrina's instigation I waylaid you. She thought I might have more persuasion in her cause with you than she herself. She wished me to approach you —and who, Miss Jeans, but you, should I approach? Standing as you do *in loco parentis*. So to speak."

Miss Jeans concealed her satisfaction. Mr. Burnaby's way was not without effect. She thought it greatly to his credit, notwithstanding his unconventional method of attack, that he should come direct to her with his addresses, recognising as he did that she, though not Sabrina's legal guardian, was undoubtedly her spiritual adviser. And her friend.

"For who—between ourselves, Miss Jeans—could call the influence of Lady Pinkerton a worthy one, or could consider her the right protector for an innocent young girl?"

Miss Jeans' sense of what was proper rose to a feeble protest.

"I cannot discuss with you, sir, the—hem!—merits or demerits of the lady in whose service I am employed."

"Bosh! Excuse me. But that has nothing at all to do with it." Gazing more earnestly than ever at Miss Jeans' averted cheek, he emphasised his words with the slightest pressure of the fingers that he held. "Miss Jeans. Does Sabrina, do you think, enjoy this empty, artificial life to which Lady Pinkerton has introduced her? straight from the wholesome influence of the country and *your*"—another pressure—"sheltering wing, Miss Jeans? Life! It isn't life. It's death. Dead-rot. No, but seriously, don't you suppose Sabrina feels about it just as I do—that while half England is dying of starvation and all nations are at war, the meaningless palaver that goes to make a London season is a little out of place? or that society might find something better to do than learn to dance the waltz or lionise a man like Byron?"

"Lord Byron is a great poet, Mr. Burnaby."

"The greatest poet never won a war, even though the pen is said to be more mighty than the sword. However, that is neither here nor there. What I wish to impress on you is this"—a squeeze so fervent of Miss Jeans' little finger that the poor lady all but shrieked—"that by hook or by crook, Miss Jeans, you and I have got to prevent this utterly disgraceful and inhuman marriage. Good Christ! A thousand pardons, ma'am: 'tis a monstrous ugly habit—I admit it. But listen—do you mean to tell me that you can stand by and see that lovely young life handed over to a fat-headed smirking toad old enough to be her grandfather? I'd sooner see her in her grave—and so would you."

The boy's voice cracked. Miss Jeans would have it that his eyes were wet. She liked him none the less for that.

He released her hand. She stretched her aching fingers. He stood up.

"Perch," he said, "shall never have her—that I swear. Miss Jeans"—his smile flashed out again to poor Miss Jeans' undoing—"there's nothing for it but to enlist your help in this. You'll not deny us? She has no one in the world but you. And me. We can't count her schoolboy brother."

"But, sir, I cannot see—in what way—" faltered Miss Jeans. "Can I assist you? How can *I* prevent—"

"Do you walk across the Park to Piccadilly? Then with your permission I will walk there, too. And I will explain exactly *how* you can assist me. I have said nothing yet."

She would have thought that he had said enough. But there was more to come. . . .

IV

The battle of Vitoria on June 21st, which added further glory to the name of Wellington, was received throughout the country with wildest demonstrations. From Carlton House, where at an open-air fête the Royal host entertained the élite of London society, to the most pauperised of dwellings, representatives of the nation that had triumphed over Bonaparte celebrated, each in his own fashion, this red-letter day.

We are not concerned—any more than were Lady Pinkerton and others to whom the price of bread meant nothing, and to whom the economic and social realities far beneath them meant still less—with the manner in which the lower class declared its loyalty to England and England's victory. To many, one supposes, the emptiness of stomachs may have quickened the more violent emotions; or it may be that a penny bloater bought in Billingsgate and shared by a whole family, even to the bones, signified for some a gala. It is not for us to say. Young Prior Wrotham at a later date may throw some light upon the subject of what he calls the 'Under-Dog.' (Is it possible he coined that word?) But he, at school at Eton, for all the letters that he writes, can tell us nothing of how his individual brothers, on that day in June in the year 1813, starved or feasted, loved or whored, worked or wept, raped or wed, were born or died, and performed the million and one acts that go to mould each microcosmic spoke in the great wheel of the universe, regardless of a nation's war or peace.

It was a day not only of importance to the history of England, but of some importance also in this narrative. For, notwithstanding that events nearer home had for the last two weeks occupied her time and her attention, it appears that owing to the diplomacy of Sir Rodney Perch, Jess Pinkerton had managed to secure an invitation to the Royal Fête at Carlton House.

"Never have I seen," she writes, "so splendid an Assembly. Every one of note was present, all in Full Dress. *Not* our friend J—rd—n. She will be green, I'll warrant, when she sees my name in the Morning Post among the lists of Guests.

"My Turquoise satin looked well with the gold Turban and the Plumes. Rodney more of a Coxcomb than ever in Corbeau-coloured coat, white satin breeches and false calves was rouged to his eyebrows and had his wig new-dyed. Sabrina still in the sulks refused to leave her room to see us go. Perch has pulled every string in London to get her a Card but Prinny it seems has not forgotten *that Affaire, nor* the name of Wrotham. There's a slur! I should have known how it would be if I were fool enough to bring her up to Town. Better far have hid her in the Country where she might have had her Burnaby or the Village Idiot for all I'd care or wear myself to Bones settling her with the finest Match in London.

"A relief indeed to get away for a few hours from the Misery of the Household and my Poor Wretch who the Dr says will not last six months. I thought as much for he is as bad as he can be and has now gone Incontinent so that a man must be ever in attendance at his bedside. Sooner than six months in my opinion and what a Merciful Release, Poor Soul, for him. . . .

"We were invited for 3 o'clock P.M. and altho' we left the house at 1.30 precisely we took a full hour and a half to drive there, so great the Traffick and so numerous the carriages ahead of us proceeding at a Snail's pace along St James' Street. The Weather was superb. Tents had been erected in the grounds under the supervision of Sir Benjamin Bl—mf—ld but to my thinking the seating Accommodation was sadly limited. I nearly fainted twice for short of sitting on the Sward there was no Seat to be had. Standing so long in the Afternoon heat is a Trial to any Female at my Time of Life.

"The Festivities were opened by dancing on the lawn. The Royal Circle was composed of the Queen, the Regent, the Princesses Sophia and Mary, Princess Charlotte and the Dukes of York, Clarence, Cumberland and Cambridge.

"H.R.H. is stouter than ever, and looks Apoplectic to my think-ing (or something worse). The Queen, poor Soul, is shockingly plain and for all her years is painted to the Skies. Princess Charlotte whose first appearance in Public this was is no Beauty, neither. I had a near view of her and thought her gown the most Hideous I have ever beheld. Her Complexion is good, and her eyes her best Feature, but she is heavily built and over-tall for her years. She danced twice, once with the Duke of D—v—sh—re and once with Lord A—y—ne. Prinny made himself very ami-able to everyone but conversed most with the Ladies H—rtf—d, Ch—d—l—y and M—ntf—d. I did not see my Lady J—rs—y, (nor the F—tz!) Brummel was there, C—ke (looking like a fash-ionable Blucher), 'Tea-pot' Cr—f—d, and 'Ball' H—h—s. Sir L—m—y, Sk—ff—ngt—n and Sc—p—e D—v—s who gave me news of Wrotham! He had met him in Brussels where he is liv-ing very well on nothing with a Countess X—r. He plays high every night and has been twice called out, so D—v—s tells me, and was himself winged once, and the other *affaire* settled without bloodshed on either side. D—v—s says he is suffering from a Disease of the Liver and is as yellow as a Guinea. He assured me also that Wrotham is too well placed with his Countess to wish to return to *this* Country. . . .

"*Later*. . . . *12.30, Midnight*.

"I was interrupted in my writing by the most appalling News. Even now I scarce can take it in. Sabrina has gone with that young Jackanapes. Eloped! Jeans of all Treacherous Bitches breaks me this Calamity with the Air of a Churchwarden pass-ing round the Box. *She* has been aiding and abetting the pair of them—by her face I knew it. By her manner. Perch has turned High-handed and ill chooses his Time in threatening to sue me for what he calls a Loan granted on False Pretences. I always loathed the Creature. Who could believe he would come at me *now* while I am *Prostrate* with Anxiety and Grief. God in Heaven what have I done that Disaster should be heaped upon me in this Fashion?

"That Odious Ungrateful girl! To behave so wicked and so False to me who have given her a Mother's Care. How I regret the day I brought her to the house. I should have known that anything begot by Wrotham would turn out Bad. Bred Bad the pair of them. She and her precious Brother. Both of a Pattern. Jeans hands in her Notice after high words between the two of us and myself in the Vapours.

"To crown all I find Pinkie's man dead drunk beside the bedside and that poor Soul trying to tell me with his twisted Tongue that he has had no Dinner. All this in my Absence. A pretty ending to the Day's Affair. . . ."

It was indeed.

We might question the tactics of Sabrina, who left the faithful Jeans to bear the brunt of it, while she, in the mail coach beside her husband, was on her way to Lynton in North Devon, where they spent a week's ecstatic honeymoon and John's extension of his leave.

'Jeans hands in her Notice . . .' Very wisely. But this would have occurred in any case. Miss Jeans, as she often told Sabrina, would never have stood by and countenanced her marriage to Sir Rodney Perch. Never in this world. "But so long as you, my dear Sabrina, needed me, I would not have deserted you. I should have been in readiness beside you always—for all time . . ."

From Miss Jeans also we have a full account of the manner in which she announced to Lady Pinkerton Sabrina's flight; of the manner in which her ladyship received it and of the scene that then ensued.

One can imagine Jess returning important from that function

in her full-trained 'Turquoise satin,' her 'gold Turban' and her plumes, with Sir Rodney smirking there behind her in his 'Corbeau-coloured' coat. We can imagine, too, Miss Jeans' 'Churchwarden' air. High words may have passed between them, but Miss Jeans declares she never raised her voice. She offered Lady Pinkerton a note written by Sabrina, and left for her to give. She stood by calmly watching while Jess read it, her head with its neat, pathetic bands of greying hair a little to one side.

One must be just. Jess had good cause enough to rave. Sabrina's behaviour, to my thinking, was outrageous. But the alternative—a marriage with Sir Rodney Perch—would have been more outrageous still. Besides which—a fact that Lady Pinkerton has overlooked—Sabrina was mad in love with Burnaby. And he with her.

Jess read the note, turned to Sir Rodney, who was taking snuff, and shrieked at him: "For mercy's sake, man, *do* something! Don't stand there like a monkey!"

Sir Rodney jumped. He had no notion in the world of what had happened. *He* had not read the note. Nor shall we ever know its contents, for Jess promptly tore it up, burst into tears, laughed, then flew at the terrified Sir Rodney and shook him till his false teeth rattled.

"Sabrina! She has bolted! She has gone!"

"Gone? Gone where? Pray, madam—please—" The startled beau released himself, rubbing at his shoulder.

"Gone, I tell you, idiot!" screamed Jess. "Gone with that Burnaby. They're—*mah— Hah-ah!*" Lifting her clenched fists high above her head, Jess apostrophised the ceiling. "Damn him! Damn *all* of you! Damn*nation!* . . . ———!"

Such scenes had taken place at Drury Lane often at rehearsal, but never to our knowledge since.

"You—" She rounded on the trembling Jeans. "You dare to

stand there and to tell— *You* knew of it. Don't presume to contradict me. Serpent!"

It was all so very shocking, Miss Jeans could find no words. ". . . Like a dream, my dear Sabrina, a bad dream. She raved and ranted like a fish-wife. She stormed about the room. Sir Rodney tried to soothe her. So did I."

Between them they got her on a sofa. Miss Jeans burned feathers underneath her nose, slapped her wrists, and bathed her temples in cold vinegar and water, the while Jess sobbed and laughed and shrieked in turn and finally together.

When her administrations began at last to take effect and she had ejected the superfluous Sir Rodney, Miss Jeans sent for her ladyship's maid, and went to her room to pack. . . .

They were married, those two children, at the church of St. Mary's-in-the-Fields. John Burnaby had been carrying a special licence in his pocket for a week. Jeans and the verger were sole witnesses. She and Sabrina left the house five minutes after my lady's coach had departed for the Royal Fête with Sir Rodney and herself inside it.

The servants who saw them go—Sabrina in white muslin with a dove-grey pelisse, Miss Jeans in cinnamon sarsenet acquired new for the occasion—thought they were bent on no extraordinary excursion. Miss was in care of her governess. All must be well.

And if it wasn't, Mr. Burnaby had been free enough of guineas to make it so.

Chapter Three

I

Two YEARS they had, less of a marriage than a lovers' meeting in the midst of war.

He was not sent overseas until October, and until that time she lived with him in furnished rooms at Weymouth. At a moment's notice he received his orders to join his regiment, at Saint-Jean-de-Luz. He fought at the battle of the Nivelle. Their letters to each other at this period I do not reproduce. They are no concern of ours. But I do think that never were two lovers more in love.

Sabrina spent the Christmas of 1813 at Wroth, with Prior. Jess Pinkerton had washed her hands of both of them. She had refused to see Sabrina since her marriage, had shut up Cheam, and remained at Curzon Street in attendance on her husband, who took his full six months to die. Wrotham was good as dead already to his children, since they had heard no word of him for seven years. Wroth still remained to them, and Hannah, both in deplorable condition but their own.

Prior, who finished finally that term at Eton, was undecided what he would do next. At one moment bent on Oxford, at another declaring nothing in the world would send him there. He would stay at Wroth and write. Or he would join forces in London with Shelley, who was sitting at the shrine of Godwin, publishing *Queen Mab* and undergoing matrimonial upheavals with his Harriet.

Or he would throw in his lot with Cobbett, who upon his release from prison was conducting a campaign on Reform, and editing the *Weekly Political Register*. It was possible Cobbett might require a subeditor, or at any rate a conscientious propagandist, to assist him. He would go north. Make a tour of the manufacturing districts. Address the crowds, make known to the so-called 'educated classes' the wrongs and sufferings of the workingman. Rich and poor were of one nation and should be of one mind. He would devote his whole life to the cause.

But for all his wild notions, he stayed at home at Wroth, and spent that Christmas with old Hannah and Sabrina.

She knitted stockings for her John. Warm ones of scarlet wool. Her first Christmas married and he so far away! If tears dropped on the needles Prior never saw them. He was deep in a work on economics, ink on his fingers and his hair on end, munching an apple and declaiming between paragraphs. He refused now to eat meat, had gone—of all things—vegetarian! Only cannibals, he argued, ate each other's flesh, and what was man but a less worthy beast than the patient noble ox, or gentle sheep? Who could stand by unmoved and see a calf torn from its mother's teats and dragged to the shambles followed by the frantic lowings of its dam? or hear the agonised shriek of a slaughtered hog as the knife stuck in its gullet? Did no man consider that even dumb beasts have souls, have instincts, finer, possibly, than ours? can feel, can suffer? While the continuity of organic life on earth, he said, persisted solely on a system of survival of the stronger, of brute force against brute force; while man remained unconscious of his possibilities *as* Man, so would life's misery in every phase continue—till the end.

This oratory was lost upon Sabrina. It was doubtful if she heard it. She sighed, blinked the water from her eyes, and laid down her knitting to stare out of the window at the grey sky, the bare grey trees against it, the cold green country, at some starlings strutting and picking on the lawn where the grass, so long neglected, had recently been sheared by Prior. There were no gardeners at Wroth.

"Like something carved from stone," she said, and sighed again.

"What is?" asked Prior testily. "You listen to nothing that I tell you."

"The landscape—and the sky. It will snow soon. I have had no news from John for two whole weeks. And I am worried."

"The mail coaches always are delayed at Christmas time." Prior finished his apple and laid aside his pen. "I have been thinking, Sab, we'll be eighteen very soon. We shall then get each a thousand pounds. That is, if Jess was not lying when she told you we would have it."

"Why should she lie?" Sabrina was indifferent. Of what use a thousand pounds or all the money in the world, when her John was at the wars and fighting—or was he fighting? Today? Out in the snow? Would it be snowing? Did it snow in Spain—or was it France? Saint-Jean-de-Luz. She never knew—just on the border, maybe. Would he be cold? How long before the summer? Six months. He would be back by summer. Dear God, send him back by then. And keep him safe. Pray God—to keep him safe. Now and for always. . . .

"One never knows with Jess," her brother said. "I've an idea, though, what I'll do with mine."

She smiled. "You and your ideas!"

"This, however, is a good one. I will tell you—"

"Put another log, then, on the fire first. It grows chilly."

The afternoon was closing in the room with shadows. The fire leapt anew under the heaped-up wood. Prior sat on the hearthrug at Sabrina's feet, his hands clasped round his knees. The flame-light flickered on his face with its high cheek bones, his deep-set eyes, under rust-coloured peaked brows, on his hair, a shade darker than his sister's, on his bare throat, exposed at the opened soft shirt collar.

"I am going to use *my* thousand pounds," he said, "or at least one-half of it, in starting a private printing press to propagate Peace among the people. Did you observe that quite spontaneous alliteration? Some writers cultivate the trick. It is a bad trick. No writer should alliterate intentionally. Did you know that? Don't laugh!"

"You make me," Sabrina giggled. "You are so ridiculous."

"To you, perhaps, because you lack intelligence."

"I am quite intelligent enough," she flashed at him. "I have a great deal better sense than you if you but knew it."

"That's as may be." Prior gazed into the fire. "I cannot talk to you. I never can. To anyone. I keep it here"—he tapped his forehead. "One day, perhaps, I'll show you. You and the world. Listen, you fool. You pimple! If all nations were agreed that there should be no wars, if one could inculcate into the pigheads of those that legislate that there is nothing to be gained by the massacre of human bodies—that so long as men have tasted blood they will hunger for it—"

She shuddered. "Prior! Don't!"

"Yes! Hunger for it. I object to war. I would not lift my arm to strike a fellow-man."

"But you would to save your country. If your country and your King were in danger—"

"My country and my King! Patriotism! Pah—sentimental folly. My King—poor devil, witless, crazed—and he who rules instead of him a profligate. Spending a nation's money on his women. What has my country and my King done for *me*—or for my starving brothers? for the very men that fight? Kept on half-rations, given tainted food, insufficient clothing—"

"It's not true! The soldiers are well cared for. Their officers look after the welfare of their men—"

"It *is* true. You know nothing. The whole world is blind and deaf. A fanatic madman sees himself a superhuman power, goes frantic with the fever for possession, sets whole nations at each other's throats, brings misery on countless homes, and death to many thousands—*one man,* mark you! And the world starts up and fights him. *That* is war. A man-made war. No sense in it. No reason—instigated at the whimsy of a lunatic—"

"If you are meaning Bonaparte," Sabrina interrupted, "he is no lunatic. He is second only to Lord Wellington, so John says."

"John says! John says! Child! You only *know* what John says. And John only repeats what he is told—"

"And sees! And does! Which is more than *you* will ever do, sitting here while men die for you. It is easy enough to talk. We want deeds—not words. You have too many."

Sabrina took up her needles; her lips were quivering as she counted stitches.

Prior considered her thoughtfully awhile, and shook his head.

"A pity. A vast pity. Is there no hope ever of enlightenment? What can *one* man do? What can a thousand do against this everlasting struggle for existence?"

"You do talk such utter nonsense!" burst forth Sabrina. "We *are* at war. And sitting there declaiming doesn't help those that are taking part in it and those that are left behind. It doesn't help the mothers waiting for their sons—or the wives waiting for their —husbands. And oh! I cannot bear much more of it—this waiting. No, I can't! They don't always—come back."

Her head went down, tears overflowed and splashed on the red stocking.

Prior shrugged his shoulders, rose from the hearthrug, put out a hand to her bent head, and with an ink-stained fingertip he stroked a curl.

"Don't cry, my pretty. He'll come back. Boney is beaten. The war will soon be over. And the country will rejoice. Great doings! And those that have eaten cow-dung may even eat bread again."

"Always with you it is the abstract," sobbed Sabrina. "You have no personal feeling about war. About *any*thing."

"Have I not?" asked Prior coolly. "We shall see."

He went back to his inkpot. Sabrina to her knitting. The door opened to admit old Daniel with the candles, come to draw the curtains, to announce that it was snowing, to peer out of the window at the darkening drive and to tell them:

" 'Tes a quiet Chrismuss Day for you two chillun! No frolickin', no feastin'. Onnat'ral for young uns not to be merry-like wi' dancin' an' sech. I mind me when we 'ad jollifyin' at me feyther's farm on Chrismuss Day. We used ter dance roun' the Punch Bowl an' play 'Down Down Derry' in the 'all. Aye! Lads *were* lads when I was one. Our 'eads were filled wi' lighter stuff nor book-larnin', Marster Prior."

"But why," demanded Prior, "should we dance round the Punch Bowl and play Down Down Derry in the hall? What *is* Down Down Derry, Daniel? And why should we rejoice this day more than any other day, for every day our brothers—*your* brothers, Daniel—die of slow starvation. Why should we fill our bellies when theirs are empty? Why should we feast and frolic and be glad?"

"Why? Thee knows why, Marster Prior—" Daniel reproved him. " 'Tes a blessed day. 'Tes the Birthday of Our Lord an' Saviour. That's why, Marster Prior. An' 'twould 'a' done you an' Missie 'ere a deal o' good to go to church once in a whiles. That it would. I bin to communion meself this marnin', an' feel the better for it—"

"And you will not go again until next Christmas Day. Come, Danny—do you really believe that—"

"Prior!" Sabrina scowled at him. "Kindly keep your beliefs and disbeliefs to yourself. Neither I nor Daniel care to hear them. Don't listen to a thing that Prior tells you, Danny. He only wants to set you arguing so that he can talk. He talks—but he says nothing. It must be as dull for you and Hannah in the kitchen as it is for us up here. Ask Hannah to let us have some chestnuts with our tea. We can roast them at the fire. Danny's quite right, Prior. We're as gloomy as two owls. We have not even a sprig of holly in the place. What do you keep looking at out of the window, Daniel?"

" 'Tes—methought I saw a 'orseman round the bend o' the drive."

"A horseman? Who would be travelling today?" Sabrina strained her ears to hear the faintest sound of hoofs on frozen ground.

She flew to the window, flung it open wide. The sound of hoofs rang clearer, and more crisp. Nothing to be seen. But her heart leapt up in sudden fierce anticipation. If it should be—

" 'Tes a traveller for sure," said Daniel.

And it was.

She saw him coming in between the tree-trunks; saw in the dusk his long grey cloak and his face muffled to the chin, a pallid blur above it. Her heart died down again. Not John! She had not really dared to hope. But if not John, then who—who in the world?

She was out of the room and at the door and waiting. Prior followed after at his leisure, old Daniel wheezing in the rear.

He was close enough now for them to see his features, his

crooked smile, his hollowed eyes under the down-pulled hat, a hand raised to it in salute. He called to them: "A most infernal journey—but I'm here!"

"God's mercy!" gasped old Daniel, " 'Tes the marster!"

When later in his study he faced his son and daughter, both could see under the candlelight how ill he looked—how grey his face and greyer still his hair. And he was thin. His hand outstretched to the fire's blaze as pale as though all blood in his veins had ceased to flow. He had refused food but ordered drink.

"If there's any in the cellar left. I'll warrant you and that precious Hannah, Daniel, have had your fill in the time I've been away."

"The cellar," Daniel replied with dignity, "is as you left it, sir. I meself 'ave guard o' the key."

"Excellent. Then bring me of the best. And quickly. Well, my chucks?"

His smile was like the grin of a skull, not pleasant. But his eyes, Sabrina thought, in sudden pity, had the look of a hurt dumb beast, with all the sparkle and the life gone out of them.

It was she who broke a silence falteringly:

"What brings you—Wrotham? Is it not—unsafe?"

"Pooh! That"—he snapped his fingers. "They can take me if they find me. I've come back to die in any case. Gad! girl, you've grown a beauty! Let's look at you. . . . And will you still address me by my name? A charming trick I thought it when you were both aged ten. I suppose you don't consider me your father?"

Her heart contracted with the first tenderness for him that she had ever known. She went to his chair and stooped her face to him and pressed her warm young lips upon his forehead. "Father," she whispered. The only time in all her life she had ever called him that. "How did you get here? How did you manage to evade the Customs officers?"

"I've a forged passport. Bah!—'tis simple. But they'll find me in good time. I care nothing. You"—he turned to his son who in the background sat in shadow, hands deep in his breeches pockets, head lowered, his eyes on watch and guarded. "Have you no word to throw to me? No word to throw to a dog—eh? Stand up. How tall are you? As tall as Sabby?"

Prior rose.

"Why, you're only half a man! And half a girl, I take it! Still at Eton?"

"I have left Eton," Prior said, "this term."

"Yes, and it's I who've paid your school fees. That's to say—I placed a sum at your disposal to be drawn on in my name by Pinkerton. Maybe that bitch of his annexed it. He's dying—so I hear. It'll be neck to neck between us, probably."

"Are you so ill, sir?"

"Ill? Do I look it?" He pressed a hand close to his body. "There's a rat inside me, son, a rat that's gnawing at my vitals. His teeth are sharp—but I've an anodyne. A drug that's made of poppy seed. It goes well with good liquor. Where's that fellow with the bottle, curse him! Will he take all night?"

"I'll go—" Sabrina was beginning.

"No, you stay here. This is an unexpected visitation—eh? You both looked scared of me as though I were the Devil. Not overglad to see me back again—is that it? I don't blame you."

Sabrina had no answer. Her eyes, pitying and half afraid, were taking in each detail of his appearance: his splashed riding boots, his buckskin breeches, travel-stained but cut—she could tell that—to perfection; his chin showing a blue stubble of beard sunk on his stock; his coat of purple broadcloth, very elegant, his greying hair and those thick black jutting eyebrows—his ironic, smiling lips.

"Father!" She spoke from her heart that was all too quickly touched. "But indeed we're glad to see you back again. We—we've missed you. Have we not, Prior?"

"We have never known our father," Prior answered quietly, "and scarcely ever seen him."

"Well then," Wrotham flashed back, "you see him now. What do you think of him? Not much, eh?"

"We think perhaps, sir," the boy's voice was sullen, his look defensive, "that even though you were abroad so long you might have taken some interest in us these last few years. Not once did either of us receive even a letter. You left us to the care of strangers and never so much as—"

A low chuckle interrupted.

"So! My son reads me a lecture! Qualifying for the pulpit, are you?"

"No."

"Not the church? The army? No—not that by the look of you. They want more brawn than you can carry. What's all that rubbish on my desk? *My* desk! The impudence! You own the house—are master of it, eh? What's all the scribbling?"

A slow flush dyed young Prior's cheek.

"I have been making some notes on economics, sir."

"God bless me! Is that your recreation for a Christmas Day? A pedant or a politician, are you? Will you outrival Grey and Grenville? You've your chance, my lad! There's not a man-jack among the lot of 'em who could make fit laws enough to run a brothel, let alone a nation. Where do you get it from? Not me! I've never had an interest in such matters. On my soul! You're a solemn enough pair. I've a beauty for a daughter, but I'll be bound she's as strait-laced as any maiden aunt, and my boy's a learned prig. Ha! Well! I've bred a better couple than I'd have thought would ever spring from my loins. But perhaps you don't."

Prior's fist clenched inside his pocket. He took a quick step forward, thought better of it, and stood stock-still—white to the lips.

"Go on, lad!" Wrotham laughed round at him. "Find out what that fool's doing with the bottle. I need it badly."

The boy, his face quivering, turned on his heel and went.

Wrotham beckoned his daughter. "Come! Come here and tell me of your conquests." He pulled her to his knee. She submitted stiffly. How strange to sit so close to him, his hand ruffling her hair! Shyness seized her, she could not look at him. The old spell of his attraction held her enthralled and half-afraid, and dazzled. "Why"—his voice caressed her—"what a sin to keep a prize like this hidden in a worm-eaten barrack! But I hear that Jess paraded you in London. You ought to be there now. I heard, too, that you were stupid and dull as an old boot. You haven't done me credit, have you? I've never known a Wrotham dull. I've known 'em mad and bad but never— Gad! What a pair of eyes she has—they'll do some mischief!"

His hands went out to fondle hers and found there her wedding ring upon it. "Why! What's this? Is it a fancy that you wear it? Or—is it—it's not your mother's?"

"No, sir, I'm married."

"Good God!" He put her off his knee and started up. "Why was I not told? You—a babe, a suckling—married! You're not turned seventeen."

"I am. We're nearly eighteen, Prior and I."

"Time goes—I had forgotten. So you are. And who's the husband? Why is he not here? Where is he?"

She met his glance clearly.

"He's at the wars—and fighting. You knew his father. And his mother—once. His name is Burnaby."

"Not possible!" cried Wrotham. "Is this a retribution—or a farce?" He laughed. Threw back his head and laughed till the room echoed, then broke off with a groan rattling in his throat. "My rat's awake," he muttered, and though beads of sweat stood out upon his forehead, his lips writhed to a grin. "I'll get no peace from him," he said, "till both of us are buried. . . . And I'm to be haunted, it would seem, by Burnabys. I'm damned if I approve it. You're under age. I can withhold consent. Dissolve the marriage. Shall I?"

She was silent. Wrotham laughed again, his hand clutched to his side. Daniel came at last with a squat, dusty bottle and some glasses, mumbling an excuse for the delay. He had been searching for the key of the wine cellar.

"So much you guard it, you old rascal!" Wrotham filled a glass and passed it to his daughter. Then he filled his own.

"To my friend, Arthur Burnaby, and to our next meeting—soon! What? You won't drink to that? I will!"

He snatched the glass away from her, drained first one and then the other.

All her life she had a picture of him standing in his purple riding coat, a glass lifted in each hand, that twisted smile on his lips, and his eyes staring past her and beyond, as though he saw the ghost of him he mocked.

He was a sick man. A dying one. But the authorities took no account of that. They tracked him down and found him, not three weeks after he had taken to his bed at Wroth.

He lingered there impatiently, waiting for the end.

During that time, Sabrina never left him. She tended him with Hannah's help as though she had been trained for sick-room

nursing. He refused to see a doctor. "I'm an outlaw, don't forget, and once they know I'm here on British soil—dead or alive
—they'll have me."

He was right.

On the morning of January 11, 1814, two officers arrived at
Wroth with a warrant for his arrest for the murder of Major
Arthur Burnaby on February 28, 1806.

Prior received them in his father's study, explained the situation, and treated them to a diatribe on his opinion of it. They
were, he said, more than polite in their insistence to see Wrotham.
And they did. They stood at his bedside taking notes and assur-
ing him that every consideration would be accorded in view of
the serious state of his health. So much so that they would advise the physician for the Crown to certify that his condition was
such as to delay the course of the proceedings for the present. At
the same time Mr. Wrotham would understand that he must remain to all intents and purposes a prisoner, and that he, his house,
and all that lay within it would be guarded.

Wrotham laughed in their long faces.

"By you, sirs—eh? My uninvited guests. Pray make yourselves
at home. I've a good cellar. But if you think that you will get me
—then you make a grave mistake. This bed will see the last of
me. A more comfortable end, however, than the gallows."

"Come, Mr. Wrotham! There is every chance of your acquit-
tal. It is extremely likely that a verdict of manslaughter will be
returned, and you may only have to pay the penalty of a fine, or
a short term of imprisonment. After all—in an affair of honour
—you must not take so negative a view."

He grinned. "I don't. My view is positive. Of your goodness—
do be seated, gentlemen. You will excuse me if I take my little
dose? An opiate that eases me of pain. I have a rodent in my
belly with teeth like red-hot sword pricks. No—I'm not delirious.

Neither am I drunk. I am dead sober. As sober as the judge who soon will judge me. Your pardon, gentlemen."

He groped at the bedside table for the small brown phial that stood upon it, always ready to his hand. He raised it to his lips and drank to the last dregs. When he replaced the bottle it was empty. It had been three quarters full.

The effect was not immediate. Those two who watched saw nothing but an added pallor, a slow drooping of the eyelids, his wry smile, nor ever guessed he had escaped them.

But they heard him laugh and tell them he would sleep. They could mount guard outside the door if they'd a mind to . . .

II

Throughout the first half of the year 1814 Sabrina stayed at Wroth. Her father, who had left his son nothing but his house and debts, had left still less to his young daughter, but they had each their thousand pounds, and she a husband generous to folly, although he, poor lad, had little enough to give her. Prior, still full of the wildest-goose notions and no practical sense at all, betook himself to London, or, to be precise, to Hampstead, where he found a cottage on the Heath only three doors from that of a young literary critic, Leigh Hunt, who for publishing his Radical views in a paper of his own printing entitled *The Examiner,* and for his libel on the Prince Regent whom he called 'a corpulent Adonis of fifty,' had been fined five hundred pounds and sentenced to two years' imprisonment in a Surrey jail. He was married to a domestic homely wife, and the father of a lusty brood of children.

It was at Hunt's house that he renewed acquaintance with Shelley. Prior's letters to his sister at this time tell of the poet's visits to Hunt's cottage, and also of his meeting there at a subsequent date with a curious personality of the name of Kell.

That year was for Sabrina possibly the happiest in the whole of her long life. The successful invasion of France by the allied armies, culminating in the capture of Paris and the abdication and imprisonment of Napoleon, had brought for her a temporary surcease from the pitiless recurrence of reunions and partings, with and from him round whom her world revolved.

All of England's triumphs were as nothing to her own. John had been given back to her, his regiment was stationed now at Portman Barracks. He had been raised to rank of captain, had gained an order of distinction, a cross for courage, and a medal for the War. Surely no woman could be prouder?

She found furnished rooms for both of them in Seymour Street.

In June, the seventh and last Earl of Pinkerton died of a stroke, and his widow decorously mourned him for a year. She shut up the house in Curzon Street, sold Cheam Royal to an East Indian merchant for twenty thousand pounds, and on the proceeds thereof departed for Paris in deepest black, with a retinue of servants, a cageful of canaries, a pet monkey, and Sir Rodney Perch.

All the world, it seems—or so Jess Barrett's journal tells us—was in Paris during that summer of 1814. Napoleon was overthrown and sent to Elba, and from London, beauty, rank and fashion flocked to the French capital to celebrate the restoration of the Bourbons.

London no less than Paris shared these national rejoicings. Sabrina, Prior, and the faithful Jeans (now installed as companion to her widowed and ailing sister in Chelsea) went to see the review in Hyde Park which was attended by the allied sovereigns, and in which John Burnaby, very splendid in full regalia of scarlet and gold braid and mounted on a coal-black charger, took his part.

She was incredibly happy. Life, she believed, could offer her no greater gifts unless . . .

But it was not until the first month of the New Year, 1815, that she knew she was to bear his child.

On the night of her nineteenth birthday John, to honour the occasion, took her to Vauxhall. It was her first visit to the famous gardens.

One can visualise those two wandering hand in hand along the darkest walks, or where the crowds were denser, his arm protectingly through hers, standing agape, the pair of them, to watch the fireworks—he despite his brave array of medals still boy enough to be enchanted at the sight of Golden Rain.

They witnessed, too, the audacities of Madame Saqui on the tight rope, and the extraordinary juggling of Ramo Samee, who swallowed seven swords. Both declared these exhibitions marvellous. Sabrina held her breath and squeezed John's fingers tighter—suppose that Madame slipped! And surely Ramo Samee was a wizard! Were those swords made of steel? And why was not the poor man cut to bits? You may be sure John told her all about it. Trickery of course. He could see how it was done—the sword closed upon a spring as it slid down—it was a matter only of good practice. These fellows spent their lives upon such antics. . . . And now what else was there to see?

There was everything to see, and she delighted with it all from the first anticipatory throb as John hurried her through the entrance wicket gate and down a darkened passage, to the moment when the many-lighted enclosure broke full upon their view. And what a view! The trees hung with twinkling lights, and candles in sconces braced to their trunks, so that they looked aflame; supper tables ranged in alcoves, all the temples and pavilions merrily lit up, blazing beneath the grape-bloom of the sky, where stars made a poor show against such rivalry, and music coming from all quarters. What endless promenades—a bewilderment of intersecting ways—the Grand Walk, the Grand Cross Walk, terminating in a statue of Apollo, and a painted vista glimpsed between three arches, representing the Ruins of Palmyra. From thence you were transported to another painted scene, this of a Chinese garden complete with little bridges, a pagoda, and all kinds of birds and flowers. And then the Wilderness—anxious mothers might seek their daughters there in vain —and on the other side of it some Rural Downs, built up from sand and covered with turf after the manner of a Roman camp. From this eminence you could look down upon the company, uplifted from the world at large to a height of twenty feet! But the pavilions were the best of all, fitted with alcoves for the accommodation of supper parties and forming a semicircle round a statue of Handel in the character of Orpheus. Each alcove was gaily lit with candles in coloured globes, and decorated with mural paintings attributed to Hogarth.

To one of these retreats designed for two, John led Sabrina, and ordered a supper of cold chicken, Vauxhall ham and punch. That notorious rack-punch for which the Gardens were so famous and which had wrought such havoc to one Jos Sedley (who even at that same moment and in the box next to their own may have been clasping Miss Rebecca in his arms, and calling her his "Diddle-diddle-darling").

Sabrina swears it was the punch that caused between these two their first and only quarrel. Certain it is that John drank his full share of it—upon an empty stomach. For it so happened that he had been detained at Barracks when he might have been at home and dining with his wife. So that when at last he did arrive he would not stay to eat lest they should miss the fireworks, the greatest of attractions at Vauxhall—after the Punch. But had *she* dined? For she must not go without *her* dinner. Of course she said she had. Oh, yes, she had . . . All the dinner that she wanted.

"And what was that? A caraway seed? A biscuit? Or two bites at an apple?"

"But indeed a big, big meal." She crossed her fingers at the fib, sighed for the duckling burned to cinders in the oven along with his own favourite kidney pudding and the cranberry and damson pie to follow. All that she had ordered for his liking done to death—and he in no mind but to hurry her away and leave his dinner to its desecration.

They were to go by water. The weather was mild enough to warrant it. He had engaged a wherry to meet them at the White-hall Stairs, and a hackney coach to take them there, already at the door.

She was wearing a new white gown of jaconet muslin under a pink fur-lined merino pelisse; and a necklace of cornelian, and gold earrings in the shape of a heart. Tied to her wrist by a nar-row pink ribbon was a reticule, hand-painted in a design repre-senting a lady seated in a swing displaying the prettiest frills and petticoats up to her knees. But charming! And evidently the smiling gentlemen in the picture who stood a little in the back-ground thought so, too. The whole a copy of the famous Frago-nard.

Earrings, necklace and the reticule were John's birthday pres-ents. Not one, but a surfeit of small gifts done up in separate par-cels, placed solemnly upon her breakfast tray and brought to her in bed that morning.

"For you see," John told her when the parcels had been opened and rapturously received, "you have only me and Prior to give you things upon your birthday—"

"And Miss Jeans," she interrupted loyally.

"I had forgotten the good Jeans. Well then, apart from Prior, whose present is not yet forthcoming, and our excellent Miss Jeans, I must make up to you for lack of friends, father, mother,

uncles, aunts, and all. I have to be everything to you except a
brother, haven't I, my lovely? But had I *my* way this necklace
should have been of pearls—and so it shall be when I take command of a battalion."

She put her lips to the scar upon his forehead.

"I would not," she whispered, "have it different for all the
necklaces in all the world."

"And I must go," he whispered back. "I am due on parade.
I shall be late. It is always a misery to leave you, but more than
ever now—on this, your birthday. . . . How can I go? Will you
let me go, my Dawn? I truly must—" But her arms clung
the closer.

He murmured: "You are happy? Do you love me? How much
do you love me?"

She could not tell him that. "If such love could be measured—"
She broke off, her lips aquiver, hiding her eyes against his neck.

It was as if their very spirits met and mingled in that sweet
union from which at last he tore himself away, and left her
dazed and tremulous with the magic of a secret shared, the joy
of life fulfilled.

And that same evening after the visit to Vauxhall they had
their first and only quarrel.

To their supper box the punch was brought and duly sampled,
not by Sabrina. She said that it would make her tipsy.

John would not countenance such folly. "Indeed you must.
Why, it's the chief feature of the place—this punch. You cannot
come to Vauxhall and not drink punch."

He filled a bumper on the spot to prove his words, then filled
another and passed it to his wife.

"Now, my dear love, we drink to your most happy birthday,
and to still happier returns."

Sabrina took a sip and made a face.

"Oh, no, John! Horrid! I cannot bear the taste of it."

Determinedly she put aside her glass.

"But that is childish of you, sweetheart," John reproved her. "Everyone who comes here drinks the punch."

"Then," said Sabrina, her face a little flushed, "I'll prove exception to the rule, and I'll *not* drink the punch."

The moment was unfortunate, for Sabrina was in the slightest mood to resent, not only John's insistence but also the implication—or so she chose to see it—that he had visited these Gardens many times before (in that dim past when neither knew the world contained the other), and in company, no doubt, with ladies more inclined for punch than she. And it was just at this moment when these ridiculous imaginings began to shape themselves into the smallest cloud to darken the sun of her horizon— just at this very moment it so happened that among the throng of people who passed and repassed before the box in which these two were seated, a young lady promenading upon the arm of a young gentleman paused in her walk to greet in the most friendly fashion the husband of Sabrina.

"La! Burnaby! Of all strangers in the world! I had thought you dead and buried."

The gentleman upon whose arm the lady clung jovially confirmed this statement.

"A resurrection, Burnaby! Damme! But we must celebrate."

"'Pon my soul! Clarissa! Allinson!" cried John, starting up with every expression obliterated from his countenance save that of sheer delight. "Well met! Come in! Won't you join us here inside? We can squeeze in a couple more of chairs."

This invitation, with a series of twittering ejaculations from the lady and some boisterous sallies from the gentleman, was immediately accepted.

Sabrina sat aghast at the invasion. In a flash between a second and a second she had noted to the last button on her pelisse every item of the fair intruder's habit; had noted not only cherry ribbons in the crown of her tall hat, but a cluster of cherry blossom underneath the brim; had decided she was painted far too high, and was maddeningly pretty; black-haired, dark-eyed, vivacious, and quite young. All this she registered the while her lips were smiling as became the rôle of hostess, acknowledging her husband's introduction.

"You must meet my wife. My love, allow me to present—Mrs. Clarissa Marshall—Captain Allinson. Late of ours."

"Mrs. Marshall. Charmed," Sabrina curtseyed.

"Mrs. Burnaby." The lady curtseyed.

"Mrs. Burnaby. Delighted." The Captain bowed and kissed Sabrina's hand, and then all but Sabrina began to talk at once.

"I had not the faintest notion you were married, John!"

"Why, damme, my dear fellow, where have you been hiding? Not seen you inside Boodle's since—why, not since— When was it?"

"God knows. But I remember the last time that we were here, Clarissa!"

Sabrina's heart gave a deep dive and then leaped up again. . . . 'The last time that we were here'? The last time *they*— Good heavens!

So there they were, the four of them. John, dispensing punch; the lady (who made no bones about accepting it); Captain Allinson, a horse-faced tall young man with hair the colour of brown treacle and looking for all the world as though it had been smeared with such before it had been powdered—and Sabrina, whose eyes were dark as thunder if John had deigned to look, which he did not, for he was looking at the lady.

Under the table Sabrina's hands were tightly locked together, the while her lips stretched to a smile that was no smile at all. Her John appeared to be transformed. Indeed, she scarcely knew him for her own, so loud he laughed, so merry were his jokes, some full—she was convinced—of the most spicy innuendoes, or so the lady and the gentleman seemed to think, the way that they received them. They spoke, too, of old times and found the topic so absorbing that her presence by all three was forgotten. And she was in two minds whether or no to overturn the table, or to box first Mrs. Marshall's ears, and then her husband's. But naturally, she did nothing; she simply sat there with a smile as fixed as though she had just seen Medusa's head.

Then, during a lull, when it did at last occur to them that she was present, and the talk began to veer in her direction, Mrs. Marshall waxed a little confidential while the gentlemen, refilling glasses and exchanging snuff, discussed the European situation, Lord Castlereagh's masterly handling of the new Alliance, and other topics of purely masculine concern.

Clarissa—Mrs. Marshall—whose tongue was loosed with punch, lost no time in accounting for herself. She was a widow—oh, dear! Yes, 'twas very sad. Widowed at seventeen, not five years since. She had been married just one year—and Mrs. Burnaby—how long had *she* been married?

"Nearly two," mumbled Sabrina.

Just fancy that! And no one ever knowing! Why had John kept his marriage such a secret? *Was* it a secret? Was it a *romance?* Was Mrs. Burnaby— Oh, but surely one might be permitted to use the Christian name—what *was* Mrs. Burnaby's Christian name? ... Indeed! How most unusual! Sabrina ... And was Sabrina very much in love? She, Clarissa, had been oh! *so* much in love, but then, between ourselves, dearest Sabrina, she was always falling in and out of love. Her poor dear husband had been *years* older than she, and had once been very wealthy; but with this dreadful war taxation all one's money dwindled, did it not?

Sabrina answered that she couldn't tell. She had never had any money either to dwindle or to increase.

But that was too distressing. Was Mrs. Burnaby—Sabrina— interested in the fashions? What did she think of these new hats? The crowns grew ever higher—all the latest styles had a military trend in honour of our brave, *brave* soldiers. . . . (That John should dare—his wife reflected—make me suffer such a fool! That *he* should suffer her was even worse.)

And if Mrs. Burnaby—Sabrina—would care to call on her one day she would be glad to show her all the latest fashion-books and modes, for such—being left a widow so very, *very* young—was Mrs. Marshall's only means of livelihood. Yes, modiste and milliner—*modes et robes*—at 111, Queen Street, in Mayfair. If Mrs. Burnaby would remember the address. She would design for her the *sweetest* hat—the very copy of one made for Lady Caro Lamb. If one might suggest that Sabrina should wear blue instead of pink—blue was the colour for a blonde— and such lovely, lovely eyes. The new spring hats were *all* in satin straw—and if Captain Allinson—Toby—John—could supply a pencil and a little scrap of paper—

Both gentlemen with alacrity complied with this request.

Then Clarissa, not to favour one more than the other, must take from John his gold-cased pocket-pencil, given him last Christmas by Sabrina, and from Toby—Captain Allinson—his card. On this she scribbled her address and gave it to Sabrina. For they must often meet for tea and talk—it was so seldom, so very, very seldom, that one came in contact with a kindred soul. Dear John (Sabrina would never mind her saying 'John'?) was such a very old, old friend.

All this while the gentlemen drank punch, and the more John's face turned scarlet, so Sabrina's turned more white.

Presently Captain Allinson suggested they should stroll in the grounds. Sabrina said that it was getting late. It were better to be going.

"Going? Going?" John banged his fist upon the table till all the glasses jumped. "Who is it says going? Why, the nigh's on'y jus' begun."

If he had not been quite so merry, or so hazy or so blind, he would have seen that Sabrina's smile was more crooked than its wont, and that the glitter in her eyes was like forked lightning. But John's head was full of punch, and he saw nothing. He did not see an inch before his nose.

Offering his arm to Mrs. Marshall, he walked her away with a laugh across his shoulder to Sabrina.

"You will follow us, my love, with Cap'n All'nson. Don' run 'way with Mrs. Burnaby, All'nson! Cr'lissa and I are goin' to see the ruins."

And off they went. John and Clarissa on ahead, and Sabrina in the rear, with rage in her heart, storm in her eyes, and her hand on the Captain's arm.

She watched her husband and the odious Clarissa swallowed up in the mass of sightseers, and not one glance behind him did John give. Captain Allinson, who was as tall as a giraffe, had little enough to say to her, but what he had to say he bawled, for the crowd was very noisy, the music louder still. When he squeezed her hand in the crook of his elbow too close against his side, Sabrina was hard put to it not to pinch him. Detestable idiot! How could John make a friend of such a simpleton? With his horse-face, and his haw-haw laugh and his stupid baaing voice. She seethed with hatred of him, and all the world.

"Now it seems that we have lost 'em," said the Captain. "I

must keep an eye upon Clarissa's hat. It's as high as a church steeple."

"I think they took the path *that* way," Sabrina said, and tugged her hand from the Captain's arm while his head was turned to look. In a trice the crowd divided them, she lagged artfully behind, and, by the time her escort had discovered that she was no longer at his side, she was running swiftly down a sidewalk in the direction of the entrance to the Gardens.

Exactly what she meant to do, she did not know. The impulse of the moment had decided her, and anger, humiliation and a fierce desire to hurt for the imaginary hurt she had received. She would teach John that he could not so neglect her, or introduce into their privacy these strangers from his past. All that was possessive in her nature rose up to be avenged, and all that was young and foolish, and in love.

If John should find her gone, so much the better. He'd be alarmed. Frightened to death, he'd be. Or would he care? He was well pleased with his Clarissa, and well tuned with his punch. That vile, wicked punch! . . . She would go home—yes, she would go straight home. Or better still, she would find a coach to take her up to Hampstead, to Prior's cottage on the Heath. There she would lie the night, and John and his Clarissa could go to— Jericho. And John would think her murdered. Dead. She wished she were. . . .

She was sobbing now, a little, as she ran, dry, tearless sobs. Couples strolling there beneath the trees turned to look at her. She did not care. Her heart was bruised. She thought it broken.

At the entrance gates a gang of chairmen surrounded her with guttural invitation. No, she did not want a chair. It was a hackney coach she wanted. Please to get her one at once.

She did not go to Hampstead, for the man refused to drive the

long distance at that hour. The watchman was calling eleven
o'clock and a fine night when she reached the house in Seymour
Street. It was past one when John returned.

She had not gone to bed, but sat in her wrapper in her bedroom awaiting him. He stood there at the bedroom door, his eyes
on hers, stony, cold, his face expressionless; and his voice when
he spoke at last, was like a whiplash.

"Is this your idea of a jest?"

His icy tone incensed her. She who in those hours of her
waiting had been utterly remorseful and in the mood to ask forgiveness, and to forgive—exquisitely. But now she flamed in
tempestuous response.

"No jest, indeed. I came away because your friends did not
amuse me."

"So?" He spoke in that stranger's voice of his, dry, staccato. "It
mattered nothing to you, I suppose, that we searched the grounds
for hours—nor did it strike you that your manner was dis-
courteous to my guests."

"*Your* guests!" She rose and shrilled at him. "Why should I
care for your guests? *I* was your guest tonight. You had no right
to bring them to our box, or to present me to such a woman. One
who has obviously been your mistress."

"You lie!" He was now as hot as she, and his eyes that had
been frozen were lit and blazing. "You have no justification
to assume—"

"The justification," she interrupted, "of a wife. A fact that
you seem to have forgotten." Her heart was galloping so loudly
she thought that he must hear it. She felt a little sick.

He was regarding her with a meditative smile on his lips that
were a narrow pallid line. She noted every detail of his bearing,
a lock of hair fallen untidily upon his forehead, hiding the scar

beneath it, his eyebrows raised, one a little higher than the other, the dust upon his boots and kerseymeres, a bleeding scratch upon his hand.

She asked him how he came by it. "Have you been fighting?" She pointed to the mark. "Or did the lady scratch you?" And she laughed, an ugly little snigger.

"I have been crawling on my hands and knees in undergrowths, scouring the hedges for you. Who knew but you had been set upon by thieves?"

"But you see," she told him coolly, "I was not."

"Exactly."

He turned on his heel and left her. She heard him in the next room moving furniture, a heavy bumping and a creaking; heard the door between them locked. Then frenzy seized her, and she flew to it and pummelled at the panels. "Let me in! Why do you lock me out? What are you doing?"

"I am going to bed," came back the chilly answer. "I am sleeping on the couch in here tonight."

It was the end of her world.

She lay awake till morning, too miserable to seek relief in tears, too proud to ask forgiveness. But she knew she had been wrong, been wicked. She was utterly to blame. She would possess him—yes, she saw it now—down to his dreams. All of his past, and all the women he had known—body, soul and all of him she drew into herself. It must not be. In that way danger lay. If she entwined her life with his too closely it would mean imprisonment from which he might at some time seek escape. But how was it possible to love with the whole depths of one's being and *not* desire a complete possession? She had discovered a new force in herself, the force of jealousy. But jealousy of whom—of what? A foolish scatterbrain, a pretty face, the distraction of a moment? Were such trivialities as these to weigh against the solid substance of their lives? She shivered where she lay in the wide lonely bed, stifling in the pillow the aching sobs that brought her no relief.

And when morning broke he came to her.

Reconciliation was worth the anguish of that brief estrangement. Never, so each vowed, should such misery occur again. He was the more contrite. He should have remembered her condition. God! Suppose that he had harmed her! Had he harmed her? Had she slept? She was so pale, and overwrought. She need never—he would promise her—meet either of those two again, had she no mind to. She was not compelled to like his friends simply because they *were* his friends. And these were but the slightest of acquaintances. Would she believe him? . . . Yes, indeed she would believe him, but had he known—would he tell her now, had he known ever—intimately—that woman? Never in this world, he swore it. Well, perhaps he'd kissed her once when he was drunk. . . . No, not last night. No! Truly not last night.

But with feminine persistence she drove home her final point.

Had he known any women—ever—in that way?

Must she ask him that? He knew no women now. None but his Dawn.

And so, like the two children they were, they kissed and comforted each other, and vowed the same eternal vows that have been sworn by lovers since time immemorial.

Looking back on it in after life, she realised that this trivial and momentary rift had drawn them even closer, had warned her where the danger pitfalls lay, had served to cement still further the foundations on which their love was built. . . . But one wonders, had they been allowed a longer span, would those foundations have endured the test?

III

It was not long after this that Prior brought to the house in Seymour Street a recent acquaintance, one Roger Kell, a man of stocky build and middle age, with hair gone prematurely white. Fresh-complexioned, rosy-gilled, he had a curious cast in one eye that gave to his expression a quality of remoteness. His voice was high-pitched and precise, slightly pedantic, as one used to public speaking. Not the least thing odd about him was his dress, of unrelieved black and an almost quakerish severity, with knee breeches and buckles to his square-toed shoes. He kept a bookshop in St. Paul's Churchyard and was a widower with one young daughter, Mary.

This Kell, it seemed, shared Prior's crazy views. A stern up-holder and friend of Robert Owen, he was in fact, instrumental in working out the details of the first Factory Bill in collaboration with Owen and Sir Robert Peel the elder, father of England's future premier. He had founded, too, a club for working-men whose premises were two large empty rooms above his shop, and there those who could afford the sum of twopence might procure a meal of meat and bread and ale, and read the pamphlets printed for their edification, and privately by Kell himself, on the subject of universal suffrage.

Idealist, fanatic, what you will, he had none the less a keen appreciation for the better things of life, whether these might be good literature, good food, or the face of a pretty woman.

All eyes for Sabrina, although his left was roving, he won her heart completely by his estimation of Prior's progress in the cause. It mattered not to her that she did not understand nor care what was this cause, so frequently alluded to and far beyond her powers of comprehension. (Something parliamentary, she deemed it, or revolutionary or such.) What mattered most was that this Mr. Kell, a gentleman, she judged, of paramount intelligence, cultured, and a scholar, too, should speak so highly of her brother.

"He should go far—it is young blood we want. Young, eager blood like his. Sincere enthusiasm, Mrs. Burnaby, and selflessness. Yet—do not mistake me—*self* cannot be denied. To find—to *know*—oneself is the chief aim of all who desire an intelligible and sympathetic vision of this turmoil that is life. For how, without a thorough knowledge of our own Ego, can we hope to give help to others?"

"Can we," Sabrina asked him, "ever know ourselves? or our own Ego? I seem to be a dozen different persons. I present a different aspect to everyone I meet—except—" She paused and glanced up at her husband's portrait on the wall.

"Except to him"—with a smile of singular sweetness and understanding Roger Kell finished her sentence for her—"who knows the truth of you. Yes, it is only by love, by tolerance, and by united effort, Mrs. Burnaby, that we may learn to know the truth that lies within ourselves, and in the souls of men."

She looked across at Prior. His face, she thought, was softer, his expression more serene than she had ever known it. She was glad of this new friendship for him, and her heart went out in gratitude to the strange, forceful little man whose philosophy seemed based on the simplest of all creeds, and yet one so seldom practised. To love one's neighbour as oneself. Who did? Was that, she wondered, what was meant by a Democracy?

When he invited her to pay a visit to his bookshop and meet his little daughter, she accepted gladly.

"Ask this brother of yours to bring you—tomorrow—if you will. Are you interested in rare editions? I will show you some exquisitely illuminated sixteenth century quartos. It has been the greatest pleasure to meet you, Mrs. Burnaby. Tomorrow then? I shall expect you."

The next day Prior called for her to take her there. Roger Kell's shop occupied the ground floor of a four-storied house directly facing St. Paul's. Sabrina thought it must be peaceful to live so close to the Cathedral, and to hear the chime of bells striking the hours from morning until night.

It was a queer, dark little shop down two steps to its interior, with book-lined walls exuding the faint musty smell peculiar to old volumes. While they waited for the appearance of their host, Prior pointed out to her a glass-covered case in which each book, he said, was a museum piece of priceless worth, but not for sale.

"See, here"—he indicated a worn, faded binding, the text upon its cover illegible with age—"is a first edition of Sir Thomas Browne's *Religio Medici*. He will never sell it, although it is worth a fortune to a collector. This shop is as much Kell's private library as his trade. . . . Ah! And here is Mary, who can tell you a good deal more about these things than I. Is that not so, Mary?"

The little girl, of about thirteen or fourteen years, who from the inner room behind the shop had silently approached them, smiled a wordless greeting.

"This is my sister, Mary. . . . Is your father within?"

"No, Mr. Prior, he is not at home, but he told me to say he will be back shortly. He has gone to see a poor man who is lying sick of a fever in Newgate Jail. They say he will be hanged. . . . Pardon me, ma'am. How do you do?" She dropped a curtsey as she spoke. Her voice had the same precise inflection as her father's. Her hair of a rich, dark brown was banded in neat braids round her head. She had a high intelligent forehead, the brows delicately shaped like the wings of a bird in flight above a pair of velvety, soft brown eyes. Over a short-sleeved dress of grey merino, she wore a little apron of black silk. She was small for her age, not much taller than a child of ten.

"Pray come in, Mr. Prior, sir, and the lady, too. Father told me to prepare tea if he should be late. But I think he will not be long in coming now."

"Is it Tom Beckett he has gone to see?" Prior enquired.

Mary nodded. "And will they really hang him, Mr. Prior?"

"For stealing five shillings from a butcher's till to buy his children bread? Yes, Mary, they will hang him."

The child's eyes filled slowly. " 'Tis too cruel," she murmured. "If he had come to father he would have given him the money. Why did he not come to us?"

Prior took her hand in his. "You would have given him every penny in your money-box, would you not, my pretty?"

"But surely, Mr. Prior—I have ten shillings still. Pray, ma'am, will you please to walk carefully—there is a step down into the room."

"Do you look after the shop in your father's absence, Mary?" Sabrina asked with a smile for the little girl's grave old-fashioned manner.

"Yes, but usually Silas—that is our handy-man—is here to help me. He has gone in the coach to Putney with a parcel of books to deliver. Please, ma'am, will you not be seated?"

While Mary busied herself with the kettle on the fire, Sabrina took stock of the room, which was furnished in the modern style with one or two fine Sheraton pieces—the only mark of antiquity represented by some faded tapestry that Prior told her was genuine Gobelin. A canary in a gilt cage hung in the bow window, and on the panelled wall above the mantelpiece the portrait of a woman whose features bore so strong a resemblance to Mary's that there was little doubt as to the relationship.

By the time tea had been placed on the table Roger Kell returned.

He began at once to talk of his interview with the man Beckett, who, he said, had been too light-headed with the fever to speak coherently of the trial that lay before him, and which at best would be the barest mockery.

"For the crime of theft"—a faint ironic smile came upon his lips—"must merit the just punishment of the law." He turned to Sabrina. "And yet, Mrs. Burnaby, in the case of a duel where a man is killed in some wanton cause, his murderer is invariably acquitted, and the affair considered one of honour, to the credit —rather than discredit—of both parties."

He had spoken thoughtlessly and realised it by Sabrina's mounting flush, and Prior's quick rejoinder: "I cannot see in what way lies the credit—either to the killer or the killed. My father was forced to live in exile, a social outcast, because his shot proved fatal. I admit he may have deserved his ostracism, yet you must remember he answered to and did not make the challenge."

"That is so, but had he stood his trial and been acquitted, he would surely have been reinstated as a leader of society. Pardon me, my young friends, if I pursue a painful subject." His kindly glance embraced them both. "But I do not think for one moment that your father would have had to pay the death penalty. How many have, within our knowledge? Take the most recent fatal duels of the present century. Do you remember—but I don't suppose you would, for I doubt if either of you were interested in the newspapers in 1810—a political duel that took place at Wexford between a Mr. John Colclough and a Mr. Alcock? For many years, it seems, a certain nobleman had monopolised the representation of Wexford, and Colclough at last determined to put the sense of the county to the proof and proposed Sheridan as joint candidate with himself. Alcock, well supported by certain influential electors, contested the county, but several tenants of a well-known landowner who had supported Alcock absolutely refused to vote for him, maintaining that they were on the side of Colclough and Sheridan. Alcock's party ascribed this complete reversion to the name of Sheridan, which they maintained was used as a decoy by the opposing party. Colclough was requested either to decline his votes, or to receive them at his peril. He chose very rightly to disregard this threat, with the result that it was decided both candidates should fight out between themselves the contested question. I am speaking now of Ireland, Prior, where extraordinary happenings are permitted; nevertheless—this is actual fact—that these two met and Colclough was killed. . . . Two hours afterwards it was announced that Alcock had been elected. At the next Assizes he was tried for murder before, I think—if I remember rightly—Baron Smith, who openly declared against a capital conviction. The jury returned an immediate verdict of 'Not Guilty.' "

He paused, thoughtfully stirring his tea; and, spooning up some melted sugar from the bottom of the cup that Mary had just passed him, he scrunched it like a schoolboy. Then: "So you see the way it goes." He glanced up and met Sabrina's clear attentive gaze with that remote look of his. "A man is hanged for taking a few shillings to buy food for his children, but not necessarily for taking human life."

"It is all most terrible," murmured Sabrina. "There seems to be no sense, no mercy in our laws."

"Not in our man-made laws," said Roger Kell, digging up another spoonful of the sugar. "Do excuse me for this childish habit —I have the sweetest tooth. No, not in our man-made laws, because mankind, not excluding those who *make* our laws, has not yet reached that state of consciousness wherein the quality of mercy is not strained. Man performs his functions and his work in life as an automaton. Totally unaware of his own possibilities, he will yet tell you glibly that he is made in God's image. . . . Did you ever know the fairy-tale of the Sleeping Beauty? I expect Mary here can tell it you—eh, my love?—of the Princess who slept until the Prince's kiss awakened her? One might liken the soul of man to the Princess who lives in a sleeping palace amidst a sleeping world, awaiting the magic moment of enlightenment." He pointed his teaspoon at Sabrina, but his eyes were half closed as though he saw—not her—but through her and beyond. "That moment," he said, speaking slowly and prophetically, "has yet to come. And it *will* come. Though the way of him who strives to waken those that sleep, may end in crucifixion."

"Please," whispered Mary at Sabrina's elbow, "may I offer you another cup of tea, ma'am?"

"Ah, yes!" Kell roused himself and smiled round at her. "That is right, my dear. Attend to your guests. I entertain them far too lengthily. Mrs. Burnaby, you will sample a slice of Mary's most excellent seed-cake? My little girl is a first-rate cook, as you will discover if you will—as I hope—sometime take dinner with us. Is your cup empty, Prior? Refill it, Mary, if you please. . . . And then you may fill mine. What do you think of this latest news of Bonaparte?"

"Is there," Prior asked, "any latest news of Bonaparte? I thought he had been silenced for good and all, though it never would surprise me to hear that he was landing troops at Dover."

"Then have you not heard the rumours that are floating round the city? . . . But it is not likely that you would upon the heights of Hampstead. By the way, how is Leigh's chill? I meant to ask you—and now, while I remember, Mary has made him a bowl of chicken broth, congealed to a jelly, so you may carry it in safety with you if you will, and give it him with my—no, with Mary's compliments. Is that not right, sweetheart?"

"Yes, please, Mr. Prior. If you will be so good as to take it to Mr. Hunt. He tasted some soup I made when he was here to dinner, and he liked it very well, so I thought, maybe, he would care for some now that he is sick. He is not badly sick, I hope, Mr. Prior."

"No, he is better. He has had his feet in a hot mustard bath for two nights before retiring, and has passed his ailment on to all his brats. Such a fanfaronade of coughs and sneezes as you never heard! In fact the whole village is rampant with this chill. I think it is a kind of plague—all complain of aches and pains, in heads and backs—and so on. But this latest news of Boney, Roger, what is it?"

"It may or may not be true—but they say he has escaped from Elba. The Stock Exchange had it yesterday morning, and there has been in consequence, or so I hear, a distinct drop in the Funds."

"God grant—not true!" broke from Sabrina.

"I am inclined to believe it is true," Prior said. "What is imprisonment to Boney? A further incentive to set his heel again upon the neck of Europe. Sooner or later he is bound to escape. He is mercurial. There is no holding him. We've not done with him yet, mark me!"

Roger Kell nodded, sitting back in his chair, his elbows on the arms of it, and his finger-tips just touching. His eyes, the one aslant, the other straight and steady, gazed before him as though he saw outside the window something other than the green buds of the plane-trees whose lower branches leaned against the pane, or the grey pigeons flown from St. Paul's to cluster on the sloping roof of a low housetop. As though, perhaps, beyond that patch of sunset sky above the budding plane-tree where, even as he watched, the darkening storm-clouds gathered, he could see a snakelike line of men marching with soundless tread. . . .

"Was that thunder?" Mary asked. "I thought I heard it."

"The sky looks threatening." Prior rose. "We had best be going, Sab, before the deluge."

Good-byes were said. Mary gave into Prior's charge the bowl of soup. Roger Kell presented Sabrina with a book, a slender volume containing some of the most recently published poems of Mr. Wordsworth.

"A great poet, Mrs. Burnaby, but then—it is an age of poets. And names that are known today will be known tomorrow— and tomorrow. Yes, indeed, pray keep the book. I am acquainted with the author. He comes to London rarely, but on such occasions as he may be induced to leave the solitude of his lakes and fells, he pays me the honour of a call. The next time you come I will show you something of more value, an early Chaucer. You have seen none of my treasures, since this brother of yours will hurry you away. You must come often. You will be always welcome. Good-bye—and God bless you."

That visit left upon Sabrina a deep impression. The calm, precise voice of Roger Kell, the words he spoke, his grave, sweet-faced little daughter, and the quiet room with its musty smell of books remained long in her memory. But she was to see her whole world crumble before she visited the shop in St. Paul's Churchyard again.

Chapter Four

I

Napoleon's escape from Elba was no rumour. Within three days the whole of Europe rang with it.

"The War-Dog is loosed from his kennel, and once more the Doves of Peace are flown." Thus, airily, wrote Prior to his sister from his cottage on the Heath (March 5, 1815). "One cannot help but admire the indomitable courage and tenacity of that little Monster. In my belief he is unconquerable. This final contest will decide the future of the world. All personal reactions upon the subject of Principle as for and against the settlement of disputes of nations by massacre and the draining of said nations' whole resources, must be relegated in face of these new and terrible activities, to the background. War to the Knife! Slay and Spare Not! He who sees himself—and acts as though he were—Jehovah, has so ordained it. I would have had my own puny share in this bloodiest of all struggles (as it will prove to be—you mark my words!) that we have yet had to face. . . . You will deem me a Turn-Coat that I do not still uphold the Principles to which until now I have so consistently adhered.

"However, John will, I know, approve me. Perhaps you too, when you hear.

"I have made the greatest efforts to enlist my services as a private soldier in three different regiments! (Mounted, you may be sure. I do not even in this heroic mood see myself on foot.) But do not, alas! put out your hand too readily to pat me on the head. I have been refused! My lack of inches tells against me (although I should have thought that upon a battle-field the more insignificant the target, the less likely to be hit).

"However, there seems to be a regulation height according to the dictum of two out of three recruiting sergeants to whom I conscientiously applied. The third was more leniently inclined to overlook my meagre stature, and conducted me before the military Medico for a more searching examination. This revealed that my heart (the merest nothing, child, do not be alarmed) does not function in the manner prescribed by the Regulations of Lord Wellington. Still, none can say that I have not at the least, made honourable attempt to exchange the sober garb of a civilian for a dashing scarlet coat. . . ."

So began those historic Hundred Days which were to end in the battle that broke the back of the Napoleonic wars.

At the end of April John's regiment was ordered to Brussels, where from Paris the whole of fashionable London had migrated, hounded from the French capital by the steady influx of Napoleon's troops.

Sabrina, in company with many other wives of officers, who could not bear the strain of yet another parting, followed soon after, attended—in view of the delicate state of her health and John's insistence—by Miss Jeans.

He had found rooms for them in the Rue de Namur, and there during those first few weeks that preceded Waterloo, all three were comfortably established.

Although she took no part in any social activities, Sabrina's letters to her brother at this time show her full of interest in all she saw around her. As in those early days in Mayfair, so now in Brussels with her good 'Jeansie' for companion, she walked in the Bois de la Cambre, fed the swans upon the lake, or drove out in a hired carriage to the villages on the outskirts of the city, there to drink milk at some farmstead or, leaving the carriage at an inn, to wander at will along "solemn avenues of poplars"—so to Prior she describes the straight long roads of Belgium, "plastered with such mud as you would not believe possible after one night of rainfall. I dare not think what it must be like in Winter. There seems to be no Enclosure here of private Land. The Orchards trespass on the road-sides without Restraint or Barrier. Surely the Belgian peasantry must be very honest not to take advantage of such Temptation. I am charmed with the native Costume of the Women, their dark crimson petticoats and bodices of black velvet with wide white sleeves. The caps—or coifs as they are called—which they wear on their heads are like the wings of some great white bird. With their wooden pattens and milk-pails against the background of this dwarfed flat country, they resemble nothing so much as the little figures in those two Dutch pictures in the Dining-room at Wroth.

"Every now and then along the roads are placed the simple Shrines dedicated to Our Lord or to His Mother, and it is a common sight to see an aged woman leaning on her staff come to kneel, or a toddling child to lay at the foot of some crude wooden Image of the Tortured Christ, an offering of way-side blossoms. A peaceful, simple land this little Belgium, even though bivouacs and horse-lines cover now its open fields, and everywhere one sees and hears the preparations of War. . . ."

II

In consequence of his preoccupation at Headquarters, Sabrina saw her husband not as often as she could have wished, but she was thankful to be near him, to await the sound of his horse's hooves on the cobbles below her window, or his step upon the stair, and for those nights when, undivided, she could hold him close, listening to his sleeping breath, his head heavy on her shoulder and the prayer ever on her lips that God would keep him safe—here for her arms—and always.

She had been in Brussels nearly two months when she received a call from Lady Pinkerton.

"I am not one to bear umbrage for ever," she confided to Sabrina over tea and muffins (an English delicacy procured from Heaven knows where by the enterprising Jeans). "I heard you were in Brussels and found out where you lodged from the wife of John's Colonel. I suppose she visits you? She was a Cholmondeley (one of the *best* families) and has great influence at Carlton House. If you have a head screwed on your shoulders and not always in the clouds—you will play your cards, my child, to gain her favour. That is, if you want that boy of yours to take his place at Court. Yes, as soon as I knew you were here, I made up my mind to forgive you and forget. What hurt me most— and this I feel I have to let you know—was your ingratitude. Your slyness! To go behind my back—"

"Dear Jess!" Sabrina broke in, her small crooked smile quivering on her lips. "I would not have hurt you for the world. But had I told you that I was going to marry John you would have hurried me to church with old Sir Rodney. You know you would!"

"Well, well!" Jess took the girl's chin between two fingers, gave it a squeeze and let it go. "What's done is done, and can't be *un*done, and it's no good crying over milk that's spilt. You've made your marriage bed and if you find it deuced hard to lie on then it's your own affair and no one else's. As it happens Perch is here now and dancing at the heels of all the prettiest girls in Brussels. But he's too old a bird to catch the early worms! He had a passion for *you,* sweetheart, because you smacked his face. 'Ods me! And how I laughed! You should have married him. You'd not have found him *exigeant*. Better an old man's fancy than a young man's fool. When do you expect, my dear?"

Sabrina's cheeks turned pink. "Am I so noticeable?"

"*I* can tell. That dress don't leave much doubt behind it. I can give you the name of a good woman in the Rue de Florence who specialises in gowns for these occasions. All the young matrons who are *enceinte* are gowned by her, and believe me the better half of half the British Army here are in good case. These long absences make husbands hot. La, child! How you blush! I wish I could. You've lost some of your looks, but they'll come back. Do you think me thinner than when you saw me last? I've been taking a remedy prescribed me by a French doctor who attends all Paris—at least all of us who *were* in Paris—for various complaints. A marvel of a man, my dear, and the greatest boon to ladies who find themselves in awkward circumstances. . . . Now tell me, have you received a card for the Duchess's ball tonight?"

Sabrina shook her head.

"Then," Jess cried with energy, "you shall have one. I'll see to it you go. I'll take you there. In the right gown you should do very well. You won't be able to show yourself much longer, but for a month or so you shall come visiting with me in Brussels. Everyone is here, the Creeveys, and the Ords—you'd like Bessy—and Wedderburn Webster—and the most delicious armies of inflammable young men to set even *me* afire!"

A gleam of mischief sparkled in Sabrina's dark blue eyes. "I thank you kindly, ma'am, but I have my own private store of fuel. To add to it would, I think, be bringing coals to Newcastle."

That was possibly the first inception of a time-worn joke. Jess had certainly not heard it said before. She received it boisterously, went off into peals of laughter, and handed it all round Brussels that same evening.

"My faith! She's coming on! You're developing a wit, my darling. You never had one. Such a trouble as I had to make you talk. Prior atoned for all you lacked in tongue. Is he as garrulous as ever? What does he do with himself now? Write? He'll never earn three ha'pence with his pen. How are you off for money? And who looks after Wroth? Is that terrible old Hannah with you still?"

Jess gave no opportunity, nor did she seem to expect an answer to her questions, but rattled them off like shot from a popgun with scarcely a pause between.

"Wrotham," she said, "left you nothing, I suppose. It's a good thing he had the sense to kill himself."

"Jess—if you please—" stammered Sabrina.

"Well, he'd have died in any case," retorted Jess, "and sooner by his own hand than the hangman's. Has this lad of yours a penny? His mother should have left him comfortable. Burnaby had quite a little fortune. I expect she ran through it all and more besides. What'll you live on? Love? That'll feed the heart but not the stomach."

Sabrina said she managed very well. John had his pay and a small income besides, and she her thousand pounds.

"When you're as old as I am, girl," Jess told her, getting up to go, "you will learn that money is the only love of which one never tires. You refuse to come to the ball tonight? So be it. You always were a mulish little wretch. But perhaps it is as well." Jess gave her a judicious glance from head to heel, and smiled. "You'd have had to spend the evening in a cloak. Yes! 'Pon my word—you're big. . . . Good-bye, my love. I'll fetch you for a drive tomorrow. 'Tis deplorable that you ride out in a hired carriage. Do you like my hat? I think this amber suits my hair.

You see I am in colours. I wore full mourning for a year, half for six months, and now I am a harlequin again. You say nothing of my hair. Did you not notice? It is auburn now."

"I thought," Sabrina answered doubtfully, "that there was something of a difference but I did not care to mention it in case—"

"I'm fifty-two and growing old disgracefully," sighed Jess.

When John came back a few minutes after Lady Pinkerton's departure, he found Sabrina laughing, and Jeans with a long upper lip opening the window. Between herself and her late employer there had been no reconciliation. The good Jeans highly resented—in Sabrina's cause—the renewal of an intimacy that she had hoped had been for all time disestablished.

"The room reeks," she told Sabrina. "With all due respect to her ladyship, there is surely no necessity to soak her person in odours redolent of a Turkish harem?"

"How do you know?" Sabrina asked her teasingly. "Have you ever visited a Turkish harem?"

"Imagination," said Miss Jeans, flinging up the window, "goes a long way. Such smells are not compatible—in my own humble opinion—with the highest moral code of any self-respecting lady. I may be wrong."

"I like the smell," Sabrina said, wrinkling up her nose. Then the sound of her husband's step upon the stair brought a sparkle to her eyes, a flush into her cheeks, and she ran to his arms, chattering gaily as she unbuckled his sword, and laid it on a chair.

"There! The horrid thing! I hate it. Only think, John, who has been here! Jess—of all surprises! You have but just missed her. Jeansie does not like the scent she left behind her. I am so glad she came. She is just the same. The most absurd, affectionate and bawdy of all creatures. I do feel that it was wicked in me to run away from her—even to you—"

She stopped, the laughter dying from her eyes that sought his anxiously. There was that in his face, his silence, in his unsmiling lips that caused her own to whiten, and her heart to miss a beat.

"What is it?" she asked him quickly. "Why do you look like that? Is it bad news? Not—not marching orders?"

For each day, each hour she expected it, and prayed it might not come.

Miss Jeans went out, leaving them together.

He took her in his arms, holding her close.

"We're to stand by in readiness. Don't tremble so, my lovely. . . . Listen, I want you to go home. At once. Back to England, and await me there."

"Not yet!" She clung to him. "Don't send me away, John, yet. Let me stay near you—not with the sea between us. I want —just to be near you—"

"Yes, my darling—but—"

"There are no 'buts.' I cannot go. Indeed, I *will* not go!"

Her body pressed to his, she overruled him, pleading, praying him to let her stay—no, he must not be so stern. She would be safe. She could not bear to leave him. Let her stay. Then she'd be brave. Much braver. . . .

So she had her way. He was powerless against the longing in her eyes, or the tender frenzy of her mouth riveted to his in mute appeal.

He did not leave that night—the night of the famous ball that has made history.

But when dawn was in the sky and the city flamed with the news that spread like fire to the sound of drums, of bugles, of bands playing, and the shrill blare of the pipes; to the sight of quiet streets transformed into a confused impression of waggons, horses, men, artillery, and tramping feet—he left her.

She saw him go.

He passed under her window riding at the head of his column on his black charger. The first rays of the sun glinted on the gay gilt trappings of his uniform, on the scabbard of his sword. She saw the eager, sharp turn of his head, his eyes uplifted, shining; she saw his smile, and her own trembled crookedly, in answer. Very white and tearless, still as stone, she watched him pass, while deep within her body she felt the stir and heartbeat of their child.

She stood there at the window long after the last horse and man had gone, and the last sound became a memory.

Then such silence fell upon the small grey city that the noise of sparrows quarrelling in the gutter over some fallen wisps of hay was loud in her ears.

III

All the better part of that day and the next found her at the open window sewing her baby's garments, and watching the endless cavalcade of troops and baggage moving up towards the Porte de Namur.

During the afternoon news of a retreat began to filter through with the slow return of those that now passed down the Rue de Namur instead of up, to the accompaniment of a sound like thunder far off, ominous, unceasing.

Some came back on stretchers, and some who had been mounted came on foot leading their wounded horses; some walked who were lamed themselves; some were bandaged, some were silent, and some sang.

Sabrina watched it all. She saw things unforgettable. A man

who turned aside to vomit in the gutter, the blood pouring from his mouth. And one who halted, to drop dead. A heavy giant of a man, he lurched over sideways like a stout tree felled. His comrades lifted him, one at his head and one at his feet, and bore him off. She saw his eyes, wide open, staring up.

She saw a horse fall, too, led by a young ensign. It stumbled to its knees and sank. The boy knelt in blood beside the poor beast's head. "I should not have tried to bring you back, dear lad," she heard him say. The horse gave a convulsive kick and then lay still. Men came and helped him shift the heavy carcass to the roadside and for a long time the boy sat there with the tears rolling down his face, guarding his dead horse. Later a cart was brought to take the thing away. They hauled it up with ropes, soldiers and civilians lending aid.

Miss Jeans, who had been marketing, came back while this was going on and closed the windows and the shutters. It was bad for Sabrina to see such sights, she said. The good soul had bought some special dainties which she herself had cooked to tempt her appetite: "For the baby's sake," she insisted, "you must eat."

Sabrina forced herself to take a cup of soup, but when she tried to swallow food she turned sick, and Miss Jeans took her up to bed.

By night all sound of cannonade had ceased, and the following day Jess Pinkerton came full of news, gleaned first hand from Mr. Creevey who had all the latest bulletins straight from Head-quarters.

Major Hamilton, whose horse had been shot under him, had returned the night before with the report that Lord Wellington was at Genappe, not thirty miles distant. The French were gaining rapidly, Blücher's army was separated from ours and the British were retreating to take up a position in advance of

Waterloo. The French would be in Brussels any hour. It was crazy for Sabrina to stay; she must depart at once, with Jeans. Jess herself was going. There was no room in her coach for more, since Rodney and two ladies were already promised seats, so Jeans must see to it at once to procure a conveyance to meet them at Ostend. All vehicles would soon be at a premium. Would Sabrina not be sensible and go? According to Mr. Creevey the cavalry had not arrived upon the scene of action. No news as yet of the Dragoons, but no news was always good—

Sabrina raised her head; in the pallor of her face her eyes seemed enormous, the pupils dilating till the eyes themselves looked black. She had heard one sentence only:

"The cavalry! Not yet arrived? What does that mean? What is the delay?"

"Now! To worry for that!" cried Jess. "You should be rejoicing. If they are not on the ground they are out of the enemy's reach, that's certain. They are taking up positions in the rear, maybe."

On Sabrina's face a smile wandered up, and faded like the flicker of a sunbeam on cold stone.

"The cavalry," she murmured, "is never in the rear."

"There, child!" Jess patted the girl's shoulder. "Your boy's all right. You'll hear from him presently. Couriers are coming with despatches twice a day. He'll smuggle through a letter, certain sure. In the meantime do you listen to what I tell you. You must go with Jeans. Yes, I insist. The French will be in possession of the city any moment, and God forbid you should be left to the mercy of those cut-throats. Do you want to be raped or murdered?"

"I want to be near John," came the low-voiced answer. "I shall not go. I shall be here when he returns—and if—" She paused, one hand crisping the folds of the tiny garment that she held.

"And if," she said so softly Jess could scarcely hear the words, "he should be—wounded—I shall be here to tend him."

Something in her attitude, the utter stillness of the child's pitiful distorted figure, moved Jess profoundly, touched to the core of her being all in her that was generous and real. Perhaps it was something in those darkened eyes upraised to hers that touched her; something remote, as though within that passionate immobility, that unnatural calm, the wells of suffering were risen to overflow and quench the springs of youth; or some glimpse, perhaps, of a spirit whose essence, undeveloped and enclosed within the limits of its inexperience, was yet to blossom, to bear fruit, to reap a richer harvest; or perhaps the mere helpless anguish of young love torn asunder and quiescent in the grip of forces stronger than life—or death.

"My poor child! My dear!" Jess took the girl's white face between her hands. "Do you think that I don't feel for you? Thank God I have no man—no son—to care for. But be reasonable, my darling. You must go. John himself would wish it."

Again that smile flickered for an instant on Sabrina's lips and died. She shook her head.

"I must be here," she said.

In vain Jess pleaded, scolded, wept, and finally appealed to Jeans, from whom she got no satisfaction.

She was there, Miss Jeans maintained, to obey Mrs. Burnaby's instructions, but her ladyship could rest assured that she—Miss Jeans—would guard Sabrina's safety as her own.

Jess was tempted to retort to the effect that Miss Jeans' own safety at the hands of the French soldiers was a foregone conclusion, but with an effort she controlled herself. The argument might have lasted the whole evening, had it not been for the entrance of a servant with a letter, which he said had just been handed in.

It was from John.

Dated Saturday June 17, with the heading 'Quatre-Bras,' much in it of official news is guarded, but I give here certain extracts deleting matters of no consequence to us:

". . . We are all in the dark as to our movements for the morrow, but I imagine from what I hear from our fellows that we are preparing for a Tussle. It has been a heavy day, Sweetheart, and I am about to sit down to supper with the keenest of appetites having had no food for thirteen hours. If you could see me now, a very Vulcan, smoke begrimed and filthy, you would not . . .

"We have had our share of fighting, and believe me the French fight like Devils, in particular the Cuirrassiers who are magnificent. Cased in mail with breast-plates like the pictures of the Mediaeval soldiers, they have the greatest advantage in withstanding our muskets. The balls positively bounce upon their armour which seems to render them invulnerable to shot. In hand to hand fighting, once unhorsed, they crack like lobsters in their shells! Enemy or no I cannot speak too highly of these splendid fellows whom nothing seems to daunt except the onslaught of our Highlanders: who with kilts flying, pipes playing, and blood-curdling yells as they rush into the fray cause even the lion-hearted Cuirrassiers to quake and turn tail! But on the whole the contest is unequal. The Enemy's forces seem to be incomparably stronger than the British. I may not be too explicit for fear this fall into other hands than yours. If only . . .

"Now I will tell you briefly something of today's activities. Our Infantry lines were formed behind a hedge with 2 Companys of the —th extended in front to guard the Enemy's approach. It was generally supposed that Boney would endeavour to turn our flank but all on a sudden his Cavalry turned to the Right and Left and shewed a large mass of Infantry who rushed forward at

full Tilt shouting *'Vive l'Empereur.'* A most tremendous Tug
ensued. They attacked our lines behind the hedge with muskets
almost muzzle to muzzle. Meantime our fellows of the —th
charged from the left flank. Although our Infantry was greatly
outnumbered they held their ground and by the time we came up
in support of the —th, the worst of it was over. You should have
seen the Frenchies turn! But instead of running they *walked* off
in close column and with the greatest decorum. We managed to
haul in near on a Thousand prisoners which makes a fair beginning, but by George, what a day! And glad I am to find it
over for I am stiffer in my joints than after a hard day's hunting
and ready enough for my bed even though . . .

"I did not tell you that we were attended by a most Terrific
thunderstorm during today's doings, as if all the Forces of Nature had joined us in Battle! I was soaked through to the skin
but my Cloaths dried on me and I have suffered no harm from
my drenching. Tomorrow I will write again and send this by a
Courier. All my heart goes with it. . . .

"Good-night, my dearest Love. God bless you."

Further extracts from a postscript dated Sunday June 18th:

"I write this in an Interval while we await [orders] * from
H.Q. Black Prince grazes here beside me at the greatest ease. He
is become a hardened Warrior and scarce lifts an ear to the fir-
ing. Our position this morning skirts the wood of [Hougou-
mont?]. Every tree is pierced with balls. In one alone I have
counted the holes where upward of 20 are lodged in its [trunk].
This shows we are [regaining ground] fighting again over the
same positions where yesterday our lines were in Retreat. We
have captured 2 [Eagles].

"W—— himself is leading our [Brigade] so we are in good

* The original is written in pencil and so faint in parts that certain words are
illegible. The brackets denote a possible interpretation.—P. J. W.

hands. In spite of tremendous set-backs we have never been shaken for a moment. I have no fear of the issue, Sweetheart.

"The day is fine after yesterday's storm and the sun is shining. . . ."

With that letter underneath her pillow she had her first night's sleep since he had left her. Intermittent sleep filled with strange dreams.

One was of John.

She thought she walked in a flowery meadow beside a river on a golden summer evening surcharged with warmth and beauty. All the brightness of the passing day seemed imprisoned in a molten radiance that spread and blossomed with each moment. Everything was marvellously still.

Just such an evening as had been given to their marriage-day when she and John walked from the inn where they had lain the night, to wander hand in hand down to this very river. . . . So in her dream did she remember it.

And presently it was as if he stood before her with the sunlight on his face. Such light was on his face and in his eyes, that her own eyes were dazzled. She ran to meet his outstretched arms, but the tranquil stream divided them. She stepped forward into that shining water and felt its touch, so chill, so icy to her feet that she shuddered and drew back. She heard him laugh and call to her: "I'll wait—my Dawn."

And woke to find Jeans at her bedside with great news of victory.

John Burnaby lay dead on the field of Waterloo, but England lived.

BOOK TWO

CLARE

Born 1822   *Died* 1904

Chapter One

I

THUS IN one day was the destiny of nations decided and an Emperor dethroned.

To this crippled country, fraught with internal strife and economic crises, recovery was slow; but step by step with the pauperised working classes marched those who championed their cause.

A new civilisation was springing up, a new morality, a newer creed. Democracy, conceived and brought forth in the agony of bloodless revolution, thrived, a sturdy infant, sponsored by such godfathers as Owen, Cobbett, Huskisson and Peel; pioneers who with their courage and idealism, their Herculean efforts to establish a more humane and intelligent viewpoint towards the wrongs and sufferings of enslaved masses, were paving the way for the builders of an Empire to follow.

In 1820 the long unhappy reign of George III was ended, and his son—prevented by a fit of gout from attending his father's funeral—ingloriously succeeded him.

The baby Princess who a few months earlier at Kensington Palace had made her first appearance in this world at a time of fierce antagonism and profoundest discontent, was considered of no great account and was forgotten in affairs of more importance.

Prior Wrotham had his share in not the least of these.

We hear of him in Manchester on August 16th, where at St. Peter's-in-the-Fields a crowd of sixty thousand composed of men, women and some children, and led by the Radical Henry Hunt, were assembled to clamour for their rights and for Reform.

At that meeting Prior spoke, or to be exact, he made attempt to do so, but was not two minutes on the platform when his speech was interrupted by the appearance of mounted troops and yeomanry sent by order of the magistrates, who had taken alarm at the sight of so great a gathering and decided to disperse it. Armed with lance and sabre, the horsemen obeying to the letter their commands, charged among the incensed multitude, who retaliated with catcalls, hisses, curses and threats, and where possible with stronger methods still. The meeting, which had begun peaceably enough, ended in a holocaust. Some hundreds, men and women and a few children, were crushed and injured in the stampede that followed, and a round dozen, mostly men, and two women, were killed. Prior had an eye gouged out on the point of a hussar's sword. He scarcely noticed he was hurt until he tasted blood. He felt a sudden stab, a sharp agonising pain, and thought his eye was closed. He had gone mad, demented, screaming to those around him: "Save your bodies, brothers, and your souls will save themselves! You have the right to live—you whose children and whose children's children will make the future race. Stand firm and demand justice—stand firm, I say! Know yourselves the stronger—those who torture you are dying—are already *dead*—"

His words were lost in the tumult. None heeded him nor saw how with blood streaming from his gaping socket and hands clenched above his head, he beat the air in helpless frenzy. His voice amid the clatter of horses' hooves, the cries of women, the shouts of men, and the terror-stricken shrieks of children, was less than the hum of a gnat in a deluge. He fell, was trampled on and lay there in the dust, sobbing with rage and impotence and pain.

A huge brawny Yorkshireman raised him to his feet.

"Thee be hurt badly, lad," he soothed him, soft as any woman. "Where be thy whoam?"

But Prior could not tell him. He had fainted.

For three weeks that fellow—Joseph Silk, his name was—cared for him. He carried him to the garret where he lived on the top floor of a house inhabited by half a dozen families. His wife, so he told Prior, had died recently of a consumption. He had taken her from the cotton mill where he had worked as foreman, and had married her. But the mill had its toll. She did not live to bear his child. He had lost his job, he said, for insubordination. He had made an attempt to lessen the working hours for children under ten. The mill-owners had vetoed it, had called him traitor, rebel and a public danger, and had turned him off without a moment's notice or his pay. He had come from Liverpool to Manchester to hear the meeting. He thought now that he might go to sea; there was no life in England and no one left to live for.

"You must come to London," Prior said, "and work with me. I am going to start a printing press. I intend to publish books by unknown authors. I shall print the books myself and I want willing helpers. I will pay you all I can, which won't be much for I have parted with half of my small capital in one scheme or another—but this latest one of mine, I think, is good. You *shall* come to London, Joseph, and you shall live with me."

"Nay, lad, what'd I do in Lunnon?" Joe Silk answered. "The Devil that ye knaw is better than the Devil that ye doan't. Thee must give thy money to they that han't got t' bodies t' work with. I 'ave, I thank t' Lord, an' a strong un, too. I'll come to no 'arm, young Prior, never fear."

"I'll give you money then, Joe," Prior offered him, "till you find work. I'll share all I have with you, and gladly. It's only right I should. Did you not save my life?"

But for all his generous impulse Prior found that after he had paid the surgeon who attended him, his fee, and stacked the garret with good wine and food enough to last ten men a month, he must deduct three guineas from the surplus he had heaped on Joseph for his trouble, to take him down to London in the coach.

On one fine September morning with tears in his one sound eye and a bandage on the other, he took his leave of Joseph Silk—whom in this life he never saw again—and himself to Roger Kell to be consoled.

For two years Prior had been employed as assistant in the shop, helping to run the Club above it, writing grandiloquent pamphlets, and learning how to print them.

"But that is not enough," he told Kell, on his return from Manchester. "I must have scope. I must expand. You and I together, Roger, can do much. I intend to be a publisher since I can never be a writer. I might have been a poet—but more gifted men than I have failed there—giving place to those who are destined to immortality. It is an age of literature. Very well then. Let us see what we can find, *not* among those who have already struck their note, but among those who are unheard of. Who knows what genius may lie hidden—undiscovered—on a dustheap?"

So with one eye gleaming, a black shade plastering the other, in the dark little room behind the shop, the excitable youth let fall his latest bombshell.

And Kell with that remote smile on his lips sat there and let him talk.

"Where is the capital to come from?" was his calm rejoinder when Prior paused for breath. "It needs money, lad, to run a business."

"Business! You talk like a city merchant. Listen, Roger. Hunt can help us here. He tells me of manuscripts submitted to him every week by men who never get a hearing. The great names usurp the markets—the big firms are already overstocked. Now

is our opportunity. We live in an age of progress, of new ideas, .
new voices. Let those be heard who have the will to speak. In
Manchester I shared a garret with a man who, given the right to
live, might be a power in the land. He could neither read nor
write, yet I have learned from him a new philosophy. Although
he has lost all that makes life good there is no trace of bitterness
against those who would have crushed him. He forgives them, for
they know not what they do. He and such as he are the new
Christs. Ah! You smile—but, Roger, I have *seen*—I *know!* This
country is peopled with such men of humble birth who, given
their chance, may rise to unimaginable heights. And some of these
—a very few—*can* write. God knows how they have learned to,
but they can. Let us help them, Roger. Let us give to the world
the words of those who have the gift but not the means to pen
them. *There is* a cause to follow! Roger—you *must* come with me
in this . . ."

In such fashion he raved on while Roger, waving aside superfluous verbosity, selected from that outburst the germ of an idea.

And thus was founded the firm still known today as Kell
& Wrotham, publishers, first established 1820, in St. Paul's
Churchyard.

II

One who lent enthusiastic aid to this departure was Mary Kell.
She it was who read the manuscripts selected by Prior from those
submitted to Leigh Hunt, who passed on such as he judged
worthy of consideration. Few enough these were, and fewer still
the signs of genius.

The first selection was anonymous and the discovery of
Mary, who in reading it was convinced that a master hand had
penned it. On the surface nothing more than a delicious fantasy,
it dealt with the problems of the day, attacking both Whig and

Tory leaders with the silkiest of satire and the choicest flow of language. Brougham was there, and Liverpool. The Duke's gossip, Mr. Creevey, and the King himself all in the most transparent of disguises, but so wittily, so jauntily displayed that none could cavil at its impudence.

Prior, reading it on Mary's recommendation, stayed up all night to finish it, and when she went to draw the curtains she found him in the morning, dazed with want of sleep and in a state of nervous tension.

"You're right, my dear—this *is* a masterpiece. But not what I intended. *This* is a polished voice that has been already heard. I'll swear Hunt wrote it, although it is not his hand. Someone has copied it for him, I'll be bound. I am too tired to think—but I believe that with this we'll make our début—or mar it! We'll arouse controversy if nothing else, and whether your father agrees with me or not I'll publish it—" He yawned, swaying a little where he stood. "And—Lord! How I am tired! I'm sleeping on my feet. I'll go to bed."

"Poor Mr. Prior!" She flung wide the window to let the cool air in. "To have turned night into day. Was that so necessary?"

She gave him her shy entrancing smile that seemed to linger in her eyes while it faded on her lips; her look the more gentle for the way he rubbed his fist into his empty socket, for the trembling of his small, slight, weary frame.

"I wish," he told her testily, "that you would not call me Mister. Why do you—always?"

He saw her, outlined against the window with the early sun behind her turning the top of her smooth brown head to gold. Her eyes were dark as shadowed pools, and softer, he thought, than velvet. He saw the tender curves of her young breasts under the tightened bodice, her white throat, and all the fresh young girlhood of her like a bud unfolding.

"Why," he said wonderingly, "you're a woman, Mary—and I never knew!"

A flood of colour rushed into her cheeks. "I am eighteen," she said.

"So you are! I had forgotten. You're so little— Now what are you doing?"

He watched her fetch a chair and place it under the covered birdcage that hung in the window, but even from that elevation she needs must stand on her toes to lift the cover off.

"Could I not have done that for you?" Prior asked. "I'm small enough compared to men, but a giant next to you."

She laughed and jumped down lightly as a kitten.

"There! It is done. Look at my little dear—how pretty the way he lifts his head up to the sun. Is it cruel to keep a caged bird, Mr. P-Prior?"

"Not if he is bred in a cage as this one was. He knows no other life. And he has you to tend him, Mary—"

Then, while he spoke, because of some strange, intangible emotion that set his pulses racing, and because perhaps he felt, rather than saw, her startled shy response to that first breath of something not yet born between them, something yet to come, he turned without another word and went away.

The mysterious authorship of the book that brought to the two adventurers who launched it the fruits of richer harvest, was eventually solved. It was not Hunt, but one whose name like his has passed down to posterity, though in that day unknown.

Later, he was to publish with Kell & Wrotham the first volume of his scattered verse and prose when, owing to the success of his anonymous 'best seller,' he was invited to join the staff of the *London Magazine.* Perhaps his works are read today less for their own sake than for the light they throw upon the character of the author, who is established in the history of literature as one of the most dearly loved among English men of letters. Prior's description of him shows us a retiring personality, painfully shy, reserved, and afflicted with an unfortunate impediment of speech, but his voice coming through his magic pen is ever unforgettable and cherished.

There came a day in February when the first specimen copy of the book arrived, unbound. Prior received the parcel, opened it, and called Mary from her duties in the shop to see. It may have been the mutual interest of that moment which brought to its full blooming the tender growth of love between those two, so gradually, so imperceptibly it flowered.

There was no need for words; all that both felt stayed in their hearts unuttered. The book opened there before them on the table served only to increase their greater joy. He hardly knew that he had spoken when he breathed her name and saw the look that trembled up at him, and all her life's sweet promise in her eyes. . . .

III

She whose life was broken on that day in June five years before, lived on at Wroth with Miss Jeans for companion.

That good soul, who since the death of her sister was possessed of a small but independent income, had offered gratuitous and permanent service to the stricken, dazed young creature whom no child lived to comfort. The budding life she carried had passed from her stillborn.

There was nothing of heroics in her tragedy, no dramatising of her loss. Only a bowed acceptance, a frozen calm, that gave to her young loveliness an austerity beyond its years as though her very heart were wintered in the noontide of its spring.

There had been some money left her, little enough but all that poor lad's own, besides her widow's pension. Prior, who was legal heir to Wroth, would have none of it. The house was hers, he said. What use had he for such a mansion? A derelict at best. She must shut up all the rooms for which she would have no use and live in those that were sufficient for her needs. Miss Jeans would help her there.

Jeans did.

She took the reins, installed old Hannah in a cottage at the gates, and set Daniel to the garden where he could dig and potter to his heart's content, for Sabrina would not hear of their dismissal. In place of these two ancients, a competent man and wife were then engaged and certain rooms redecorated. In this Jess lent a hand, hoping in her kindness to offer some distraction to "that piteous poor Child whom it breaks my Heart to see so brave and uncomplaining" (from her journal dated July 14, 1815). "She never speaks of him nor says his name. One would think her Callous but for the Look in her great Tragic Eyes. Alas! That War should bring such Devastation to blight the Flower of Manhood in its Prime and rob young Wives of Love and Mating. For never, that I swear, have I known a couple more devoted. I cannot blame her now for such a Choice. Had it been otherwise she would have been spared this Grief but would have missed a sweeter taste of Life for all it turns so Bitter. Her case is not Singular. There is poor Cr—v—n (Lord Sc—sd—le's heir) who left a young Widow in similar Case. She was brought to Bed last Week of a fine Boy but my poor Child is denied that Solace. Heroic Tales filter through from Cr—vey. A Col. M—l—r of the first Guards requested a last sight of the colours under which he fought. He kissed them fervently and begged that they might be waved over him till he expired. Poor P—ct—n was killed while leading the head of his Division. I supped with him at the Duchess's Ball on that unforgettable

Night before the Battle. I count a Dozen friends among those killed. Life in Town is dreary, and half of us in Black. I am for Bath so soon as I have seen my poor Sabrina settled and in better Health. Jeans is with her for which Thanks Be, tho' for myself I would not abide that Pinch-Face near me. . . .

"The morning has passed in chewsing Patterns for Wall-papers and new Curtains, but I doubt that she will take an interest. Nevertheless her rooms are not fit in their present State for Human Habitation. I have chose for her Bed-room a silvered Bed raised in an Alcove to be lined with white fluted Silk bordered with Silver Lace. The Curtains are Rose-coloured which when drawn enclose the whole concealing the recess. The Window-curtains are to be of rose-pink Satin with embroidered Muslin Curtains inside trimmed with Pink-dyed Lace. A Carpet of uncut Pile (Rose du Barry) and a Chandelier of Lustre, the whole costing me a Fortune, but if it give her Pleasure I do not grudge it.

"For her Withdrawing room I have chose a Paper in a Chinese Design, this to match the Chinese Chippendale Suite which poor Pinkie gave to his Daughter with her Dowry. The Curtains are of Rich Blue Silk lined with Ivory Satin. I sent her also two Jardinères and the Oval Mirror which Rodney gave me set round with Dresden Cupids. . . ."

So with good friends beside her she found peace at Wroth. No grief endures for ever, and youth's rarest treasure is its power of recuperation. Each year that passed, each miracle of the recurrent seasons, brought its own healing. Each spring with its unfolded sweet deliverance of bud and leaf and blossom; its wild ecstasy, its wistful yearning, its gleam and song and shadow. Each lingering summer of slumbrous golden days and breathless nights, heavy with muted passion, empty of love. Each hay-

making and flower-scented warmth; each ripening harvest, each
fall of leaf burned red in autumn sunsets; the laden apple trees,
and smell of wood-smoke in the sodden lanes. Each winter,
slowly passing; the short, sharp days, the white shroud of their
snows, the swifter meltings; and one grey frosty morning when
the huntsman's horn rang clear and brought Sabrina from her
bed to stand barefoot at the window, ears pricked to hear it, and
the thought leaping within her—to be out there riding with him
and his hounds would be so joyous! She who had thought all
joy for her was dead. . . .

And as the years receded life began to quicken with rebirth.
As some young tender shoot thrusting shy fingers through the
frosted ground, there came to her spirit an expansion, a passing
out from shadow into light. The routine of the days held for
her a new significance, familiar objects a new shape. She would
rise early, saddle her little mare and ride out into the morning
alone, but not now lonely.

The gentle countryside, the gracious repetition of field and
wood and meadow, presented ever some fresh surprise of form
and colour. Delicate outflung branches lit over with the first
green flush of leaves; the magic of an apple bough in bloom;
grass-blades the greener for the arrowy rain; a latticed window
wreathed in jasmine; red rose and white around a cottage door;
the piping of a chaffinch; cows knee-deep in clover, and everywhere fulfilment between the land and sky. The dragging moments were replenished with perpetual motion, a weaving and
interweaving of new thoughts. She began to chafe against inertia.
There was not enough to occupy the hours with Miss Jeans re-
lieving her of household supervision.

At this period she read extensively, ransacking the library at
Wroth of its store of mildewed volumes. She found an early
Pepys, unexpurgated, and from him to Bacon and Sir Thomas

Browne, revelling in contrasts, feeling the first wonderment
of words.

So to the poets.

Here Prior helped her with all the latest products from those
new masters of the age, Shelley, Wordsworth, Coleridge, and the
then almost unknown Keats. For Byron she had the scantiest
regard, allowing perhaps her personal reactions from her one and
only meeting with him to temper criticism.

"A Reprobate and superficial Versifier." So she describes him
in a letter to her twin dated March 1, 1820. "It seems to be the
Fashion now for young Gentlemen to put their travels into Verse
like *Childe Harold* and Lord Nugent's *Portugal*. But your
storm-wracked Shelley is a mightier Proposition altogether. I
have just finished *The Cenci*. What dark and noble Tragedy is
there! Tho' I mistrust such Genius and the sombre Depths of
thought that must have fostered it. Infidel, Blasphemer though
he be, he is yet greatest of all living poets. To think that you
have known him and have conversed with such a Mind. Would
there be ever the possibility that I might have the Privilege of
meeting him? You say he is at Pisa. I am tempted to pack Baggage and embark with Jeans on a Pilgrimage to Italy. . . . Who
is this Keats of whom you write with such Enthusiasm? Yes,
indeed, send me the Volume of his Poems which you tell me
are just published. What an Age we live in! Every man turns
Poet unless he turn Annihilist and shake his fist at Monarchy
or God. . . .

"How fares it with you and your Mr. Kell in London? So
little I see of you of late, my Dear, I confess to jealous Pin-
Pricks. Does the new Venture usurp *all* your thoughts and time?
And the sweet Mary, who must be fully grown by now? I will
pay you a surprise Visit one of these fine days.

"Did you go to see the Funeral Procession? Poor King! So

long a Reign and so unhappy. What of His New Majesty? Is
it true that he seeks a Divorce from the Queen? Jess writes me
all the latest gossip. She says H.M. is determined to rid himself
of his Poor Wife and that he will have her name omitted from
the Liturgy as past Praying for. Poor Hunted Creature with
every man's hand against her and such Trumped up Evils spread
about her name. Jess writes in highest indignation all in favour
of the Poor Lady. H.M. seems as unpopular upon the Throne as
off it. (I pray you guard this letter lest I be accused of Treason!)

"We live so quiet here, Jeansie and I, like a pair of Nuns. Hannah is full of the Rheumaticks and has taken to her Bed. I
visited her yesterday and took her some Hare Broth. She will not
last the Winter through, I fear. I have engaged a child from the
Village to tend her for she cannot now be left. She sends you her
Dear Love and hopes you come to see her when next you visit
Wroth. And when will that be, you Wretch?

"I read in the copy of *The Times* that you have sent me (and
for same I thank you greatly) of this Cato Street Conspiracy. It
is most Infamous. I hope, my Dear, that you are not on nodding
terms with the Chief Instigators! One hardly dare to ask you
knowing your mad Notions. I read in Fear lest I see your name
in the lists of those that have been arrested in some Riot. However, this monstrous Plot is not, I trust, in your most wild
Province. To think that those Good Ministers and our great
W—— might have been most foully murdered but for Discovery
at the Eleventh Hour, makes my Blood run cold. I suspect that
Thistlewood and his Accomplices will be hanged, and surely
they deserve it sooner than the poor man who steals a small
crown piece. Pray, my dear one, curb your *too* Radical sympathies for see to what terrible Results such advanced Views may
lead. Before you are aware you may be embroiled in some serious
Complication. But I know such Fears as these are foolish and

unfounded. You follow the true Spirit of a Christian Brother-hood that marches towards enlightenment holding on high its colours of Faith, Hope, and Charity and you would never coun-tenance and participate in premeditated violence. Ever since that shocking Affair of Peterloo last August, and its so sad results for you, I have been set about with Worries. You might have been more injured than you were—God forbid you might have lost *both* eyes—or even have been killed. You are no Revolutionary, my dear Prior, altho' you speak as such sometimes, but I who know you, know that your Tongue gives Utterance for the sake of words as much as for your thoughts.

"Lord! What a homily! I can see you frown on this. Forgive me, little Brother, and answer this letter soon. . . ."

He answered it in person a week later, arriving unexpectedly one night in a blizzard, just as Miss Jeans and Sabrina were re-tiring to bed. He had come by stagecoach which had set him down at St. Albans, and from there he had walked across coun-try in the snow the whole of the remaining distance of ten miles.

Once dried and fed and warmed, and Miss Jeans disposed of, he announced the news of his betrothal.

"I had an idea that this would come about," his sister said. "For I have seen when you speak of her an expression in your eyes—your— Oh!" She knelt beside him where he sat, his wiry hands clasping his crossed knee, lips pursed in an elfish smile, his one eye peeping round at her. She kissed the other. "Poor lost eye!" she whispered. "You're to be happy now, my dear. You *shall* be happy. Does she love you—enough?" (Can anyone but me, she thought, love you enough?)

"More than I deserve she loves me," Prior said, taking her chin in his hand to smile down at her. "Why! Are these tears—silly one! Aren't you glad for me?"

"So glad—but perhaps—afraid to lose you."

"I had to lose you to your John when I most needed you," he told her.

With a trembling lip she asked him, "Did you mind, then, when I married John? You never said—"

"Why should I say?" He tweaked a curl of her hair. "But you won't lose me more when I am married than you have lost me now. You haven't lost me yet, and if you like," he added quickly, "you can come and live with us. Not here. Wroth is too far away from town and much too big for anything so small as Mary. But you can share our home with Roger, for we shall live with him. You can be a literary adviser to the firm as Mary is already. Yes, we can all keep house together. That, I think, is a capital idea."

"Lord! How he talks!" She laughed though tears still stood in her eyes. "No, Prior. You must keep Mary to yourself. No sharing of homes. That can never answer with two women. With her father—yes. That is another matter—but not with me. I am a jealous cat. We should be scratching and spitting at each other in a week. You know I can be quarrelsome."

"Mary," Prior said, "could never quarrel. You don't know Mary. When you know her you will love her—as I do."

"Yes," she assented with emphatic nods, "I shall. I am quite sure I shall. But how do you know that Mary will not want to live at Wroth? The house is yours and should be hers by rights."

"That is all settled. We don't want Wroth. It is imperative we remain in the centre of things in London—where our work is. And Mary is a Londoner, you must remember, not a bumpkin like yourself. What would she do here? She can't ride; she would be scared—bless her—to go near a horse. She knows nothing of the country—and cannot tell a wheat field from a cabbage patch.

We will come here for holidays, and Wroth remains yours, unless"—he paused—"unless you should marry again, my dear."

"That—never," Sabrina answered quietly. "I wish," she sighed, "you had sufficient means. What will you live on, Prior? I will help you all I can, for I need nothing here—"

"Hush!" He put his hand over her mouth. "Do you think that I would take from you?"

"Do I not take from you?" she flashed at him. "Your house and all that's in it."

"That is different."

"How different? Absurd! Just because I am a woman—we should share equally. We always did as children."

"I shall make money, never fear," her brother told her stoutly. "A fortune for us all. This new book that we shall publish will make the biggest noise in prose since *Waverley*. We shall rouse endless wrangling in cause of it, and maybe find ourselves in—"

"Fond as I am of Jess," Sabrina interrupted, pursuing her own thoughts, "I cannot help feeling aggrieved that she has managed to secure for her own lifetime the income that by right of inheritance belongs to you. I do not know if I have told you this— but I always had an idea that poor Grandpapa meant to provide for both of us, and would have done so if he had kept his wits. The very day he was taken with a seizure—even at the moment of it—he was mumbling something to me, I remember, to that effect, but at the time I paid no heed. I have often wondered since if he knew then that he had not been fair to us."

Prior shrugged his shoulders. "I don't need an inheritance to help me. I have always hated this system of handing property from heir to heir. No man of wealth should have the power to will to his descendants his entire substance, but should be taxed according to the sum of it. The greatest mistake this country ever made was to abolish Pitt's property tax after the war. Such fools as we have in power—who will never realise until they may be forced to—that we live in an age of transition, when a policy dictated by a small class whose experience and interests are limited only to their own environment, can no longer hold in check the increasing demands of a population. Every dog has his day and the under-dog will yet have his—mark me! By God! When I think how *blind*"—he brought his clenched fist down upon the chair-arm—"how *doubly* blind—not one-eyed like myself—are these governing swine—"

"Well, then, don't think," Sabrina soothed him, rumpling his hair, "or at any rate not at this hour. Look! It is long past midnight."

Prior rose to his feet. "Yes, if I begin to think I shall never sleep. And believe me, I need it."

"You get yourself too overwrought and too excited," his sister said. "You take to heart the whole world's woes. There!" she kissed him. "Go to your bed. It is warmed and waiting for you. Sleep very well, my dear."

But she did not. She lay awake till morning, filled with her thoughts of him and her own memories.

The marriage of my grandparents Prior Wrotham and Mary Kell took place at St. Martin's Church on June 25, 1820. For some years they shared with my great-grandfather his house above the bookshop in St. Paul's Churchyard; and there in due course was born to them a daughter, Clare.

Chapter Two

I

HER EARLIEST recollections are of books, and yet she never read one; the smell of books, their dusty bindings, the dark shop, her Grandpapa upon whose knee she rode, crowing with laughter and thumping her small fists on the open pages of some rare illuminated treasure brought from its case to show her, a privilege which none but she had right to.

For nearly seven years she reigned supreme, and queened it over all of them until the appearance of a rival, Anthony.

Clare could not believe that he had come to stay. There had been two more before him, and one had stayed a week, and one had stayed a year. But these visitations were forgotten in memory so faint that she was never sure she had not dreamed them.

It was her Aunt Sabrina who first presented her to Anthony, down in the parlour on a Sunday morning, in November of the year 1828. That memory was certain—not a dream. It began with Eliza telling her while she buttoned up her drawers—the long white Sunday drawers that came down to her ankles and pricked her legs with their stiff starchy frills— "Now, my lady, *your* nose is out of joint."

The announcement was alarming. Even the reassurance of the looking-glass that her nose seemed much as usual did not allay her fears that the feature in question had undergone some drastic change, mysteriously due to the advent of this new ugly little brother who lay squalling on a cushion in his Aunt Sabrina's arms, shawled to his chin and bright scarlet.

Clare was aghast. "Goodness gracious! Where can he have come from to learn such shocking manners? And why has he no hair—nor any teeth?"

"Because," it was explained, "he's very young. Teeth and hair take time to grow."

"How young, then, is he?"

"About four hours," she was told. That, Clare admitted, was young.

"Has he come to live with us? I tell you—we don't want him. We're very well just as we are, I think."

"Would you like me to take him," her Aunt Sabrina asked, "to be my little boy?"

Clare would with pleasure, and offered there and then to make a parcel of him in the basket that Eliza had brought the cat in.

"If we doubled him up he would fit in nicely—"

Her aunt laughed so much at this that she nearly dropped the baby, and then Papa came to hear about it, too—and he must laugh—and lift Clare to his shoulder and tickle her ribs where he held her, so that all three were laughing, Clare loudest of all. But the very young Anthony cried.

"He protests," Clare's Papa said, "against his share in the problems of the universe. Is that not so, my son? You did not ask, nor possibly desire this ejection from infinity into a world of sorrow. But by George! His lungs are sound enough. Ought he to howl like that, Sab? Do you think he's got the gripes?"

"He's got no gripes, a-precious. Merely an appetite. He's asking for his dinner—and you shall have it, my sweet life. And-yes-you-shall-then. Come to his Mamma-a-lovely," said Aunt Sabrina, speaking, as Clare observed with some disgust, in a fashion most ridiculous when addressing this new Anthony.

"He is lucky," remarked Anthony's Papa, with one of his funny looks, "to be able to procure a meal simply for the asking. There are a million or so in England today who may ask but will not get."

Everything her Papa said was, to Clare's thinking, droll. A trick of speech, a turn of head, his lips pursed comically, and his one eye quizzing her as though he had a joke on hand for all he spoke so solemn.

It took some time to become reconciled to the stranger, who grew surprisingly apace, and developed soon a soft brown fluff on his bald head that stiffened and turned black.

"You are dark enough," Clare's Mamma told her. "But he's a little nigger. He takes after your dear Papa's papa, I think— in looks."

And in looks only, pray God, breathed Mary to her heart.

"Nigger! Nigger!" jeered Clare, poking at her brother. "Solemn-face," she called him, kneeling by his crib. "Great big Round-eyes. Hi! Look at me, will you? What are you staring at up there on the ceiling? You're like a monkey—an ugly little monkey. I don't believe you're young. You're old—older than me—older than Grandpapa. Aren't you? Why don't you speak? You have no sense at *all*. Why could they not have given me a puppy? . . ."

Clare was eight years old and Anthony nineteen months when George IV died, unmourned; and the last of the Hanoverians, driven almost crazy at the honour of such unexpected elevation after sixty-five years of insignificance, sat in his brother's place upon the throne of England.

With an elderly buffoon at its head, whose absurd antics and eccentricities made him the laughing-stock of his subjects and the consternation of his Ministers, the country under the new reign was moving rapidly in the direction of Reform. Bad trade and general economic misery fostered the predisposition of the middle classes to unite in their efforts to enforce upon a sluggish government the necessity for granting their demands. The agitation in France that culminated in the "Revolution of July" bid fair to spread infection. In England, in the north, social war loomed red on the industrial horizon, while in the south the ruined peasantry sought vengeance for starvation wages—or no wages at all —in rick-burning and riots. Parliament dissolved and was re-elected with Wellington resigned, Grey high in office, and the Whigs and Reform in tow.

Such was the state of affairs when William IV was crowned, and Kell & Wrotham removed from St. Paul's Churchyard to more extensive premises in Soho Square. The house above Kell's bookshop was not now large enough to meet the requirements of an increasing business and a family.

In the last ten years the firm had made some rapid strides and was becoming recognised as publishers of quality, if not commercial value. Although since their first discovery they had produced few outstanding successes they included in their lists names that are now household words. The introduction of a quarterly review entitled *The Magpie* and edited by Prior, created a furore in 1832.

The first number, issued in January of that year, gives as contributors Charles Dickens, a solicitor's clerk, and one W. M. Thackeray, a young law student whose aptitude for caricature illustrated his burlesque of the prize poem on the subject of Timbuctoo which had been won two years before by Alfred Tennyson, and which we reprinted in *The Magpie*'s first edition. The rising stars of these two obscure young gentlemen, hitherto unheard of and still of no account, were totally eclipsed by such a galaxy as Hazlitt (posthumously represented in an essay entitled "Mademoiselle Mars"); Edward Bulwer, then editing the

New Monthly Magazine; the much talked-of Lady Blessington, who made her début in print in that number of *The Magpie,* and Landor, whose first instalment of *Imaginary Conversations* had appeared that year elsewhere.

The freehold of the mansion in Soho Square which was to serve its dual purpose as head office of the publishing house, and household, had been bought for a song by Roger Kell of the executors of the late Sir John M——, Bart., who had died bankrupt. No sooner was the agreement signed than Roger made it emphatically known that he refused to leave his house above the bookshop. He was too old to transplant his roots, he said.

The news came as a bombshell to his daughter.

"But it was understood," protested Mary, "that you should come with us. You, who have shared everything—all our ups and downs—all our joys and sorrows—and now just as we turn the corner on the road to real success you desert us. How can you do so, Father?"

"But who says that I desert you?" smiled Roger Kell. "You speak as dramatically as Prior. We have lived together under one roof for nearly thirty years, and more than ten of those have been your married life. Now is the time come when you should —as it is said—cleave unto your husband. You can leave me Eliza as housekeeper, Silas as watchdog, and my books for company. What more can man desire? Besides which, I am in charge, you must remember, of the trade department here—and after all—what should I do in the world of fashion?"

"Is Soho Square," asked Mary fearfully, "the world of fashion?"

"More so than the Churchyard of St. Paul's. You may soon find yourself entertaining literary lions and their attendant female adorers," her father teased her. "To say nothing of the dandies led by D'Orsay."

"I shall be miserable if so," sighed Mary. "I can never adapt myself to such surroundings. I wish that we could have remained here, but the children, bless them, take up so much space. The house grows small as they grow big."

And to Sabrina, Mary wrote in one of her rare letters a week after removal (undated):

"Such a muddle as you never saw! We are without Domesticks save for Eliza whom I borrow from my Father to lend a daily hand. I have engaged a Cook, two Housemaids and a Butler (very Gentlemanly) who frightens me to Death by addressing me as *Madame* with the most Frenchified of Airs.

"This change from our simple Mode of living to a scale more elaborate fills me with Concern. Prior says that it is necessary in view of the increase in Business to live accordingly, but I misdoubt this strange Revulsion of ideas for it is not compatible with our dear Prior's Views to live to such High Standard. He has his reasons for so doing I presume, though they be beyond my Calculations. Where the money is to come from to support a staff of servants, to say nothing of the upkeep of this House, I do not know, for our joint capital is all sunk in the Business. Do not imagine we are grand, although we inhabit a grand Mansion. Most of the rooms are without carpets (Prior says that we may keep them so for the floors are laid in Parquet) but not even a Rug conceals their bareness. We have brought with us such Movables as belong to us, and some that Father gives, but I have scarce the Heart to re-arrange them here. None of our old things looks the same, so out of place and Shabby, which makes me love them more and grow to dislike in Proportion the pretentious Rooms that hold them which I fear can never be a Home. I hope in time to grow accustomed to the upheaval, and would not for the world have Prior know that I am not entirely content, for he seems so, thank God. He suggests we furnish from the rooms at Wroth that still remain unused. I understand that this first

suggestion did originate from you, or I should not now have
mentioned it, and would take it more than kind if you could
advise me as to what I should choose from the furniture stored at
Wroth. I would like, if it will not incommode you, dear Sabrina,
to come and spend a day or two at Wroth in the near future
when we could take stock together of such Articles as you think
best suited to our new Abode. At present the House looks like a
Mausoleum. The Children, I am happy to say, have settled in
most comfortably. Clare plays up and down the stairs all day,
and gets under Eliza's feet in the Kitchen, which swarms—con-
ceive it—with Cockroaches! Can you or Miss Jeans advise me of
an efficacious Remedy for getting rid of these noisome pests? We
were happily free of all such horrible invaders in the old house.

"Anthony has a slight chill so I keep him to his Cot today. He
is a little peevish cutting a large Molar. I must find me a good
capable Woman as Nurse to them, for even if Father had not requested that I spare him Eliza, I do not think she is the Right
Person for the care of my two Darlings. I came upon her yesterday whipping Clare for stealing Jam from the Store-Cupboard,
and as you know I do not at all approve of Corporal Punishment
for young Children. Is there any linen to spare at Wroth for I am
short of Bedding? . . ."

II

This letter—in the nature of an SOS—brought Sabrina and
Miss Jeans to the rescue, who between them piloted Mary through
uncharted seas of domesticity and brought her safely into harbour.

When the servants were installed, the house furnished, and the
family well settled in, the Wrothams gave their first reception.

Here again Sabrina's aid was called upon.

"For without you beside me," Mary said, "I shall never face it."

She was pale with apprehension on the evening of the party, to

which half literary London had been invited from the list supplied by Prior.

"Although it goes against the grain in me," he told his wife,
"to pander to the conventions of society, I think that it is necessary
up to a certain point to do so. Publishing after all is nothing but a
trade, and a tradesman has to advertise his wares, so must I as a
tradesman display my authors in the flesh to critics who may
remember the good wine with which I've filled them when writing their reviews. And perhaps by such foul means we may de-
ceive prospective applicants into the belief that the capital which
supports us is greater than the overdraft which in actuality it
represents. You are silent. You disapprove. You think such methods of coercion contemptible. You're right. They are."

"I don't know anything about your methods of coercion," Mary
replied with her slow smile. "But I do know that I'm scared to
death of playing hostess to a grand assembly. To meet an author
in a friendly way at dinner in the old house was a different matter,
and one that I can cope with, but to meet a hundred in this mansion is for me an ordeal. I am unused to company. I shall have no
words for your guests."

"Pooh! That! You need not fear—*they* have the words. Give
them enough to eat and drink and lead them to their 'I'—for that
is all they talk. 'I.' 'My.' They're swollen with self-love. They'll
be too taken with themselves to worry you, my pretty."

But Mary was not reassured, even with Sabrina at her side to
help her in her preparations, in a gown new for the occasion, of
lavender crêpe with a long heart-shaped corsage that proved too
much for Mary's modesty, who after one glance in the mirror
made haste to cover her white shoulders in a scarf of printed
gauze.

"I am no lady, Sab," she confided, blushing. "I assure you I'll
be wretched the whole evening if I go so exposed."

"Why! Silly one," laughed Sabrina, "to call that glimpse of you 'exposed'! Then what am I with so much bosom? Shameless?"

"A goddess," Mary told her, lovingly. "Proserpine."

"What! To spend six months of every year in the dark regions with old Pluto! ... Spare me that, I pray you. Never Proserpine."

"Ceres, better, then?"

Sabrina shook her head. "Not I—unfruitful."

"Then be yourself, my darling." Mary took her hand and kissed it. "For you are always lovely."

"Still?" A faint shadow crossed Sabrina's face. "Am I still beautiful?" she repeated wistfully. "Not withered—old? I'm thirty-five."

"You're ageless," Mary said.

Sabrina turned to her on a quick, indrawn breath, and her eyes darkened in a lost, abstracted look that raked Mary's heart to see. "It has been said to me before—once—long ago," Sabrina whispered. " 'You're ageless.' "

Her gaze came back to Mary's with the smile to her lips. "I wish we might stay young. I do not wish to grow old and see all that is familiar pass from me. I would like to see the face that John—that he—knew and loved—stay just as it was, for ever."

"As he will always know and love it," said Mary softly. "As he first saw you, so you are, and so you will always be—for him."

"Mary, do you believe there is an afterwards?"

Mary's brow grew thoughtful. "I believe that nothing dies; but in what form it lives, or on what plane of existence it continues —that is the question. My father often says that although human intelligence can only be aware of three dimensions, there is no reason to suppose that there is not a fourth, a fifth, a sixth—or even more. I wonder! Such a theory," Mary mused, "might carry one to the verge of extraordinary discoveries. Height, breadth and length are the dimensions that we know—but there surely must be others in a universe that has earth and heaven for its boundaries. Do you think a worm is unaware that it inhabits a world of even three dimensions? It can only know the surface over which it wriggles—so to the unknown quantities above, perhaps, we too are worms."

"Why, Mary!"· Sabrina gave· her a whimsical glance. "Have the learned hearsays of Prior and your father turned you agnostic? And would you forsake the older worlds for new? For myself, I only feel that I would like to know the why and wherefore of my being—and if there *is,* perhaps, a mind that rules this universe of which we know so little—or whether everything—you and I—life, death, birth, sun, moon, stars, are not all the outcome, merely, of some colossal accident—and that we—our comings and our goings, are as inconsequential as the touch of pollen carried by the bee to fertilise a flower."

Mary nodded her head. "Perhaps. Just that. And some pollen gives us ugly weeds—and some pollen gives us lilies."

"True. And the lilies·toil not, neither do they— No! Surely, it cannot be an accident. Only God could make a lily! But how serious we have become! Listen to our talk! We might be a couple of grey-headed old philosophers discussing riddles that not even a Solomon could fathom—instead of two decked-up matrons— one of whom is middle-aged and should know better than to dance around in frills and furbelows. I should wear a cap and shawl—more fitting to my years."

"Good gracious, Sab!" cried Mary. "One would think that you were fifty. How can you be so ridiculous! And you do not look your age in any case."

"Aha!" laughed Sabrina. "Now we are back again just where we were before this profound discussion started. Are we not truly feminine? A woman's age, once she is past twenty, is always her most vital question. And she is as old as she looks, they say."

"Then tonight you're twenty-five, my dear," said Mary.

Indeed she seemed so. Time and sorrow had laid their lightest touch upon her to linger round her eyes like a caress, and in that look of hers, far-off, remote, the look of one whose life is not so lonely as unshared by others. She had ripened but retained the quality of youth arrested. Her creamy pale skin was smooth and clear as any girl's, her eyes more lovely for their shadows.

She stood before the long wall mirror in her grey, full-skirted gown, the bodice of which was cut in accordance with the fashion of the times, to display to best advantage the wearer's bust and shoulders. And Mary, who watched how with dainty precision she arranged a white flower in her fawn-gold gleaming hair, worn parted on her forehead and in ringlets at each side, thought that surely never had there been such waste of womanhood—wed to the past—and unwed in the present, that like youth fled by too soon.

"There!" Sabrina turned to her. "I can do no more to beautify myself. Now Clare must give me her approval. I promised she should pronounce judgement on my finery. But before I go to her—there is one thing, my dear, that I forgot and meant to ask you. Is Jess Pinkerton invited to this gathering? For you know she is in London."

"Yes, I do know," smiled Mary, "and she has received an invitation which she accepts. She called on Prior, as it happens, at the shop a week ago, and she made him bring her instantly to see me here in her carriage. What a character she is! That is actually the first time I have ever met her though I have heard so much of her it seemed that I already knew her. She has not seen Prior, she told me, since he was a boy, and she petted him as though he were still ten. She was horrified to see he'd lost his eye, and she was quite enchanted with our Clare, thought her manners fit— she said—for Court already. She ought but to see her other times when not on best behaviour! And she nursed Anthony on her lap, like any old wife from the country instead of a fine lady from town. *Now* if you talk of age! Although she is so buxom her face is unlined as a child's, and for all her nonsense as ingenuous. I should say she'd been a beauty in her time, though she must be old in years."

"Yes, she must be nearing sixty. Dear Jess! I am glad she has been here, and I hope she comes tonight. It is long since I have seen her. And now I must to Clare and you to your post, my love, ready to receive your guests."

"Not yet!" cried Mary in a fluster. "It is not time. Don't leave me, Sab, to face them all alone."

"I'll be with you presently—and you'll have Prior beside you."

"Prior! He is not yet dressed. I'll wager he'll forget to change his suit and come ink-covered and in buckskins. Oh! Mercy! I'm terrified of this! Come quickly when you've said good-night to Clare. She should be fast asleep by now."

But Clare was well awake.

Sabrina found her pirouetting before the looking-glass in the large white-painted bedroom on the third floor that had been set aside as nursery for the children.

She came prancing to Sabrina's side barefoot and in her night-gown, over which she had hung from her shoulders the quilted bedspread that trailed behind her like a train. A broad ribbon sash was folded turban-wise around her head, confining her bobbing curls.

"Now look at me! *Look* at me!" squealed Clare, pulling at her aunt's hand. "Look how I'm dressed for the party. Why can't I go? Look at my cloak. Isn't it like the pictures of the King and Queen in their coronation robes? Am I not el'gant?"

"Very elegant, you baggage! And without slippers, too! Do

you want to catch your death? Get into bed this minute. Who gave you that ribbon?"

"It's my best sash—see! It is hand-worked in a design of daisies on blue silk. Mamma bought it for me in Paternoster Row. I wore it to church last Sunday. Isn't it fine?"

"I rather fancy, Clare, that you think too much of finery for such a little girl."

"I'm *not* a little girl. I'm big. I'm old. I'm nine. Soon I shall be ten. I think it unkind in Mamma," Clare pouted, "not to let me come down to the party. Can you not ask her to let me? I'll sit quiet in a corner and not stir or speak. I will be very good."

"That," remarked Sabrina, "would be a change indeed. Let me see how good you can be now by putting slippers on your feet or else jumping into bed—one or the other."

Clare chose the lesser of two evils and scampered to the cupboard to find her slippers, tripped on her 'train' and fell knocking her head with a great bump against the fender. Sabrina picked her up in a storm of tears.

"Pride has to fall. Fie! A great girl like you to make this noise. Have you not just said how big you are—and elegant? Now! Now! You're not really hurt. Hush! You'll wake Anthony."

But Clare only roared the louder. She *would* go to the party. Yes, she *would*.

"Ah! So the party is the trouble." Sabrina knelt, regardless of her frills, to sop up tears with her new lace handkerchief. "I thought there was more in this hullabaloo than meets the eye. Suppose we bring the party up to you? Some comfits and good things to eat and perhaps some orange wine? But," Sabrina added in a hurry as Clare's sobs lessened, and smiles never far away shone from behind the tears, "only if you take off that pretty sash and fold it nicely, so that it does not crease, and then get into bed at once. *Vanitas vanitatum.*"

"What is that you say?" Clare asked, all woes forgotten. "What language?"

"A language whose roots are in all other language and it means that you're a little Madam. Now off with you. Why— What? Oh! Cupboard love! For shame! Well then, one kiss."

Sabrina was enveloped in a fragrant bundle of clinging arms, warm lips and silken curls.

"I love you next Mamma and Papa best in the world," Clare whispered.

"Grandpapa before me, surely," Sabrina whispered back.

"Not even Grandpapa—well, yes, then—both the same. Do you love me better than Anthony? You *must* love me more than Anthony."

"As much more," Sabrina said, "as you are big and he is little. Are you so greedy, then, for love? Perhaps . . . so are we all. . . . Now you must let me go, my darling, for Mamma is waiting for me down below."

Clare tugged at her hand. "Please to untie this sash. It is knotted."

Sabrina smiled at the child's unconsciously imperious manner. Eyes coloured like her own gazed up at her, but there resemblance ended. Clare was a gipsy girl, dark-haired, and warmly tinted, with something of her father in face and nothing there of Mary. She lacked her mother's calm. Clare was all movement; eager, fluid, vital. She infected others with her energy.

"And don't," said Clare, "forget to bring the party up to me."

III

In the large panelled drawing-room, Mary with Prior at her side stood to receive her guests. The ground-floor rooms used as offices for the firm had for this occasion been set apart, the one for refreshments, the other as a smoking-room for the gentlemen, with four hired men in livery in charge.

To Mary it seemed that most of the people who bowed before her there were utter strangers, although Prior appeared to be on affable terms with each, and as greatly at his ease when addressing lions, as when in company with the members of her father's club, whose premises since some years back had been extended to a house in Seven Dials.

Of all versatile creatures, Mary thought, her heart swelling with love and pride, timidity and excitement, and the sudden awful fear that the refreshments provided might not last the evening out.

Her father, who arrived with Leigh Hunt, was wearing full dress for the first time in his life, which unusual departure from the conformity of years served to increase Mary's sense of unreality and embarrassment. Hunt, on the other hand, had not abandoned his usual garb and was in shabby buff-coloured pantaloons and a none too clean frilled shirt-front. Mary, however, who had known him all her life, was glad enough to welcome one face she recognised among so many never seen before.

"But why," she asked him, "did you not bring Marianne? Is she unwell?"

"Yes, and besides—" Hunt did not finish his sentence; his eyes had wandered, and his mind, she knew, had followed them. He looked ill and harassed; his black bushy hair was turning grey. It was said that he had never recovered from the shock of Shelley's death during that nightmare visit of his to Pisa, when he had seen the beautiful drowned body of his friend dragged from the sea and flung to the flames of a funeral pyre on an Italian shore.

He apologised vaguely for his unconventional attire.

"I did not intend to come tonight. I was at supper with your

father. He insisted that I should. I did not think to see so many—
I am not dressed for the occasion."

"You are best as you are," Mary reassured him. "And welcome
always."

She turned from him to greet a new arrival, whose name
though shouted at her by the hired flunkey at the door she had
not heard. A young man of most singular appearance, dressed as
if for Court in white satin breeches, with jewelled buckles to his
shoes, and a coat of royal blue. He wore his dark, well-oiled hair
arranged in curls, had rouge on his cheeks, and diamond rings
outside his white kid gloves. He bowed very low, and kissed
Mary's hand in foreign fashion, when Prior presented him as
"Mr. Benjamin Disraeli."

The gentleman's acknowledgement of the introduction was as
elaborate as his costume, his speech as oily as his hair. The pleasure of meeting Mrs. Wrotham, he said, was only equalled by his
enormous admiration and regard for her husband's excellence,
both as publisher and as man of parts.

Mary, who had no words to offer in reply to this effusion, was
spared the pains of attempting any by the entrance of another
guest, whose dress and manner were scarcely less extraordinary
than his.

This a lady, very old, diminutive and stout, in a gown of stiff
white satin, and a monstrous silver turban surmounted by three
black ostrich plumes, which had the effect of making her appear
top-heavy. She addressed Prior with the greatest animation,
poked him in the ribs with her forefinger, and in a genial but
gruff voice like a man's which was surprising coming from so
small a body, she told him:

"You'll be glad to hear I've hung red flags out of me windows
with the Bill, the Bill and nothing but the Bill scrawled over
them in golden letters. Is this your wife? You look eighteen, my

dear. You can't be. I don't look my age either. I'm eighty-odd—but *how* odd—and now that's talking! I'm writing a book of memoirs and if I make love to this young man of yours d'you think he'll publish them? I don't know that I want him to, I'd rather Murray's. They've more money. Wrotham! Introduce me—you're not a host unto yourself!"

"Pray excuse me, ma'am," stammered Prior, put completely out of gear by the old lady's downright manner. "My love—allow me to present you—Lady Cork."

But her ladyship did not wait for this; she had sighted young Disraeli and waddled after him to clutch him by the elbow and to tell him loud enough for all the room to hear that her grey parrot had that morning laid an egg. . . .

Sabrina sat apart and watched the company with Roger Kell beside her.

"Is it," she asked him, "part and parcel of your trade to entertain so varied a menagerie?"

"Menagerie?" he laughed. "That is it, my dear. You have the correct word. Lions, lionesses, jackdaws, jays, to say nothing of some Gadarene swine. Yes—what a gathering! Prior, let me tell you, is nothing if not thorough in his undertakings. No half-measures here—he suits his person to his company. In casting his net upon the seas of literary society who knows but that he may not catch a whale? There is one, for instance—that broad-browed young man who stands shrinking in a corner by the window with his frayed cuffs two inches short of his raw wrist-bones. I'll wager he hired that evening suit from old Sol's in Petticoat Lane. Do you see him? Very awkward, to be sure, to find himself among such company. He, unless I'm much mistaken, is some giant fish in embryo. He passes all his days perched on a high stool in a lawyer's office—but he will write," said Kell impressively, "books that will hold the world entranced. Books that will live when you, when I, when generations after us are dead. That is great praise, you think? Ah! But I have seen a manuscript, the first fumblings of a mind that is not yet aware of its own capacity. He is no scholar, he has little or no education, he has no erudite philosophy to support him; he merely writes of what he sees and knows and feels. Vignettes of London life as observed in his own law-courts, or among the urchins of the street, the small shopkeeper, or the city merchant. Life as one-half of England lives it, and with a whimsicality, a tenderness, a humour that in my opinion may never be surpassed. He does not know it, but the world will one day tell him."

"What is his name?" asked Sabrina.

"It will convey nothing to you. Charles Dickens."

"No, I've never heard of him. And who is the gentleman talking to Leigh Hunt? The one with the thick spectacles."

"That is Benjamin Haydon, the artist. I use the word advisedly for he *is* an artist—there are many painters who are not. He, poor fellow, is continually in and out the Fleet for debt, but what of that? He has been extolled in verse by his many friends the poets. Keats once wrote to him from Teignmouth when he was sent there for his health, the most charming doggerel. Haydon showed it me, some years ago—and I was so enchanted that I asked to be allowed to copy it. Now let me see if I can recall a verse or two:

"Here all the summer could I stay,
        For there's Bishop's Teign,
        And King's Teign,
And Coomb at the clear Teign's head;
        Where, close by the stream,
        You may have your cream,
All spread upon barley bread.

"Is it not delicious? There are several other verses, but one in particular I must really quote you:

"Then who would go
Into dark Soho,
And chatter with dark-hair'd critics
When he can stay
For the new-mown hay,
And startle the dappled prickets?

"And that," added Roger, with a twinkle, "might have been written expressly for tonight's occasion. Don't you agree?"

"Yes, indeed. Delightful." Sabrina's answer was abstracted. Her attention was not now fixed on Mr. Haydon, nor on a poet's rhyming, nor on Roger Kell himself; a newcomer had claimed it, one who caused her to turn sharply to her companion and to ask his name, not so much from the desire to know it as to hide the queer emotion that had seized her at first sight of him.

"He," Roger told her, "is the son of a rival firm of publishers. Young Marriott."

"Ah!" Sabrina released a breath. What was it she had seen? A look, a turn of head, a flying glance . . . A youth, tall and well proportioned, head well set upon broad shoulders, his chin a little raised, and lips that tilted upwards at the corners—like a faun's. Did memory play tricks, read into any face the likeness to another's, or was the likeness true? Her eyes sought eagerly the answer in the delicate bone structure of jaw and modelled cheekbone, the square, cleft chin, the impudent blunt nose—found nothing of resemblance, not even the similarity of colouring, for this young man was dark as that other had been fair. . . . Nothing at all. Imagination merely.

And dragging her eyes away from that boy's laughing face, she heard Kell saying:

"Will you, my dear, excuse me if I leave you for a moment, for I have to talk with—"

"Yes."

Her fingers loosened on her fan; one of its ivory sticks was broken, so tightly had she held it. A fan that John had given her —how many years ago? . . . And as she sat apart there in that crowded room, it seemed to her, looking back upon her life, that she had now completed one whole cycle of it, and that the long empty years which she had striven to replenish with impressions drawn as much from external influences as from the visionary world presented to her through the thoughts of poets and philosophers had brought their own fulfilment. Life had enriched itself through suffering and loss, and if—as Mary had said earlier in the evening—if there were continuity of existence on some other plane, then one might know that nothing *could* be lost, merely set apart and waiting as in an interval between one act of a drama and the next. To pass that interval in listlessness, in self-pity, or in some narrow chamber of the individual mind, was a sin against life itself. Life must be lived, fresh contacts must be made, experience ringed round with quickened consciousness must multiply and draw into the spirit each contribution of the senses, until the one is merged into the other, and the whirlpool of thought and feeling is intensified.

Something of this was in her mind as she sat there, unobserved, withdrawn into herself; a dignified quiet figure with a rare untouched beauty of its own, as of some cloistered painting by an old master's hand, her lovely lifted head haloed in gold from the shaded candlelight behind her, and a white flower in her hair. So Stephen Marriott first saw her.

To Prior he said quickly, "Who is she—the lady in grey sitting alone at the far end of the room?"

"That is my sister," Prior told him, "and my twin."

"You are not much alike."

"No? Perhaps not. . . . Ah! Jess—at last! Sabrina has been asking for you. She will be delighted you have come."

Young Marriott drew back. This was no time to force an introduction, but he must know her—he *would* know her before the evening ended. She put every woman in the room to shame. All looked commonplace beside her. Not young—and yet—the feeling there of youth, of girlhood, a half-virginal worn sweetness, a far-away look under brows arched as though in faint surprise. What should surprise her? What did she see? Not him, for certain. Or did she? Could he catch her eye? Almost he believed so, and reddened to the ears, his heart racing underneath his shirt-front. Her lips were smiling a very little, crookedly. Was she married? Certainly she must be. But he *must* know her, talk to her, tell her—

"It's your father that I want—not you, young man!"

The voice of a macaw that seemed to rise from somewhere near his knee, croaked startlingly. Stephen looked down as old Lady Cork looked up.

"My father is not here, ma'am—I regret—"

"Tell him from me that if he don't publish my memoirs Wrotham will. For mercy's sake, child, find me a seat. I cannot stand for long or I get palpitations. The room is full of swells. Have you seen the Blessin'ton? Such a dress! Where does Wrotham find 'em all? I should have thought he was too busy throwing stones at other people's glass-houses to spare time to go a-hunting. Don't you dare publish *her* if you value your reputation—though *she's* got none to lose. Give me your arm."

There was no shaking off this venerable lady. She liked young men about her and could entertain a dozen with her tongue if their thoughts were not divided as were the hapless Stephen's. Hiding his discomfiture beneath a sickly smile, he resigned himself to a most wretched evening.

Meanwhile Jess in full fig was bearing down upon Sabrina. Her hair, which of late had been allowed to whiten, was partially concealed beneath a cap of tinsel gauze. Her bosom displayed jewels that might have graced a begum. Her gown of purple satin, with enormous sleeves puffed to the elbow, served to increase both bulk and stature. She was laced so tight that all her blood was in her face, and powdered so heavily that the shade of her complexion matched her dress.

"I came just for a sight of you, and only you, my darling!" Jess exuberantly declared. "And you look blooming. To think of Prior holding forth as host on this grand scale! Whoever would have thought it? There must be a method in his madness. He has all the advantage on his side—born to it, so to speak. Your father, for all that his name stank, had London in his pocket, and there's breeding on both sides of the Wrothams, or else you may be sure my Lady 'Corky' would not be here. She boasts of rubbing noses with the Radicals, but if truth be known she's as great a snob as any Tory in the town. Just look at her marching that young man away! He's fairly caught. They say she's going daft in her old age, and steals like a jackdaw. Yes, I assure you —kleptomania! Considerate hostesses leave out their best teaspoons, but she always gives them back again next day. She's not the only one—ha! ha!" laughed Jess. "Do you remember how as a child you stole my vinaigrette? I have your letter still, confessing it, scrawled over all in blots, stuck in my journal. You should keep a journal, love—'tis most diverting to read over what the years have got to tell. I've kept one, on and off, since I was twenty."

"Have you really kept that letter, Jess? Yes! I remember, how disgraceful of me! And I sent Daniel with it to you the next morning—all unaware of what had happened—and yet I witnessed the beginning—and never have forgotten it." The blue eyes darkened. "Only think! If things had been ordered otherwise, if on that night Wrotham had not—"

"Had not entertained too lavishly another fellow's wife," Jess supplemented as Sabrina paused.

"Well, yes—to put it so. If the duel had not been fought—if Wrotham had not left England—I might never have been godmothered by you, nor taken to that masquerade at Richmond. And so I might never have met John."

Yes, and you might by now have been a happy wife and mother, Jess told her silently. It is not too late, if she could only know it. Unnatural to live so long alone. I should have died without a man beside me. Men—even the worst of 'em can have their uses, and I've made use enough of them in my time, goodness knows. And she has not, I'll wager, by the look of her.

And—"Do you stay long in London, love?" Jess asked her, fanning her hot face. "Such a racket as is going on in town—one had best be out of it. There's nothing spoke or thought of but Reform. My carriage was held up on the way here by a demonstration passing along Piccadilly. A torchlight procession and the greatest noise! All of 'em yelling blue murder till I thought the horses would take fright. Lady Jersey's had her windows smashed, they say, and they've put up bars outside the Duke's at Apsley House."

"No! Truly?" exclaimed Sabrina. "I can't think why the Lords oppose the Bill so long. The country is in an uproar. One wonders what the world is coming to. What with these new railways! I would give anything to travel in one. Prior did, last year. He went to Manchester to see the opening of the new railway run from there to Liverpool."

"Yes, so he was telling me. And it's a mercy *he* wasn't struck dead like poor Huskisson. I call it flying in the face of Providence to take up with such mad newfangled notions. The Duke, I hear, is all against steam, and received such a shock when he saw Huskisson killed that they say he refuses to travel in any other fashion but by post. As for me, nothing would induce me to go within a mile of a steam engine. I don't want to be blown up. But of course Prior *would* be on the spot," Jess added grimly, "when it's a question of high explosives. He has only himself to thank for the loss of his eye. I hope that he's too occupied with this publishing business to run wild as he used to at those meetings. I am not surprised," Jess shook her head resignedly, "that he should turn out unaccountable, with such a father. I wonder he's no worse than he is. That mousy little creature seems to dote on him. He ought to have aimed higher than the daughter of a shopkeeper."

"The daughter," retorted Sabrina with some warmth, "of a scholar and a gentleman—and to aim higher than Mary would be aiming at the stars."

"Tut, child! how you colour up! She has a friend in you! Still, you must admit that she's no beauty, and no bigger than my thumb. . . . Ah! Look who arrives now! My faith—I'm most diverted. D'Orsay himself! That brother of yours, my girl, has his head screwed on his shoulders for all the screws may be a little loose. He knows his way about. With Blessington and D'Orsay in his favour he can snap his fingers at the rival firms. She'll bring the authors, and D'Orsay will bring the cash. I should not be at all surprised if the *Beau Comte* is backing him."

Sabrina gazed with interest at this famous elegant of whom the whole town talked; and surely he deserved it, for there was no denying his extraordinary good looks. His abundant chestnut hair was arranged in meticulous curls above the high, intelligent forehead, his eyes were the clearest hazel, his lips curved and bow-shaped, too red for any man's. His dress outrivalled the young Disraeli's in cut and dandyism, with a coat of skin-fitting lilac cloth and white trousers strapped so tight beneath his instep that not a crease could show, and one wondered indeed how he might bend his knee; the whole completed by a blue brocaded waistcoat and a pair of pink kid gloves.

"It seems to me," Sabrina said, "that gentlemen today care more for dress than do the ladies."

"If I sit here much longer I'll explode," exclaimed Jess unexpectedly. "It's me new stays, my dear, which that fool woman of mine laced far too close. Can we find a man to take us to the buffet? Prior don't look after you at all—he hasn't introduced you to a soul."

"I don't think," Sabrina smiled, "there is a soul I wish to know."

"Not even D'Orsay, prince of dandies?"

"He least of all. He is too gorgeous. One can scarcely believe him human."

"The Blessington seems to find him so," Jess remarked with a sly look. "I wonder how she likes giving bed-room to her stepdaughter. There's a coil! Have you heard the latest of *that*—"

"Come, Jess, enough of gossip," interposed Sabrina. "Let us find the buffet for ourselves since there is no gentleman to escort us."

"Ha! See how she puts me down," beamed Jess, not in the least resenting the rebuff. "You'd never shine in the *haut monde,* my love; your tongue is too well guarded. Give me a hand, for I'm swelling fore and aft. *Ups*-ee-day!"

It was no easy task for Jess to raise her weight from off the sofa, but the feat at length accomplished, the ladies edged a way through the groups of chattering guests, in the direction of the door. Here Jess met with an acquaintance, an elderly gentleman in a wig with heavily dyed whiskers, whom she hailed with every expression of delight, forgot Sabrina's presence, and walked off upon his arm downstairs.

The room in which refreshments were being served was not too overcrowded, and, mindful of her promise to Clare, Sabrina soon procured a plate from one of the hired servants, filled it with cakes and bonbons, and with this in one hand and a glass of orangeade in the other, she made her way back to the staircase. But here there was congestion, someone knocked against her elbow, the plate dropped, the cakes and comfits scattered, and the orangeade was spilt on her new gown.

A pretty how-d'ye-do!

Sabrina surveyed the ruin of her dress in consternation.

He who had caused the trouble was profuse in his apologies. Relinquishing old Lady Cork to the arm of another victim, he was on his knees and offering his handkerchief, and himself along with it for all the world to see.

"Truly, madam, I am more ashamed than I can say, but some clumsy rascal jostled me—my back was turned—unpardonable that I should not have known—should have been unaware—"

So on and on most happily he floundered, blocking up the staircase there at Sabrina's feet.

She laughed. Almost she laid a hand on that dark bent head of his, as one might caress a schoolboy—or a son.

"Do not allow the matter another instant's thought. The damage is nothing that cannot soon be remedied."

But the plate that had held the eatables was broken clean in half. One of the hired footmen came to clear away the bits.

"I must make another effort," said Sabrina, "to take the party up to Clare."

Reluctantly young Marriott rose from his knees.

Seen nearer she was even lovelier than he had thought her at a distance. A very gracious lady. "You said?" he murmured, watching her red mouth and the play of its charming smile.

She laughed again, softly. "I see I must enlighten you. There's a young person some three flights up who, if not asleep—and Heaven send so, to be sure, by this time—is waiting for me and my promise. Woe betide me should I break it!"

"But it would seem to be already broken, or at all events that part of it which is the most important. Can I fetch you," Stephen offered eagerly, "a fresh relay of stores? I undertake it shall be delivered in all safety."

Sabrina looked at him. She saw his parted lips, his young hot eyes, and read in them more than his lips dared utter.

And because for so many empty years she had not seen—nor had she cared to see—that message in the eyes of men, which to women is the breath of life for all they may deny it, the blood quickened in her pulses and raced to her cheeks in a warm flood of glowing colour.

This is folly. He's a child, her heart whispered. I am mad. . . . But if this, she said, is madness, then sooner be mad than sane.

IV

Clare lay in her bed with a finger propping up each eyelid. She would not go to sleep. She was waiting for the party. The rushlight burning in the wash-hand basin shed the dimmest glow upon the shadows in the room, intensifying all the blackest corners so that one might imagine the tallboy was a nasty fat old man, and the clock upon the top of it his face. An old man with brass buttons down each side of him—but of course they

were nothing of the sort, those were the handles of the tallboy—
and even if the firelight flickered on the wood, so that it seemed
to move ever so softly with no sound at all, and the face above
it grinned and nodded in a most knowing fashion, one had only
to get out of bed and look and make quite sure—and Clare
would certainly have done so if she had not just then found herself upon a cloud and sailing through the sky on a very dark
blue night. . . . The stars were little moons, and the moon itself
gigantic, and the sun was shining somewhere too, just like a big
sunflower. She was eating a cream-tart. . . .

Someone poked her in the back. "Wake up, you haven't had
the party." The cream-tart was left suspended in mid-air. Her
heart was pounding in her ribs. Of all tremendous jerks! Surely
she had tumbled? No, she was safe in bed and staring at the
ceiling on which a glimmer from the rushlight formed a pale
circle, the colour of lemon curd spread on a slice of sand-cake.

She could hear sounds below of voices buzzing loud as bees.
Oh! to be there! Not here in this stupid silent room, all white
and ghostly except for the black corners, and the tallboy (who
really was so very like an old man) and Anthony in his crib
there, fast asleep. He'd sleep through anything, the silly! She
called to him, for although he could not answer and was so very
young, he was better than nobody to talk to.

"Hi! Can you hear me? There's a party on downstairs. Much
you care, you baby. You great slobby-flobby baby! Aunt Sabby's
going to bring me comfits and a glass of orange wine. Would
you like some, stupid? You're not asked, *you're* not. You can't
eat lollipops. You can only chew slop food that's been minced
up for you. Hi! Listen. Why can't you *answer* me? What a
*simple*ton you are! Why does Mamma love you? I don't."

Clare flung off the bedclothes and got out of bed. Lying
there and jeering at her unresponsive brother was a poor game.

At the foot of Anthony's crib was placed a screen covered with coloured scraps that had been pasted on to form a pattern. This screen was Clare's delight. The leaping flames of the fire seemed to make the figures in the pictures come to life.

She plumped herself down on the floor beside the screen and began to play the game of which she never tired. This was to pretend that she was part and parcel of those pictures. There was, for instance, the gentleman who sat inside a tub. Her Papa had told her that his name was Dog-on-Knees. All the time and always he sat inside that tub. He must be cramped in that position. It gave Clare pins and needles to sit for half an hour on her foot—but in a tub! Dear me!

After a minute or two of sharing his tub with Dog-on-Knees, Clare found his company a trifle flat, and passed on to another picture of the infant Moses in the bulrushes, who looked the living spit of Anthony, but uglier if anything, and there was Pharaoh's daughter very fine in yellow, kneeling by his side.

The next picture was of Lazarus being raised up from the dead, while Martha in purple and Mary in pink stood by in great surprise. Lazarus looked quite alarming in his shroud and very thin, and Clare passed quickly to another which was no happier a choice, for it depicted a bad boy in a pillory with his eyes rolled up, his tongue stuck out, and a gallows in the background. Under this edifying spectacle was printed in black letters:

How shocking, Dear Children!
This Boy. is a Thief:
He stole from the Butcher
A large Joint of Beef.

"One more for luck," Clare muttered in a hurry, for she wished no part in *that,* and chose a lady and a gentleman standing by a

stile. Her head was on his shoulder, and his arm was round her
waist. This picture never failed to produce in Clare the strangest
feelings. She could not have told why, but there it was. Feelings
that ran up and down your spine in a queer tickly sensation, not
unlike the feelings that came to you in church when you listened
to the organ. Pleasant. Very.

The gentleman was most elegant in a cocked hat and blue and
white striped pantaloons. The lady wore white muslin and black
mittens and had the loveliest golden curls. Clare thought that it
must be delicious to look just like that lady with a fine gentleman
to hold you round the waist and give you such enjoyable sensations. But a low gurgle from behind the screen soon dispelled
enchantment and brought Clare to Anthony's crib-side with
the question: "Are you awake, you Ugly? Did you speak to
me?"

No answer.

Could a person ever be so plagued by such a dumb useless
creature?

"Talking in your sleep, I think." Clare prodded him in great
contempt. "Ho! Won't I have a thing or two to tell you when
you're *my* age? More than two years you've been with us, and
what use are you to anyone? What can you *do?* Nothing but
twiddle your thumbs all day and stare. Or cry. Or eat. Wake
up and *listen!*"

Another prod and, to be confessed, a pinch in the most fleshy
part of her small brother's person. This time she got more than
she had bargained for, when the outraged Anthony, dragged
from his snug oblivion to this most rude awakening, protested
with the full force of his lungs.

"Now! Now!" cried Clare, giving him a slap. "I won't have
it, do you hear? Nobody hurt you. Hush! You'll rouse the house,
and then *I'll* get the blame. Not you. Oh, no! You're *never*

wrong. You're everybody's Darling, and Mamma's Angel-Boy. Little Pig-face. Stop it, will you? Oh, deary-me! For shame."

Such a noise now filled the nursery as might well have been heard not only in the room below it but by the watchman at the corner of the street, whose announcement of the hour was drowned in Anthony's howls.

Then, while Clare strove alternately to scold and coax him into quiet, the door opened and her aunt—at last!—came in followed by a gentleman whom Clare had never seen before.

He it seemed had brought the 'party,' a dish of lollipops, a slice of almond-cake, three ratafia biscuits, a ginger-nut, and a glass of orange wine.

Back in her bed with this fine choice of edibles about her, Clare rapturously sampled each in turn and chattered gaily to the gentleman, who, had he worn a cocked hat and striped panta-loons, might have passed for her hero of the picture. She left her Aunt Sabrina to deal with Anthony, who when he had been walked around the room a dozen times on his aunt's shoulder, and talked to in that softy-softy voice that they all used to *him,* and cuddled and petted and kissed till Clare felt sick, did at length consent to be returned to sleep. Then all was amiable and happy, and Clare in seventh heaven, until her aunt told her: "We have eaten enough goodies for the middle of the night. Suppose we save the rest until the morning."

"No, no, *no!*" Clare protested very loud.

"But I say yes, my darling." And Clare knew exactly what that meant. There was no wheedling her Aunt Sabrina as she could wheedle her Mamma. Better give in without a fuss while every-thing was pleasant.

"And now," said Aunt Sabrina, shaking up the pillows, "bid good-night to the party and to Mr. Merry Hat." (The queerest name!)

"Stay by me till I go to sleep," Clare pleaded. "See how quickly I will go to sleep."

She put her head down underneath the covers, and shut her eyes up tight, then opened them to peep above the blankets, and laughed and laughed because she was so happy, and because Aunt Sabrina looked so happy, too. Her cheeks were round and pinkish, and her eyes had a tiny candle-glow in each of them, Clare saw as she bent over, as though the rushlight in the basin were reflected in two polished dark blue stones. "How pretty! And how sweet you smell," Clare murmured, "like sweet William in a garden!"

Her aunt laughed and kissed her forehead and kept her lips there awhile. Then the gentleman bent down to kiss Clare, too, which made her hot all over. He kissed exactly the same place where her aunt's lips had been. How pleasant it all was and warm and cosy! . . .

The room was growing misty, the figures of her aunt and the gentleman, on either side the bed, dwindled till they were no bigger than the pictures on the screen. And why! Dear me! How droll! Here we were all three of us back again beside the stile with Aunt Sabrina in white muslin and black mittens—how strange that was, to be sure!—and Mr. Merry Hat in blue and white striped pantaloons.

Now she could hear each word that both were saying. Two voices in the distance that mingled like a song.

"You are strangely like—and yet unlike—someone—"

"That you know?"

"Someone that I knew."

"How long ago?"

"Many years ago."

"If only I might ask you—"

"Pray ask me—what?"

"Ah! If I dared!"

"Am I so formidable?"

"No—enchanting."

"And you, sir, are too bold."

"Was that too bold? Then I must crave forgiveness. I think you have bewitched me. I saw you the moment I came into the room. I longed to know you. Perhaps you saw me, too? I dare to hope—"

"But all this has happened"—the merest breath, so soft that Clare could scarcely hear it—"has been lived before. . . ."

And now it seemed that Clare was no longer in the picture. She was floating on a wave, a watery silver wave, rising and falling, ever so gently, down and down and down.

Chapter Three

I

THE YEAR 1832 that produced the first number of *The Magpie* may be said to have set the firm of Kell & Wrotham on its feet, both financially and as publishers of note. Manuscripts by well-established authors who were inclined to look askance at a house run by a crank bookseller and an eccentric jackass—for so they had chosen to regard the partnership—were now equally inclined to modify their views and to concede it at least good taste and enterprise. Then, shortly after the first issue of *The Magpie,* came the announcement that the house in Soho Square was to have the honour of publishing the forthcoming novel of one whose name even in those early days of his career was known to thousands.

When the book appeared in January and went into three large editions in the first week—an unprecedented sale for the times—those who, even if they could find no cause for disagreement with their present publishers, would sooner or later inevitably discover some (for such is the way of authors) were disposed to include Kell & Wrotham in their calculations as a possible and future substitute. The firm's fiction list grew apace. By the autumn of '32 it numbered in its ranks no fewer than half a dozen names of note, among which two were women.

Prior, who although now more identified with his own activities than with the state of the British Constitution, finds time to write this to his sister (May 21, 1832):

"The Cabinet resigns, and the Political Unions have in hand the situation. Riots everywhere! The working classes are fighting not so much for this Bill or the Ten Pound householders as for their Liberty. It is bound to be carried, nothing now can keep it back and Heaven knows we need a thorough enough cleansing of the Augean Stable filth that has accumulated under the *Ancien Régime*. All our hopes lie in this regeneration after these muddled years of instability. Grey through it all, however, keeps his head, and offers the King fifty new Peers which 'Billy' in a rage rejects.

"Macaulay (they say) is responsible for this commentary on the current movement:

> "What though now opposed I be?
> Twenty Peers shall carry me.
> If twenty won't, thirty will,
> For I'm His Majesty's Bouncing Bill,

which fitly meets the case though not in the author's usual vein, I think!

"We are all on Tenterhooks as to what next. Wellington it seems is next and goes warily, telling all who care to hear him that he'd sooner tackle Waterloo twice over than this present Kettle-of-Fish. Navigation is not so much in his line and it is no easy task to steer his cockle-boat between Scylla and Charybdis where it is like to split on both rocks any minute! There'll be nothing for it but that our 'Billy' must down on his knees and get Grey back to office. If I were ten years younger it would please me greatly to head a demonstration as did young Brighton (Steyning's son) waving a red banner, and was walked off to jail between two Peelers for his pains, with a broken head from a stone thrown by one of his own company—not at him but at an Anti-Reformist's window—which took him by mistake! I fear that the youthful zeal that drove me to hard measures in former years has died on me, and also I have Mary now to hold me by the tail. But the Spirit remains willing!

"Young Marriott was asking after you when I saw him last night at the Bulwers'. He tells me that his father is negotiating with a view to a deal with the present owner of Cheam which I understand is up for sale. Since when? This is news to me. You tell me nothing, but perhaps you did not know of it. Marriotts' must be hauling in the Shekels over their latest triumph, and a more villainous bad book has never yet been printed. Have you read it? If not—pray don't! 'Undying Flames' by one Eustace Smedley. An ill-chosen title for *his* flame will be as dead as mutton in a year. Nevertheless their methods serve to bring them in the wherewithal to lay down a cool twenty thousand which is, I hear, the *prix fixe* by the tea-merchant next door.

"Is it possible that Marriott Junr. exerts pressure on his fond Papa in view of near proximity to his fair neighbour? You seem to have made a high impression in that quarter, and if you were a few years younger I might remind you that it is a firm of great solidity, even though its taste in authors is too catholic for mine, and that the young man is in for a large fortune—not entirely from the brains of better men, but partly from his grandfather's estate, who was a landowner of considerable means. Do you see how the rôle of *Pater-familias* takes effect? Soon—as time flies—I shall have a marriageable daughter of my own. That Minx grows daily more self-willed and more self-centred and withal as sweet as honey! What to be done with her? I am for sending her to Boarding-school but Mary cries her eyes out at the thought of it. But the boy shan't go to Eton, and there Mary all contrariwise says Yes! Still, these are early days to talk and I wander from the main object of my letter which is to tell you that Mary sends you some Rose-point as a much belated Birthday present and souvenir of our united love. . . ."

The present owner of Cheam Royal, a Mr. Grimsby-Hogg, was the husband of an ailing wife and father of a dozen children of all ages from two years to twenty. He spent what time he passed at Cheam in fox-hunting and village inns, and the rest of his leisure in London, where from all accounts he had been losing heavily at Crockford's.

His lady, who stood in greatest awe of him, was a colourless, dowdy little woman to whom Sabrina paid two duty calls a year, receiving the same in due return from her.

It was on the last of these occasions, shortly after Prior's letter, that the two ladies met across the tea-table in the drawing-room at Wroth. Mrs. Grimsby-Hogg, who was accompanied by her eldest daughter, a strapping girl of nineteen with a loud laugh and the manners, in Miss Jeans' opinion, of a stableboy, confirmed the rumours that were already round the village.

"Yes, it is true. We have sold— My husband—that is to say—"

Mrs. Grimsby-Hogg had a nervous habit of never finishing her sentences, which her daughter Leonora finished for her.

"Is about to sell, you mean, Ma. And I for one will not be sorry. There's not enough life in this hole-in-a-corner. Don't you agree, Mrs. Burnaby? You must find the neighbourhood very dull, living as you do alone, or"—with a glance at Miss Jeans' uncompromising face above the tea-tray—"almost alone. If it were not for the huntin' I'd have gone mad, particularly when the boys are all at school. But you can't hunt in the summer, and then I'm sure one might as well be dead."

"My dear," her Mamma feebly ventured to reprove her, "you do say such—"

"Well, it's true! Cheam is just about as lively as the tomb. My Papa is going to take a smaller place in Leicestershire, Mrs. Burnaby. There'll be some good huntin' there, that's one thing in

its favour. He can't afford to keep up such a big house as Cheam
Royal with six sons now at Harrow."

"Six!" echoed Sabrina. "Dear me! I did not realise there were
so many."

"And two more yet to go when they're old enough. But two of
the six are twins. Nine boys and three girls, and we've not finished
yet, have we, Ma? I've got a bet on the next with my eldest
brother, Tom, as to which gender it will be. If it's a girl I shall
lose five guineas."

"Hem! May I fill your cup, Mrs. Grimsby-Hogg?" Miss Jeans
enquired, awfully.

"Thank you. I—Leonora!" gasped her mother. "So dreadfully
outspoken! I don't know where you learn—so many brothers,
Mrs. Burnaby, and her two little sisters only babies yet. *Most* in-
delicate, my dear. Yes, Miss Jeans, thank you—I think I—cream,
yes, if you please—and sugar. So we thought it best—Mr.
Grimsby-Hogg and I decided when we heard of the offer of this
place in Leicestershire—"

"To sell *our* house to the highest bidder, and there's only the
agreement to be signed now, so it's as good as fixed. And such an
elegant young gentleman, Mrs. Burnaby—at least the son is. He
came here with his father a week or two ago to see over the place,
and they stayed the night at Cheam. They publish books, so perhaps you know them as Mr. Wrotham is in the same trade—"

Miss Jeans hemmed again at this. Trade, indeed! If publishing
were trade, then what was tea? And—"Your cup," she said, "Miss
—Hogg?" with a pause that might have been deliberate before
dehyphenation.

"No, thank you." All undaunted by acidity, Leonora babbled
on. "Their name is Marriott. Young Mr. Marriott is most entertaining, Mrs. Burnaby; you will be charmed with him I'm sure.
He has three sisters, and he's the only son. I almost wish we were

not going to live so very far away, for now there will be no lack
of company. Although I understand that *young* Mr. Marriott will
be in London most of the time, or so his father said. Such goings
on in town over the Reform Bill. Just fancy! And I never knew it
had been passed till Mr. Marriott told me. My Papa says it means
ruination to the country and that we shall all be paupers, but then
he's been saying that for the last twenty years—or at any rate ever
since I've been born—and I don't see much signs of it as yet."

"That will do, Leonora. You talk too— Yes, so we shall soon be
on the move. I cannot say that I look forward to— No, thank you,
Miss Jeans, no more. I have done very— A delicious cake, dear
Mrs. Burnaby. Almond flavouring, I think? I wonder if I might
dare to ask you for the recipe, though I doubt if my cook could—
she has such a heavy—"

"Hand. Oh, dreadful! Her pastry is like lead. Aren't your roses
lovely, Mrs. Burnaby? May we walk a little in the garden? And
can I go round to see the stables presently? She is a sweet pretty
thing, that new mare of yours. A thoroughbred, isn't she? I want
my Papa to buy me a thoroughbred. He has a beauty, a straw-
berry roan named Captain."

"Yes. I've seen him. A handsome creature. Will you not take
another slice of cake, Mrs. Grimsby-Hogg? No? Then if it will
not tire you to walk in the garden—"

"Not at all. I—"

And, rising from their seats, the ladies collected scarves and reti-
cules and adjusted more firmly on their heads the wide-brimmed,
much beribboned hats that were fashion's latest fancy. Indeed
poor little Mrs. Grimsby-Hogg in hers, which sported, in addition
to its yellow ruchings, three large magenta dahlias and several
ears of corn, was almost entirely extinguished.

Great improvements had been made at Wroth in the last fifteen
years, and the garden was Sabrina's pride. Not now neglected,

overgrown with weeds, uncared for, its profuse flower beds and grassy yew-lined walks showed everywhere the evidence of loving ministration.

The visitors dutifully offered rapturous comments, and received in return a bouquet each of choicest blooms. Leonora visited the stables, and in her absence Mrs. Grimsby-Hogg confided that it really was a most inconvenient time to move, owing to—but that she hoped she would be comfortably settled in the new house before—

Sabrina profoundly pitied the timid, negligible little woman whose life was one long agony of childbearing and who accepted such without complaint as her own rightful share in the matrimonial alliance to which it had pleased her God to call her.

After the Grimsby-Hoggs had gone she sat a long time in the garden under the chestnut on the terraced lawn, watching the golden afternoon pass to its sunset end. Beyond the yew hedge where the lawn dipped to the spinney the cuckoo's note piped, deepening, and in the field below where the three tall elms stood sentinel, old Butterfly grazed, cropping the last of the buttercups, her white tail swishing at the flies. How old she was! Twenty-eight. As old as a woman of ninety.

On Sabrina's lips a smile came and faded. It was so beautiful, this quiet countryside in which her life was rooted, that perhaps her heart ached a little from sheer love of it, and for the knowledge that each year led her a step further from the pulse and urge of youth and from youth's glamour.

Youth and Love. The two went together hand in hand.

But what was love? A strange, sweet thing, haphazard, swift, a meeting and a parting, an interlude, or a bright eager flame, a dying down, a passing out and then—forgetfulness? Such grades of love as went to make that word so glibly used, so seldom known; a kiss, a touch, a whisper—was that love? So called. Ah!

but she knew. No matter that all future life were lonely or that each summer brought its own remembrance to mock her days with shadows and her nights with waking dreams, she had known love's fulfilment; no transient dream-phantom, but a steady, sober burning, an unquenched spark, which would endure beyond the mortal loss of it that must leave her spirit always a little empty and on her soul a scar.

The sun sank lower. From near meadows came the heavy scent of new-cut hay and clover, from each tree an evensong. Gnats danced in a bar of light that looked like gilded honey, a ladybird settled on her arm. She watched its tiny rust-red wings, black-spotted, fold together; there it stayed, the fragile fairy-creature. Where did it come from? Where would it go? To drift upon the air for one short day with some such fairy-mate and then—to die at the moment of its union? Perhaps man's life is of so brief a spell viewed by that Source within whose sight a thousand years are but as yesterday, and man himself no less infinitesimal to the whole great scheme of things than is this tiny insect—Sabrina mused—to me . . . which even while she wondered at its exquisite perfection, painted surely by some super-craftsman's hand, spread its small wings and vanished.

The sky was reddening; the sun fierce in the last of its strength seemed to draw from all shapes a clearer outline, from all colours richer hue, from each opening flower a more fragrant breath; and beneath that close embrace the tranced earth lay surrendered. Webbed in the shimmering haze, she could just discern the chimneys of Cheam Royal rising above the belt of woods that girdled the base of Cheam Hill. Between woods and uplands lay Cheam Valley, watered by the Lyme whose narrow stream divided the two estates. And while she gazed into the still radiance of the early evening, watching the flight of swallows, the slow dusky flight of bees, watching the shadows lengthen; hearing the pigeons croon, the song of late larks and bird-calls in the spinney, and all the throbbing undertones that spoke through summer's voice, her thoughts that since a certain episode had been barred from a direction which she had sternly told herself must be for ever out of bounds, stirred in her heart and whispered there, insistent.

She recalled those three weeks spent in London at her brother's house in Soho Square after their first meeting. There was no gainsaying him; he had an ardent, gay impetuosity so reminiscent of that other lost young love that her spirit swooned to see it, and in sheer self-defence she meted him a gentle series of rebuffs that served only to inflame his ardour more. Such was youth's way, and so must youth be served with its own fever, its own joy, its own intoxication. This she had striven to point out to him: "But not with me, my dear—" Each word that had passed between them on that April afternoon when he had stolen in upon her, unannounced, where she sat in the half-deserted, and still half-furnished, drawing-room, dressing a doll for Clare, came back to her.

She remembered details: the bits of coloured stuffs strewn about her on the sofa, and the sofa itself, with its rolled head cushion at one end, its slender framework, and starry-blossomed chintz; the naked wax doll on her knee, its painted face and glassy eyes staring unwinking and with a grotesque, puppet reality at the cornucopia; her workbox with its inlaid lid open at her elbow; how he had swept aside both doll and workbox with a fine disregard for either and offered there and then his hand and heart in the traditional grand manner until, the stilted phrases broken, he dropped his speechifying and stammered that he loved her, loved only her—would love none other while he lived. Could she not feel that this was truth? And dared he hope that she was not—entirely indifferent?

Had he stirred her? More than her silence, the drooped lids that hid her eyes would ever tell him. But her answer when it came was cool enough.

"Do you know that there is"—she had hesitated for a scarcely perceptible moment—"ten years' difference in our ages, Stephen?"

"What of it? Yes, I do know—or I guessed. The first time I ever saw you, your brother said you were his twin. I knew you must be older than myself. How can it matter? You see that it has made no difference. If you were fifty—"

"When I am fifty you will still be in your prime."

His face darkened. He was unaccustomed to denial. Sullen-mouthed, he asked her: "Is that all the hope you give me? You find me then—too young?"

"No, but myself too old."

Then for an hour he had pleaded, raved, shifting his tone in turn from tenderest persuasion to impassioned violence, his grey eyes smouldering between their jetty lashes. His hands, intelli-gent-looking, slender-fingered hands, felt feverishly for hers. "Such an objection! If only *that* is the objection—then there can be no possible objection. We have the same interests, the same pursuits. We could live in books together. Look how we read—"

True. They had read. He had come to her with offerings, with first editions; one of the *Bourgeois Gentilhomme* which he read to her in French. He spoke the language like a native, but her own knowledge of it was too slight to provide her with much entertainment. Twice he had caught her in a yawn, and at the third he laid down the book, rose, bowed, apologised for his too lengthy visit and left her in high dudgeon, to return an hour later on his knees. Did grown men behave so? But for all this— for his absurd inconsequence, that bewitching trick of his faun's smile, so like and yet unlike a living memory—she loved, and dared not love, him. So, sooner than enlarge upon a fantasy, she erred upon the safe side of discretion.

She may have been hypercritical, too well aware of her own weakness, and his. She saw him spoiled of the gods, perhaps of women; generous, impulsive, acutely sensitive, arrogant, too sure of himself and his opinions, and—irresistible. Yet she resisted.

He took it hardly. She heard no more of him for quite two weeks. Then came a letter all in the same strain, and to effect that life was now unbearable. He was sincere. Why did she doubt him! If disparity of years were the only barrier between them, surely his deep regard and heart's obsession could overcome it? If she considered such declaration importunate, then he must crave her pardon. To her he was no doubt ridiculous, but with all his soul he loved her. Would she not give him hope, a word, a sign that he might live again? For this was Death.

She gave him nothing for a month, then replied as cold as he was hot, in brief: that she appreciated the great honour he had paid her, but that her decision must remain unchanged. Perhaps some day he would realise that her attitude which now appeared so stern was truly for the best. She begged him to believe it and would always be his friend.

That must, she thought, have finished him, for no more was heard until ten days ago, when after his visit to Cheam Royal he had called on her at Wroth.

He was terribly in earnest. She began to think her tactics had been wrong, that by her very reticence she had stirred fires in him stronger than the ebb and flow of passion. Because so nearly he had lost her she embodied for him now not the mere form of Beauty, but the shape of an ideal. His love expanded, a blent mixture of the sensuous and the intellectual. Opposition, it seemed, had humbled him, and from this new humility sprang a more impersonal emotion, a more sober understanding. She may have guessed that what he sought in her was more the fruits of her experience than experience itself. To share with her a harmonious completeness, not only of the senses, but of that rarer quality of the imagination when things visible to sight and touch are dissolved within an inner world of thought and feeling, seemed to him now the acme of desire. He tried to tell her so, could form but broken phrases, and stood before her clumsy and dumb.

They walked together, she remembered, in the garden, here on this very lawn. She strove to keep the conversation insignificant, avoiding the deeper currents that flowed between them, chattered of nothing, and turned to her flowers to relieve the tension.

. . . Those green spikes would soon be lilies. Did he not think those tulips were like footmen, so tall and dapper in their flaunting scarlet? Was there anything so sweet in all the world as the scent of gillyflowers? Unless perhaps of stocks when dew is falling. Would he, please, admire this portulaca? She had reared the plant herself. That hedge was berberis. The honeysuckle had been earlier this year. Would he care to see the spinney?

As she wished—he bowed.

A slight wind was swaying the long grasses; there under the beeches the last crop of bluebells lingered. "We had a shocking gale here some two years back. Do you remember the inclement weather of that winter? Look!" She pointed to three bleached birches stranded in the glade, wrecked like a brig at sea. "This is all that we have left to tell the tale."

He had not heard a word, but he had turned and faced her. She saw that he was trembling; there was something resolute and desperate in the way he took her hand and crushed it between both of his; she felt the fever in his blood, and her own leapt up to meet it.

"Must you," he whispered, "trifle with me? Have you no heart? And yet I know you are all heart. I love you so completely. . . ."

It seemed he had grown older. All that he was feeling had carved faint furrows from his nostrils to the corners of his mouth, not lifted now; close-lipped.

She longed to comfort him, to give him what he needed and what he dared not ask. At the thought so sharp a pang pierced through her that the breath fled from her body and the colour from her cheeks; voiceless, her unveiled eyes answered his. And in that unguarded moment he had shattered her defences. With his arms about her, his hot eager mouth on hers, triumphant, close, he held her. In those seconds of her yielding it seemed that time stood still. . . .

Her gaze fixed on the blossoming sky, she relived a ghostly rapture, its slow enchantment, and swift recoil from the storm that it had roused.

Where would such madness lead? To what end this sweet dark fever that fired her veins and his, and filled her with unutterable longing? To what was she committed? What promise had she given? None, but the sense and touch of her—withheld.

Lifting her face to the sun she closed her eyes. A sound as of low laughter, half a sob, came from her parted lips; and her cheeks were flushed as though the sun had burned them.

II

The five years that elapsed between the passing of the first Reform Bill and the death of William IV were years of social and psychological significance to a nation that was only just emerging from a state of semi-paralysis to a wider understanding of the possibilities of progress. The voice of the populace had carried further than the opposing resistance of the old order entrenched behind the House of Lords. Desire for change was paramount and everywhere a forceful eagerness to break the chains that bound the active present to the oppressive and unworthy past.

The government that during this period abolished negro slavery, amended the Poor Laws and passed the first Factory Act prohibiting employment of infants under nine, was to define afresh the country's whole perspective. Utilitarianism was the order of the day; the invention of the steam engine and industrial machinery inspired visions to revive the tempo of the world. The Whig followers of Grey and Althorp, supported by the recently emancipated middle classes, reinforced the weakened spine of England, and for the first time in history the nation became master in its house.

The ailing old King, who, peppery and ridiculous though he was, had nevertheless won the hearts of his people by his genial bluff good-nature, died on the anniversary of the Battle of Waterloo, and the girl princess of Kensington on whom all eyes were turned and who wrote that day in her journal, "I shall do my utmost to fulfil my duty towards my country; I am very young and perhaps in many, though not in all things inexperienced," was called from her bed at six o'clock in the morning to be told that she was Queen of England.

My father, Anthony Wrotham, a boy of nine or ten, was taken to see her coronation procession. From accounts that I have heard from him and from Sabrina that day, the 28th of June, 1838, lives almost as vividly for me as for those who witnessed it.

Sabrina, who was staying at Soho Square for coronation week, had secured a balcony in St. James's Street. "As some little return," I remember her telling me, "for the hospitality I received so often from your grandmother. Your Aunt Clare was then about sixteen."

The balcony was on the first floor of a house whose lower part was occupied by a wine merchant, and directly opposite Crockford's, which was extensively decorated with flags and preparations for the evening's illuminations. Small coloured lamps outlined the words 'Victoria Regina' and each of the letters was at least three feet in height, the two words separated by an enormous crown surrounded by laurel leaves.

The party consisted of Prior and Mary, Roger Kell, Sabrina, Miss Jeans, Jess Pinkerton, Anthony and Clare. They had with them luncheon baskets, and my grandfather Prior had brought the manuscript of a short story recently submitted to him for *The Magpie* which he read aloud, although none but Miss Jeans listened, while they awaited the return procession from the Abbey.

Lady Pinkerton arrived late, on foot, and in a state of agitation. Her carriage had been held up by the crowds in Piccadilly and there was nothing for it but to get out and walk, accompanied by two flunkeys, who carried between them reinforcements of provisions, a relay of little flags, and four magnums of champagne.

She was splendid in a gown of blue silk poplin with trimmings of scarlet and white, the whole combination, one presumes, a compliment to the national colours. Her blue poke bonnet (a revival of the fashion of twenty years before) was adorned with three white ostrich plumes. She was seventy-six and looked no more than fifty. Painted to the eyes and quite amazing. She wept without restraint when the procession passed. "Too moving! Such a fool as never was, but I can't help it. I always cry at weddings —and this is worse—"

With the tears making rouged rivulets down her cheeks she waved a scarlet handkerchief, squeezed Sabrina's hand, inhaled smelling-salts, and told Roger Kell he was the coldest fish. "Have you no feelings, man? Look at her! Eighteen!"

To the vast populace who watched that radiant fair-haired child driven for the first time through the streets of her capital as its anointed sovereign, there was something more than the sentiment of patriotic frenzy that echoed through the city in a thunder of massed voices from a million throats. The years of suffering and distress that had accompanied a succession of debauched old men who stood for monarchy were gone, and to the mighty multitude who greeted her she expressed the symbol of their springtime, a rebirth; regeneration. She came, passing through the shouting streets in her golden coach, drawn by six cream-coloured horses. Behind her came her Guards, her Grenadiers, and her Hussars, a glittering scarlet pageant. Kings and Princes followed her, and Ministers of State, and those who had made history, and those who had fought by land and sea to save her country, any of whom would on that day in June have laid down their lives for her. In those small hands that held the orb and sceptre, lay England's future, and the whole of England's pride.

A mist blurred Mary's sight of her. So young! So pitifully young, for all that grandeur.

Monarchy! thought Prior. Barbaric. And yet without it—what?

From Sabrina came a whisper, "The merest child!" She was storing up impressions to tell Stephen. She would write this all to him. He was in Paris. He had gone to see Dumas about the translation of the author's latest novel *Pascal Bruno*. He wanted her to join him there. Why not? All would be so easy. Jess still retained in Paris her apartment in the Faubourg Saint-Germain. She had a standing invitation to visit there whenever she wished. She had spent three months last year in Paris with Jess and old Sir Rodney, who survived at eighty, still giggling, though decrepit, and notorious for his absurd extravagances, his mania for

perfumes which were specially distilled for him in the flower
fields of Grasse, his collection of canaries, and the private zo-
ological gardens on his Devonshire estate, where he kept two jag-
uars, a leopard and an aged bear which he had rescued from a
baiting a dozen years ago. He could not suffer cruelty to dumb
animals; for all his nonsense he had that much to his favour.

Jess had said she was going back to Paris for July. Rodney was
ailing, he had sent for her. Would Sabrina not go, too? Here was
the invitation ready to her hand; the game continued to be played
with circumspection, as it had been played these last six years
without reproach. And again—it would be easy to evade with
lies, with superficial subterfuge the outrage to convention. She
knew even while she hesitated that he would have his will
of her—for just so long as he would need her. But with a deep
accepted certainty she knew, too, that there must come an end to
all illusion. She had snatched at a glamorous bubble, had built
her castle upon sand. If it crumbled, who to blame but herself?
Not him. One must pay for happiness, or its spurious reflection.
She was prepared. She had enriched him. She would have no re-
grets. She might as well have married him, and defied her better
judgement. But was it a better judgement? Had she been too cautious in denying herself that much indulgence—for his sake—or
her own? He was only now twenty-seven, and she—yes, she had
been wise and overwise, and yet not wise enough.

A deep sigh passed from her on a whispered breath: "She looks
the merest child—"

Another burst of cheering rose, splintering the air, drowning
the clatter of horses' hooves, the braying music, the joyous pealing
of bells near and distant. The cheers swelled to a climax.

"That's for Wellington," said Roger Kell. "There he goes."

Jess Pinkerton removed her handkerchief from her eye to replace it with a spyglass. "How he has aged! Well—he's seventy.

I remember him in Brussels—what a man! There's Marshal Soult behind him—he looks older than the Duke, but they were born in the same year. Ah! Lord! We none of us grow younger."

How wonderful to be a Queen, thought Clare.

Anthony craned his neck to see—saw nothing. He was too small. His sister Clare was squashing him on one side, Miss Jeans upon the other. She stood there like a tower, very stiff. In front of him, brushing his nose, was a bulky mass of blue, fold upon fold of silk that smelled as ladies' dresses always smelled—hot and dusty, with a smell behind the dust like vinegar and barley-sugar, sweet and sour.

"I can't see nothing," whimpered Anthony.

"Now don't begin again," his sister warned him. "We've had quite enough of you for *one* day, thank you."

That was because she had locked him out of her bedroom while she dressed. And he had kicked at the panels, kicking off the paint, shouting at her: "Booby-Face and Missie Cock-Eye. What a Guy! Put her on a *bon*fire and *burn* 'er. Guy! Ugly. Nosey. Pug-nose. Guy!" All the names that he could think of to make her wild. What she hated most was when he copied her sitting at the table. Folding his hands as she folded hers. Blinking at the ceiling. Putting his lips the way hers went when she was talking. That day the gentleman Papa called Stephen came to Sunday dinner—*how* he had copied her then. And *how* she had blinked and smiled, and then looked up and caught him mimicking and went as red as the red ribbon in her hair. And he loathed her. He loathed the way she stood there now beside him with her chin up and her eyes looking down at the procession which he could only hear and could not see.

He hated her new bonnet. It had a rose under its brim; he loathed her curls corkscrewing on her neck. How glad he would have been to pull them off! His fingers ached to do it. He had

watched her at the looking-glass, brushing those same curls round
her finger with a brush dipped in sweet oil. *He* knew how much
she loved herself, and those dark shiny curls; how she smiled in
the looking-glass and spoke to the face inside it. She had a new
pink dress with lace let in the skirt all the way up showing blue
silk underneath, and at her waist a rose to match the one under
her bonnet. He would have liked to take a knife and slash holes
in that new dress. *Then* she'd be a Guy. Hoo! Wouldn't she be
wild! She had spoiled his new kite. He'd pay her out—one day.
He had left the brand-new kite his Grandpapa had given him
lying on the tallboy. Its tail had got caught—somehow—in the little private drawer she usually kept locked. And what if he had
opened it to see? Yes—well! And he had found a piece of note-
paper with forget-me-nots all round it and some writing he could
read. Hers. He could always read *her* writing if the words were
not too long. These weren't. These were easy. Only two. Dear
and Dear-est. And a heart with letters in the middle. S and M.
She had drawn a heart with letters in its middle like the pink
lozenges you buy with 'Love Me' and 'I Love You' written on
in red. She was always buying those pink lozenges and sucking
them all day and taking them out between the sucks to see if 'I
Love You' came off. It never did because Anthony had sucked
one down to nothing and the words stayed on right through. Yes.
And he thought it would be grand to tie her forget-me-not note-
paper with the heart onto the tail of his kite. She came in while
he was doing it—and squealed. And boxed his ears. He kicked
her hard for it, and then she took his lovely kite and tore it clean
in half. That was a week ago. He had not forgotten—never
would forget. He didn't forget things quickly. Oh, dear, no!

"I hate you. Pig!" said Anthony to Clare.

She didn't hear. She was smiling down at the procession, her
head held very high, and every now and then she slowly bowed

with a smirk upon her face that made Anthony long to scratch it. But nobody cared. Nobody looked at Anthony. Nobody saw him. He might have not been there. Fury raged in him. And hate. Hate of the sun that was beating down on his new sky-blue cloth cap with the white tassel. A handsome enough cap. He had been glad to have that cap. His Mamma had bought it new for him to match his new blue suit. His trousers were too tight, they made his legs feel sticky. They tickled his calves as if ants were crawling up them. The smell of ladies' dresses was hotter than the sun. Inside his stomach was a queer bad sickish feeling. His hands went cold, his forehead damp, he knew what was going to happen pretty soon.

Then what was going to happen, did.

"Oh, my angel!" cried his mother.

"You little Horror! My new *dress!*" screamed Clare.

"I'll see to it. . . . Dear me!" said good Miss Jeans.

His sister was in tears, and Anthony the centre of attraction. He no longer hated Clare. He was avenged.

III

Clare at seventeen was sent to Mrs. Galloway's Academy for Young Ladies at Missel Kempton, the most select of finishing schools. Situated on the borders of Herts and Bucks, its easy accessibility to Wroth made it possible—with the gracious permission of Mrs. Galloway—for Clare to visit her aunt during term time, and spend a night or two from Saturday till Monday.

Clare's bosom friend at this establishment was Theresa Marriott who lived at Cheam Royal, and how delightful that was to be sure! To have one's dearest friend living next door as it were, to her Papa's own house.

"For Wroth *is* my Papa's own house," Clare confided to The-

resa in the first week of their acquaintance. "Although my Aunt
Sabrina lives there when she is not visiting in town. She is a
very elegant and distinguished lady, my Aunt Sabrina. She travels abroad alone. She is rather old but very beautiful."

"Not as beautiful as you, *I'm* sure," said dear Theresa. "And
how can anyone who is rather old be beautiful? I hope to die before I'm forty."

Clare—with intermittent lapses—kept a journal during the
three terms she spent at Mrs. Galloway's. It had been a birthday
present to her from Lady Pinkerton, who was, as everybody
knew, quite crazy, and the *vulgarest* old creature. Nevertheless
it was a charming journal, bound in blue plush with a real gold
lock and key. Clare wore the key on a ribbon tied to her garter,
for safety. For it would have been a calamity too shocking to
contemplate should any prying person come upon that key, and
unlock the blue plush journal, and read within its pages such
revelations as could never be divulged to any living soul except
Clare's most bosom friend, Theresa. Or perhaps the narrator of
this history, who nearly a hundred years later came upon that
very journal in an old oak chest in an attic here at Wroth.
The blue plush is faded, and between its yellowed leaves some
dried rose petals fell to ashes at a touch. And the gold lock is
broken.

"There is no accounting for Tastes," asserts one entry—undated. "I for instance could *never* fall in Love with Mr. Lee.
And I cannot say that whan I marry I would willingly chewse
an Undistinguished Drawing-Master for my Husband not if he
were ever so—and Mr. Lee is *not*. His hair is sandy and his eyelashes are white. He is too thin, and he has a long sharp nose.
But Theresa says he writes the *sweetest* Letters. If Mrs. G. finds
out dear T. will be expelled and so will Mr. Lee. I have no doubt
I am prejudiced in favour of S. beside whom all men appear as

Reptiles. Is it not wonderful and strange that I should come to this Detestable School and find here the sister of Him whom for two years I have adored? Surely this is Fate? When we read in Class to-day that Speech from Shakespeare She never told her love but let concealment like a Worm in the Bud feed on her Damask cheek, I could not contain my Tears. At tea at Wroth last Sunday when he rode over with those grapes from his Mother for Aunt S. he scarcely looked at *me*. But one day he *shall* look at me. My dearest T. has promised to invite me to stay a week at Cheam next vacation. I am marking off the days on my Calendar. There are forty-two more. It is Valentine's Day to-morrow. If only I dared send him a Valentine! T. is sending one to Mr. Lee. Mamma has given me a new dress for Dancing-class. Blue Tarlatan with three flounces and a pair of satin sandals. I shall not wear it for dancing-class but shall keep it till I go to Cheam. I had a bad Mark to-day in History class for inattention. But who cares to hear about the Past? I do not want to know Past History. I want to know the Future. *My* future. T. says that her old nurse can tell Fortunes in the Tea-cups and with Cards. She shall tell mine when I go to Cheam. *When* I go to Cheam! How long to wait! If I had not seen him last week I might have been able to *bear* this Misery but now it is all *Woken up again,* and I am in *Torment.* He thinks I am a child. I am not. I am seventeen. Aunt S. was married when *she* was seventeen. Can I help it if I do not look my Age? If only I could grow. Why am I Little. Why am I not like Aunt Sabrina. Theresa says that tall women are odious and that all men prefer *Petites.* She says that I am more than merely pretty and always so well *soignée* which is so important. I use the orange flower cream that old Lady P. gave me last Summer on my hands and arms every night and morning. I wish I were white-skinned like T. T. says she is convinced that I have French or Spanish blood, but I do not think that we can trace any Foreign Extraction on either side. T. says that men *adore* French women. . . .

"We are having Presentation classes with a Madame du Bois to teach us how to curtsey and to Kiss the Hand. We walk round the room with calico trains suspended from our shoulders and curtsey to Mrs. G. who sits in an armchair on a platform looking utterly ridiculous and imagining I am sure that she's the Queen. I know that Mamma will not let me be presented. T. is going to be presented, but my Parents are so *dreadfully* unfashionable. Why cannot Mamma be more like T's Mamma. It was only through Lady P's persuasion that I was sent here to Mrs. G's. Mamma would have kept me at home sewing *Hems* and reading the Classics. Who wants to read the *Classics.* Neither Mamma nor Papa have any Social Amenities. Our subject essay this week is on Social Amenities. I do not in the least know what to write. I shall begin this way I think. Viz:—

"'By Attention to the Social Amenities is formed the character and Disposition of a Lady. Social Amenities do not only include Good Manners and Upright Deportment but a consideration for the feelings of others. Also it is necessary to chewse with Taste and Discretion one's companions. A Lady is always known by the Company she keeps. That is why in Court Circles only the greatest Ladies in the Land are permitted entrance. Bad Manners and Slovenly Deportment are Indicative of Bad Character. . . .' I am sure mine will be a bad Essay. I *cannot* write this silly stuff. How I loathe School. I had the most Delicious Dream of Him last night which I dare not even write in my Journal. It was too excruciatingly Divine. T. has revealed to me the most wonderful secrets about Life and Men. She has been kissed by Mr. Lee. Just fancy! I could never—not with Mr. Lee. She says that if your lover kisses your lips that you are pledged to him for ever. I shall die if I am never to be kissed except in Dreams.

I must keep this book locked for if it were ever discovered . . . I have tied the key to my garter."

And this, later, still undated.

"Aunt S. writes that old Miss Jeans is ill and that I cannot go to Wroth on Saturday. How tiresome and *Dreadful*. I was longing for another glimpse of Him. He would have been over some time for sure, or I might have met him riding like I did before. *Miserable* Miss Jeans. Why should all my Hopes be shattered because of old Miss Jeans. I am writing back at once to ask if I can come and be of help to Aunt S. for with sickness in the house she might be glad of my Assistance.

"Papa said I was a Perfect Nurse when he was laid up with his bad Heart. But I should hate to nurse Miss Jeans. . . ."

IV

"Snowflakes are always charming," said Miss Jeans.

She sat propped up on her pillows, smiling, warm and quite content. She had been cold—so very cold. For was not the weather very cold?

"Indeed so cold, my dear Sabrina, that one might believe the earth had cooled and become a second moon. For as you know —as I have so often told you—the moon according to some scientific theories was once upon a time another sun. I admit I find such hypothesis extravagant."

"Try not to talk, dear," said Sabrina.

Miss Jeans, still smiling, closed her eyes. "The tables turn," she murmured. "You govern me. On the whole I think that you were tractable. I took to you from the first, although your manners and your language when I came to you were shocking. I shall never forget how when I heard you say some dreadful word beginning with a *B* it went right through me—like a knife."

And like the knife, added Miss Jeans silently, that is turning
at this moment in my breast. My bosom. For 'breast' was a word
used only by the poets—or a mother. And since, whispered Miss
Jeans, I am neither of these things, then what am I?

Behind her closed lids slow pictures moved, faces, lives—of
others. Not Miss Jeans' own life, for that was finished. It may
never have begun. "A figment merely of imagination," breathed
Miss Jeans. "For what *is* life but sheer imagination?"

One might believe that one had been a messenger from the
gods upon Olympus, chosen on a day in—when? How many
years ago? In a cinnamon-brown dress—or was it that the young
man's suit was cinnamon? How soothing to sit quietly beneath
green trees holding a young man's hand! Have I, too, had my
moment, asked Miss Jeans. But in any case such behaviour is not
at all in order. Most indecorous to stand about the streets outside
the house for hours. Miss Wrotham's window, sir, is at the
back. . . .

'And I returned and saw under the sun that the race is not to
the swift nor the battle to the just but time and chance happen-
eth to them all.' Each of us in life, my dear Sabrina, has his time
and chance. My time and my chance are coming. They are near.

Miss Jeans was struggling to speak.

"May I trouble you—for a—sip—of lemon-water?"

Sabrina rose and went to the bedside. She slid her arm under
the old woman's shoulders and raised her, holding the tumbler
to the dried, quivering lips.

"Refreshing," said Miss Jeans. "Thank you, my dear. You are
very good. There have been moments when I feared for you.
You should have married that young man—so many years acquainted—to fly in the face of all convention—pardon me. I will
never speak of this again. The mother of my last pupil Elizabeth
who married—you remember—Captain Ffoulkes of the Dragoons

—I went to see her wedding—six years older—Elizabeth's mother, my dear Sabrina—the Honourable Mrs. Sloane—was six years older than her husband. You will never—would never"—Miss Jeans licked her lips—"do anything that would bring me down in sorrow to the . . . thank you, I have had enough. My mother used to tell me that lemon juice is good for the complexion . . ."

"Try not to talk," whispered Sabrina, "you are tiring yourself."

"Tired. Yes."

Miss Jeans' lids drooped again over her fading eyes. Sabrina smoothed the stiff grey hair back from the lined forehead and took a seat beside the bed. The doctor would be coming soon to pay his second visit. But there was nothing to be done. Her good Jeans was leaving her. Jeans, who had stood beside her through nearly all her life, had helped her to her happiness, had watched her in her anguish, had seen her son born dead. She who had spent her whole essence in service and devotion, to be repaid, Sabrina told her achingly, in such small part. For what has been given you?

On the threshold of eternity the spirit of Miss Jeans was marking time. The body that still contained it lay outlined upon the bed, a long gaunt shape under red blankets and a patchwork quilt. Her body felt at ease, impalpable and airy. Like this it might be possible to fly. From behind sealed lids she watched the snowflakes falling, and that was strange for the curtains had been closed a long time since, and the room was full of shadows. But the spirit of Miss Jeans, straining at the leash that bound it to the present and the past, could see beyond closed curtains, beyond the shadowed room to the uttermost depths of that pure darkness which is the beginning and end of all things.

"She is going."

A man's voice spoke the words at Miss Jeans' bedside. A man's hand touched the secret places of her heart. She was consumed in flame, swept up on a tremendous wave, dissolved upon an ebbing tide of bliss; and as the last slow throbbing of her blood died down, a great triumphant sigh broke from her.

. . . I too have had my moment, said Miss Jeans.

v

Clare was dressing for the party. Her dress, the blue tarlatan that she had saved for this occasion, lay upon the bed in Theresa's bedroom. Theresa's old nurse Betty was in attendance on the two young ladies. She laced Theresa's stays.

"That's as tight as I can get you, lovey, and it's as tight as you can bear."

"It's nothing of the sort," replied Theresa stoically. "Try again, Betty, if you love me, and pull hard."

Betty tried again and pulled so hard that Theresa had to cling with both hands to the bedpost for support while she inhaled and held a long deep breath, released at last upon a groan.

"Your waist is like an angel's," Clare assured her. "I am nowhere beside you."

Clare was already laced. The compression across her diaphragm felt as though she were encased in bands of lead. When Betty fastened her bodice over the stiff-boned corset she scarcely could repress a shriek. Betty had taken in two inches of that bodice at the seams, and boned it more severely, acting upon instructions from Theresa who had such perfect taste, and who declared that *il faut souffrir pour être belle*. Theresa was full of elegant French phrases. She'd had French governesses since she was ten. Clare, too, was learning a few French phrases.

She said: "You are *tellement chic,* tonight, Theresa love."

She envied Theresa's *chic*. Theresa's dress was incomparably more *chic* than her own. Lilac taffetas with three deep flounces of cream lace stiffened inside with whalebone bands to produce that *chic* new hooped effect. Skirts were growing wider every season, worn over six silk petticoats at least. And I, reflected Clare, wear only three and none of them are silk. How cruel of Mamma to send me to my first dance dressed like a charity-school child! Mamma has positively no *savoir-faire* at all.

Theresa was pinching her cheeks and biting her lips to make them glow the redder, while Betty dusted Theresa's shoulders with powdered orris-root. Clare envied besides Theresa's dress, Theresa's milk-white skin, her swanlike neck, her dazzling complexion.

"How hideous I look!" Clare murmured as Betty left the room. "I am dark as a mulatto next to you."

"How can you be so wicked!" exclaimed Theresa, "to complain because you are brunette. I would far rather be a brunette than a blonde, and Stephen thinks that you're bewitching."

"He!" Clare's hands leapt to her bosom, her eyes sparkled. She was breathless. "Don't *torture* me, Theresa! You know you only say such things to please me. He never said—you can't tell me that he really *said* I was—"

"Bewitching? But he did. Would I tell fibs to please you? You think me insincere. A hypocrite. You don't trust me. Very well." Theresa pouted and, watching the effect in the looking-glass, decided that her lips might still be redder and began biting them again. "If only," she sighed, "I had thought to buy some coral salve. Mamma has a little pot of coral salve, but she won't let me use it. It is the most delicious stuff and smells of roses."

"He really said the word—bewitching?" faltered Clare. "But how? In what connection?"

"When he was watching you at archery this morning. Do you think my hair is curled too tight? I look horrible. It *is* curled too tight."

"It isn't. . . . Theresa! *Don't* tell me he was watching. I am so shocking at archery. I have never made a higher score than three. Was he really watching?"

"But you know that he was watching. You saw him on the lawn. Do you like my hair best with this rose-wreath or without it?"

"Let me see without it. . . . No, I like it better with. Tell me, Theresa, did you ask him? Confess that you first said to him 'Isn't she' whatever it was—and that all he said was 'Yes.'"

"No, he said it first. I shan't wear this wreath. It makes me look too young. I shall wear nothing in my hair at all."

"May I try the wreath then, if you're not going to wear it?"

"You are distinctly better without a wreath. I think that I shall wear it after all. It was sent to be worn with this dress, and Madame Lalli has the best of taste. Who made yours, my love?"

"Oh, nobody. One of Mamma's frumpish little women. She is always finding frumpish little women who are poor and come to her with tales. She is the most gullible creature, my Mamma. You cannot think how she is imposed upon by servants and poor people. My Papa is, too. We would be much richer if he were not always giving money to workingmen and starving authors. Your parents are so different to mine, Theresa, especially your Mamma. No one would believe she could have a son as old as Stephen. She is so youthful and so gay."

"Yes, but you see she was only sixteen when she married my Papa. Just imagine! Younger than we are! And she had three children in two and a half years—Stephen is the eldest, then my two sisters. How thankful I am that they're married! It would be dreadful to go to parties with two old maid sisters—and when I was born—oh! long after the others—my Mamma nearly died. I do think ladies are greatly to be pitied. The men have all the pleasure and we have all the pain."

"Theresa!"

"Are you shocked?" Theresa giggled. "You needn't be so prudish."

"I am not in the least prudish," retorted Clare, a little nettled. "I am very interested. Nobody but you ever speaks to me of such intimate facts of life. But I have often wondered—Theresa—is it possible to—have a—a baby from being kissed?"

"Oh, yes!" replied Theresa confidently. "Quite possible—if one is kissed upon the lips. That is why it is so dangerous and wrong to be kissed upon the lips before one has a husband. I was terrified when Mr. Lee kissed me on the lips. Don't you remember in the Bible it says, 'Let him kiss me with the kisses of his mouth'? The whole of the Song of Solomon deals with the marriage of a bride and bridegroom, although of course we are told that it is the love of the Church for our Lord."

Clare's hands leapt to her bosom a second time. Theresa did say the most audacious things.

"Then I shall never, never, *never* let myself be kissed that way. Not until I'm married. Not even if I am engaged."

"You won't be able to help yourself, my dear, if you're in love."

"Theresa! This—this conversation," panted Clare, "is giving me the most extraordinary sensations."

"Then you *are* in love," declared Theresa. "The first sign of love is an extraordinary sensation. That is why I knew I was in love with Mr. Lee—because he gave me such extraordinary sensations. Clare. Is it not peculiar that when Betty told your fortune in the cards you had the nine of hearts crowning you? Hearts mean success in love, and spades mean disappointment. I was crowned with disappointment—the nine of spades—which of course means that I shall be an old maid all my life."

"Theresa! You must never even *think* it! You will never be

an old maid. You are far too fascinating to be an old maid. It is
only hideous old horrors with beards like poor Miss Jeans who—"
Clare put a hand over her mouth and tittered. "How wicked of
me to talk about her beard when she is dead! But she did have
one, you know, horrid grey hairs sticking out of her chin . . .
You mustn't give up hope because one man turns out to be a
Monster. You are getting over it a little now, are you not,
Theresa? The agony is not quite so unbearable?"

Theresa shook her head.

"Unbearable as ever. Because I do not talk of him you immediately imagine—"

"I don't, Theresa! I don't imagine anything. . . . Oh! Mercy!
My stays are much too tight. It hurts to breathe. . . . You know I
ache for you, Theresa. But I do think that such a creature is
unworthy of another thought. Odious man. What horrible deceit to make love to you when all the time he was betrothed to
another! Shall you ever forget when Mrs. G. announced that he
was going to be married to Miss Ayr? and asked us all to sub-
scribe two shillings each for a wedding present? What irony! To
have to give two shillings for a wedding present for Miss Ayr
and Mr. Lee. And fancy! Miss Ayr! How *could* he after swear-
ing that he loved you and kissing you—like that—turn from *you*
to hideous Miss Ayr and all her pimples?"

During this sprightly monologue Theresa's face had undergone a change; her charming features stiffened; her lips became
a hard pink line, her face a mask of ice.

"I have no doubt," observed Theresa in an acid tone, "that you
find my downfall comic. Very droll." A hollow laugh broke from
her. "Such a dear friend."

"The*resa!*" Clare swept across the room and flung her arms
around Theresa's neck. "How can you so accuse me? You know
how full of sympathy I am. Don't be so *cruel*, Theresa!"

Theresa disengaged; she rearranged her ribbons and observed with frigid calm:

"You crush my dress. How much you do enjoy making a scene!"

"I am *not* making a scene," denied Clare loudly. "It's you who make the scene. I never made a scene. What have I said? What have I done? How very strange you are, Theresa!"

"I am. I'm very strange," was the sinister rejoinder. "But not so strange that I can't see through a brick wall." And Theresa put her lips together as though she never meant to open them again.

"What do you mean?" Clare tempestuously demanded. "Why do you look like that, for Heaven's sake? Anyone would think—"

"Anyone *may* think." Theresa's glance stabbed like an angry swan's. "But what *I* think is quite a different matter. You can't tell me you didn't gloat."

"I didn't—*what?*"

"You heard," replied Theresa inimically.

"You think I—gloated?"

"Yes." Theresa threw the word at her as though it were a brick. "You—gloated."

Clare stood trembling in horrified incredulity.

"You can say that to *me!* How vilely unjust—how perfectly abominable! Such a thought was never for one moment in my mind. I swear—"

"There is no need to swear. And why be so dramatic? You are always so dramatic. You roll your eyes," Theresa stated loftily, "like a third-rate actress on the stage. You don't look at all fetching when you do that, I assure you, so I advise you not to practise it on Stephen. You should study self-restraint a little more."

It was too much. Insult heaped on injury scattered the last

shreds of discretion. Clare rushed upon a precipice and hurtled over.

"Self-restraint, indeed! Ho! *Should* I? I have more self-restraint than you, from all accounts. You and your Mr. Lee! I would not so demean myself as you have done with a sandy-haired, long-nosed drawing-master. . . . *Kissing!*"

Too late for recall. Clare could have bitten off her tongue for that unwary outburst. To quarrel with Theresa, in whose good favour lay her fondest hopes, was madness. She choked and tried to speak, said nothing, and gazed dumbly at her dearest friend, who in the shock of this attack had closed her eyes; she opened them again to deliver herself between clenched teeth of one brief, pent-up explosion.

"Snake!"

Then, gathering her skirts and without another word, Theresa billowed from the room and banged the door.

How far that difference of opinion between these two dear friends was responsible for further complications, is not for me to say. I merely state the facts, gleaned from the blue plush journal which gives an accurate if hysterical account of them, written, it would seem, that very night.

There is no doubt Clare felt herself hard put upon; no doubt, too, that Theresa undeniably had scored. To be attacked with vile opprobrium, to be misjudged, insulted, for no reason at all was an intolerable outrage, unjustified, and not to be endured. The more Clare brooded on her wrongs, the more painful became the weight of disillusion, until extinguished, she flung herself upon Theresa's bed, and wept.

This welter of emotion may have lasted for an hour, or it may have lasted two. She had no idea of time. She heard the mocking music far away, and sobbed in greater anguish. What to do? She could not join the party and face importunate enquiries—if indeed enquiries were made at all. For nobody had missed her. She was outcast, a nonentity, a fool. And what a fool! To have placed her trust in that False Cat. She would put an end to this most sorry business. She would not stay at Cheam another night. She would leave at once. Ring for Betty to come and pack her boxes, and go home to Wroth and Aunt Sabrina with a tale. She would tell how she had been treated—and as for Steph—Theresa's brother, she must forget him. He had never given her a second's thought. Theresa probably had lied when she said he used the word—that he had used. He has never even looked at me, Clare moaned to the soaked pillow. Why should he now? To have waited a whole term for this occasion, to have saved her new blue tarlatan to wear tonight, to have lived on air all day until the moment—which now would never come—when he would ask her for a dance—was too unbearable. Sobs ran through her frame like waves.

A discreet tapping at the door brought her head up from the pillow with a jerk.

"Who is there?" she quavered. For if Theresa she would not yet forgive. Oh! no. She would have her on her knees and grovelling before she would concede one inch.

Slowly the door opened, and in the candlelight upon the wall appeared a shadow. A voice spoke—not Theresa's.

"I have been sent to bring you to the party."

He leaned there in the doorway, and at that sight of him and of his tilted smile, his laughing eyes that drew her own to his and held them, helpless, drowned, the child Clare became a woman.

He went over to the bedside, sat down upon the end of it and watched her. Had he observed that strange transfiguration? Perhaps he saw her then for the first time; the quivering soft mouth, those drenched, ink-coloured eyes, the foolish tear-stains round them. Ridiculous young creature! Ridiculous and yet pathetic with the wistful, half-comic pathos that is youth's as much as are youth's poignant ecstasies and unfulfilled desires, its fear-encompassed hopes, its dazzled moments. . . .

And Stephen, watching, smiled.

"This," he said, "is not the first time that I have met you at a party."

She stared up at him, lips parted, irresistibly.

"Not—when?"

"A long time ago, to you. But not long—in years—to me. Do you remember when you were very young, a good deal younger than you are today—drinking orange wine, and eating lollipops in bed—out of all hours when you should have been asleep?"

She put a hand up to her throat, where a small pulse beat and fluttered. Stephen's eyes, still watching, narrowed. "Do you remember, little Clare?"

She nodded, swallowing. "I do—I thought—I always thought," she whispered, "that I dreamed it."

"And sometimes," Stephen said, "our dreams come true. . . . Can you hear the music playing 'Invitation to the Waltz'? May I have the pleasure of a dance?"

VI

Sabrina was at Curzon Street staying with Jess Pinkerton when the young Queen's marriage to her German prince took place. There are no accounts in Wrotham annals to tell that any member of the family witnessed the wedding procession, although it is believed that Jess secured a window in Piccadilly for that purpose and cancelled it the day before, owing to indisposition. We know that she was taken ill about this time, that eminent physicians met in consultation, that she was plastered, bled, forbidden wine, and had a gouty toe.

Confined to bed and fed on pap, she entertained familiars in her room to morning chocolate. In her old age Jess as a society 'eccentric' bid fair to crush the memory of Lady Cork. She held something of a salon at the house in Curzon Street. Disraeli described her humour as the purple vein in Phrygian marble, and sent her a signed copy of *Venetia.* D'Orsay visited her on several occasions, and was said to have declared her the only woman in all London who could make him laugh. She gave him a dozen pairs of gloves.

"Six lemon coloured *shammy*"—so she tells us in her journal, "and six French kid. He'll never wear them. . . . Lady B. is editing the 'Book of Beauty.' I gave her my Recipe for the Complexion cream that Rachel uses daily. The poor Soul is hard put to it with D—r—y's debts. I hear he hides in G—— House gardens most days of the week while Creditors line up outside the door. The Dr. finds that I have Gall-stones. . . ."

"Too much port, the rascal says," Jess confided to Sabrina after this diagnosis had been verified. "I used to drink Madeira. Perch loathed the stuff and laid down in my cellar a whole pipe from Oporto. Poor dear Perch!" Jess picked a tear out of her eye. "The sweetest funeral you ever saw. *That* shattered me. I'm old."

So was Sir Rodney when he died in Paris in December, '39, of eating crab.

He left Jess half his fortune.

"I could have married him," she said; "he was on his knees to me this last ten years. But to tell the truth, my dear, there's more cachet to a countess, and Perch always was a fishy name to my mind. He was extraordinarily devoted but as mean as mud— God bless him!—till he died—when he did handsomely by me—

at all events. Extravagant in the grand manner but would haggle over sixpence. You could have altered that. He'd have given you the moon." Jess heaved the deepest sigh. "Well! It's not all of us can say they've kept a man under their petticoats for sixty years—"

On another occasion she told Sabrina she had made a will.

"I've left you every penny that poor Rodney left to me, and your grandfather's estate to Prior. But he don't need it now. He's making money hand over fist, so everybody tells me, and giving it away to those damned Chartists. I hear that secret meetings are held above Kell's shop. And what a pompous ass that man Kell is! Mary brought him here to see me with a bunch of flowers in his fist, and he droned on and on until I fell asleep. Is it true that Prior is writing inflammatory articles in *The Magpie* signed 'The Torch'? He'll get himself arrested."

Sabrina could not enlighten Jess for certain on this point. She had not read the articles in question, but she thought it more than likely that Prior's hand was in them. She had met for the first time in Soho circles one Feargus O'Connor, a barrister, who preached the socialistic gospel from the hearthrug, backed up by measured commentaries from Kell and laudatory declamations from her brother.

O'Connor was a man of gigantic build, with a fiery tongue and a delightful brogue. He it was who had led and ultimately ruined the Chartist movement which had already received its first death-blow, though it was said it had nine lives. Read in the light of today, the appeal, as presented in the People's Charter, is not so unreasonable as it appeared to the hidebound politicians of a century ago, when among its 'six points' were emphasised the right to vote by every male over twenty-one; vote by ballot; and the payment of Members of Parliament for their services —this last the greatest outrage!

So in the face of popular agitation the Whig Ministry found itself in a tight corner. Melbourne's position was tottering; not all his charm and wit nor the good favour of his Royal pupil could hold him to her side. Defeat was certain. The Queen watched with apprehension the growing antagonism to her beloved 'M.' The Chartist movement had been the thin edge of the wedge. Sterner methods must be adopted to silence once and for all the ugly clamour of the people. The new age was bringing in new masters. A young man of Scottish extraction, but born in Liverpool, one William Ewart Gladstone, had made the ablest speech ever heard inside the House. The dazzling Disraeli whose novels and whose waistcoats made the whole of London talk, and who had just married an old wife, was in the running for election to the Ministry. The world was turning topsy-turvy. Such changes everywhere as in Sabrina's knowledge had never been before. England was changing. Everything was changing. Sabrina too was changing. She had no mind for Chartists, for new Ministers, for the problems of a nation. She was riddled with her own.

Jess talked on. Although in bed she was in highest spirits. She wore a transformation, recently acquired, with a centre parting and rolled curls on either side. "The colour I was born with, love," she told Sabrina. "Gustave made it for me, and here I'm reproduced—eighteen—and rising eighty. I was never one to look me age—except in middle life. An awkward time for ladies. You—" She stopped, and took a pastille from a gold bonbonnière on the table by the bed.

"Yes, I am middle-aged," Sabrina said.

Jess coughed, swallowed her pastille, spluttered, rubbed her chest. "You'd best forget it," she rejoined when she could speak. "I remember poor Rodney used to say that a woman is not as old as she looks but as young as her lover sees her. And he'll see through her soon enough," Jess enigmatically added, "if her heart gives up the ghost. Are you going to marry your moon-eyed young gentleman? It's time you did."

"And it's time"—Sabrina rose and went to a side table—"you took your medicine, my dear."

"Drat the medicine! If you don't nail him some young miss will, and one that's not so far away from all accounts. *She'll* not go back to school." Jess chuckled grimly. "I had Mary creeping in this morning with a dozen new-laid eggs. Yes! You were out. That woman for all her bread-and-butter airs and Puritan high notions has a head screwed tighter on her shoulders than her husband's or than yours. You Wrothams see no further than your noses. Never did. Your father was the same although he was a wrong un. And there was Mary," Jess continued with some malice, for she had not forgiven Prior for marrying in trade, "looking like a mouse and clutching an umbrella—what a sight! Why don't you make her dress? All in a flutter—this and that— and Missie such a trial pulling in her waist—it's a pity Mary Wrotham don't pull in hers—and a certain party calling three days in a week. To see Prior? Oh, dear, no! To play marbles on the floor with Anthony . . . I laughed! Good God!" The force of the ejaculation hoisted the old lady from her pillows. Her eyes still clear and shrewd strained sharply for Sabrina's. "Harken here, my girl! Love behind the curtain to a woman over forty is like beer without a head. Ought I not to know? And you—you fool—have caught him young. I caught mine old. You're lucky."

"Must we"—all colour had slowly faded from Sabrina's cheeks —"discuss this question now? Here is your dose."

"Pah! I've no patience!" Jess snatched the proffered glass and dashed it to the floor. "That for me physic! Pull the bell. I'll have a bottle if it knocks me dead—confound you! . . ."

Later in her own room Sabrina sat long at the window which now overlooked the street, the room in which old Pinkerton had died. In the early dusk of a cool March evening the sky was opalescent; a faint afterglow of sunset brushed the housetops, thinly, fading as she watched, and while impressions crowded to her consciousness with microscopic clarity, her mind, detached and resolute, faced at last the conflict between self and self.

This moment which for eight years of uncertainty she had deliberately shunned, thrusting aside the pietistic scruples distilled from the teachings of Miss Jeans, and perhaps some lingering strain of prudish adolescence—this moment long dormant, long delayed, now sharpened by the dread of separation, had arrived, must be attacked and fought to a decision. What had brought about this disenchantment? A careless word, her own heart's fears, the sands of the hourglass running out, or some remote dark signal warning? Seated at the window in that dusky stillness, her eyes followed abstractedly the passing panorama of the street, stray atoms from the condensed multitude of a city whose inexorable murmur pulsated with the throb of human passions, the never-ending process of existence, each unit a life-force, each force a cosmic atom of an individual whole. The grey pigeons strutting on the cobbles, the clear whistle of an errand boy, a rattling cart, a dowager's barouche, a little milliner with a bandbox on her arm, bright eyes glancing roguishly from under her poke bonnet; a horseman from the Row curbing his restive bay; a lady in a pea-green mantlet who bowed to him—his hat raised in salute; a footman in gold and scarlet at a door—the lady entered —the door was shut, the weaving pattern shifted. The sky paled and turned cold.

Sabrina closed the window but still stayed there on its cushioned seat staring through the glass at shadows.

She had only to be resolute, to take what was—what had been
—hers. . . . Had been and was no more. Remorselessly she accepted the inevitable; she had known that it must come, known
too that she must be the first to make the challenge. That much
for her pride. Pride! A false illusion. Had they not shared the
same security of comradeship, the same delights? The same—
and not the same—for she had grasped at youth and warmth, had
rekindled a dying fire at his flame, had made him hers, her own
creation. She knew that she had built an image in his likeness,
endowed it with the qualities he lacked; she knew him weak and
strengthened him. She knew that beneath his impish arrogance
lay a curious distrust of himself; she gave him faith, fulfilled his
spirit's craving, his deep need of her, superimposed her will on
his, even at the moment of surrender. Or perhaps she had never
utterly surrendered, never yet known the completeness of abandon, held back by relics of lost maidenhood, cloistered in the
fastness of her dreams. Was all her life a dream, an unreality,
fed from the past and nurtured on ephemeral desire? What had
she gained from these tense years of living? A loneliness of mind
and soul, her spirit's flagellation. Were these brief ecstasies, the
drift of fragmentary acts of sight and thought and passion, be-
littled in the narrow way of subterfuge? And yet that way was
of her own discretion. She could not lay to his account the
limited confinement of their loving. He would have taken her
before the world had he had his will of her. A thousand times
she asked herself—had she been too cautious in resisting? Was
the mere difference in age a justification for refusal? Fourteen
years—and she had told him ten. That much had she lied to
him, being all woman.

"There is ten years' difference in our ages, Stephen."

The argument—as so often he had argued—bore no weight.
"You are inconsistent"—so he had raged to her at the beginning.

"For if you consent to come to me, why not come to me as wife? The relationship is of your choice, not mine. I am yours—you know it—whichever way you take me. Dear—do you not feel it? Why do you doubt? Do you regret? I know I am not worthy."

Those were the moments when she weakened, when his endearing charm, his loving-kindness tortured her, while her whole essence craved towards him for the memories that he evoked. Perhaps those very memories held her apart and guarded, even though because of them she loved him.

The room darkened and she rose; went to her mirror, lit the candles on the table, searched her face closely. . . . Yes! But if that were all, her beauty still might hold him. She had ripened. The faint coinlike stampings round her eyes and mouth caressed and softened, gave dignity, did not at all detract. She was still desirable. . . . Or was she lying to herself, afraid of truth? If now he saw her for the first time, would he lay before her his young homage, his eager adoration? Mercilessly she forced herself to see the grey among the gleaming gold, the dimmed contours, the slow tracery of change, undeniable and bitter. She saw with quivering prescience the strain of future years, the struggle to retard that cruel slow finger, to set her pace to his. It must not be! Youth must have youth. Such was the law of life. Inevitable. Certain.

And from that mirrored face that watched her she turned her eyes away. It was as if something there had died.

They met that night. He had rooms in Duke Street. A confidential manservant with downcast look and closed impassive mask silently admitted her.

Once Stephen had told her that this very secrecy added

piquance to the situation. ". . . If you were mine before the world we might lose the spice of love."

Then, for he had seen the mortification in her eyes, he was at once repentant.

"Dearest, you know I honour and adore you. You are too sensitive, sweetheart. You give me so much—too much. I had no right to take you even at your will." Who could withstand him? He ravished her with his naïve abandon, his awareness, his complete response. His boy's face that seemed to grow no older, his boy's mouth that smiled like a faun's and could exhaust her lips and body at a touch.

He was at his gayest when she came to him that night; his room was full of flowers. Daffodils and flaming tulips, white hyacinths, a bowl of violets whose perfume drugged the air.

"All this for you," he whispered while he unfastened her wrappings. "Spring flowers and loveliness—for you. I was at the Coal Hole in the Strand last night, and stayed till morning: How your eyes look at me! Was that so wrong? I saw the sunrise above Covent Garden. I was not too drunk for that, and I had won a pony. The flower waggons were unloading—I must take you there one morning to see the carts come in. I bought a barrow-load and gave an armful to a trollop. She swore at me— for guineas. Ah! Now you shrink. You are disgusted. Do you think my pleasures take me whoring?" He shook her shoulders gently. "Look at me! What have I said? You are like a statue. Cold. Come back to me and smile."

She moved away and sat down in a chair by the fire. One candle only lit the room, burning in a Florentine lantern hung from the ceiling. Books lined the walls, and two prints by Morland, a miniature of her; no other woman's picture.

Her eyes strayed to the mantelpiece. There beside the glass-

encased gilt clock was something that attracted, something new,
a daguerreotype photograph, the first that she had ever seen although she had heard, as had all the world, of Monsieur Da-
guerre's great invention. She got up to look at it, to take it in
her hand.

"You see who it is?" asked Stephen, coming up behind her.

"Yes." The ghost of a laughing face gazed back at her, the
features indeterminedly etched, dark upon dark, filmed in dulled
silver lustre. What wizardry of science! To produce on metal
by exposure to the light the reproduction of the living form.

"When was this likeness made of Clare?" she asked him.

"Recently."

Sabrina replaced the daguerreotype where it had stood.

"Prior," Stephen said, "is having pictures taken of the whole
family."

"I had not heard of it."

He put an arm round her shoulders.

"Sit down again," he murmured. "You are so far away from
me tonight. We have not met for nearly a whole week. Have
you not wished to see me?"

"If you have wished it so."

"Ah! Now! Unjust of you to take that tone. You know I have
been busy. A round of entertaining. Our authors expect it of us.
Do not blame me for attending to my business." He knelt before
her on the hearthrug, looking up, his eyes bright and mischievous.
"It is my business to be pleasant to every man jack of 'em, so
long as their stuff sells. When it don't—well, that's another matter. Do you know I nearly cornered Dickens at a dinner? I sat
next to him and talked—or rather listened to him talk—of
Carlyle's petition to Parliament for granting copyright to authors, and was so entirely sympathetic that I left him with half a
promise to sign up an agreement with us when the book he is

doing now is published. He is calling it 'Barnaby Rudge.' What a name! Prior is hot on his track, too, I hear; but we are aiming at the stars, we'll neither of us get him. . . . And *now* what are you thinking? Not of me or anything I tell you, I'll be bound. You hate me!"

Leaning forward, he crushed his mouth to hers. Her lips were closed against his lips' demand. He released her suddenly and drew away, brows lowered, eyes darkening beneath them. "So! You feel no more for me than that! Am I dismissed?"

She held her palms against his cheeks and looked at him clearly, so clearly that his own look flinched.

"Stephen, I have been thinking. . . . Once, long ago, we both agreed that if we felt there was no more to give on either side we should be honest with each other." She paused. "It seems the time is come when we must face the truth—and ask ourselves—what is there left to give?" The sound of her voice was disconcerting. The stilted phrases coming from her lips were not her own. She had not known that it would be so glib, like a learned lesson. She felt weak and empty and unpained, as though she had been drugged.

He was staring at her in shocked surprise, his mouth a little open, his jaw a little dropped.

"You are not serious?" He spoke sharply on an indrawn breath. "What do you mean? Is this some peevish trick? You are annoyed at what has seemed my negligence. I have not seen you for a week—but you used not to be exacting. Someone has gossiped. Lied about me. Why do you stoop to petty, small revenge?"

"My dear." She laid her hand upon his head, stroking back the crisp dark waves of hair above his forehead. She knew that she had hurt his pride—but had she hurt his love? "If in these years of our association I have given you something that is real, something that you will remember and look back upon as a *good* thing, then it will mean I shall not yet have harmed you."

"Harmed!" He caught roughly at her wrist. "What words you use! *Yet* have harmed me. What whim has taken you all of a sudden? Are you playing with me? Acting? Are you mad?"

Her smile trembled crookedly. "Too sane, dear love. But we have been both—a little mad. No, hear me out, then you may talk." She watched his widening eyes, the twitching of a muscle in his jaw, and hardened her heart against that look of his.

"Stephen. When you came to me so young—so heart-breakingly young—I struggled long against my instinct—but not long enough to overcome it. I felt that you could give back to me all that I had lost. All my lost youth, all my lost love. I wanted to relive my past in you. Was that wrong? I have sometimes felt it so, for you were twenty-one. A child. . . . And I was—thirty-five."

He jerked his head up sharply. "You were not! You were thirty. You said that you were thirty. Why all this now? What are you trying to tell me?"

"The truth."

She saw the quick colour mounting to his eyes, a darkened frown between them.

"What of it? All women lie about their age. I knew you were ten years older than myself. Say you were twice that. Must we," he cried impatiently, "go over this old ground again? Believe me it grows stale. You know you have had all of me. Was that not enough?"

"More than enough. No woman could have wished for a more dear lover. I needed just such love. A boy's love. No man's love would ever at that time have stirred me. Does that seem strange and inexplicable to you? There is so much in myself I cannot understand. Why did I go back? Why did I not go forward?"

The words died on a whisper. She spoke not to him but to herself, and her face was drawn and ashen. He stared at her relentlessly.

"So! I see! I have served your dead John Burnaby. Each time that you possessed me, it was not I you took—but him. You were the stronger always. I knew that. I was your ape. Your fool. Don't! Don't touch me!" He pushed her hand aside and started up. "By God! But it's incredible that you should do this thing to me. You make your age your whole excuse, because you never loved me—have never given to me one inch of your body. Your dead husband has overlain us both. He has had each moment that was mine!" His voice cracked hysterically. "It's hideous! Obscene. . . . I was mad for you—you made me mad for you. So that you—and he—" He broke down, leaning his arms upon the mantelpiece, his head bowed to them. "You have not had sufficient faith in me or in my love." The muffled words wrenched at her heart and tortured her. "If we had married—"

"It would still"—she rose and went to him—"have come to this."

All the woman in her was dissolved in love and pity. He was suffering because of her, and she dared not comfort him. But through all her agony she was conscious of a feeling of triumph. He still needed her, cried out for her, wanted her—for his pride's sake. But she had saved her own.

She laid her lips an instant to the dark hair that crisped in the nape of his neck, felt his quivering response and drew away.

"I am leaving London for Bath with Jess next week," she told him quietly. "I shall be gone some months." Her glance fell on the daguerreotype of Clare upon the mantelpiece. "A whole life can be changed in a few months," she whispered, "—in a few moments."

He did not lift his head, made no reply. Perhaps he had not

heard her. For an instant then, she wavered, but he did not move. She slipped out silently. One gesture from him would have weakened her. He could have taken her, held her, kept her there for ever had he wished it. But without another word he let her go.

Chapter Four

I

On an afternoon in April, 1848, a hackney cab drove up to the house in Soho Square, and deposited a young gentleman at its door. He wore a suit of dark grey broadcloth, and on his left arm a mourning band of crape. He had with him no luggage, and apparently no money, for after some leisurely searching of his pockets which produced no more than a jingling of keys, he bade the cabman "Wait a jiffy," ran up the steps and beat a peremptory tattoo on the door, which was immediately opened by a grave-faced personage in black. The features of young Anthony Wrotham assumed an expression equally grave.

"Good morning, Parkes. I find I am out of cash. Pay the cabman for me, will you? And see that he don't rook you. The fare should be half-a-crown." And having issued these instructions in the manner of one accustomed, in that house at all events, to having his word obeyed, he proceeded on his way upstairs.

His mother and sister, both dressed in deepest mourning, rose as he entered the room.

"My darling boy!"

"Poor little mother!" Anthony bent his head to receive her kiss, warm and clinging, in the middle of his cheek. "There! There!" He patted her shoulder. "Don't upset yourself. Where's the Governor?"

"Your papa has gone to see the Reverend Mr. Armitage about the—the service," faltered Mary, gazing up at her tall son with

227

tear-dimmed, adoring eyes. "You have been very quick coming up. We didn't expect you till this evening."

"I came by train."

Mary shook her head. "I don't like those trains. Did you have a comfortable journey, my lovey?"

"Goodness me, Mamma!" cried Clare. "Anyone would think he'd come from the North Pole, instead of from Oxford. I hope you've brought a black suit with you, Anthony. You can't go to the funeral like that."

"I've brought no luggage at all," replied her brother crossly. "How do you suppose I had time to pack anything when I received that telegraph message? I suppose it was Stephen sent it. I can tell you it created a tremendous stir in college. The first telegraph wire ever received in Balliol—anyway in my time. I was nearly mobbed when I drove off."

"As it happens," Clare told him coolly, "it was not Stephen, but I who sent that telegraph. So now! And if you haven't a decent black suit, you'd better go out and buy one—hadn't he, Mamma?"

"I refuse to wear reach-me-downs," retorted Anthony. "I shall go as I am, or borrow one of Stephen's. We're about the same height. When is the funeral?"

"On Friday. Mamma! Do tell him—he *must* have a black suit."

"Oh, my darlings!" Mary groped blindly for a chair, and sank down in it, her handkerchief to her eyes. "Must we have this wrangling? I am not in a fit state—"

"There now!" shrilled Clare, glaring at her brother. "How can you be so tactless? Worrying your mother like that the moment you set foot in the house. Where are your smelling-salts, dearest? Anthony, bring Mamma's salts. They're on the davenport."

"Have you dined, Tony, love?" His mother asked him faintly,

submitting with closed eyes to her daughter's hurried minis-
trations.

"Of course I haven't dined," Anthony returned, aggrieved. "Do
you suppose they give you dinner in a train? I'm hungry as a
hunter."

"My poor boy!" His mother started up and was promptly suppressed by Clare.

"Pray sit down, Mamma. Anthony! Go away. You fidget her.
Stephen's downstairs, somewhere. Go and talk to him. And for
goodness' sake see about your mourning."

With a muttered commentary on the fussiness of women, Anthony departed to his father's study. There in an armchair, his
feet stretched to the fender, his chin sunk on his chest, his
brother-in-law lay dozing. A bottle of port and a half-filled glass
stood on a table at his elbow. Anthony drank the contents of the
glass, refilled it, and drank that. Thus fortified, he addressed the
supine figure in the chair.

"Wake up, old cock!"

Stephen opened an eye.

"Hello, young feller. When did you arrive?"

"A few minutes ago. Such a to-do upstairs—your precious wife
ruling the roost as usual—hustles me out of the room, gives my
mother the fantods and blames it on to me, and finally decides
that I'm to go to my grandfather's funeral in your best black
suit."

"She does, does she?" grunted Stephen. "I doubt if any suit of
mine, best black or otherwise, would fit you. You're grown out
of all knowledge. How tall are you now? Six foot?"

"And three-quarters," said Anthony proudly, "with a chest
measurement that can beat yours by an inch. Not bad for my age.
Nineteen last November."

"Last November, was it? Well! Well!" Stephen poured himself another glass of port and raised it to the light, with an appreciative eye for its warm colour. "Did you receive a tip from me —or not? It's rather late in the day to ask."

"Never too late to mend," grinned Anthony. "But Clare sent me a pair of doeskin gloves and a silver-mounted riding crop with your love. I have two already."

"I see." Stephen's lips twitched as his hand went to his pocket. He produced a leather purse and counted out three sovereigns. These he tendered with a twinkle.

"You're unlucky. This is all the gold that I have by me for today. You can spend it on cigars."

"Thank ye! I'll bear in mind, sir, your instructions. There's a capital brand to be obtained at Hanson's. Much obliged to you, Stephen. But tell me"—Anthony lowered his voice. "I daren't ask upstairs in the midst of all that racket. What did the poor old fellow die of? I always thought he'd live to be ninety—never showed a sign of age. And then to go off suddenly like that. Was it heart failure?"

Stephen shook his head thoughtfully before replying: "Your grandfather, my boy, died in harness—so to speak. He caught a chill standing out on Kennington Common to watch that madman Feargus O'Connor mustering his forces for the final rally. The whole thing was of course the most absurd fiasco—"

"I wish I'd been down last week," Anthony interrupted. "I'd have joined the special constables. By George I would! Were there many casualties?"

"Nothing to speak of. Don't you read your *Times* at Oxford? When the hour came for the procession to start only about twenty-odd people were present, most of whom were onlookers and idlers. Whether your father and poor old Roger intended walking with the procession to Westminster, I cannot say, because

the procession as originally intended never took place. The whole
thing collapsed like a pricked bubble. Both sides were made to
look ridiculous—the Chartists for their grotesque mishandling of
the situation, and the defence for its unnecessarily warlike display. You never saw anything like it! London armed to the teeth
—bristling with artillery, cannon mounted on the Tower, sand-
bags guarding the Bank of England, and the Duke himself in
command of the troops."

"Wish I'd been there," repeated Anthony. "It must have been
a grand sight."

Stephen poured himself another glass of port and sipped it
meditatively. "H'm. And all for nothing. A flash in the pan. The
Chartists are done for. This last explosion is their death-knell.
. . . Yes, your father and the old man returned in a sad plight:
your grandfather shivering and cold as charity. Your mother put
him to bed in your room here—she would not let him go back
to his own house—and next morning he was in a high fever.
They had two doctors to him, but there it is. Snuffed out," murmured Stephen, "like a candle in the dark. And if the poor old
fellow had not been so overzealous in a misguided cause he might
have been alive today."

Anthony nodded gloomily.

"Misguided is right. Between ourselves, Stephen, I think my
father has a screw loose in the upper story to go siding with that
truck. I don't say so much against my grandfather's views. He
belongs—or did belong—to the people and as such he was justi-
fied in upholding them—bred in the bone as you might say; but
my father, sir," stated Anthony with solemn emphasis, "my father
is a traitor to his class, and that in my opinion is unforgivable."
He paused, waiting for some comment from Stephen; but since
none was forthcoming, he proceeded warmly: "And don't you
make any mistake but that *I* suffer for it. I can tell you it don't

do me much good to be associated with firebrands even if they don't burn. Why, only last week a feller came up to me in the grounds of my college—a feller of the name of Lamb in my year—relative of Melbourne's as it happens. 'Are you signing your name to the petition?' he asked me, very sneery. 'What's that to you?' I said. 'Nothing,' he said, 'except that in the interests of Alma Mater we don't altogether welcome piebald Radical-Tories here, y'know.' 'Oh, you don't, don't you?' I said. 'And what do you think you are, anyway? The Master of Balliol or Lord God Almighty?' He told me what he thought he was and what he thought I was—and what he thought my father was. 'Piebald Radical-Tory,' by gum!" Anthony's hands clenched in his pockets at the memory of that impertinence. "Gad—sir, but he paid for it! I laid him one in the jaw that put him down properly. He didn't get up in a hurry. And *that*," concluded Anthony, bitterly, "is what I have to contend with as the son of a crank father. The name of Wrotham has been in none too sweet an odour for the last two generations. Glyn Wrotham was an outlaw and my revered sire is—"

He stopped abruptly as the door opened and Prior came in. He looked tired and ill. Greeting Anthony with a curt "So you've arrived," he sat down in the armchair vacated on his entrance by Stephen, and glanced interrogatively first at the empty bottle of port, and then up at his son.

"I fear I am the culprit," Stephen said, his smile answering the glance. "I took the liberty of ordering—"

Prior waved this aside. "But of course, my dear fellow. An excellent good vintage, too. It was merely that the sight of it reminded me I have not yet paid this young gentleman's wine merchant's account at Oxford. About as heavy in three months as mine is in three years."

"Perhaps, sir," Anthony ventured mutinously, "if you conceded me an adequate allowance in accordance with my increased expenses, I might be permitted to pay the account myself and so relieve you of the responsibility."

"Such filial consideration," drawled Prior, "overwhelms me." He leaned back in his chair, a wizened midget of a man, his shoulders drooping wearily, his one eye closed so that he seemed to sleep.

"Here! You had better come along with me," Stephen addressed the scowling Anthony. "And if you care to call at my house, you can ask my fellow if he can fit you up with trappings for the funeral. He will find something for you, I've no doubt."

"Hearses, plumes, and mourning black," murmured Prior, "revolting travesty of death." He opened his eye and fixed it on his son, who stood uncomfortably straddling the hearthrug, his hands in his pockets, his dark brows lowered in a frown. "When my turn comes, see that I go unadorned. No mutes. No mourners. And no flowers—by request."

"I shall endeavour to carry out your instructions, sir," replied Anthony, with haughty insolence.

"Come along then, if you're coming," Stephen put in hastily, aware that a storm was brewing between these two who, for some inexplicable reason which Stephen was not psychologist enough to know, could antagonise each other with a word, a look.

Prior stayed where they had left him, sunk in his chair. The tragic events of the last few days, culminating in the death of him at whose side he had worked for nearly thirty years, seemed now to oversweep him with renewed force.

Roger Kell was gone, and it was as if something of his own life had gone with him. He was stricken not so much with the sense of loss, as of futility. The fervour that had propelled him in his youth towards some visionary objective, had been devoured in its own flame. The drift of vague ambitions had passed in unfulfilment. And in this utter failure of the Chartists' last, chaotic effort to reorganise the world, he seemed to see a symbol of the human spirit, striving in purposeless flight to attain some new horizon, passing swiftly from point to point in the blind endeavour to see and touch, to draw from each impression something permanent and solid; only to find that the image vanishes, the colours darken, the whole scope of life is narrowed to the limits of external influence, and all perception dimmed.

Yet he had prospered. Failure lay not in material collapse, but in the gradual fading of ideals and the hardening of the dream substance that had moulded them. He remembered how triumphantly he had set forth on his magical first venture, which was "to give to the world the words of those who have the gift but not the means to pen them." Ah! But it was not so easy to search among a voiceless multitude. He had succumbed to the louder trumpet-call, had followed the nearer herd, had been drawn into the whirlpool of competition and the pitiless struggle for survival—but would he, in the end, survive?

He stirred uneasily in his chair, his thoughts turned towards his son. There again—frustration! Long accumulation of small differences had resulted in a submerged hostility sprung from the conflict of two opposing wills. The boy was arrogant and stubborn. From the first he had developed an individuality that would brook no interference or repression. So with his daughter Clare, who, imperious, high-spirited, self-willed, tempered her concession to parental discipline with a good-humoured tolerance that disregarded it. Thus, and in this manner, had she taken Stephen Marriott for husband.

Prior rose and went to the window. The blind had been drawn down in deference to the unburied remains of Roger Kell. He pulled it up with an impatient jerk. The April sky had clouded and a thin drizzle of rain was falling. He stared sombrely at the plane trees in the Square, misted over with a budding of faint green. . . . That marriage! Even now he wondered why he had not more emphatically withheld his consent, knowing what he knew, and what Mary to this day had never known.

He remembered a letter from Sabrina urging him to an unbiassed decision. "For all things in this world," she had ambiguously ended, "work together—it is said—for good." And no further explanation had she offered, nor never since alluded to the past.

Clare's wedding, which took place in December, '41, had been a fashionable affair, and well attended by representatives not only of the literary world but of society. The newspapers were full of it. The young couple spent their honeymoon at Nice. The following year Marriott senior died, and Clare became mistress of Cheam Royal and a house in Berkeley Square. Within six years she presented her husband with two daughters and a son. All was very well, and Stephen the most exemplary of husbands. There was no rift in any lute.

But Sabrina no longer lived at Wroth. She had remained with Jess. The old lady had wept so bitterly and become so utterly hysterical when, after their visit to Bath, Sabrina had suggested returning to the country that she had not the heart to leave her. So it had gone on, and Sabrina stayed beside her to the end.

First Jeans, then Jess. . . . Her vitality, so Prior mused, had been sapped, of latter years, by these moribund old women who drew the last breath of their bodies in her arms. Her life was spent in giving.

Jess died at eighty-five of syncope, brought on in a tantrum with her maid.

"I'm done for this time," she told Sabrina while two doctors worked on her either side the bed. "They can manhandle me till they're black in the face, but they won't keep the Devil from his due." She chuckled, closed her eyes, and fell into a coma from which she never woke.

She bequeathed to Sabrina her house in Curzon Street, an income worthy to support it, her jewels, and all her personal effects. To Prior the surplus from his grandfather's much decreased estate, and the position of Trustee. Her will, written in her own hand, and drawn up, one surmises, without legal supervision or advice, is an amazing document. She left to Mary: "Any such or one of my Articles of Household Furniture as she may wish to select as a Memento with exception to any such or one of my Journals which bespeaks a Record of my life for these last Sixty years and any such or one of my personal possessions bequeathed to Sabrina Harriet Burnaby (née Wrotham) which she may wish to select with Permission of said Sabrina Harriet Burnaby, To my maid Smollet in Recognition of her Services and Forbearance my Canaries together with an Annuity of Fifty Pounds Sterling."

There follow bequests to various charities and to certain protégés of Lady Pinkerton who during her lifetime had considerably benefited from her erratic generosity.

To Anthony Wrotham—"The gold Repeater appertaining to his late Lamented and Deceased Great Grandfather, the seventh and last Earl of Pinkerton together with the sum of One Thousand Pounds Sterling to be held in keeping of the Trustees hereto under-mentioned in this my last Will & Testament until he shall attain his Majority."

Clare's name for reasons best known to her ladyship and to Clare's greatest indignation is not included as a beneficiary under the will, which ends with solemn instructions as to the laying of the tombstone—"which shall be of Rose-veined Marble with plain Slab beneath no flowers nor grass to grow neglected there and my Body not to be laid in the Family Vault at Cheam but in the Churchyard of St. Mary Ovary in the Borough in which Neighbourhood I passed the first Ten Years of my Life and at which Church I was subsequently Baptised. On this same Stone omitting any Reference to the Age of the Deceased shall be writ these words:

SACRED
TO
THE MEMORY
OF
JESS
COUNTESS OF PINKERTON
Live and Let Live
Die and Let Die
Not to Awake
Only to Lie
in
Peace."

It may be that Jess derived a certain macabre enjoyment in the writing of her own epitaph, which can be seen to this day on that same 'Rose-veined Marble' by any who care to visit the little known churchyard of St. Mary Ovary in the Borough.

As a consequence of the death of Lady Pinkerton, which left Sabrina in possession of the Curzon Street house, the question of selling Wroth arose. It was too far from town for Prior to take up residence there, and Mary was as unwilling after twenty years' inhabitance to leave the house in Soho Square as once she had been to leave her father's.

Clare settled the matter for them. Her arguments admittedly were sound—too sound, Prior commented, a dry smile twisting on his lips at the recollection of the scene in which Clare in her new rôle of matron had spoken her mind on her return from her honeymoon seven years before.

"It is quixotic and ridiculous enough, Papa, that you should have given up your home for all these years, but it would be still more ridiculous for you to sell it. Our grandfather bought it for your mother, and you are the rightful heir even though for the last thirty years Aunt Sabrina has usurped your place. In a hundred years hence it will have become the ancestral seat of the Wrothams. Cheam Royal will come back to us—through me—and you have a right to keep Wroth House for Anthony. It would be madness to sell. Don't you agree, Stephen?"

Stephen had of course agreed. He was sufficiently in love, Prior reflected grimly, to agree to any suggestion offered by his dominant young wife. The minx had him completely under her thumb. She ruled him as she had ruled her parents with a tenacity of purpose that would permit of no denial. She knew exactly what she wanted and would get it. Her small delicious body sheltered an inexorable will. To Stephen such petticoat government was delightful.

The really excellent way in which she managed not only him but his affairs, his servants, his children, and the family at Soho Square, to say nothing of her position as mistress of two fine houses, filled him with admiration, while her little conscious airs and graces never failed to amuse. If his love for her was not on the highest emotional plane, it was none the less vital enough to content and hold him. The marriage was eminently successful, thanks to Clare, whose husband, Prior must admit, was no easy customer to tackle. Yet Clare had tackled him with understanding. . . . Sabrina had been wise. She knew.

A carriage which he recognised was stopping at the door. Prior's face lightened. He had hoped that she would come. None but she—not even Mary—could guess to what extent this sudden loss of Roger Kell must leave him lonely.

He turned from the window and went quickly to meet his sister.

The political unrest that had attacked the whole of Europe in the year 1848, culminating in the revolution in France and the

flight of Louis Philippe to England, threw the entire Continent
in confusion. In city after city barricades were rising; nation was
arming against nation and class was arming against class. European princes dared not call their thrones their own, and the
despotic tyranny of governments was tottering.

Divided from the conflict by a few miles of sea water, the British watched with interest but not very much concern. We would
never be embroiled. Our troubles lay behind us. The attempt
of the Chartists to bring about a revolution here was memorable, not only as a failure, but a joke. Its leader O'Connor
had gone mad as a result of it and was shut up as a lunatic
for life.

Our affairs were well looked after. The influence of the
Consort was being felt as much throughout the country as
the Court. M.'s light had been extinguished. He had become
'That poor Lord Melbourne' to the Queen, who wrote him kindly
letters on his birthday. Little Lord John Russell was made leader
of the Whigs, and poor 'M.' was never even asked to join the Cabinet. He died of disappointment, and Victoria forgot him in adoring
her good Albert. She had produced a Prince of Wales, was
already the mother of five children. She was simple, she was
homely, she was kind. No fuss, no ostentation. The Royal household was a magnified replica of a million other homes furnished
in keeping with the German taste for woolwork, wax flowers
under glass, and horsehair sofas. Mahogany was coming in and
walnut going out, and Chippendale was hidden in the attics. A
prim solidity was shown, not only in the furniture, but in the
heart of the whole nation. The lingering mildew of the Regency
had vanished. The country shone with conscious virtue as polished as its sideboards. The great Victorian era was climbing to
its apex, and under the auspices of Albert, in 1851, its triumphs
were exploited to the world.

II

When, in due course, Anthony came down from Oxford and entered the firm of Kell & Wrotham, it was evident that he meant to reorganise the whole concern. Their methods, he maintained, were a hundred years too late. "They stink," he told his father, "of the Churchyard." All very well to start as booksellers behind a counter, but you could not possibly conduct a firm of these dimensions on the same principle. The whole outlook of the business wanted widening. The firm, as far as Anthony could see in the short time he had been associated with it, had a reputation for too exclusive publishing. It had spent time and money on unnecessary output such as quality of paper, binding, and the finest print. And to what purpose? The public did not give a fig for the quality of print or superexcellence of binding so long as the reading matter was acceptable. And that again, in Anthony's opinion, needed a thorough overhauling. Their fiction list was cluttered up with names you'd never heard of, and books that cost more to produce than the authors ever earned. The public did not want to wander in transcendental fields. Give 'em a *story*. Give 'em something that was going to keep them up at nights reading in their beds, something that was going to advertise itself by word of mouth. Cut out one-half your fiction list and fill it up with Names. Even if you have to pay through the nose for them. Why, you'd get it back on the first edition. Don't print five hundred, but five thousand as a send-off, and print them cheap. Exclusive publishing be damned! It was *sales* they were after, sales to attract the bigger fish. What were Kell & Wrotham thinking of to let another firm get hold of Currer Bell? And now this woman Gaskell who had actually sent 'Mary Barton' *here*—to be refused! Not that Anthony believed in women writers, but there seemed to be a vogue for them at present. Not one of 'em would live—but what of that? Make hay while the sun shone. It was preposterous to see the way that this concern had been mishandled. Would his father give him—Anthony—*carte-blanche* to redirect?

"For how you ever made it pay," young Anthony exploded, "fairly beats me. You seldom find our books in any bookshop."

"And in the oyster seldom any pearl—among those one eats at table," answered Prior.

Anthony crimsoned with exasperation. And hunched in his chair, his wizened face lined as a medlar's under its shock of whitening hair, one eyebrow cocked above his one sound eye, his father watched him. Smiling a little, Prior drew from his breastpocket a silver snuffbox, and delicately took a pinch of snuff.

"You prefer the full aroma of tobacco, do you not?" enquired Prior gently. "I see that you have recently invested in a hookah. Try this." He offered him the box. "The perfumes of all Araby—"

"Damnation, sir!" blazed Anthony. "Do you refuse ever to talk sense?"

He flung out of the room and banged the door.

It was, however, due to his endeavours that the firm of Kell & Wrotham were represented in full force at the opening of the Great Exhibition in 1851.

He had moved heaven and earth to get a stall erected, for Industry, not Art, was the order of that day. The staff was sworn to secrecy. No blabbing among travellers in public houses. We were to be the only publishers in London showing books at the Crystal Palace, in Hyde Park, that first of May.

The vigorous youngster had them all behind him. Even the elder hands were much impressed. Young blood—y' see? Modernity. Progression. The Gov'nor was getting old. Played out. And to most minds had always been too highfalutin. Faddy.

This lad was a winner. . . . And they backed him to a man. For weeks young Anthony was full of it. He talked of nothing else, and his father wisely let him have his head. The most important feature was to be a miniature printing press—the whole process of production must be shown. As illustration he would use the original manuscript of *The Golden Calf*—that anonymous best seller which had launched the firm upon its maiden voyage. Perhaps its veteran author might be induced to autograph copies of later editions to be exhibited for sale. Then there must be on view the first copy of *The Magpie*,* which contained the earliest printed works from the respective pens of the two great rival lions of the day. He ransacked for first editions the library of Roger Kell which had been bequeathed to Prior, found the rare Sir Thomas Browne, a Shakespeare Quarto also acquired by his grandfather—in 1826—and an illuminated Chaucer, all of which represented capital to Anthony. The firm's reserves. Gilt-edged Security—which was to be his creed. Exhibits such as these would bring advertisement. There was no end to the possibilities entailed by such a venture. The publishing trade would stand agape and green with envy. And Anthony was to be in charge of the whole thing. . . .

Mary, writing to Sabrina, who was staying at the time in Bath, taking the waters—she was inclined to be rheumatic—gives an account of the event which was to bring all nations together in friendly competition, revealing to the world for the first time the mechanical forces that controlled it.

"How I regret, my dear Sabrina, that you were not with us," writes my grandmother on May 2, 1851. "For it was a spectacle such as one may see but once in a life-time. No words of mine can describe the magnificence of that immense structure built

---

* This magazine, which expired in 1872, was resurrected some fifty years later as the *Quarterly Review of Art & Literature*, first issued by Kell & Wrotham, in April 1920.—P. J. W.

entirely of *glass* with the trees of the Park actually enclosed *inside* it! Fountains and statues abounded in this Fairy Palace and aisles of stalls filled with Merchandise and Spices from all corners of the Earth. The whole effect was like an Arabian Nights' Dream.

"We had a splendid view of the opening ceremony and saw the Queen quite plainly. She was wearing a dress of pink watered silk Brocade, and for all her small stature looked very elegant and regal with her diamond ornaments and the Order of the Garter.

"The Prince Consort in full dress Uniform led by the hand the little Prince of Wales, a fine upstanding boy wearing a Scottish Tartan. We could not hear very distinctly the Prince's opening speech for we were too far away and also he has a *very* pronounced German accent. I was quite bewildered by the glittering display of jewels and Orders worn by the Ladies & Gentlemen of the Court, and by many representatives of Foreign Countries, some in their native costumes. It really was a sight worth seeing, and one which I shall not readily forget. To think that in comparatively few years (since in our time we can remember a very different life to that which is lived to-day), such wonderful discoveries have been made and such great achievements accomplished. There seems to be no end to the astonishing results of modern invention. Steam, machinery, this new gas-lighting—the rate of progress is quite alarming when one remembers the days before such innovations had been thought of. We live in a new age and the younger generation does not let us easily forget it! They know so much more than their parents ever did—God bless them!

"Prior, I am sorry to say, did not accompany us. He has not been feeling at all himself lately, and I have begged him to consult a Doctor, but you know how little attention he pays to his health. Yesterday he was taken with a slight fainting fit—nothing to be alarmed about, my dear, or you may be sure I should not have left him. I did not think, however, that he would be equal to the excitement of such a day as yesterday, and persuaded him, much against his will, to stay at home.

"Our party consisted of Clare and Stephen, Stephen's younger sister, Theresa Macfarlane, and her husband, and a young lady who is a cousin of Captain Macfarlane's—a Miss Helen Paxton— no relation of the Horticulturist who is responsible for the rear- ing of the Victoria Regia Lily which is so *gigantic* that one can only suppose it to be the Eighth Wonder of the World!

"After the opening Ceremony we were free to wander about and examine the exhibits. Stephen bought an elegant little ame- thyst brooch for Clare from Hunt & Roskell's of Bond Street, whose stall exhibited the most beautiful display of jewels imagi- nable. And for me, from Elkington's, a pretty silver pin-tray. I bought some exquisite fine Bed-linen, pillow-cases, and sheets to match stitched in drawn-thread. I bought also for you, my dear, a Paisley shawl which I ordered to be despatched to Bath. An- thony received from an Indian Potentate an offer of *Ten Thou- sand Pounds* for the Chaucer and was very put out that Prior had forbidden him to accept or even consider the sale of any of my dear Father's cherished collection. It hurts me more than words can say to see the Discord that exists between my two loved ones, and I am so grieved at the manner in which Anthony treats his father with the scantiest Respect. Between ourselves, my dear Sabrina, I fancy Prior's collapse yesterday was due to the fact that he lost his temper with Anthony over some question or other of a prospective Agreement between us and a Mr. Anthony Trollope. However I am not very clear about it and did not care to ques- tion Prior on the matter while he was so poorly. I daresay I shall hear more in good time.

"When all was over we repaired to Clare's house for a cold Collation. I noticed that Anthony appeared to be very taken with this Miss Paxton who is a charming young lady, very modest and unassuming, no great Beauty, but has pretty fair hair and a good Complexion. She is the only daughter of Colonel Robert Paxton, of Gadsby Hall in Yorkshire, and is a Macfarlane on her mother's side. I understand that Clare has invited her to stay at Cheam for Whitsuntide, and as we shall be at Wroth and Anthony so attentive I should not be surprised if something were to come of it. . . ."

And what more suitable? A young lady of good family, well dowered and charming—"no great Beauty, but has pretty fair hair and a good Complexion."

The portrait painted in the first year of her marriage, which hangs here in my study, shows a large-eyed, childish face with drooping curls on either side of it, and a milk-white neck and shoulders. The smiling lips are just a little wistful, the eyes a thought too grave.

It may have been her very frailty that lost Anthony his heart; those great grey long-lashed eyes of hers, her slight hesitancy of speech that was almost but not quite a stammer; and the way, perhaps, she looked upon him as a creature from another world, as indeed to her he was, flattered and fed his self-esteem. From the moment that he saw her, he knew that she was his, to make, to mould, to mar to his own pattern.

An only child of elderly devoted parents who had married late in life, she passed her first seventeen years in the depths of the North country and seclusion. Her first introduction to London Society must have been, to the shy young thing, a torture. And the visit to Cheam no less, in spite of the fact that the magnificent, handsome, dashing Mr. Wrotham lived within calling distance.

I have a full record of that visit. She wrote a letter every day to her parents beginning, "Dearest Darlings," and ending, "Always your adoring & devoted Min." Why 'Min,' we never knew, and none could ever tell us. Pet names were not in use at Wroth in my day.

"I have just arrived," she writes on June 3, 1851, "after an *insufferable* journey by the *Train* with Uncle Mac & Aunt Theresa. We had a specially reserved compartment, but oh! my Darlings, such *horrible* discomfort & such a smell & noise which has given me the Headache very badly so that I can hardly see out of my eyes to write & am quite dizzy with *Sal Volattely.*

"I have a pretty room overlooking the very beautiful gardens. Cheam Royal is a much larger place than ours but not nearly so homely & the country round is more enclosed & wooded & I miss our wild open moors. I am *desperately nervous* of being here alone, although M[rs] Marriott is very kind.

"Uncle Mac & Aunt Theresa are going back to London on Thursday & I am to stay here for another week. M[rs] Marriott's maid has just brought me a can of hot water & has asked which dress I will wear to-night. If only I had my dear Annie with me! This maid is French & I am sure she thinks—& rightly so!—that I am nothing but a *Country Mouse.*

"M[rs] Marriott is very elegant & pretty, small, dark and vivacious. I am *tongue-tied* in her presence! She wears the most beautiful dresses. I told her maid that I would wear my poplin, & now I am wondering if it is sufficiently *dressy,* but I have only the choice between that, my ball-dress, which is much *too* dressy, and my pink, which I am saving for a more formal occasion. M[rs] M. expressly said that the dinner to-night was to be *in*formal. . . ."

One presumes, however, that both the poplin and its wearer met with Anthony's approval, or so the remainder of this letter, written later in her bedroom before retiring, leads us to believe.

They walked together on the terrace, "while the Company played whist. As you know I cannot play, & Mr Wrotham did not care to. He complimented me upon my dress. Fancy! That dowdy poplin! I wore the chaplet of gardenias that you gave me, dear Mamma. Mr Wrotham thought they were *real* flowers. He told me a g^t many interesting things about books & authors. Only fancy! Currer Bell is a lady! She lives not far from us & I never knew! Mr Wrotham asked if he might present me with a copy of 'Jane Eyre' but I told him that I was not allowed to read it. Do you think I might be allowed to now, Mamma? He— Mr Wrotham—has met a g^t number of celebrated writers. His conversation is v^y interesting. . . ."

I have no doubt it was. So lordly and superb a creature had never looked at her before, much less spent an entire evening at her side. She was both terrified and dazzled. He had the way of his paternal grandfather with women; those dark blue Wrotham eyes, Glyn Wrotham's smile. She was as powerless against his wooing as a harebell in a storm.

He stayed at Cheam a week and rode over every day to see her with offerings of fruit, of flowers, books. His name appears on every page and in almost every line of all her letters.

"I am reading the latest poetry of Mr Browning," she tells her parents. "Mr Wrotham has given me a copy, bound in Blue Calf. Do you think it was unbecoming in me to have accepted it? It was *v^y ķind* of him, I'm sure. . . ."

And: "To-day we went to church. I sat next to Mr Wrotham. . . ."

Sharing, possibly, a hymn-book, and trembling from head to foot to find herself so close to him, his arm against her shoulder where he stood—so tall above her—those spun-glass ringlets hiding her flushed cheeks, and her heart breathing its tender secret in her prayers.

We have it on the best authority that Anthony declared himself that very Sunday evening.

To her "Dear—her dearest Darlings," my little mother writes a blotted letter.

"These are tears of joy," she tells them in a postscript, "so please excuse so many smudges. I am y^r *Happy* Min." "I c^{ld} not," she says, "have believed such Happiness existed. Please do not think it wrong in me or my dear Anthony not to have spoken to you first of this *loveliness* between us. I dared not hope that he w^{ld} pay me this g^t *honour* of asking me to be his *wife*. I pray with all my heart that you will approve of & give y^r consent to our *Engagement* & crown this *happiest of all days in my life* with y^r dear *Blessings* & y^r love. . . ."

My parents were married at St. Margaret's, Westminster, on April 15, 1852. And at the house in Great Cumberland Place—presented to them as a wedding gift by my maternal grandfather, Colonel Paxton of the Twenty-first Hussars—my two brothers, who died in infancy, my sister Charlotte, and myself were born.

Chapter Five

I

> Theirs not to reason why
> Theirs but to do and die. . . .

IT HAS become a legend, immortalised in doggerel, the most hideous blunder in the whole history of war. Of those six hundred and seventy-two who went forth unquestioning upon their fatal ride, only one hundred and ninety-eight returned. And yet a small enough toll to us who sixty years later were to see the massacre of millions.

In that famous charge at Balaclava my grandfather Colonel Paxton met his death. The news of it nearly killed my mother, about to be confined with her second child, a boy who survived just long enough to be baptised and who lies buried here in Cheam Churchyard beside his brother Robert Anthony, aged one year and eight months.

The gross mismanagement of affairs in the Crimea had kindled a feeling of distress and indignation throughout the country.

Reform, which had brought about a reorganisation of commerce, Parliament, municipalities and the Church, had not yet touched the British army. He who had pitted his iron strength against Napoleon had died in '52 and left behind him no successor but tradition. That same tradition that has kept alive the soul of a great nation never yet known to yield, and which kept alive the spirit of the British soldier fighting through the horrors of a

Crimean winter under conditions that threatened to exterminate —according to *The Times*—"the noblest army England ever sent from these shores."

Every day came fresh tidings of privation, sickness, death; of unspeakable neglect and carelessness, of the appalling sufferings of our wounded, dying like vermin for lack of proper surgical attention; of tents standing in pools of water for want of implements to dig trenches; of medical stores decaying at Varna when they should have been sent to Scutari; of the farcical delivery of a consignment of boots ordered for three regiments, and all for the left foot.

But out of those great evils arose a greater good, destined to affect all future generations, both military and civilian; destined to affect humanity throughout all time to come. She who raised the first sign of the Red Cross at Scutari; she whose name has been for ever blessed not only by British soldiers, but by the soldiers of every nation in the world. If during that deadly campaign our generals and statesmen lost to us something of our prestige, the name of Florence Nightingale has restored it. She stands triumphant and alone.

Sabrina, although nearing her sixtieth year, had by repeated efforts, and with incredible difficulty, at last obtained permission to join the gallant band of women who accompanied Miss Nightingale to the very seat of war. Her letters written from the base hospital at Scutari give the most reticent account of her own work there; but of her fellow nurses and their noble leader she writes:

"Such utter selflessness and devotion is beyond all words of mine" (dated Nov. 6, 1854, after the Battle of Inkerman). "Many of our women have not taken off their clothes for two whole weeks, but have worked day and night with short hours of intermittent sleep on the hard wooden boards of the huts. As for our beloved Chief, I can only believe that she is inspired by some Higher Power, for her spirit and her strength never falter. Yesterday she stood for 20 hours seeing the wounded brought in and providing them with the accommodation which is so sadly lacking. My work here is largely administrative, and as the oldest member of our Staff I am accorded certain privileges, which go much against my will to take—such as a truckle bed raised from the wooden boardings of my hut, and extra blankets. The other ladies and Miss N. herself sleep on sacking, but I am not permitted to do so owing to my rheumatism, which I have scarcely noticed since I arrived here, and which is less troublesome now that I am occupied than when I sit at home in an overheated atmosphere. Thank God I am hardy and robust and have been so all my life. I have had my small share of the nursing, although again I am not permitted night work, unless in the event of being short-handed through sickness, and I am now called on to attend our own women of whom several, I regret to say, have been indisposed with Fever and Blood Poisoning.

"We shall soon be receiving a fresh contingent of Volunteers and, Alas! we need them badly. The cold is bitter. Outside our huts the snow is a six foot frozen wall! The soldiers have dug us an entrance, and have made paths to take us back and forth from hut to hut. I go muffled to my eyes in furs like a Russian Bear! If it were possible, my dear Mary, to send me any spare blankets, rugs or woollen comforters, or mittens for our poor men we should be more than grateful. . . . I trust that all our dear ones are keeping well in health & spirits. I fear that dear Helen must be undergoing a great strain since the Colonel left for the Front with his Regiment, and it is so bad for her in her condition. I was greatly distressed to hear that Prior has had another attack, & am of your mind entirely, my dear Mary, that he should take a complete rest, & not attend to the business until he has completely recovered . . ."

II

He never recovered. The attack alluded to in Sabrina's letter was the beginning of his end. A sudden end as he would most have wished. Against all doctor's orders and his wife's entreaties, he refused to remain at Wroth that winter, and brought Mary up to London in November, to stay at Soho Square. He had recently discovered a new author, a young man 'From the gutter,' to quote Anthony, a consumptive lad of twenty-two, who had written an amazing novel. An epic, Prior called it, in three volumes.

The author was none other than Mortimer Rudd, and the book *The House of Hur*.

"The manuscript of *The House of Hur*," states William Cator in his *Biographies in Brief*,* "was bought outright by Cartwright's for a hundred pounds after having been refused by every other publisher in London. Not until the reviews which were to hail him as a new star on the literary horizon, had begun to filter through, did the publishing world consider him as a coming proposition." And then it was too late. He died, according to Cator, a week after the completion of *Dandy Commons,* in extreme poverty, having spent his hundred pounds within a month.

But to us was given the first offer of *The House of Hur*.

"Fantasy! Impossible! We can never put it over," was Anthony's verdict when the dubious reports of our readers had been submitted. He went forthwith to his father to tell him so.

---

* Kell & Wrotham, 1925.

He found Prior at his desk in the room that once had been his study, but which, because of necessity for further extension of the premises, had been turned into a ground-floor office.

"This manuscript—" said Anthony, and flung the bundle of bound pages on the desk.

Prior, sharpening a quill pen, smiling at nothing, and looking for all the world like some elderly malicious gnome, made no comment to this preliminary, beyond a gentle "Ah?"

"Now, sir—" Anthony stood before his father all important, his fine shoulders under the well-fitting broadcloth slightly squared, as always when ready for attack. His chin, that showed a blue shadow of beard which no shaving could erase, squared too.

"You'd make three of me," said Prior unexpectedly. "I never carried brawn. They would not let me join up for a soldier in '15. Your aunt has gone at sixty."

"May I crave your attention for a moment?" enquired Anthony impatiently.

The thought occurred to him, as many times it had before, that the old man was not altogether sane. That shock of wild white hair, those rust-grey brows jutting like peaked eaves above the sunken sockets, that twisted smile, and the gleam of his one sound eye, gave to his father's face an eerie, unaccountable expression.

Anthony cleared his throat.

"I understand that you want to publish this."

"That?" Prior cocked an eyebrow, nibbling at his pen. "It's grand. By God!—it's— Have you read it?"

"As much as I could wade through. Not quite half. The blatherings of a lunatic. You can't cover three thousand years within eight hundred pages. Starting from the Book of Genesis, leaping from age to age, and finally ending up a hundred years ahead of our own time with futile prophecies of war in the air. The whole thing's crazy."

"You think so? I'll guarantee," meditated Prior dreamily, "that there's not a statement in this book that will not be fulfilled. Winged boats are not beyond the scope of human enterprise. Man will never be content until he has conquered the air as well as the ocean. We already have balloons. Leonardo made a flying ship. I myself have thought—"

"What I am trying to point out to you," Anthony interrupted firmly, "is that you cannot ignore the reports of two expert literary advisers who both declare that this stuff is not only unsalable, but rubbish. If I may say so, you are interested because the author expresses throughout your own extreme political opinions, which at a time like this when England is at war"— Anthony squared his shoulders—"I consider would be very ill advised to bruit abroad."

Prior nodded. "A good phrase that—'to bruit abroad.' I always had a fancy for words that trip upon the tongue." He took up from his desk a glass paper-weight and balanced it upon his palm. Enclosed within its crystal walls was planted a miniature tree, bearing on its tiny branches fairylike golden fruit. " 'A word fitly spoken,'" murmured Prior, " 'is like apples of gold in pictures of silver.' . . . This is delicious, is it not? My sister bought it me in Brussels nearly forty years ago." He replaced it. "Yes. . . . The author dines with me to-morrow. He coughs deplorably. He won't live long. But his book will. And we shall publish it."

"We *cannot* publish it!" exploded Anthony in desperation. "Really, sir, you try one's patience beyond bearing. Don't you see," he queried violently, "that we jeopardise our name by association with such stuff? The whole thing cries out rank socialism on every page. It is utterly destructive, and the man who wrote it is a lunatic. The prestige of our firm would be at stake."

"Prestige!" Prior started up, a deep flush spreading to his forehead where one vein stood out like gristle. "Almighty Christ! You—*you*—to stand there and dictate to me—you and your prestige! At what altar do you worship? Mammon? God? Or grovelling hypocrisy? You and such as you are our destroyers!" His voice cracked on a high falsetto note, and hideously he began to laugh. "*You!* What do you uphold? What have you at stake to gain or lose? All—all—that all my life I have striven to de*feat*—"

In hysterical frenzy he seized the paper-weight and hurled it with all his puny strength at his son's head. The startled Anthony ducked. The crystal crashed against the wall and was splintered in a thousand fragments. . . . "To find myself . . . de . . . feated!" Prior gasped.

His face turned grey. From his lips issued an awful sound. His head lolled forward, and, clutching at the air as though to save himself, he dropped like a log.

"Father!" screamed Anthony. "Father!"

He was on his knees, fumbling at studs and buttons. One glazed eye stared up at him. The writhing lips strove to utter, but no words came. A spasm shook the shrunken body. And when Anthony's hand had found his father's heart, that heart had ceased to beat.

BOOK THREE

CHARLOTTE
Born 1858

Chapter One

I

My sister Charlotte's first appearance in the Wrotham family occurred some several weeks too soon and on the first day of the New Year 1858, at between three and four o'clock in the morning.

It was prophetic of Charlotte to arrive at the most inconvenient time she could have chosen, and to herald her approach by alarms and excursions at a New Year's Eve party, given at the house of her Aunt Clare.

"A family party," so the invitation to Helen had been issued. "And you need not have the smallest *honte* as to your condition, my dear, for it will only be ourselves."

But Helen, it seemed, had been misled. "Ourselves," were much in the minority, and consisted of Mary Wrotham, looking very frail and accompanied by Sabrina Burnaby; Elizabeth and Diana Marriott, Clare's two elder daughters aged fifteen and sixteen respectively, and Theresa Macfarlane and her husband. Apart from these, too familiar to be at all intimidating, the room—when Helen entered it on Anthony's arm, and wearing a carefully adjusted crinoline—was occupied by a horde of total strangers.

"But nobody," Clare whispered, swooping down upon her in a wonderful creation of amber and black lace, "that you need mind. Only a few dull authors. No one of importance. Let me introduce Mr. Hodges to you. He is the editor of *Woman's Words*. Anthony! That young man, Algernon Swinburne, is here—look—over by the fireplace with Stephen. Go and talk to him."

And Helen found herself wrenched from her husband's side to be presented to a pigeon-chested gentleman with sandy whiskers, a monocle, and a dazzling smile that displayed two rows of the finest porcelain teeth.

He talked without a pause for full ten minutes, of himself, his magazine, of Anthony, of a seedy-looking, dark-bearded individual wearing the shabbiest of evening dress and a morose expression, standing sombrely aloof in a corner by a palm. He was, so Mr. Hodges said, the most powerful literary critic in all London, and had most unkindly treated Mr. Hodges' own one attempt at fiction—*The Trumpeter*—a copy of which he would be proud to present to Mrs. Wrotham and which had been produced a little late in life, but none the less creditable, he hoped—for that. No doubt his dear Mrs. Wrotham would realise that an editor cannot indulge exclusively his own creative inspiration—he must be for ever nurturing the art of others. Perhaps he had not been over-tactful in his attitude to the gentleman in question—for it was an unwritten law that one must take critics up tenderly, treat them with care. Ha! Ha! To the finest of fine dinners—the best wine. Would Mrs. Wrotham sit?

Most thankfully would Mrs. Wrotham sit.

She was feeling rather tired. The day had been a trying one, and the least bit catastrophic, beginning with Anthony's breakfast, which it seemed had been served cold.

Anthony had been annoyed, and justly. The cook had been sent away the night before, having been found lying in the pantry by the beer barrel. It happened that Anthony was presiding that evening at a dinner of the Writers' Club, and the butler in his master's absence had announced to Helen the news of the calamity and left her as mistress of the house to deal with it.

Having descended to the lower regions, taken one look at the snoring figure on the floor, and suggested that the woman be carried to her room and dismissed with her month's wages at such time as she should recover, my mother promptly fainted. A scene may or may not have ensued on Anthony's return; we know that Helen did not appear at breakfast with the ill-served ham and eggs, and that the master of the house was much put out; that he forcibly declared his wife to blame for all the trouble; that her servants were incompetent, her household a disgrace, and if half a dozen maids could not serve a dish of ham and eggs, then she might have made attempt to.

Helen admitted that. The sense of her shortcomings weighed as heavily upon her heart as Charlotte in her womb. She gave Anthony just cause to be so angry. She was aware she irritated him beyond endurance. Her childish simplicity, delightful in a maiden, was out of keeping with her status as a wife. She must learn to overcome it, to be sensible and bold, and capable and elegant, like Clare. How tolerant and patient her dear Anthony had been when she remembered how she jarred at every turn! ...

The poor child must have suffered a destructive loneliness in the first years of her marriage. Her mother's death, following within a few months of her father's, brought to the bewildered, grief-dazed 'Min,' whose whole life had been encircled by parental loving-kindness, her first lesson in endurance. The loss of both her infant sons—a bitter disappointment not only to herself but to her husband—had almost broken her. Almost, but not quite. She had yet some way to go.

"Helen, my dear, how very nice to see you!" Anthony's Aunt Sabrina took her seat at Helen's side. "And how low and comfortable these new *fauteuils* are! Once in them one cannot get out of them again."

Helen looked up gratefully. Anthony's Aunt Sabrina was always very kind. A remarkable woman for her age, so everybody said. And fancy going out to nurse the soldiers when she was nearly sixty! Helen wondered she was still alive to tell the tale. She must once have been a beauty, Helen thought, and was quite handsome still. A most distinguished-looking lady, with an elegant upright carriage, that the drooping Helen envied. Her dress of thick grey silk had a bertha of Brussels lace, cut not too décolleté, as befitting her years, and to hide any deficiencies around her throat—which was astonishingly white—she wore a black velvet band. She had a charming smile, slightly crooked, her eyes were clear and bright, and despite her silvering hair there was nothing of age about her; as a tree that is past bearing fruit and yet is evergreen.

"Clare told me there wer-would only be ourselves tonight," said Helen in her soft hesitating voice. "I did not know it was to be a party."

"Clare probably changed her mind at the last minute," Sabrina answered. "She likes entertaining. Where is Anthony? Did he not come with you?"

"He is by the fireplace talking to Ster-Stephen, and that strange-looking gentleman. Who is he?"

The gentleman in question was a round-shouldered, under-sized young man with a pale, weak-chinned face framed in a shock of violent red hair. His long thin fingers were for ever clutching at his tie, or fidgeting with the buttons on his coat, while his colourless eyes blinked nervously like those of an epileptic.

"I believe he must be that young Mr. Swinburne of whom Stephen was speaking so enthusiastically," observed Sabrina, after a prolonged scrutiny. "Stephen seems to think he will be one of the greatest poets of the century."

"Fancy that!" murmured Helen. "And such a funny-looking

little man. You can't jer-judge by appearances, can you, Aunt
Sabrina? Do you know that I cannot even now—after being
married all this while, and having met so many fa-famous writers
—I cannot even now become accustomed to the kind of ker-
company that Anthony keeps. I feel so dreadfully—always"—
stammered my mother in almost the longest speech that she had
ever made—"that I am a failure as a hostess. I have nothing to
say to these people who are so brilliant and so witty. I am ster-
struck dumb when they talk to me and I feel the greatest idiot
in the world. I can't think why Anthony ever wished to marry
me. I am quite unworthy of him—I know that."

The childish lips quivered. Helen looked down into her lap
where her small mittened hands were folded close together.
Sabrina covered both with one of hers.

"Come! Come! We mustn't indulge in foolish fancies. What's
amiss?"

"M-my cook—last night—was t-tipsy," said Helen, driving back
her tears. "She was quite dreadful, Aunt Sabrina. She was lying
on the floor."

"How most distressing! What did you do?"

"I sent her away, and now I have no cook in the house at
all."

"Then I will send you mine until we find another," offered
Sabrina briskly. "She is a treasure, I assure you. Is that all the
trouble?"

"Yes—trouble enough, I think. Don't you?"

"Trouble enough, indeed. Servants can be the greatest nuisance."

And what now? Sabrina wondered, pursing up her lips, with
a sideways searching glance at the downcast quivering young
face beside her. What a child it was! At twenty-four she looked
about sixteen.

And if it is the onlooker who sees most of the game then Sabrina had formed her own conclusions as to the players' parts in this. Certainly, she granted, Helen might be a little irritating. Spoiled all her life, adored by those two old fogies up in Yorkshire—poor Paxton! God forgive her that she should speak against the dead, and so heroic in the charge as he was—but what a bore of a man with his tales! And then the mother. A stupid, garrulous person, very gushing, as Sabrina remembered her on the few occasions they had met—and only this little one to spend their love on. And their money . . . Trust Anthony for that! The girl had come into a fortune. A pity women were not allowed to keep their own. Anthony, in this, his aunt reflected shrewdly, had not done so very badly for himself, for all that Mary never ceased to make of him a martyr for marrying "a helpless little fool." Granted that the little thing *was* helpless as a kitten and utterly incapable of running any sort of home, what did it matter? Anthony could well afford a housekeeper—on Helen's money. This she had pointed out to Mary: "And you must remember she has been brought up on swansdown—waited upon hand and foot. Give her a chance to learn."

"Learn!" The gentle Mary was unwontedly inflamed. "I have given her every chance to learn. I have no patience! I ran my father's house when I was ten, and unused as I was to the ways of big establishments, I ran the house in Soho Square as well— once you and poor Jeans showed me how. But no one can show this girl how. She has no intelligence. She lets her servants rule her, and Clare does her accounts. She doesn't know a rib of beef from leg of mutton. She cannot even rear her children. She has lost my poor boy two, and may yet lose him another—"

"That is unjust, my dear."

"Unjust, it may be, but it's true. The girl's a fool. And I regret the day he ever met her."

Mary would not see reason over this. Recalling that discussion, Sabrina realised with a slight sense of shock how much Mary had changed since Prior's death; as though the tissues of her soul had hardened with the tissues of her body. Have I too changed, she wondered, or is it merely that as we grow older we grow more insensitive—to our own suffering as well as to the suffering of others? She glanced across the room at Mary, who, with her young granddaughters beside her, sat gazing up with adoration at her son where he stood, with one arm on the mantelpiece, talking to Stephen. Mary, although four years Sabrina's junior, looked a good deal older. Her hair under the widow's cap was white, her little body shrunken, her skin brittle and dry as a faded leaf, and she wore spectacles, for her sight was slowly failing. She lived with Clare now, at Cheam Royal, or at the house in Berkeley Square.

She had no interest in life beyond her children. She had sunk into the apathy of age.

Clare was busy with her guests, talking to each in turn, and supervising the handing round of cakes and tea to the ladies, and sherry to the gentlemen. Just before midnight the company—twenty-five in all—were to go down to the dining-room and to stand round the punch bowl, clasping hands and singing 'Auld Lang Syne'—or so Clare had planned it. She had foreseen no hitch in her arrangements, nor had anybody else; she least of all who was the cause of it.

At a quarter to twelve the company descended. Sabrina with Helen came last accompanied by Stephen, who, Sabrina noted with concern, was not looking too well of late. His cheeks had hollowed, and his hair was grey; his shoulders stooped a little. She had heard rumours that he was speculating on the Stock Exchange. The upkeep of his two houses must cost a deal of money, and Clare for all her competence was extravagant. Sabrina did not doubt that he lived beyond his means, though this was not the time to tell him so.

His hand was on her arm.

"I want a word with you," he whispered hurriedly.

His eyes, she saw, were haggard, his face a little drawn. She was conscious of a sense of shock, and of foreboding.

"Stephen—what?"

"Nothing. Nothing that I can speak of now. I am desperately worried. Your advice may help me."

So it had been before, so it would always be. Her influence still persisted, only its quality had changed, and from the ashes of a long dead passion had arisen, phoenixlike, a living friendship. Both had discovered how much of life lay beyond desire, beyond fulfilment, and beyond regret. Both knew—perhaps had always known—what each from each demanded.

"My advice is yours—if you will take it, Stephen. I have so often begged you to be circumspect in all your dealings. I have a horror of gambling whether it be with stocks and shares or cards—or—"

"Not cards this time, Sabrina."

"Not? Then I am glad to hear it. But you have not been looking at all yourself these last few weeks—I guessed something was amiss. Does Clare know that you are troubled?"

"No—not a word. She must not know until—perhaps—she's forced to."

Sabrina's eyebrows lifted. Was it as bad as that? A low cry behind her arrested on her lips the words she would have uttered. She turned quickly to see Helen, whom both she and Stephen had forgotten, clinging to the rail of the staircase a few steps above, her face ghastly pale, and her eyes wide with fear. Before either Stephen or Sabrina could reach her she had collapsed in a dead faint.

"Fetch Anthony at once and find a carriage," commanded Sabrina, taking in the situation at a glance. "There is no time to be lost. Don't stand there like a dummy," she added with impatience, for Stephen was agape. "Help me lift her to that sofa on the landing. No, leave her be—I'll see to her myself." Men were worse than useless in emergencies.

II

Family affairs of a disastrous nature entirely usurped the interest that in happier circumstances might have been occasioned by the birth of Anthony's daughter. Charlotte lay in her cot, and Helen in her bed, impervious to the bombshell that had fallen.

Stephen's hints of a catastrophe, which had so alarmed Sabrina, were at last resolved in plain and awful fact. He had been speculating. There was nothing new in that. He had been doing so for more than twenty years. But to sink the best part of his capital and the reserves of his own firm in the most gigantic fraud of recent times was another proposition altogether. The bogus company, which had been formed within the last six months, self-styled the Imperial Mercantile Association and floated by men of social standing and repute, numbered among their victims, not only Stephen's, but greater names than his. The chief perpetrators of the outrage fled from justice and the country, leaving the duped shareholders to pay the piper.

The newspapers were guarded. The Sadleir affair which had involved the loss of a hundred and fifty thousand pounds and the trial of the man Robson, who received a sentence of twenty years' transportation for larceny and forgery upon the Crystal Palace Company, were still fresh enough in people's minds for dinner-table talk. Panic must be avoided at all costs. The depression of trade mainly consequent upon the recent war, and mutiny in India, the failure of some millions of the Western Bank of Scotland, the equal failure of American banks, and the embarrassment of American railways, caused increasing apprehension, both at home and abroad, and this last colossal hoax was the climax.

Clare seemed to be less shattered than her husband by his downfall. She was Wrotham enough to take what life might offer, whether for good or for evil, and with a bold front for both.

The family, who discussed in Helen's bedroom as often as elsewhere the all-absorbing topic, were of one mind as to the best thing to be done.

"Cheam must be sold," Clare decisively suggested, "and the town house as well. We will live in Hampstead. Old houses there are cheap. The girls won't need a governess much longer. I shall manage with two maids, and George must go to Westminster instead of Eton."

Mary removed her spectacles to wipe her eyes. "I can make you an allowance, love. I don't require half the income that your darling father left me."

"And I can educate the boy—it would be my pleasure," Sabrina offered quietly.

"Thank you, Aunt. It is more than kind of you, I'm sure, but we have not sunk so low, I hope," flashed Clare with a fine colour in her cheeks, "that we need ask charity from our relatives. Not even from you, Mamma. We must shoulder our own burdens."

Anthony nodded his approval. He was inclined to regard both swindlers and swindled as equally criminal in their intent. There was no excuse in his opinion for foolhardiness.

"It seems to me," he said, from his position on the hearthrug where, with hands under his coat-tails, he stood commanding the attentive gaze of all his audience including that of his infant daughter, who from her crib stared up at him with eyes as wide and solemn as his own, "it seems to me that there is only one course open for Stephen to adopt, and that is to turn Marriotts' into a limited company, nominating himself as managing director at a moderate salary, which could be increased when the firm's reserves have been refunded. There are at least three men of my acquaintance—men of sound business acumen and substance—who might bite at the offer of directorship. I myself would willingly invest a thousand."

Stephen left the room. He had borne about as much as he could stand; and not the least of it his wife's reproaches, who though she had displayed an admirable fortitude in the crisis did not hesitate to remind him that had he only asked for her advice instead of taking such a step without due consideration, he might have averted the disaster.

Clare's attitude of tolerant contempt made him feel that he had failed not only as a husband and a father but as a member of society itself, for in Clare's opinion—as in Anthony's—ruin and dishonour walked together, hand in hand.

Seated there in Helen's bedroom on that January afternoon, her small head lifted and her small chin squared, and on her lips that twisted smile of her father's which was with both a signal of defence—none would have guessed that Clare had watched her whole world torn from its foundations and the background of her life recede. None guessed, unless it was Sabrina —who would not offer pity, and dared not offer more.

III

Charlotte, so the family decided, must be a throw-back to Cheam ancestry, for no Wrotham had been known to have red hair. There is, however, a red strain among the Cheams. The miniature of Harriet, Glyn Wrotham's child-wife, shows Charlotte's selfsame colouring; but Harriet had great beauty, and Charlotte had not much. The lovely Wrotham eyes were not her heritage, for Charlotte's eyes were frankly green; her skin, as milk-white as her mother's but with a tendency to freckle. Her hair—as fiery a red as would have rejoiced the hearts of the pre-Raphaelites—was her Mamma's despair. As also were those freckles. How many quarts of buttermilk, of distilled orange-water, how many pots of ointment concocted by Nurse Annie, who had been her Mamma's maid, were consumed in the endeavour to erase that facial blemish, none will ever know. Certainly not Charlotte, who suffered all such treatment with a stoical indifference, and who freckled every summer like a sandboy, just the same.

Her sex was to her father a source of deep resentment. He had hoped for and been expectant of a son, and was hard put to it to tolerate a daughter—and a daughter, too, with such outrageous hair!

But despite parental disappointment Charlotte grew apace. The most exemplary of babies, she escaped the worst of infant ills, took whooping cough and croup, and learned to speak before her teeth were cut. She had a ravishing wide smile, and a trick of crinkling her nose up when she laughed. She laughed silently, not often, but she very seldom cried.

She was the strangest little child. Completely self-sufficient, she would play about for hours quite happily in a world of her own making in the gardens here at Wroth. She preferred Wroth to London. The house in Great Cumberland Place was dark and tall and gloomy. Her nursery windows looked out upon the street and were enclosed in iron railings. The whole of London seemed to be enclosed in iron railings. There were railings to the houses, and railings in Hyde Park, and the flowers massed behind them stood as stiff and brightly coloured as the ladies in their crinolines who promenaded.

Once the railings at the entrance to the Park were all torn down and broken. Charlotte, walking with her parents on a Sunday morning after church, asked—had there been an earthquake?

Her Papa told her: "No. That is the work of wicked men who wished to get inside when the gates were locked against them."

"Why were the men wicked to want to get inside?" Charlotte always had a ready thirst for information.

"Because they were disobeying law and order, and the Government. And men—like little children—must be taught to obey the powers in authority."

Such long words her Papa used! Charlotte pricked her ears.

"Is God a power in 'thority?"

"Of course."

"Are you?"

Her Papa strode ahead. Her Mamma said: "Hush, my darling, you have annoyed Papa."

Charlotte tucked her hand under her Mamma's arm. She could feel the thinness of that arm under the slippery silk.

"What did I say then to annoy Papa?"

Her mother pressed the little hand against her side and made no answer. Her Papa had turned, was waiting for them both and frowning at the broken railings with a dark look on his face, frowning, too, at the crowd of staring loiterers who with him surveyed the ruins.

"That," he said, pointing with his cane and addressing no one in particular, "that—if you want to know—is the peevish gesture of the spoiled child. The rod has been too often spared. That is a direct result of Mr. Bright's most kindly interest in the welfare of the workingman. Let us hope the Government has learned its lesson."

"What lesson?" queried Charlotte.

"Come home to dinner," said Papa shortly. "It is past one o'clock. And you, miss, will eat yours in the nursery."

"I always have mine in the dining-room on Sundays," objected Charlotte.

"Today will prove exception to the rule, and teach you to remember to be heard a little less than you are seen."

Charlotte turned upon her father her adorable wide smile. She found most things he said extremely droll. He had never yet succeeded, for all his loud pomposity, in arousing in his daughter the very slightest fear. When he roared at her she stared at him, with a wondering, large look, and on the rare occasions that he whipped her she was silent. He whipped her conscientiously with the flat of his hand across her shoulders, and painlessly at that—for Anthony had strong views as to the methods of correction. To frighten, not to hurt, was his maxim. He alternately bullied her and petted her. He may have even loved her in a guarded fashion of his own. He had little sense of humour, but her queer old-fashioned ways, her ridiculous red hair, and perhaps the fact that she had a will every bit as strong as his, although a more endearing way of showing it, served equally to pique and to intrigue him.

Until she was twelve Charlotte enjoyed the distinction of being, not only her grandmother's youngest grandchild, but the youngest by some fourteen years. Her cousins Diana and Elizabeth Marriott both married before twenty, and to the little Charlotte those rare occasions when they visited her Mamma were confusedly connected with voluminous silks, sugary smells, boxes of lollipops and kisses. Their brother George, having distinguished himself at Westminster by gaining a scholarship for

Cambridge, startled his family into eruption by announcing his intention of studying medicine at Guy's. Clare, who maintained that only three professions were open to a gentleman, the Services, the Church and the Bar, rigorously opposed her son's decision and was loyally supported in the disagreement by her husband. Since his financial collapse Stephen had become more of a cipher than ever under his wife's dictatorship, and only at the intervention of Sabrina, who pointed out the advantages to be gained by entering the boy for a profession in which such rapid strides had been made within the last few years, did Clare give in. Nor did she afterwards regret it. George Marriott does not figure to much purpose in this history of the Wrothams, but the history of medicine holds his records for all time.*

Thus it will be seen that Charlotte's childhood was singularly devoid of young society; her environment included none of her own age. While in London she received instruction from a daily governess who drilled her in a grammatical knowledge of the English and French languages, in needlework, the use of the globes and music. She worked samplers for her mother, and learned to play tinkling tunes on the piano to be exploited on Sunday afternoons to her Papa, who dozing in an armchair would rouse himself to tell her: "A wrong note, Charlotte," or "For mercy's sake, don't thump. Hold your wrist loose, not stiff like a ramrod. No! *No!* I can't stand any more of it. This noise is getting on my nerves. Stop!" So Charlotte would have to stop, and Papa would go to sleep again, and Mamma would put her finger to her lip for Charlotte to stay quiet and would sit in her own chair with her hands folded in her lap and her eyes staring at nothing, with the look that never failed to bring an ache to Charlotte's throat. She could not have told why.

---

* Sir George Marriott, K.C.B., M.D., F.R.C.P. See his *Life and Letters* by his son Stephen Marriott, published 1918.

She was so undemonstrative in her affections that none could guess how fiercely Charlotte loved her pale little mother whose voice was like a sigh, and whose eyes were often wet with tears for no reason at all. And when Charlotte saw that she would blink her own eyes in sympathy and tell her Mamma gruffly:

"I think I have a cold. Have you?"

"Yes, my dear love."

"You haven't. Neither 've I. You're crying. Why are you crying? Has my Papa been cross?"

"No, Charlotte—cross? Why should Papa be cross?"

"Is my Papa a good man?"

"But what a question, Charlotte! Of course he is. A ver-very good man. An upright, honourable man. And if—sometimes—your dear father seems to be a ler-little strict with you, it is only because he loves you so and wants you to grow up a good, obedient little girl. Will you remember that?"

"Yes."

"Even if I'm n-not—here?"

"Yes." Charlotte jerked her chin up, her mouth fell open. "What do you mean, if you're not here? Where will you be, then? Are you going away?"

"Perhaps. . . . Who knows?"

And her Mamma's eyes would moisten once again, and Charlotte would clench her small fists against her sides, and say loudly:

"Don't look like that! *Don't,* I tell you! You're not to look like that! I don't like it."

"Hush! Don't be so noisy, love. You speak like a little boy—not like a gentle well-behaved little girl. Try to be gentle and quiet, Charlotte, won't you—for my sake? And try not to answer back when Papa scolds you. *That* makes him angry."

"Does it? Angry with you? Then I won't. I'll hold my tongue.

Look! like this." And Charlotte would solemnly hold her tongue between thumb and forefinger, until a smile came upon her mother's face, and then both would laugh and Charlotte would be happy.

At Wroth no less than in London, Charlotte was singularly bereft of playmates. The vicar of Cheam was a bachelor, the doctor childless, though to be sure at Cheam Royal (which was owned by a Mr. Louis Mendoza who had bought it from Stephen Marriott for what Anthony called "a song") there were boys and girls enough. As long as Charlotte could remember she had been aware of a troop of dark, gipsy-looking children to be met with in the lanes at Wroth. She had learned to know their names, Rachel and Esther and Ruth, Ferdinand and David, but for some reason or other best known to her Papa he would allow no intimacy there.

Charlotte was all eyes and ears for the Mendozas. The thought of meeting them enriched her daily walks. They were unlike any other children ever seen. True, Rachel and Esther and Ruth did not remain children very long. Between a summer and a summer it seemed that the swarthy-skinned chattering little girls with tightly curled black ringlets on their shoulders, incongruously dressed in frocks of Stuart Tartan, were transformed into demure young ladies in wide flounced skirts down to their ankles, broad-brimmed hats with floating ribbons, and their hair done in chignons on their necks. Ferdinand was a sad boy. He had something the matter with one of his legs, which was encased in a great iron cage. Annie, Charlotte's nurse, said he was "backward" and much older than he looked. He had too big a head. Sometimes he walked, dragging his lame leg; sometimes he rode on a white donkey with a page in buttons holding the bridle-rein. Such a dark mournful face he had, and such a large top-heavy head for his narrow dwarfish body. Charlotte could scarcely bear to look at him, he was so ugly and so strange. She was sorry enough for Ferdinand, but sorrier still for David, who was not deformed and little, but tall and straight and proud. David always walked alone, lagging behind the others, never speaking, never looking round about, unless to search among the hedges for birds' nests or wild flowers. Charlotte had often seen him contemplating in the palm of his hand a tiny egg that he had found, only to replace it very gently in the nest, and walk on without a glance at her, for all she stared at him so hard. Then Charlotte would know where the bird's nest was and go herself to see, and find all the little eggs safe there and warm and cosy.

She did not know—could not have said—why David made her sorry. Perhaps it was his eyes, his great dark lonely eyes; or perhaps some look behind them, over-solemn; or the way he walked so proudly, never speaking to the others, and no one ever seemed to speak to him.

Charlotte often wondered why she was not allowed to talk to the Mendozas. The fact remained and was accepted as a law to be obeyed.

There came a time when the Mendozas all wore black. Rachel, and Esther and Ruth, who walked always with a governess, had long black crape streamers hanging from their hats. Ferdinand in a black suit looked uglier than ever, and David was nowhere to be seen.

"Where is he? Where is David? Do you think"—her heart was bumping with a breathless kind of fear—"do you think that David's dead?" Because she knew that when a person died you wore frightening black clothes. Charlotte had worn black for her Poor Grandmamma. She remembered how at her Aunt Clare's house, they all sat at a long table very sad and drinking sherry. Charlotte drank ginger wine. She knew her Grandma had been taken very ill, and Annie told her when she dressed her in her new black clothes that her Poor Grandmamma had died and gone to Heaven. That was last year. And she was terribly afraid now that David must have died and gone to Heaven. But he'd only gone to school. They were in mourning, Annie told her, for their mother. Annie had a useful fund of knowledge. "A great invalid, she was, and never went about. They say he doted on her."

"Who doted on her?" Charlotte wished to know.

"Mr. Mendoza. They say she was a regular Madam for all she couldn't walk. She ruled the house and everybody in it. She laid on her back ever since the birth of David. He's the youngest."

"Is David much older than me?"

"There's two or three years' difference," Annie said. "He was in petticoats when you were born. We brought you down 'ere with the 'oopin' cough. You were just three months. You took it early and never gave us any trouble with it, but it must 'a' got round to them, and the Lord knows 'ow for your Ma ain't one to talk nor me either—but one day there came a note along from Mr. Mendoza saying not to bring infection to the village as he had a delicate son. That would be that Ferdinand—and what an 'eathen name, too! Ferdinand!" Annie's round red face expressed profound contempt. "It put your Pa in a rare state to get that letter, I can tell you. He ain't never forgiven nor forgotten it. I must say myself I thought it uncalled for."

"Is that why I mustn't talk to the Mendozas?"

"Not that only," Annie answered with a knowing look. Which was all that Charlotte could get out of her.

Shortly after this—in the May of 1870 to be exact—Mr. Mendoza paid a call upon the master of Wroth House.

Charlotte, in the garden with her Mamma that afternoon, could remember seeing the Mendoza carriage drawn by two spanking greys with a powdered footman in plum colour on the

box, come smartly round the bend of the drive and stop before
the door. A thin dark gentleman with a black pointed beard got
out, and walking up the steps, looking neither right nor left,
waited for the door to open.

At the sight of this unusual visitation, her Mamma who was
seated in a wicker basket chair on the upper lawn under the
chestnut tree, and sewing, so Charlotte recollected—some mysterious small white garment—uttered a faint exclamation and let
fall her needle in the grass.

"Mr. Mendoza! What can he want?" breathed Helen in a
flurry. "Can you find my needle for me, darling? Your eyes are
sharper than mine. Fancy! Mr. Mendoza!"

"It's a much finer carriage than ours," Charlotte said, flopping
down upon her knees, but not to find the needle. She was staring
at the champing horses, at the coachman and the footman, at the
shining paint and harness all so new and spick and span. The
Mendoza carriage was not often seen about the lanes at Wroth.
When in residence at Cheam, Mr. Mendoza drove a phaëton, or
rode a big bay horse.

The visit, clearly as ceremonious as it was unexpected, lasted no
more than half an hour, nor did Mr. Mendoza stay to tea, although with the table spread out there in the shade of the flower-
ing chestnut Anthony could do no less than offer a frigid invitation, to be as frigidly refused.

Mr. Mendoza from his open carriage bowed low to Helen on
the lawn, smiled at the staring Charlotte, and sat bareheaded,
very upright with his black hat in his hand, until the bend of
the drive concealed him.

"What did he want, dear?" Helen asked, passing Anthony his
cup.

"What do you suppose he wants?" rasped Anthony. "To
feather his own nest, of course, by plucking mine. What else

should he want? The impudence of the fellow! To come here—
here—to *me*—"Anthony gulped his tea and set the cup down in
the saucer with a violent grimace. "What the deuce is this? Dishwater?"

"Oh, dear!" Helen lifted the lid of the teapot and gazed help-
lessly at its contents. "Yes, it *is* weak. I'm afraid they've brought
China instead of Indian. The doctor said, if you rer-remember,
that I was to drink China while I was—Charlotte, love, run in
and ask for some fresh tea for Papa—Indian."

"Never mind. Never mind." With an air of conscious martyrdom Anthony replaced cup and saucer on the tea-tray. "If you
can drink this filth, well and good. I can't. I'll go without tea. It
is rather remarkable, however, that although I pay some several
thousands a year for the upkeep of two houses, I cannot even be
provided with a drinkable cup of tea."

"Yes, love, I'm very sorry. Charlotte, do as I—" Helen's eyebrows telegraphed the remainder of her sentence.

"Haven't I just this instant said," demanded Anthony, his forehead reddening with irritation as he intercepted this wordless
message, "that I will go without tea? Yes! A most infernal impudence! But what can you expect? There's no suppressing them.
They worm their way in everywhere. The whole country's over-
ridden with them. To come here," continued Anthony, his gaze
fixed sternly on his wife, "—to dare to come here to *me* with his
preposterous suggestion—"

"What suggestion, dear?" Helen fluttered to enquire as he
paused.

"You wouldn't understand if I told you. You can pour me a
fresh cup of that dishwater. I suppose I must drink something."

Helen refilled his cup. Charlotte passed it. Anthony sipped it,
and made a face more violent than before. Charlotte's nose crin-
kled. She covered her mouth.

Her father eyed her with disfavour.

"You have never heard of the Orange Republic, I presume?" was Anthony's next enquiry of his wife.

"The Orange—" Helen refocused her attention.

"The Orange Republic," Anthony vouchsafed, "happens to be situated in South Africa. Does that convey anything to you?"

"Of course! How stupid of me! Pass Papa the bread-and-butter, lovey."

"I don't want bread-and-butter. Do you," Anthony enquired loudly, "wish to hear why the present owner of the ancestral seat of the Cheams should honour me—a Cheam descendant—for the first time in fourteen years with a wholly gratuitous visit—or do you not? If Charlotte will kindly stop fidgeting."

"I do, dear. Yes, Charlotte, you may have some cake. No, I'll cut it."

"Three years ago," resumed Anthony with praiseworthy control, "a man called O'Reilly—this may be of some interest to you, Charlotte, when you have done filling your mouth beyond its uttermost capacity—a man called O'Reilly saw the child of a Dutch farmer playing with some pebbles in the neighbourhood of Hopetoun near the Orange River. So struck was he by the singular appearance of— Are you listening, Charlotte?"

"Yes, Papa."

"So struck was he by the singular appearance of these pebbles that he took them to a certain Dr. Atherston—a scientist—for examination. And this Dr. Atherston, an expert in mineralogy, pronounced them to be, not pebbles at all, but"—Anthony paused to impress upon both his hearers the full value of his words—"but —*di*amonds."

"Diamonds!" echoed Helen, with flattering amazement. "Fancy that!"

"Yes. That," said Anthony, glaring first upon his wife and then

upon his daughter, who returned him a wide smile and, uncon-
cerned, munched on, "that was the beginning of the discovery
which since you"—to Helen—"never read a paper will convey
nothing whatsoever— Is it necessary, Charlotte, to show the entire contents of your mouth when you eat? That," Anthony continued blandly, "was the beginning of the discovery of the diamond mines of South Africa, which may possibly transform the
most obscure of our colonies into the wealthiest of all British possessions."

"Isn't that wonderful?" breathed Helen. "And all from pebbles."

"As you say," returned her husband, holding himself in, "all
from pebbles. So much interest you take in current affairs that
you have never even heard of the Orange Republic. I will now
have a slice of that cake before Charlotte devours the lot."

"Then has Mr. Mendoza's visit anything to do with the Orange
Rer-republic?" faltered Helen, when the slice of seedcake had
been passed and Anthony's appetite appeased.

"Indirectly. Mr. Mendoza had the audacity to suggest that I
assist him and his associates in the promotion of a company
for the purpose of establishing a mine in the area of Kimberley." Anthony uttered his snorting laugh. "Hah! To be first
in the diamond field with Mr. Mendoza! To propose that I—*I*
invest my substance in an enterprise backed by the Jews! What
does he think I am? The man must have a skin like a rhinoceros
hide to come here to *me* with his oily propositions. And as I
pointed out to him I have seen enough of foolhardy speculation,
on the part of my half-witted brother-in-law, to make me slightly
cautious of placing my money in the melting-pot—or the pocket
of Mr. Mendoza."

"One can always be wer-wise after the event," Helen tremulously submitted. "I am sure you are quite right, dear—"

"Right!" Anthony rose abruptly from his chair. "Much you know whether I'm right or wrong. It isn't that I'm so averse to a little flutter, mark you, so long as I can be sure I'm on to a sound concern. And I don't say that the diamond industry is not going to *be* a sound concern—in the future. But at the present it is in its infancy. Half the mines sprung today may prove to be Dead Sea fruit a year hence. Besides which"—Anthony squared his chin— "I do not care to have the name of Wrotham associated with the tribes of Israel. Find me," Anthony magisterially pronounced, "a good solid, British-run and British-backed syndicate, and I don't say that I would not—perhaps—be persuaded to consider a judicial—small—investment. I said per*haps*. But not in coöperation with a Mendoza."

"Please may I leave the table now?" asked Charlotte.

"Yes, love. . . . And so that's what he called to see you for?" murmured Helen. "Ver-very odd of him I'm sure!"

"Odd? It's a damned impertinence! And so I told him—more or less. Hah! I don't think he'll come here again in a hurry."

His feelings thus relieved, Anthony stalked off to interview the gardener.

His wife sat very still, her head a little drooping and her face a little drawn. The chestnut bloom was falling; one stray petal drifted down to her uncovered hair, and lay there like a flake of snow among those spun-glass threads. She watched Charlotte with her skipping rope, her flaming curls atangle on her shoulders. With a delicate instinctive gesture Helen laid a hand against her body. Her lips moved in soundless prayer.

". . . If it be Thy Will that I give a son to my dear husband, let me bear him safely, and let his hair—not—be red."

That prayer in part was answered. She gave Anthony his son, and lived long enough to hold him in her arms while from her breast he sucked her life away. So softly did she die, they thought she slept, until her baby, waking, found her cold and cried for her.

His hair was never red. It may have once been flaxen. A photograph discovered in an album shows him at the age of five, or thereabouts, wearing a pre-Fauntleroy velvet suit and curls upon his shoulders. And his father named him Prior John at the wish of his Aunt Sabrina.

Chapter Two

I

A NEW decade had dawned, and unhampered by the shadow of the Franco-Prussian War, England entered upon her thirty years' prosperity.

The sweeping changes marshalled by the daemonic fervour of a Gladstone, the agitating atmosphere occasioned by reform and nothing but reform—in the Irish Church, in education, in the Services, in the administration of justice—was dissolved in the general election of '74. Reaction was inevitable, the Liberal tide must turn, a wave of Tory supremacy was advancing. The mission of that over-zealous enthusiast who felled his trees at Hawarden with the same singleness of purpose as he had felled the more obstreperous branches of the Irish grievance, was now accomplished. His axes blunted, he had none to grind.

And that extraordinary being who succeeded him, not as an alien arrivist full of arrogance and epigrams, but as a conquering hero with the angels on his side, an earldom on his head and Royal favours in his buttonhole, held the key to a great empire in his hand.

He had asthma and was seventy, but, undaunted by the trouble down in Turkey, he kept one eye on India while Russia went to war. His rival in retirement at Hawarden wrote pamphlets denouncing the Bulgarians and had his house stoned for his pains by the grandsons of those who had stoned Wellington's.

'Dizzy' stayed cool; the Tsar sent him a General Ignatiev to

secure a promise of neutrality, and Victoria was raging. . . . Her
beloved Albert had *so* disliked the Russians. She would lay down
her 'crown of thorns' if England kissed Russia's feet. The Prime
Minister was in a quandary. His 'faery Queen' must be placated,
the Russian General no less. And while the Royal blood rose to
the boil he played his master-stroke. Four millions borrowed from
the Rothschilds as the price of the Suez Canal!

Charlotte read in *The Times* a report of Beaconsfield's first
speech as leader of the House of Lords. She had, of course, no
right to read the papers. Nothing enraged her father more than
to see her read the papers. He held the strongest views as to the
limitations of woman's province, which certainly did not include
affairs of state or political discussion. It was deplorable, he said,
to see the manner in which the woman of today overstepped the
bounds of feminine prerogative, striving idiotically to ape the
man. And why, in Heaven's name? Did not life essentials lie in
the contrasting element of man to woman? The feminine brain,
Anthony declared, was not fashioned to permit of the introduction of problems purely masculine. This talk of equality of the
sexes inaugurated by that canting humbug Mill, was having the
most pernicious effect upon the younger generation. Equality!
Freedom! Emancipation! Bosh!

Which outburst drove Charlotte to her father's library in his
absence, there to ransack his shelves for Mill, for Darwin, for
Huxley and much else that was taboo, and that gave more food
for thought than her young mind could well digest.

She had none with whom to talk of these daring modern writers
who advocated Women's Rights (and what were they? she wondered) and who told you that your ancestors were apes. None,
that is to say, except her great-aunt Sabrina, who was as interested
as Charlotte in the topics of the day. Between the woman of nearly
eighty and the young girl not yet eighteen, existed an intimacy

not at all affected by disparity of age. It was Sabrina who six years before had insisted that the grief-bewildered child be taken from that lonely house where, bereft of the timid presence who for twelve years had filled her life, she mourned her mother's death, uncomforted.

"For she can't stay here," his aunt declared to Anthony, when after the funeral she installed herself at Wroth to set the household wheels in orderly rotation. "She can't stay here with all the past about her. It is shameful"—the old lady minced no matters when dealing with her nephew—"that you deny her young companionship. She should be with children of her own age. Do you want to see her melancholy-mad? I suggest you send her to a boarding school where she'll forget her troubles and herself."

"It is natural," Anthony said coldly, "that a right-minded child should grieve for a dead parent."

"Less natural for a child not to cry," was Sabrina's sharp retort. "It hurts me beyond words to see her in this state. Natural, you call it! She's suffering more than *you* will ever know, or understand—or feel."

Perhaps Sabrina was unjust in this. He may have felt more than was apparent. He had lost the one creature in the world who believed in him as she believed in God, and even the son he had so long desired could not atone for that. His bed and his heart were empty. He was greatly misunderstood. He raised a fountain to her memory in the garden: two alabaster angels weeping either side an urn.

"Very tasty," said Sabrina. "And when does Charlotte go to school?"

She had her way at last, and Charlotte went—to a Miss Leigh-Sanderson's at Bournemouth, a lady in advance of her time, whose interest in the higher education had actually gone to the length of establishing a debating society among the elder girls!

But of this defiance of his code, Anthony knew nothing, for Charlotte never told him, nor did anybody else.

And there she stayed until such time as she became a grown young lady, with a bustle at the back of her, and her red hair in a bun.

Clare, whose daughters were well settled, and whose son had taken his M.D. and married a wife with money, vied with Sabrina in sponsoring her niece. "She must be given every chance," so Clare told Anthony; "with that hair she won't stand much. I'll let it be known that she will be well dowered. She must have *some*thing since she has no looks."

To Clare's conception, possibly. Charlotte's freckles, her little, heart-shaped face, too broad across the cheek-bones and too narrow at the chin, her greenish eyes tilting slightly at the corners under peaked elfish brows, and above all, that shocking hair, did not conform to any known type of beauty. The girl, according to Clare's standard, was unfortunately plain; her figure, with no curves at all, deplorable. Breastless as a boy she was, and like a boy's her manner—too downright, too direct. She rode fearlessly to hounds (and, thanks to her who taught him, the little brother learned to ride as soon as he could walk), groomed her own pony and jumped him cross-saddle in the paddock, in a pair—would you believe it!—of those Bloomers!

Her father was in London when this happened, or there might have been the deuce to pay for that. Anthony stayed in London most part of the year, coming down to Wroth for week-ends to see his son and daughter. He had let his house in Great Cumberland Place, and had a bachelor suite in St. James's where whether or no he found some consolation for his widowed state was nobody's business but his own—and possibly his sister's.

Between Clare and the astonishing Sabrina, who at eighty could

walk ten miles and get the better of an argument with Anthony
—between these two existed, it seemed, a rivalry as to which
should see their young niece launched upon the world.

"It is ridiculous," Clare insisted to her brother, "that Aunt Sabrina at her age should propose to bring her out. Why must she
always have a finger in *our* pie? Let me have Charlotte up at
Hampstead, and if you pay me an allowance for her clothes—
she goes in rags at present—I'll see that she is introduced to the
right sort of people. I would like to keep her well away from the
literary set. You don't want her to make a fool of herself with
some shoddy unknown writer. Later in the season you will have
to give a ball. . . . It might be possible to dye her hair."

Then Sabrina had her say. She descended upon Anthony one
morning in his office at the house in Soho Square, forced on him
an entrance, sent his clerk away, and stood leaning on a gold-
topped stick and smiling as crookedly as ever. Her hair was
white under a bonnet beaded in black jet, her skin coloured like
old ivory in which showed scarcely a trace of wrinkle; her ink-
blue eyes, curiously penetrating and unfaded still, seemed to note
and watch not only things visible but those that did not come
within the range of sight. And standing there supported by her
gold-topped stick, Sabrina spoke her mind.

So forcibly, it is presumed, that Clare's plans were all exploded.
It was Sabrina who took Charlotte to stay with her in Curzon
Street as sixty years before Jess Pinkerton—to that same house—
had taken her.

II

Charlotte would have sooner stayed at Wroth. Life for her at
that time presented an entirely new aspect. She no longer studied
Mill. Mr. Darwin, she decided, was a tiresome old bore, and his

theories she dismissed as sacrilegious. She devoured, surreptitiously, the much discussed *Poems and Ballads* of Swinburne, which were creating shocked furore; she read Ouida, and marvelled at the side-light thrown thereby upon a world as far removed from hers as was the planet Mars; a world inhabited by guardsmen, with flowing long mustachios, and swooning heroines whose loveliness and charm imbued her with desire for emulation. She began to take an interest in her clothes. She went so far as to order, without Anthony's permission, a new best dress for Sundays from Carter's of St. Albans. A magenta "faye" (according to the modiste) striped with yellow, with an avalanche of flounces at the back suspended from a bustle, and a corsage padded in the bust at Charlotte's own suggestion, to "take away the flatness."

Thus attired, with addition of a hat adorned with yellow roses and ostrich feather tips, Charlotte accompanied her father to church and sustained his comments on the subject with tranquillity.

What mattered though her Papa said he was ashamed to be seen out with her? that she was grotesque enough already without making of herself a laughing-stock in front of the whole village? To choose *that* colour of *all* colours to shriek against her hair! He refused to pay the bill for this monstrosity—and what a hat! If she must have clothes, why for heaven's sake could she not consult her Aunt Clare or her cousins? And how dared she order dresses without first asking his permission? She was getting altogether out of hand. The sight of her beside him decked out like a barbarian made him—he declared—feel positively bilious. And thus and so on—all the way to church.

The tirade may have rankled. Was she so ugly then? Grotesque—a laughing-stock? My hair—thought Charlotte, kneeling in the Wrotham pew at her father's side—my hair is my Calvary.

Why am I so disfigured? Does *He* think my hair so shocking?
Was he lying when he said that it was glorious?

Her heart swelled beneath the padding of her bodice at the
memory of the way he'd said that word. No one had ever in her
life before called her hair glorious. Every possible term of opprobrium and disparagement, perhaps, but never that. Even the
village boys when she was little, she remembered, had called after
her when she was out with Annie: "There goes Ginger."

Was it possible that he was making fun of her? Her face crimsoned, she covered it and prayed: "O God, don't let him make
fun of me, don't let him hate my hair. I pray you please, God,
not to let him hate my hair. . . ."

Her father was intoning the responses; she glanced aside at
him. His chin! Why did it always make her want to giggle the
way he thrust it forward? She wondered if her Papa believed in
God, if he were really praying when he put his hands over his
eyes. And as for that—could God hear him, whether he prayed
or not? or me—or anybody here inside this church, or anywhere
in all the world? For if we were descended from the monkeys,
which of course we couldn't be (*he* at any rate was descended
from the Kings of Israel—of that Charlotte felt sure)—if we were
descended from the monkeys and were only higher apes as Mr.
Darwin said, then how could God as God exist at all? Except as
a First Cause—a wriggling, unholy proto-what's-its-name. In
which case, what exactly was the meaning of Immaculate Conception? . . . But this, Charlotte said determinedly, is blasphe-
mous and especially so in church. . . .

On the other side of Charlotte sat her little brother. One cheek
bulged suspiciously. Mercy! Was he eating sweets? She thrust a
hand down to his pocket—that bulged, too; something ominously crackled. A faint odour of peppermints arose.

"*Spit-it-in-your-handkerchief,*" chanted Charlotte into Prior's

ear under cover of the psalm. *"And-don't-let-your-father-see. . . .*
Praise ye the Lord."

On the way home from their devotions the Wrothams encountered two horsemen: one an elderly sallow-complexioned
gentleman with a greyish pointed beard, the other a slightly built
young man of somewhat foreign appearance who wore his seal-
smooth black hair aesthetically long. Both gentlemen removed
their hats as they passed by, and Anthony returned a chill acknowledgement. There was nothing to be sure remarkable in
that; nothing, that is to say, more remarkable than the fact that
Charlotte's cheeks had turned from white to red, and that little
Prior, striding manfully beside his tall Papa whose gloved hana
firmly grasped his own, enquired: "When's he coming to ride
with us again?"

"What?" thundered Anthony, flinging aside the hand he held
as though it were a hornet. "He? Who? Who has been riding
with you?"

"Him what went by on the grey horse," replied the innocent,
unheedful of his sister's agonised grimaces. "He said he was—"

"Look at that darling little black-cap!" screamed Charlotte.
"Prior! Quick!"

"That's not a black-cap, it's a sparrow," Prior told her, peering. "Don't you know a sparrow from a—"

"He who went by, not *him what* went by," his father mechan-
ically interrupted. "And once and for all I forbid— Charlotte!
Will you pay attention when I speak to you?"

"I didn't know you were speaking to me, Papa."

"Once and for all I for*bid any* intimacy with these people on
any pretext whatsoever," emphatically stated Anthony, his tone
gathering vehemence as his pace increased. "You understand
me? And if I hear that this young man has had the impudence

to intrude his company upon you and your brother in your daily rides, then I shall forbid you to ride again unless accompanied by myself or Baxter. So now you know. Prior! Wipe your nose!"

"I've lost my handkerchief."

"Here, take mine," offered Charlotte in a hurry, while disgustedly her father strode ahead, and she added in a whisper as she manœuvred her young brother to her side, at the same time emphasising the words with a painful grip of his arm: "If you dare let on that he comes out with us *ever* I'll tell Papa you were eating sweets in church."

"No!" shouted Prior in a rare fright, for if that misdemeanour were discovered it would mean for sure, a hiding. "I won't— Ooh —you're hurtin' me! Let go of me-ee. I won't—I've told you that I—*wo*— Oooh!"

"Is it necessary," demanded Anthony, rounding at this juncture on the stragglers and speaking with the patience born of long-suffering, "is it necessary for this abominable child to yell to high heaven on a Sunday morning? That is all I ask. Is it necessary?"

"You see?" muttered Charlotte as she released the chastened Prior's arm. "Making that silly noise. Now be quiet."

In silence the cavalcade resumed its journey home, and Charlotte spent the remainder of the afternoon learning by heart 'An Interlude' by Mr. Swinburne.

> In the greenest growth of the May-time
> I rode when the woods were wet . . .

It had in actuality so happened, with exception that the month was April and not May.

They might have been a Montagu and Capulet. The feud existent between the two houses and fostered by a grossly exag-

gerated racial prejudice on the one side, and by a dignified isolation on the other, was in itself cause enough to embue the situation with romance. He came, or rather rode, into her life at
a time when for Charlotte the world was very dreary. Prior had
the measles and she, in accordance with the strict injunctions of
the doctor, was in quarantine. The house reeked of carbolic, and
Annie who guarded the nursery regions appeared only at grim
intervals to address her from the top of the stairs, if she had occasion to speak to her at all, and then only to send her to the doctor's surgery for medicine, or to the farm for eggs.

Anthony had spent that week-end at Wroth and visited his
son each day to assure himself (after swallowing a dose of cam-
phor by way of disinfectant) that the rash was fairly 'out.'

Her father, Charlotte remembered, had been more than usually trying during those few days. His ill-humour, manifested in
a series of complaints directed against herself, the servants, Annie,
the doctor—whose treatment, Anthony decided, was absolutely
wrong—finally culminated in a telegram despatched to his nephew
George, who might perhaps—he said—know more about his job
than this half-witted numskull.

In answer to the summons George Marriott arrived on Sunday morning, inspected the invalid, and having pronounced the
treatment perfectly correct, the attack extremely mild, and taking
its most natural course with no cause whatsoever for alarm, he
pocketed his uncle's guineas and stayed to Sunday dinner.

Later in the afternoon Charlotte accompanied her cousin to
the station. George Marriott had not inherited the good looks
of his parents. He was loose-limbed, bearded and untidy. He had
a pair of quick responsive eyes, a smile as crooked as his great-
aunt Sabrina's, and no memory for unimportant things. He
would tie knots in his handkerchief to remind him of a social
engagement, but he never forgot a case. His mode of speech was

brusque, and he had a most sarcastic tongue—a valuable asset in
the lecture room but not conducive to a bedside manner.

For this comparatively unknown cousin Charlotte entertained
a furtive admiration. Perhaps because he dared to contradict her
father. They had argued all through luncheon over politics, it
had seemed, Anthony attacking the Liberal Party with violent
Tory invective, while George retaliated with a biting comment
on "Dizzi-ben-Dizzi, the Orphan of Bagdad," and enquired if
his uncle were taking shares in the "Empress Hotel Company—
Limited?" The gist of these remarks was lost upon the silent Charlotte, but from the effect of them upon her father she judged that
Cousin George was scoring heavily. Anthony sulked for the remainder of the meal, denied himself his favourite Stilton at the
end of it, and leaving his nephew to drink port alone, he retired to his study to read manuscripts, saying curtly: "Charlotte
will accompany you to the station. Your train leaves at three
o'clock."

Having seen her cousin into his train and received at the last
minute five golden sovereigns dropped into her palm ("Your
father's fee, my child, to buy yourself some fal-lals—you needn't
tell him that I've given it to you; and don't go and get the
measles"), Charlotte returned elated to the carriage.

The afternoon was sunny; in the morning it had rained. The
road reflected splashes of blue in every puddle, the apple trees
were coming into blossom, and everywhere, in every bird-call, in
the whisper of young leaves, rose the sense of spring's unfolding.
No day, Charlotte thought, had ever smelled so sweet, never had
the fields and meadows seemed so gracious. It was as if she saw
the world for the first time; the familiar landscape, the tender
shapes of hills—all the infinite gradations of light and form and
colour presented to her sight an entirely new aspect. In the dis-

tance, above the rumble of carriage wheels, and the steady rhythm
of the horses' hooves, she could hear the sound of church bells.
The momentary pleasure occasioned by that unexpected gift of
five pounds from her Cousin George diminished; she was sad.
The piercing beauty of the day, that distant, wistful chiming
sharpened her loneliness. Why was she lonely? What right, she
asked herself, had she to feel lonely, to bear an incessant grievance
against what—or whom? Her father? He was difficult, admittedly,
but well-meaning even though at times he was ridiculous and
shouted. She had a lovely home—thousands of poor girls, said
Charlotte, would think themselves in heaven to live in such a house,
with horses to ride, plenty of food to eat, servants to wait on them.
She must not, she sternly argued, give way to stupid fancies. She
must learn to control her moods, not to indulge in self-pity. Was it
not Marcus Aurelius who said that self-pity was the greatest form
of cowardice? She had recently discovered in her father's library a
volume of that Stoic's views on life, and was of a mind to re-
mould her own accordingly. . . . And I must not be a coward,
Charlotte said, rapidly blinking her eyes. If I do not take myself
in hand I shall turn into a Mrs. Gummidge—or a *Miss* Gummidge, for it is doubtful if I shall ever be Mrs. *Any*thing. . . . To
be married. To be loved. And to love. . . . But what would love be
like? She had loved and been loved by her mother, her frail little
mother, nothing to her now but a white ghost in memory. She
loved Prior and the horses, she loved her Aunt Sabrina, and she
loved Annie, she supposed: she quite certainly did not love her
Papa. She did not even very much respect him, although she
often felt a little sorry for him. She could not have told why.

She sighed and wondered—what had made her speak to Cousin
George so openly during the drive with him to the station? To
none but old Aunt Sabrina, and only guardedly to her, had she

ever dared to voice those chaotic thoughts and feelings that came to her at times so overwhelmingly. What made her tell him even that much? Perhaps because he was a doctor and could understand a mind as well as he could understand a body.

"If only," she had said, "if only there were some work, some aim or purpose to be found in living—I mean—more than just to be alive . . ."

Yes, she had said that apropos of those interesting remarks he had made with reference to the work that women of today were undertaking. (How strange it had seemed to be talked to as though you were a creature of intelligence, instead of being made to feel that you did not exist at all except as an incumbrance and mistake!)

"Woman," Cousin George had told her (this in answer to a question she had put to him as to whether or no he was in favour of the founding of these new women's colleges at Oxford and Cambridge, a movement which had been greatly opposed by her father, and indeed by public opinion generally), "woman is only just beginning to emerge from the mollusc stage. The process of transition is slow, but very sure; and as the scope of feminine vision widens and the desire for expansion develops, so will she adapt herself both outwardly and inwardly to her revised conditions. And in a hundred years from now"—he had ended with a quizzical glance from those deep-set keen grey eyes of his, "the women will wear our trousers and we will wear their skirts."

"Yes, but how," Charlotte frowningly persisted, not to be diverted by such flippancy as that, "how can we revise conditions? Take my own case, for instance, Cousin George. Here am I, living in my father's house, but not considered capable enough to run it. A housekeeper does everything that I ought to do. Not that I should be much use, I am afraid, but I am not allowed even to *try*. I am kept down"—the words had tumbled out of her in a breathless torrent—"I am kept down and treated like a child. I am not a child. I am eighteen. My mother was married before she was eighteen. And I have read books, Cousin George, philosophy, science—I've tried to understand why we are *here,* and how we are born. I know how we are born. Is it shocking that I should know that? I have read Mr. Darwin's 'Origin of Species,' and unless you are a fool—and I don't think I'm a fool, although Papa is always telling me I am—unless you are a fool you cannot possibly *not* understand certain facts of life from reading Mr. Darwin. And I've read John Stuart Mill and I *do* think, Cousin George, that there must be something more for one to do than just to be a lady. Because, suppose one isn't married—and it is quite likely I shall never be with my freckles and my hair—what other thing is left for me except to wither up and grow old and die? Can't one *do* something, Cousin George, some work? Some ladies, I know, are authoresses, and some, I believe, are studying to be doctors. But they are clever and I am not. And oh, dear!" Charlotte breathlessly concluded, quite overcome with her own verbosity. "If only there were some aim or purpose to be found in living, Cousin George, more than just to be alive—"

And to that, as the carriage drove up to the station entrance, he had enigmatically replied:

"To be alive, young lady, is a big enough aim for you, and it takes a lifetime to learn how."

Charlotte covered her hot cheeks with her gloved hands as she recalled that so unusual conversation. A queer excitement seized her. To know, to feel, to think—for oneself! To widen the scope of feminine vision (was not that what Cousin George had said?), to develop outwardly and inwardly, to emerge from the mollusc stage—

On an impulse as sudden as it was violent, Charlotte started up. She poked her head out of the brougham window, and addressed the coachman: "Stop! I am going to walk. You can drive home—and tell my father I shall not be back for tea. . . ."

The process of transition had begun.

A daring enough gesture. Not to be at home for tea on Sunday was an inexcusable offence. Her father always had been adamant in respect of Sabbatical observances, existent in that household since Charlotte had been born. She, as perfunctory hostess and in her best silk dress, must be ready to receive unlikely callers. Prior must be put into his velvet suit, and his curls must be recurled round Annie's fingers, to dangle revoltingly upon his shoulders and halfway down his back. And in the gilded drawing-room—redecorated since our father took up residence at Wroth—a photograph album on his knees and blackness in his heart, the wretched boy would sit, seeking diversion from the silence by simulating hiccups, or alternatively plucking horsehair from the cushions, and making faces at his sister while she read—the Lord knows what—concealed within a binding from the works of Hannah More.

In an armchair, a bandanna handkerchief across his forehead, his head on the antimacassar and his feet on a woolwork stool, Anthony dozed, and nothing above a whisper from those uneasy two must be uttered till he woke.

It will be seen then that her defiance of all regulations on that Sunday afternoon was an action worthy of a Casanova.

When the carriage disappeared—she had stood to watch it go and to ascertain that it was out of sight—Charlotte climbed a stile, crossed a meadow and three fields, and passed by way of stepping-stones over the stream that divided the Cheam estate from Wroth; and there, abandoned to her villainy, she trespassed in Cheam Woods, and on the private land of the Mendozas.

Barbed wire was no deterrent. She scrambled under it on all

fours, shamelessly. She had removed her hat, and was in mad mood enough to have removed her skirt if it had unduly hampered her. She was wearing, we are told, her Sunday best silk dress, not the magenta with the yellow stripes but a subdued and chaste dove-grey. Its bodice lay as close to her slight figure as a glove upon a hand; its skirt was frilled and bustled at the back, and from a small ruching of white lace fastened with a cameo brooch that once had been her mother's, the white column of her throat rose, pure as the lily tower of Giotto—or so it may have seemed to him who saw her as she came along the bridle path swinging her hat by its strings.

Her uncovered head blazed against those green-grey beech boles; shafts of sunlight thrusting through the feathery tree branches crowned her with fiery gold. She was too elated with herself and her adventure to hear the sound of a horse's hooves on the damp moss; in the stillness of those woods even the birds were muted. The path was narrow and, on either side, the serried ranks of tree trunks receded in green distance like a retreating army. The scene was admirably laid, and the players played their parts in it, perhaps not all unconscious of their setting. However that may be, she was well aware of her own wickedness, and this, the culminating point of it, sooner or later to be paid for in good fee.

She was always a little vague as to how exactly it had happened. She saw him first when he was so close upon her that he might have ridden her down. He too was hatless, the backward sweep of his shining blue-black hair revealing one of those pale egg-shaped foreheads beloved of Morales. Charlotte knew nothing of the Spanish painters, but she knew that he possessed some rarer quality of form and feature than was ever seen among the few young men that she had met with on infrequent visits to her Aunt Clare's Hampstead house. His eyes were dark and guarded with the wisdom and remoteness of the ages in their shadows; the high-bridged curve of his nose was repeated in the fuller curve of the short upper lip, and breeding stood in every line of him as proud as that of the black-pointed bay mare he rode.

Charlotte had no doubt of his identity although, when she had seen him last, David Mendoza had been a boy, and now he was a man. She had heard that he had gone abroad after he left school, and that she should be the first to speak, denying any formula of mere convention and parental discipline, did not at all surprise her. She had already burned her boats and, exalting, she added fuel to the fire.

She asked him—quite unnecessarily—the time. Unnecessarily, in view of the fact that a gold watch on a gold chain was hidden in her waistband, and that she knew the time of day as well as he.

But what she did not know for all that she had read her Mr. Darwin, was that she had succumbed to discipline much stronger than her father's, and that the laws of natural selection cannot be disobeyed. She did not know that she, the predatory young female, had been chosen from a cosmic void and flung into that lovely wood with as fine a disregard for the proprieties as might be shown in a pond of water when two amoebas meet and merge in protoplasmic frenzy. All one to nature, the mother democrat, who chuckles as she hides in her own tracks and makes of commonplace occurrences a miracle, and of man a deity.

He dismounted to tell her it was four o'clock. Why did he dismount when, having politely answered her, he might have ridden on and left the incident suspended with for them no further issue? Because, one presumes, those forces that had brought these two together to perform their dual miracle in this vast scheme of things, ordained it otherwise. So he dismounted.

She thanked him for his information, stroked his horse's nose, said that she must hurry, and stayed just where she stood. "And I suppose," she said, "I ought to make apology for trespassing."

"Pray do not. Our woods," he told her gallantly, "have already made you welcome, and you surely have more right to them than we."

"More right? How? Why?" Her chin lifted to the question, and her eyes were lifted, too; his drowned in them a second; they both found that a very new sensation.

"Because your family," he answered—his voice was curiously monotoned, yet not monotonous—"have owned this land for generations. We are the trespassers, not you."

"My family," she contradicted, "have never owned Cheam Royal. The Wrothams were connected with the Cheams by marriage once. Lady Harriet Cheam was my great-grandmother."

"And you are very like her. There is a miniature I found in a secret drawer of an old bureau stored in one of the attics, with other lumber that must have been overlooked in the clearance when my father bought the place. I would like to give it back to you—it is a lovely thing. She has the same glorious red hair as yours."

She thought he mocked her and stared at him with tears of indignation burning in her eyes to dry in their own heat when she saw by the look in his that—amazingly—he meant it.

They spent the remainder of the afternoon together, he leading the bay mare. When they found a sunny clearing where the moss was fairly dry, he hitched his horse's reins to a tree branch, removed the saddle, and laid it on the ground for her to sit on like a queen.

What did they say, there, to each other? Nothing, it is certain, of the clamour in their hearts. It is possible that they discussed the bay mare's points. Charlotte was told of her fine pedigree: her grandfather had been a Derby winner; she was part Arab, three years old. He had broken her himself, he was going to ride her in a steeplechase. No, he had never hunted. Hunting was to his mind a cruel sport, he said.

She would have none of that. How, if he had never hunted, could he tell if it were cruel or not? The fox always had a chance to get away—and what would the farmers do if the crops were all destroyed by the wretched creatures? Think of the plunder to the farmyards, too, to say nothing of preserves. Why, there wouldn't be a pheasant left—and so on. It was unfair to make a sweeping statement of that sort unless he had confirmed it. Why should he not come out cubbing in September and judge hunting for himself?

Because he would not, he thought, be here in September.

He was going away? Her voice flattened on the question.

He was going to South Africa, he said.

Indeed? So far? Her heart beneath the grey, demure silk bodice had at those words of his turned faint, had almost ceased to beat; but she gave no sign of it, only sat up more primly.

Yes, it was a long journey, he agreed. He was going there on business. His father was interested in certain mines near Kimberley on the Orange River. He would be going out there to inspect them in the autumn. "And he wishes me," said David, "to accompany him."

"That, I am sure, will be a great experience. I—I envy you," said Charlotte.

He plucked a primrose, nibbling the stalk between his teeth, with an oblique glance at her from under his long curved lashes. "I am not sure," he said, "that I am anxious now to go."

"Not?" She twined the ribbon of her hat around her forefinger, untwined it, and then most foolishly began all over again. For a while he watched this strange performance, until, moistening her lips, she repeated rather faintly: "Why not? I should be. You are very lucky to have the chance."

"It is not the kind of chance I want. I would rather stay at home and study music."

"Do you play?"

She spoke coldly in that same flattened voice. He seemed already to have placed the ocean between himself and her. She hardly heard him tell her that he played the violin; that he had composed a violin concerto—that he had been studying these last three years in Munich under one of the finest teachers in Europe, Herr— The name pronounced in guttural German left her completely unenlightened.

She had already discovered that he was supremely egoistic, yet his egoism was not so much an inflated sense of his own importance as an inherent desire to stand well before her and before the world. She resented his absorption in himself, for she was individual enough to lay claim to primary attention; and too inexperienced to know that the surest way to a man's heart is through a sympathetic ear.

She stirred restlessly, and he, quick to perceive her change of mood, paused in the middle of a sentence to state a little hotly:

"But I bore you!"

"No, indeed." Such direct address was slightly disconcerting. "I am very interested, although I don't know much about music. I play the piano badly, and I have never been to a concert in my life."

"I would like to play to you," he offered sombrely, "out here in the woods. I would like to improvise a rondel to your hair."

She could not help blushing at that turn in the conversation, as pleasurable as it was uninvited. She looked at him again with kindliness.

"You improvise? compose—all in a minute? anywhere, in any place?"

"If anywhere, in any place, I can find inspiration. You"—a smile flashed into his fine dark eyes—"shall be my inspiration."

"I think," said Charlotte stolidly, "it must be time to go." Her face betrayed nothing of the agitation that his words had roused. She stood up, smoothing out the creases in her Sunday best silk frock. Did he take *too* much for granted? Had she cheapened herself by giving him two whole hours of her company without even a formal introduction? Could such behaviour mean that they were—flirting?

"Please don't go yet. Tell me that I may see you again soon. Tomorrow? Shall I bring my violin out here? Would you really care to hear it?"

She had never said she would.

"It might be difficult for me to meet you in this way," she answered, all confused. "My father—and yours—"

"Yes!" he cried impatiently. "Our meeting, in so far as their insane attitude drives us to deceit, will make matters no worse so long as they don't hear of it. But if you will pardon me, I might suggest that this mutual boycott was in the first place started by *your* father, not mine."

She coloured at the challenge. "That may be. However—it does seem quite ridiculous. Why, since we happen to be neighbours, may we not be friends?"

"The enmity between our fathers," he said quietly, looking not at her but past her and beyond, where the golden light was deepening behind the close tree stems, "has endured for nearly twenty centuries; it will endure for twenty more, or until such time as the world may learn that a Kingdom divided against itself is brought to desolation, and a house divided against itself will fall . . ."

Charlotte was moved; also she was embarrassed. She had not thought a Jew would quote the word of Christ.

In all ways this young man was most unusual.

When later in the library she faced her father to receive the full explosion of his wrath, none to see her would have guessed that she carried in her heart a burden of emotion as bewildering as it had been violent. The countenance presented to her raging parent was calm, almost expressionless, her smile detached and vague as of one who, having spent three hours (or three years, since time is relative and to lovers non-existent) in a world of incredible and exquisite unrealities, has passed into the light of common day still bearing the impress of its magic. Perhaps only to the most astute observer might her increasing pallor have denoted that her blood was turning from red to whitest heat, and that her silence, which her father took to be repentant, hid a process of elaborate hypocrisy far beyond his calculations.

She uttered no word, made no defence before that flood of concentrated fury, until he paused for breath, and then she ventured gently:

"But, Papa, I sent the carriage home so that I might take a walk. I needed exercise."

"Exer—" Anthony choked upon the word. "Are you preparing for a Marathon? You ride each morning—isn't that exercise? I never heard such stuff in all my life. To send Baxter home to me with a high and mighty— Who do you think you are— Queen Victoria? Good God above!" Anthony raised his eyes and voice in supplication to an unseen Presence. "What have I *done* to be victimised—yes—*vic*timised by a monstrosity? You're a mon*strosity*," shouted Anthony, lowering his range of vision to the level of his daughter's hair. "You *look* like a monstrosity and you behave like a—like a harlot. Trapesing round the country on a Sunday afternoon."

"Papa," said Charlotte, ominously quiet, "calling me bad names does no good either to yourself or to me. You are not only offensive but absurd. I did not behave—and have no intention of behaving—like a harlot. Yes, I know—but it was you who used the word, not I. And since we're on the subject," she proceeded, ignoring her father's explosive attempts to interrupt, "let me remind you that I do not think that a harlot—as far as I am qualified to judge—would care to spend a Sunday or any other afternoon in her own society—and I did!"

And having uttered this stupendous lie in conjunction with a speech of incalculable impudence and daring, Charlotte hurriedly departed, leaving Anthony in a state of stupefaction.

III

It was his first experience of an opposition from which he had emerged defeated; his first contact with an unsuspected personality at large in his own house; one that from a dove had been changed into a serpent, who attacked with open venom, and who in one brief but sharp encounter had stung deep. He was both shattered and humiliated; more, he was alarmed. The startling rebellion of his hitherto submissive daughter emphasised a problem that until now, and in spite of the repeated intervention of his sister, he had not severely tackled, the problem of her future and his own ability to deal with it.

He knew his limitations, not consciously perhaps, but with an inner sense which warned him that, if he wished to maintain his dignity and profound belief in himself, he must be rid at all costs of this menace to his leadership. He would not perhaps have put it so, he was not and never had been perspicacious; he was merely a product of his time, slightly exaggerated, maybe, but not unduly when one remembers that the natural reaction to the example of that turbulent idealist who had been his father, must be the inevitable swing of the pendulum in the opposite direction, and that such reaction must occur as often in the lives of men as in the lives of nations. When therefore a few weeks later he took Charlotte up to Curzon Street, he was thankful enough to shift the immediate burden of responsibility to one who, in spite of her advanced years, was more capable than he of undertaking it.

"You will find her no easy proposition," stated Anthony when, Charlotte having been sent upstairs to superintend the unpacking of her boxes, he found himself alone with Sabrina in the drawing-room. "She is obstinate and headstrong, and must be kept in check. If she should prove too much for you, Aunt, I trust that you will tell me, and I'll have her back—or you can pass her on to Clare. She'll know how to tackle her. It is hard," he added in an injured tone, "for a man to be left without a wife, and with two children—and one an unmanageable daughter—on his hands."

"Very hard, I'm sure," his aunt agreed, and over her face a trembling passed that was nearly, but not quite, a smile.

Anthony cleared his throat; he was never entirely at his ease in the presence of Sabrina. It was as if she were sizing him up, faintly mocking, taking him never so seriously as he took himself. "But you can always get another wife, you know." And this time there was no doubt about her smile, slightly crooked, very sweet. "I don't suppose you would find it difficult. You would be considered a good match, financially, and you're young enough yet, still in your prime."

"I'm forty-five," retorted Anthony. "One can hardly call that young."

"To me," smiled Sabrina, "you are very young."

"Well! Well!" Anthony stood up, squaring his shoulders. "I must be off. I have a dozen neglected appointments waiting for me. And don't forget—if Charlotte worries you—"

"Worry me? Why should she worry me?" Sabrina interrupted

briskly. "It is you young people who find everything in life a worry. You are always so dreadfully concerned with the future, whereas we old ones have no future to worry about at all and live quite happily in the present—and the past."

"Yes, but you are an exception for your age," conceded Anthony. "Your mind is as active as a woman's of fifty."

"Thank God, yes, my mind still serves me—and my body," said Sabrina placidly. "My rheumatism is sometimes a little troublesome, but George has given me a capital medicine for that and has told me what I may—and what I may *not*—eat. Did you know that the wrong kind of food has a great deal to do with our ailments? I eat no red meat, and drink no red wine, and I do very well without both, I find. But that, I am sure, does not apply to you. Will you not take a glass of something before you go? Port, Madeira, sherry?"

Anthony thought perhaps he would. A glass of port.

"Yes, we live in the past," Sabrina murmured when, the order given and the port produced, two glasses of the same had been appreciatively sampled by her nephew. "And history repeats itself. I remember staying here in this house when I was Charlotte's age, or younger. Jess Pinkerton—you scarcely knew her, did you? you were only a little boy when she died—a remarkable woman—one of the characters of London—used to keep a very varied company. Byron visited here when I was a girl. He was all the rage. He came in with the waltz. Jess used to give waltzing parties in the morning. I could never learn it."

In Sabrina's eyes the fading colour deepened and a light, as though some distant torch had been rekindled, glowed anew in each. "I remember the first time I saw the waltz danced by Caro Lamb and a young man whose name I forget—one of her admirers. It was a much wilder dance than it is now. It used to make me giddy just to watch. Those were gay times. I think the young people enjoyed themselves a good deal more than they do today. There was not so much restriction."

"You should write your memoirs." Anthony twirled his empty glass between a finger and a thumb. "A capital wine, ma'am—this. Where do you get it?"

"I really couldn't say. I think it was laid down by my grandfather Pinkerton—your *great*-grandfather. Or was it old Sir Rodney Perch—who gave a pipe to Jess?"

"H'm! Well—whoever it was, he knew a good wine when he saw it. May I help myself?"

"But certainly, my dear. Don't say 'May I?'—take all you want. I will send you a dozen since you like it. The cellar is well stocked."

"That is very kind of you, Aunt, I'm sure. Yes, if you were to write your memoirs," pronounced Anthony, upon whose humour, as well as on his palate, the wine was having a mellowing effect, "I guarantee that I would sell several thousand copies for you. There are not so many left today who can remember Waterloo, and who were actually in Brussels at the time. You were, I believe?"

"I was," replied Sabrina quietly. "I saw them go. They went so bravely, singing their songs. Thackeray wrote an excellent description of it in *Vanity Fair,* but it is not quite the same. . . . I saw them come back after the first battle, all those poor wounded boys, and the poor horses. . . . My husband never came back. War is very cruel."

"Yes, and we've only just escaped another by the skin of our teeth"—Anthony lifted his glass—"thanks to Beaconsfield."

"He used to visit here, too," mused Sabrina, "but I first met him at a house-warming your father gave in Soho Square. It is a pity you could not have had *him* on your list. He was a catch."

"Only for his name. He is a far greater talker than he is a writer. If he were not Disraeli his books would never have been read, and possibly never published."

"He was made much of as a young man," Sabrina said. "He and D'Orsay were in great favour with the ladies. They wore such amusing clothes. I can remember—"

"H'm! Quite. Well"—Anthony set down his glass, and pulled down his waistcoat, unceremoniously waving aside these reminiscences, which he had heard often enough before, for Sabrina, in common with all old people, was a little inclined to repeat herself—"I mustn't dawdle, much as I should like to. And if you go buying any frocks or fal-lals for my young person, send the bill in to me."

"Must I? We'll see about that." Sabrina's eyes overlooked him quizzically. "I am not to be dictated to, you know. Good-bye, my dear." And to her pursed lips she tremulously applied a lace-edged handkerchief, before implanting a kiss, firm and dry, on her nephew's proffered cheek.

In that room where she had seen the first waltz danced, Sabrina sat still and very upright in an armed Chippendale chair. She found it less tiring to sit upright than to loll—a hard chair-back rested her spine, which sometimes ached a trifle. Nothing in that house had been changed since Jess had died. Curtains and coverings that needed renovation were procured as near to the original in texture and design as was possible at a time when over-ornate decoration and monstrous patterned wall-papers were considered things of beauty. Sabrina held no brief for cumbrous carved mahogany, for heavy sideboards, and draped overmantels. They harboured dust, she said, and was greatly in favour of the attempts of William Morris and his followers—which had not yet been accepted by the masses—to introduce into an age of ugliness a new aesthetic sense.

And seated there on that late spring afternoon, while Anthony's
'young person' unpacked her trunks and wrote a letter which
concerns us not at all, Sabrina's thoughts went roving. She was
full of plans for Charlotte, and so happy to have her here. Far
better than that Clare should have taken her to Hampstead, for
Clare was the least bit domineering and the poor child had too
much of that at home. She should be allowed a little freedom
now, and young people round about her. But where, Sabrina
wondered, shall I find them? However, time enough to think of
that. A hint dropped to Clare or, better still, to Diana and Elizabeth (one did not want too much interference from a certain
quarter), and no doubt one might be able to introduce a few
young eligible men. One might even give a little dance. Certainly some dinners. It was a long time since there had been any
entertaining in that house, with exception of a few old cronies
to tea, all grandmothers. . . . One might invite their grandsons
here for Charlotte. Yes, she must pay some calls and take the
child with her—let her be seen. And later on, in August, instead
of going to Bath she might take Charlotte for a holiday abroad,
perhaps to Baden. These trains were so comfortable now for
travelling. Life in general was much more comfortable than in
the old days. Although, Sabrina must admit, it was not by any
means so lively.

She wondered what her dear Prior would have thought of the
England of today. Would he have been as much at home in this
new world of prosperity and wealth and ease, as in those days
of unrest and agitation and continued riots—in which he himself
took part? Such a violent young man—always ready to join
forces with the downtrodden in that everlasting struggle of the
people against those who would have crushed them. . . . To
Sabrina, who gleaned her information more from the cartoons in
Punch than from the leading articles in *The Times* (and she

could remember when that consisted of one double page, and was easy enough to read, whereas now with all these long discussions and wordy talk one really found it very difficult to concentrate), comfortable though this world of today might be to live in with gas-lighting and nice clean sanitary arrangements, and tidier streets and not all those unpleasant smells, it did seem as though something of the spirit that had prevailed in her youth were lacking—an indescribable something that was not entirely due to change of modes and customs. It was as though the spirit of the world had aged; as though the spirit of youth and youth's idealism were dying. Young people were not young enough, that was the pity of it! Everywhere a hypocritical respectability pervaded. The most simple facts of life were surrounded by a prudish mystery. Young ladies must know nothing of the shocking practices involved by marriage. Childbirth was spoken of in whispers as unseemly, and men were sanctimonious humbugs who took their pleasures furtively from women of the streets, and came home with saintly faces to their wives. Yes, life had been very different in Sabrina's youth, when wives were not ashamed to allow their bodies to be worshipped in the way God meant them to, and were not less womanly—and not less loved —for that.

Well! There it was, and times must change, and ideas too, and old people must be careful not to grow intolerant. What was it Stephen had said the other evening when he and Clare dined here? . . . 'All ages think their own age is the best, and we forget that youth today will be ourselves tomorrow.'

Stephen, she thought, was looking not too well of late, so yellow and so lined: he had that kidney trouble, and was older than his years, older than she herself, although—fourteen years younger. He had never quite recovered from that financial shock, had never quite been reconciled to his failure. Marriotts', as publishers, still flourished, but he was not the head of it. A salaried servant merely—or so he called himself, and his heart was nowhere in it. He was not cut out for business. He would have preferred to skim along life's surface, dipping here and there to test the underlying currents, but not to be submerged. A life, Sabrina mused, that had, perhaps, been wasted, but no more, she said—than I have wasted mine. We all waste life for want of knowing how to live it. . . . As Prior used to say, 'Man is not aware of his own possibilities, for he is not yet awake. We sleep in life more soundly than we sleep in death.' Or was that an idea of Roger Kell's? *He* had no fear of dying, nor, Sabrina said determinedly, have I. Death is as natural as birth—which reminded her of the pending christening of her great-nephew George's baby twins, a dear little boy and girl. And she was their great-great-aunt! Twins run in families, they say. She herself had been a twin and now these little darlings, not yet two days old! She hoped the flowers sent to George's wife had been received quite safely. Tomorrow she would call. . . . That child was a very long time upstairs.

And rising rather stiffly and reaching for her cane, Sabrina went to find her.

IV

During the course of the next few weeks Sabrina seemed to have taken on a new lease of life. The little dinners that she gave to introduce 'my great-niece—my nephew Anthony's girl'—the shopping expeditions, visits to the play, to concerts at the Philharmonic or St. James's Hall, the hundred and one daily activities which kept her occupied, so far from overtaxing her abundant energy served rather to invigorate both mentally and physically. The old lady accompanied Charlotte everywhere, and indeed seemed to take a more lively interest in the social round than did Charlotte herself. Clare's daughters, Elizabeth and Diana—the one married to a rising young barrister, the other to the son of the proprietor of the *Daily Echo,* Sir Ronald Garstin, who generously entertained for their young cousin's benefit, reported to Sabrina that they found Charlotte 'a trifle heavy on the hand.'

According to their lights she may have been. She had no parlour tricks, she was not at ease in drawing-rooms, she could neither play nor sing. She was not popular with the opposite sex and made no attempt to be. Her abrupt mode of speech and her lack of feminine foibles were somewhat disconcerting to a young man's gallant efforts to amuse.

Rinking at that time was all the fashion, and this Charlotte greatly enjoyed; she soon became proficient in the art of roller-skating, and in the costume chosen by Sabrina (an ankle-length skirt, severely tailored military bodice, and a very small hat perched on a very large chignon) she looked her best, for frills and fripperies never were her style. But, after having suffered a few awkward tumbles and severely sprained her wrist, she preferred sailing round the rink alone to accepting the aid of a partner brought there for that purpose under the chaperonage of the indefatigable Sabrina.

She did not care for croquet and did not hesitate to show it. Once at a croquet party given at Diana's house on Campden Hill, she disgraced herself by missing every hoop and saying, "Confound the thing!" for all the lawn to hear, and finally by throwing down her mallet in the middle of the game and declaring to her partner that she felt like Alice playing with the flamingo. He must find someone else to take her place, she said. To an indignant Diana she made excuse that she had eaten too many strawberries for tea and might be ill at any moment. And to crown this misbehaviour she drove off in a hansom cab alone.

That night after dinner when the lamps were lit, and Sabrina with her knitting and Charlotte with a book were seated either side the bearskin rug in the morning-room that once had been Lord Pinkerton's own sanctum, Sabrina offered a tentative reproof.

"I think you ought to know, my dear, and if you don't then I must tell you, that it is not considered correct for young girls to drive alone in hansom cabs in London. Also it is never ladylike to lose your temper, whatever the cause may be. And in this case it seems to have been because you were playing badly."

Charlotte's eyes widened, but to that questioning stare Sabrina, intent upon her knitting, gave no response.

"But how do you know all this?" Charlotte, after a pause, demanded. "You were not there."

"Perhaps a little bird told me," Sabrina insinuated gently.

"I know!" Charlotte jerked her chin up. "It was Aunt Clare. She was watching and she came straight to you! I wonder she has nothing better to do than to take so much interest in me. Besides, it wasn't because I was playing badly, but because I detest croquet. I have always hated croquet."

Receiving no reply to this defence beyond a mild irrelevancy—"Do you mind, dear, picking up my wool? I think you kicked the ball aside with your foot and it has rolled under the sofa"—Charlotte proceeded like a hurricane: "Croquet at its best is a slow, silly game. And I couldn't bear the man I was playing with; he kept calling me 'Miss Charlotte' and making fatuous remarks, and he lisped and he had pimples."

"Young men often do have pimples," murmured Sabrina, adjusting her spectacles which were sliding down her nose (she had not yet become accustomed to wearing the wretched things recently prescribed by George for closely applied work), "—and young girls too, sometimes. But you are one of the lucky ones. You have a beautiful complexion."

"I haven't. It's all over freckles . . . Aunt?"

"Yes, my dear?"

"I find Londoners very disappointing. I have not met *one* person since I've been here who seems to have an ounce of sense."

"I think, as far as I remember, that I made a similar observation when I first came to London. Might it not be"—Sabrina hid a smile—"that we ourselves are just the least to blame?"

Charlotte wriggled an uncomfortable shoulder. "Yes. I dare say. But still I do think, considering Papa and Uncle Stephen know all these writers and editors and artists and everybody and that you yourself must have known a lot of famous people, too, that I might have met some of them. But I haven't yet. All the people I meet are very ordinary and boring."

"I am so sorry, Charlotte, that you find us so."

"Not you!" protested Charlotte, flushing. "You know I don't mean you. You are *never* boring. You and Cousin George— whom I hardly ever see—are the only persons I can talk to about anything that matters." (Except one other, she added silently, and at the thought so deep a thrill pierced through her that the surprise and pleasure of it left her breathless.) "But you know, Aunt—I'm afraid—I shall never be a social success. I'm not interested in the chatter that goes on at parties. I don't like these silly men who twist their moustaches and say 'Haw!' and 'Hah!' and imagine that they're the heroes of a novel by Ouida. Do you read Ouida's books, Aunt Sab?"

"No. I must confess I am not quite so up to date."

"She is very sensational. I had quite a craze for her a short time ago. But I find that when you've read one, you've read all her books. I am reading a life of Beethoven now. Don't you think it must be wonderful to be a great composer—or a great musician? I do wish," said Charlotte, looking pensive, "that I knew

more about music. I love concerts. I never went to one before
I came to stay with you."

"Is that so?" Behind those uncompromising spectacles gleamed
a twinkle. "Then I am glad we have found something that
merits your approval."

"I don't want you to think me ungrateful," Charlotte returned awkwardly, "but honestly, Aunt, I can't be like all these
girls I meet who flutter their eyelashes at men, and look coy and
blush and giggle. The silly things! I've no patience with them—
no wonder men imagine they're the lords of all creation. Take
my Papa for instance. I'm sure he thinks he's God."

"That, Charlotte, is not a very pretty way to speak of your
dear father."

"It wasn't meant to be. Nor is my dear father a very pretty
person. Now I'm shocking you. Am I?"

"I find you somewhat"—Sabrina cleared her throat—"somewhat
rebellious, I must confess."

"I never used to be so. I couldn't say Bo to a goose at one
time. I've changed a good deal lately"—Charlotte pursed her
lips and nodded. "Even a worm will turn. And I've turned on
my Papa. Yes, I have. I won't be called wicked names and
shouted at. He behaves like a lunatic when he's the least put out.
Aunt?"

"Well, my dear?"

"I want to know," said Charlotte violently, "why, just because we're female, we should be treated like nincompoops—
poor little weak things that have to be protected, which means
being bullied and crushed and made to feel inferior, like the
Chinese who drown their surplus girl babies."

"My dear child! Where in the world did you get that idea?"

"But don't they? Anyhow I know it is a cause for wailing and
tearing of hair when a girl is born in China. And I do really

think, Aunt, that the reason for all this eye-blinking and silliness
that I see among the girls I meet is due to the attitude of the
men who won't grant us the same level of intelligence as themselves. Was it like that when you were young?"

"When I was young," was Sabrina's calm reply, while her
fingers darted nimbly to the clicking of the needles, "conditions
were altogether different. For one thing, England was at war,
and we lived feverishly from day to day, never knowing what
the morrow might bring forth. I think women were more advanced in their general outlook than they are now. We were
certainly more outspoken. There was not so much squeamishness
and prudery—but perhaps that was because men and women met
and mingled and exchanged ideas in a way they would not
dream of doing today. It was the fashion for hostesses of that
time to hold salons, and a certain standard of intelligence was
demanded by the women as well as by the men who attended
them. I was a shy, awkward girl and had very little to say for
myself; but we were not all like that, and I remember I was
often astonished at the wit and conversation of some of the
fashionable young ladies I used to meet here in this very house.
There was a Miss Milbanke who married Lord Byron. And what
a life he led her—poor soul!—although she was inclined to be
hoity-toity and self-opinionated but very intelligent and cultured.
And then there was Lady Caroline Lamb—a most extraordinary
young thing *she* was, but she seemed to fascinate the men, and
she wrote books and poetry and published them, I believe—but
she was not what you would call a bluestocking—she was very
gay and violent-tempered too, if I remember rightly. She was
supposed to have attacked Byron in one of her rages, at a party,
with a carving knife—and she was up to all sorts of tricks. She
used to dress as a boy and go and wait for him outside the
houses that he visited—got herself quite a bad name at one time.

Dear me! Yes!" Sabrina paused in her knitting to remove her spectacles, while she looked away past her young listener as though to some remote and inner distance. "How it all comes back to me! . . . But you see, my dear"—she returned her gaze to Charlotte's, and her spectacles to her nose—"I am speaking of one class only. In those days there was great class distinction. The middle and lower classes were so suppressed that one was hardly aware of their existence, except when they rose in revolt and broke our windows, or stoned our carriages as we drove by."

"Fancy!" Charlotte's eyes widened. "It must have been quite dangerous to go about."

"It was, if you drove out in too grand a style along the poorer quarters. This generation," stated Sabrina with quiet emphasis, "has no conception of the poverty and misery that the working classes suffered in my youth. But then, as I say, most of us never heard of it. I did, because your grandfather was a great champion of the poor and so was Roger Kell, your great-grandfather. He was a true philanthropist. I was always hearing of his schemes and plans for this and that, and I'm sure they did a deal of good; but it takes time for these ideas to become rooted and to grow. They neither of them lived to see the results of those great reform movements of their day. . . . My poor Prior!" The lace at her breast stirred on a sigh. "Always aiming at the stars and never reaching them. He lost one of his eyes in a shocking riot at Manchester when he was only a boy. And he might have lost his life."

"How interesting it all is!" exclaimed Charlotte. "And how I envy you your experience, Aunt Sabrina! You who have seen so much. Fancy going out to nurse in the Crimea, like you did. *That,* I think, was wonderful."

"Not wonderful, my dear, only what was done by a number of other women who felt they might be of some use to their country, and the splendid men who fought for it. And as for experience, that can come to all of us who live as long as I have, even though"—Sabrina achieved a little joke—"I *am* only ten years old."

And at the girl's puzzled look she smiled and explained. "Given my threescore and ten, and ten years over, so that I start again. And now you know why old age is called a second childhood."

Charlotte jumped up, and, unwontedly demonstrative, she kissed that smooth old cheek. "You are a sweet! I believe I could tell you anything—*any*thing—and you would understand. I've longed to tell you something ever since I've been here. May I tell you now? It's a—it's a secret."

Sabrina laid aside her knitting to gaze searchingly into that eager, flushed young face.

"Of course, my love. It's a long time," she said, and her heart was beating oddly, "since I was told a secret."

"Oh, Aunt Sab!"

Charlotte knelt suddenly and hid her face in the old lady's lap. "You won't be angry, will you?" came the muffled whisper. "But I do want you to know."

She felt a hand laid gently on her head.

"It began in this way . . ." said Charlotte.

Sabrina passed a sleepless night. Her mind, shocked into activity by Charlotte's startling confession, revolved in an agony of unrest and confusion. The child had become engaged to be married—without her father's knowledge—and to one of those Mendozas! Could anything be more deplorable? Not that she had anything against the family beyond the fact that they were Jews. And why—lying there in the wakeful dark, she argued—why should the question of the young man's race present a prob-

lem? The family—these Mendozas—were respected. They were
wealthy and well-born. One of the daughters had married a
Lowenthal whose Art Gallery in Bond Street was world-
renowned, and who was considered one of the greatest living
authorities on primitive Tuscan art. Everybody knew the Lowenthals. Their soirées in Park Lane were attended by notabilities
from Royalty downwards. The Prince of Wales was notoriously
hand in glove with Jews. The wealth of the nation was in the
hands of Jews—look at the Rothschilds! Disraeli was a Jew even
though he did not live according to the Jewish rites. And if it
came to that, Our Lord Himself . . .

And all this had happened, most incredibly, at Wroth before
Charlotte ever came to town. In a few weeks—so Sabrina gathered—meeting by appointment in the woods, or going rides together (and was that so very shocking?) accompanied by the
little brother Prior. And why not in Heaven's name? Youth
must have its way, and the way of youth was Love. She, too, had
taken love where she had found it, and for love's sake had defied
convention and authority and had lived the fuller for it. Twice—
twice in her life, she had found and known that blind sweet
thing whose origin and destiny has no ordained coherence, but
whose savour and whose spirit outlive age and memory—and
death.

Nevertheless one must be practical. The child, while she
stayed beneath her roof, was her responsibility. What should she
do? Inform Anthony at once? No! Not that—for she had promised, and besides she could not really face a scene—so loud when
he was angry! Write to the young man's father forbidding any
further communication between the two? No—not that, either.
Mendoza would no doubt be as violently opposed to such a match
as Anthony. From all accounts the family was orthodox, and
would never countenance a marriage with one outside their race.

Dear! Dear! How troublesome the whole thing was—and how very hot the bed!

Sabrina sat up, turned her pillow over to find a cooler spot for her cheek to rest upon, and thumped it violently as though by doing so she might thump away the worry. . . . A stifling night and far too many blankets! Suddenly peevish, she flung the bed-clothes back and left nothing for a cover but a sheet. And now she would catch her death of cold, so she must pull the eider-down over her again and try to sleep for mercy's sake. . . .

It was that moment between night's ending and the dawn, when the first veil of dark is lifted and stars are dim, when late revellers, returning, disturb the soundless streets of a great city, and in quiet country farmyards the first cock crows; that moment when life's ebb is at its lowest, and the flickering pulse of age grows weak and very weary; and lovers, dreaming, lie more close, to wake—and love again.

v

Charlotte, coming early to Sabrina's room that morning, found her so pale and strengthless that she was quite alarmed.

"Are you ill? Oh, poor Aunt Sab! Have you been worrying over what I told you? How wicked of me to tell you overnight. I should have waited till today. You look as if you hadn't slept a wink."

"I have slept well enough, my dear," indomitably returned Sabrina. "Old people do not need as much sleep as the young. I am just waiting for my cup of tea which Agnes will soon bring, and then I shall get dressed."

"Why not stay in bed today?" entreated Charlotte, with an anxious glance at that parchment-tinted face outlined against the pillow under a nightcap no less snowy than the tendrils of hair that escaped its stiff starched frills. "I am sure you overtax your energy. You ought to take your breakfast in bed. Don't, please, get up for me. I am used to breakfasting alone. You ought *never* to get up for breakfast," scolded Charlotte. "Aunt Clare never does, and she's years and years younger than you."

"Your Aunt Clare," Sabrina stated firmly, "does as *she* likes, and I do as *I* like. I am not bedridden yet, and I have no intention of becoming so. I shall get up for my breakfast so long as I have an appetite to eat it. You are dressed early, are you not? It is barely eight o'clock."

"Yes. Oh, dear!" sighed Charlotte. "I do feel so very guilty having worried you. I do wish I hadn't told you—or rather I wish I hadn't told you last night. Then you'd have slept. I know you haven't. Shall I fetch you mv lavender smelling salts? They are very refreshing."

"No—thank you all the same, my love—but I don't need smelling salts. I am perfectly well. And I am very glad you told me. It was the right and proper thing to do. I have been wondering—" With an effort Sabrina sat up, drawing a Shetland shawl about her shoulders. "I have been wondering, Charlotte, what would be the best way to deal with this situation. I certainly think that the young man ought to be received by some member of the family. I don't at all like the idea of these clandestine appointments—and as your father, for the time being, seems to be out of the question, how would it be if I were to invite young Mr. Mendoza to come and see me here? Is he in London?"

"Oh, yes! Oh, Aunt!" Charlotte squeezed her hands together in an ecstasy. "Oh, *thank* you! How can I thank you—*ever?* He came to London the day before yesterday, and we haven't seen each other yet—and oh! Will you write him a note and send it this morning by hand so that he gets it at once? I'll give you his address—have you a pencil?"

"Now, now, now! All in good time," Sabrina interrupted warningly, as the door opened to curb this outburst and admit a rosy-cheeked young housemaid. "Here comes Agnes with my tea. What, I wonder," she said, smiling, as she took the proffered tray, "would we women do without our tea? It is to us, I think, what wine must be to men. Thank you, Agnes, this is very nice. . . ."

Her vitality was such that by midday she had completely recovered from her lack of sleep, and lunched heartily on a Dover sole and a baked custard. A note sent to the Mendoza mansion in Grosvenor Place brought David to the house in Curzon Street that same afternoon, for Sabrina had already decided that if she were to act at all it were better to act quickly.

There is no doubt that Sabrina was quite charmed with him. She had always favoured good-looking young men, and this one, she was relieved to find, had an undeniable air of distinction. Although a trifle foreign in his gestures, he was not at all a pronounced Semitic type. His hair he wore, she thought, a shade too long, and the signet ring upon his finger might have been a little less ornate, but his hands, she noted with that quick perception for detail which had been hers all her life through, were expressive, with long nervous fingers, and soft-skinned as a woman's. He was dressed rather oddly in a short coat of black velvet, black and white checked trousers, and a flowing tie like an artist's. He might, in fact, have stepped directly out of a drawing by that clever Mr. du Maurier whose sketches in *Punch* were so amusing and delightful. He could talk well, too, and entertained her during tea while Charlotte sat unusually mum—to his own views on present international affairs.

He had spent some time in Germany, it seemed, and held the highest opinion of Prince Bismarck.

The greatest giant of the age, who utilised despotism, not—he said—as a weapon for the supremacy of one class only, but as a motive force in the general activity of the nation against all other powers. But he played his game *too* skilfully. By making friends of his enemies, he made enemies of his friends. This League of the Three Emperors was a farce. Austria and Russia were, in spite of it, at loggerheads, and the war with Turkey was only the thin edge of the wedge to a war with the whole of Europe.

"Dear me!" exclaimed Sabrina, impressed by the young man's flow of language and his graceful Continental gestures, which were a little reminiscent of Disraeli's. (He might, she thought, do well in Parliament. To a member of the House of Commons, whether Jew or Gentile, even Anthony could have no strong objection.) "You cannot seriously mean that such a disaster could be possible? Particularly since we have so carefully avoided implication with Russia and Turkey. Let us hope that what you suggest, Mr. Mendoza, will never come about. I know what war means—and you, happily, do not. I only pray that I may never live to see another."

"War, Mrs. Burnaby," David answered gravely, "will always come about so long as each nation covets another's possessions. There is no preventive unless Europe should emulate the example of America and become a United States, and that would be impossible while each speaks a different language. But I do feel that we in England are inclined to underrate the Prussian mentality, and perhaps the mentality of all nations other than"—his smile was faintly ironic—"our own. Believe me, the Germans are not all they seem. We have been taught to regard them as a home-loving, phlegmatic race of people who live on sausages and beer in snug little houses on the banks of the Rhine, play the loveliest music in the world, and provide obscure princes for our royalty to marry."

"Not all so obscure," demurred Sabrina. "The Prince Consort

was a very brilliant man. I have heard it said that he was the power behind the throne. Why, the Queen herself and all the Royal family are half German. I am quite sure that England will always be on friendly terms with Germany, at any rate while our Queen lives. She would never countenance any unpleasant relations with us in *that* direction, if only for the sake of her dear husband's memory."

An almost imperceptible shrug moved David's shoulders. "I do not think—if I may say so," was his smooth reply, "—that in spite of the recent hideosity created to it in Hyde Park, her dear husband's memory would prevent the Germans from making an attempt to attack England as they have attacked France. The Prussian mind, my dear Mrs. Burnaby, has a penetrative quality that the British lacks—a kind of sixth sense, for which in England we have no word, but which the Germans call *Geist*—a dangerous asset to a nation that has a genius like Bismarck for its leader."

"You speak of him exactly as they used to speak of Napoleon," declared Sabrina, who was beginning to form the conclusion that this mere boy, for all his charming manners, was a trifle too assured. "But Napoleon never conquered us, although he was supposed to be the most powerful enemy Britain ever had to reckon with since the time of Julius Caesar—or so I used to hear them say. The whole world was afraid of him, except the British soldier—and Lord Wellington." Sabrina's eyes were glowing and her faded cheeks were flushed. "Now! There was a leader and a strategist—*and* a politician—if you like! There is none today can hold a candle to him. . . . Waterloo! The greatest battle ever fought and won. My dear husband was killed at Waterloo. . . . He was just about your age . . ."

Scarcely a word of this conversation had come to Charlotte's ears. She sat through it all as though in trance, while inwardly

she burned with a fever of impatience. How was it possible that
he could sit there politely drinking tea and discussing the remote
chances of a war with Bismarck—or Napoleon—or Heaven
knows who—when every nerve and pulse and fibre of her body
was aching to be with him—in his arms. Only once had she
known the ecstasy of that unique experience—on that day in the
woods at Cheam before she had left Wroth—the day that he
proposed. . . . No! He had never proposed. It was all so utterly
unlike any love scene she had read in books, or lived in her
imagination. He had neither raved, nor pleaded, nor vowed with
blazing eyes that he adored her to distraction, as did the guardsmen heroes of romance conceived by Ouida. He had simply
taken her and held her and said nothing for a minute with his
lips against her hair, until presently when the green world around
them steadied and her heart's throbbing had died down: "I cannot bear to lose you," he had whispered. "We must be together
always—all our lives." And holding her away from him to search
her dazzled eyes, he told her: "You are all the dreams I've ever
dreamed, come true. I said 'she must be swift and white and
subtly warm and half perverse'—you know how Swinburne has
it? . . . 'Sweet like sharp soft fruit to bite, and like a snake's
love lithe and fierce . . .' And brave and ravishing and lovely—
and absurd. I think that I shall love you more than anything in
all the world, except my music—and your hair."

It was the supreme, the perfect moment of her life. And at the
memory of it and of her first surrender, of her own lips' breathless yielding to the fervent touch of his—the knuckles of her
fingers which twined together in her lap, whitened, and her
small, dilated nostrils whitened, too. . . . From incalculable distance she heard her Aunt Sabrina say:

"I confess that I am not a great admirer of Wagner's music."

Napoleon to Wagner! Would this talk never stop?

He had been recently to Bayreuth and had seen there the new theatre, just completed, where nothing was to be performed but the works of this greatest of all modern composers, whose orchestral innovations had aroused world-wide controversy. This year would see the first production of *Die Götterdämmerung,* when the *Ring* in its entirety would be presented. Mrs. Burnaby should make a point of going to Bayreuth to hear it.

"Well, now—since you mention it," smiled Sabrina, "I *had* considered the possibility of taking a trip abroad this summer. It would certainly be an interesting change for Charlotte—although at my age something of an undertaking. I am not eighteen, remember."

"I do not forget it, ma'am. But I am willing to believe that any undertaking which is possible at eighteen, might—in your case—be possible at eighty."

"Dear! Dear! Compliments *are* flying," laughed Sabrina. "Even though one-sided. You give with one hand and take away with the other. Do you mean to say you guessed my years? And would you really put me down as eighty?"

"Shall we say rather that I guessed the wisdom and experience of eighty," he suggested with artful gallantry, "allied to the spirit of eighteen?"

"Now! Now!" she wagged a finger, and was roguish, almost coy. She had always been a little prone to flattery. "You shouldn't poke fun at an old woman. You've been kissing the Blarney stone, young man!"

"Something warmer than that, I hope."

She found him most diverting and was sorry when he rose, upon those words, to go; but to Charlotte's eager questioning as soon as the door had closed—"Do you like him? Don't you think he's clever? He can talk on any subject. And if you could only hear him play! You will one day, won't you? You *do* like him, Aunt Sab?"—she answered with some caution:

"Yes, my dear, I like him very well. A self-possessed young man, and quite amusing. Perhaps his politeness is a little overdone. He can turn a pretty speech—I'll say that for him."

"And is that *all*," pouted Charlotte, "you can say for him?"

"I think it enough, don't you? I certainly would like to hear him play. We might arrange a little social evening and invite him —and his violin. How would that suit you?"

Charlotte clasped her hands in rapture.

"Oh, divinely, Aunt Sabrina. And will you speak to Papa and try to persuade him to give his consent? We will break the news to him gently and then let him *meet* David. I'm sure, after he has actually *met* David, he can no longer object to my choice. Why! He ought to be *proud* to think that I am going to marry anyone so clever and so—"

Sabrina nipped this fond exuberance in its bud.

"If you take my advice you will say nothing to your father until the young man comes back from South Africa. Then, if you are both of the same mind—"

"But of course," flared Charlotte, "we shall be of the same mind. What a thing to say, Aunt Sab! As though our minds would change!"

"Such things have been known to happen," Sabrina ventured mildly.

"Yes, but not in this case," snapped Charlotte; and the colour in her cheeks now matched her hair. "Of course I realise it will be *tor*ture to be separated for six months, but I know it won't make any difference to our feelings. What really worries me, if you want to know, is not my Papa's attitude so much as Mr. Mendoza's. He will be even more difficult to deal with. Papa will storm and rage and shout and probably turn me out of the house when he hears of it—and that won't be much penance—but Mr. Mendoza won't shout. He'll simply put his foot down and be in*ex*orable! David says he has a will like iron over certain principles he holds, and one of them is that David shall never marry anyone who is not a Jew."

"—ess," Sabrina mildly corrected. "So I gathered However, time will show. These are early days to talk. Will you pull the bell if you please, my dear, for James to take away the tea-things?"

With a total disregard for this request—"If we don't talk now we never will! You take it all so *calmly!*" burst forth Charlotte, on whom David's visit and her own reaction to it had produced a state of nervous tension that bordered on hysteria. "Don't you see how terrible the situation is for us? Could anything be more bigoted and vile and revolting than this hideous attitude of our parents? There's no sense nor reason in it. To have to bow down to prehistoric religious tradition—that's all the Mendoza objection can ever be—and the whim of a narrow-minded autocrat like Papa— Oh! It's no good making a pretence." Charlotte's lower lip slackened ominously, her whole body was trembling. "There's no hope for us as far as I can see. Why should my life be ruined?" she violently demanded. "It's my own life, and I shall live it in my own way. I won't be ruled and dictated to and crushed and beaten any longer. I won't! I won't!" All the submerged hostility of years rose to the surface and overflowed in an avalanche of long pent-up emotion. "I *hate* my father!" yelled Charlotte, her face distorted with uncontrollable passion. "I hate him and everything he stands for. I hate his ideas, and his outlook, and his small petty mind. He's smug and he's beastly, and he's bad—"

"Hush! Charlotte," gasped Sabrina, "my dear! Control yourself!"

"I won't control myself! He *is* bad! He's bad because he's stupid—there's no excuse for his stu-pidity." A great tearless sob tore at her throat and broke the word in two. "He killed my mother with his vile bullying, he crushed the spirit out of her, and he's trying to do the same with me. But he shan't. I won't let him. I don't care whether he or David's father give their consent or not—I don't care, I tell you!" shrieked Charlotte, stamping. "I'm going to marry David whatever they may say. We love each other and we're right for each other, and no one on earth can keep us apart. And if my Papa likes to turn me out into the streets—he *can!*"

And she dashed like a whirlwind from the room, slamming the door behind her with a violence that set the pictures shaking on the walls.

Sabrina, who had risen, sank down in her chair again. Her heart was beating in her side like a sledge hammer. . . . What a virago! Goodness gracious, what a temper! Still waters *do* run deep! She had no idea, but had always heard that people with red hair . . .

So overwhelmed by this time was Sabrina that she was of two minds whether to laugh or cry. For some seconds she did both; then sternly, with an effort, she pulled herself together.

One hysterical woman in the house was quite enough, she said.

As Anthony had foretold, his daughter was no easy proposition.

Chapter Three

I

Greenery yallery
Grosvenor gallery . . .

AESTHETICISM WITH the eighties had arrived.

From Belgravia to Battersea, from Bayswater to Mayfair, the vogue for Beauty flourished. Whalebone and bustles were replaced by sinuous garments of mediaeval cut, peacock feather fans were all the rage: Drawing-rooms were curtained in strange, unheard-of colours, designs by William Morris patterned every wall. Kensington spoke with reverence of the 'mystic view' at Chelsea, seen from the Embankment in 'exquisite Whistler fog.' Every suburb had its poet. The offices of Kell & Wrotham were invaded by troops of soulful-eyed young men, who offered sheaves of transcendental verse. The name of Oscar Wilde was heard in social circles as often as the names of Gladstone and Parnell; and although the Phoenix Park affair created a sensation, Wilde's latest epigram created more.

But such wayside diversions are not of great account in the long march of a nation or the long reign of a Queen.

She was beset with troubles, was aging and was stouter. Her grey hair was turning white. Her dear Lord Beaconsfield had died—at Peace—with Honour. She missed him sorely. That dreadful Mr. Gladstone was Prime Minister again. The Prince Imperial of France, whom she had loved as her own son, had been killed in the recent Zulu War. Her own life had been in

332

danger from the attempted assassination of a lunatic—or so according to the verdict of the jury. But the pistol had been loaded, the crime premeditated, and it went much against the Royal grain that so debased a criminal should be allowed to live.

War in the Sudan followed skirmishes in Zululand, and to crown all a serious situation had arisen farther south.

For some years the Orange Free State had been questioning the British interest in diamonds. The Transvaal Republic also maintained that their rights had been impinged, and the terms of the Sand River Convention broken. Hundreds of British mining companies possessed disputed territory, and matters over there were looking grave.

The disaster of Majuba Hill was atoned for, to some extent, by Wolseley's victory in Egypt over Arabi. But that affair of Majuba had far-reaching results, and the concessions which granted independence in their own appropriated land to a few thousand Dutch farmers did not, as intended, establish more friendly relations with the Empire, but served rather to embitter a long grievance.

Disturbances, however, so very far afield did not affect society at home. The followers of Beauty were still as often to be found in studios, at private views, or strolling up Bond Street to look in upon the brothers Dowdeswell; or to meet Symons at the Grosvenor, or take an apéritif at the Café Royal with Jimmy Whistler.

Kell & Wrotham kept pace with the new movement. Anthony, quick to seize upon a passing phase, turned out volume after volume of *extravaganza* in verse and prose. But at a time that fostered giants—when Meredith, Hardy, Walter Pater, and George Moore were at the height of their achievements; when the young Kipling was using verse for imperialistic propaganda, Adams for revolt, and Carpenter for democracy, we might perhaps have offered more worthy competitors to head our list, than for example these two novels,* although each was a best seller in turn.

It is interesting to note that despite my father's attitude in respect of feminine activities, the authors of both these books were women.

Anthony had not yet recovered from the shock of his daughter's runaway marriage with David Mendoza. He in due course returned to England from South Africa, without his father, who had died from enteric contracted while on a tour of inspection of his mines in the Transvaal. It may be that Louis Mendoza had some inkling of the liaison, as he added to his will a codicil to the effect that should his son David marry out of the Jewish faith he would forfeit his inheritance. Such threats, posthumous or otherwise, were no deterrent. Letters between those two had cemented the affair beyond the possibility of breach. Opposition served only to inflame them more.

Sabrina, who by that time heartily regretted her share in the débâcle, was called upon to act as go-between. In a historic interview with Anthony, it appears that she intrepidly set forth her own views on the situation, warned him that to withhold consent would only drive them closer to each other's arms, reminded him that the young man was as well-born of his race as the Wrothams were of theirs—and that the question of his disinheritance might be the making of his character. He'd have to earn a living now, instead of having it earned for him. And since his love for Charlotte had been weighed against a fortune, such love was worth to her a fortune, too. But putting sentiment aside, it would be as well, Sabrina said, if Anthony gave in with a good grace, since, whatever his objection, the young people would almost certainly take the law in their own hands.

* *The Obelisk*, translated from the French of Mlle. Laure Gaston by Ella Roche; published May, 1882. *Yellow Rapture*, Anon.; published October, 1883.

He replied most noisily that he'd be damned before he would give in one inch! His daughter was a ——. The word had not been uttered in Sabrina's hearing since the days of dear Jess Pinkerton. He would never, he repeated, give his consent to her alliance with a Jew. And as for family—what Jew could be wellborn? They all migrated from the East—or the East End. Rothschild? Disraeli? Absurd comparisons! Name *one* then other than these? You couldn't. Very well! And if his aunt believed him prejudiced, intolerant, bigoted (and what else, pray?), she was at liberty to do so. Each was permitted his own opinion, he supposed. Rubinstein? What argument was that? Yes! And supposing he had called him the greatest living pianist—had he ever said the Jews were not musically gifted? His whole objection was that he did not approve of intermarriage. The objection of Mendoza himself, which he entirely respected, was founded on the same principle. A sound principle. . . . Montefiore? Why bring up Montefiore? Certainly a great philanthropist—had he ever denied it? "But," roared Anthony, "is that the point? Does my daughter propose to marry Sir Moses Montefiore?"

Sabrina held her peace.

"I have you to thank for this," he stormed while she sat in frigid silence. "It is entirely due to your kindly intervention, my dear Aunt, that Charlotte has got herself mixed up in this preposterous entanglement—and from the bottom of my heart, let me tell you, I resent it. I entrusted her to you, and you betrayed my trust. Very well then! There is no more to be said."

There was, however, much more to be said. And Anthony said it, on several occasions, and with increasing violence, his sister Clare joining forces with her brother, while the two young people settled the question, in the meantime, for themselves.

On a Monday morning in the March of 1878, Charlotte ordered the carriage to take her to the station to catch the eleven o'clock train. She was going to meet her aunt in London for a day's shopping, so she told the housekeeper, and would be back in time for dinner. This meal she took alone, except on those occasions when her father came to Wroth for the week-end. According to the housekeeper, she departed with no luggage, but Annie tells the tale of how she came up to the nursery before leaving, and how she kissed the little Prior good-bye. Annie thought this rather strange, for Charlotte never had been one for kissing. And— "Don't you turn against me, Annie dear," so it seems she said, "whatever they may say to make you hate me."

If she had not had one of her sick headaches on that morning, Annie might have been more spry. But what with that sick headache and Prior waking with a cough that had ended in a whoop, which might mean whooping, she was not so much up to the mark as she should have been. She had known of course of all these goings on between those two, of their meeting in Cheam Woods—they'd been sweethearting together for two years, but not likely that she'd go sneaking to the master to bring the house about her ears—let well alone was Annie's maxim where the master was concerned. All that worried Annie was that Ferdinand, the elder brother, well over thirty then, was as simple as a child of thirteen. And with grim conjecture she might hazard a guess as to how many others of the family had been that way before him. To have Charlotte go and marry where there might be something wrong (she'd heard it said that one of the sisters had been put away for a short time) and to be given idiot children— God forbid!—that's all that Annie cared about, as some years after she told Prior when, home from Eton for the holidays, he would visit her up there in the nursery, while she darned his socks and mended his shirts and gave him tea with her special home-made jam. . . .

So Charlotte left the house that morning, and from the nursery

window young Prior watched her go. She turned to wave her
muff at him as she stepped into the brougham. All his life he has
remembered it—the sharp, upward turn of her head, the flame
of her hair under the fly-away hat, the trim, short plum-coloured
coat she wore—of velvet, he believed—the tight swathed skirt beneath with all that drapery and what-not up behind. (What a
fashion!) The fur-caped coachman on the box, the brougham
turning at the bend of the drive, a last wave of the muff and
she was gone.

He did not see her after that for many years, although she often
wrote to him from Germany, from Italy, from France. It seemed
they travelled. They had no money, when her father turned her
off as no daughter of his. He had washed his hands of her and of
the Jew she'd married. He, forfeiting his fortune, had nothing
but a pittance, a hundred or so a year, which had been left him
by an uncle. His sisters offered monetary assistance, in the form
of a small annual allowance. Sabrina stealthily supplied Charlotte
with a bank account, and for the first three years or so they lived
on charity.

He did nothing, but was full of plans. He would compose an
opera, and worked at it for months, then discarded it before he'd
reached the end, in favour of a ballet inspired by the lives of the
Medici. They were living in Florence at that time. The ballet
shared its predecessor's fate, was never finished, and to this day
may still be seen in manuscript at Wroth. Or he would give concerts, chamber music, tour Europe with a quartette. He would be
the violinist. The scheme must be financed, of course—the Lowenthals would help him—and he wrote a letter to his sister Rachel. She wrote back that the family had now decided he must
stand on his own legs, it was no use depending upon others for
support. Neither she nor her sisters were disposed to grant him
any more allowance, nor finance concert parties for his pleasure,

unless he proved that he had sufficient stamina to support himself
and his wife without their intervention.

"Rachel always was a miser," David said when he read this.
"And considering that my sisters share between them my inheritance, I should have thought the least they could have done
would have been to help me in so modest a request. What's a
few thousands to the Lowenthals? To him that hath, much shall
be given—from him that hath not, it shall be taken away. Which
I have always thought absurd. So I suppose now—or very shortly,
—you'll see me fiddling for coppers in the street."

It almost came to that.

They were neither of them practical, had both been accustomed
all their lives to wealth. He, in particular, had no sense of the
value of money. While his quarterly allowance had been paid into
his bank, he spent it as it came, without a thought. They lived in
suites at the best hotels, hired a carriage for the duration of their
stay in whichever capital they might be visiting; he denied himself and Charlotte nothing, but would buy whatever took his
fancy, from a blood-mare to a pin.

For the first year they lived in Paris.

The honeymoon weeks spent there were to Charlotte, fresh
from Wroth, an unceasing wonder and delight. The dizzy life of
the capital enthralled her. She existed in a feverish whirl, tasting
pleasure with an almost painful ardour; each day, each hour was
filled with joy, whether driving in the Bois, or promenading the
boulevards on David's arm, or gazing in rapture at the shop-
windows, or dining in famous restaurants, eating exquisite food,
visiting the Louvre to see the pictures and art treasures of which
David knew so much—then back again to the hotel to dress for
dinner and the play—Bernhardt was at the Théâtre Français—or
(this to her most daring) to call in at the Moulin Rouge where
women pranced about the stage in tights and so very little else

that even one initiated in the mysteries of marriage might blush unseen in the darkness of the auditorium, the while assuming, as did her husband, an air of blasé indifference to indecency.

She knew neither fatigue of body nor of mind. Conscience did not trouble her. London, Wroth, her father, were forgotten. She was supremely, radiantly happy, utterly entranced by that joyous new existence. David was a demonstrative lover; she, responsive as he was eager. They lived only for each other and their own demands.

Their first few days in Paris were spent in buying dresses. She found his extravagance delightful, although she thought the price he paid for everything exorbitant. He did not hesitate to tell her that she had no taste for clothes, "which only makes you more—to me—adorable," he added to take the sting out of his words, and drove with her to the Rue de la Paix, there to visit the salons of famous dressmakers, who to Charlotte's satisfaction raved with French abandon about her hair *"si ravissant."* David had his own ideas on how to show to best advantage his wife's colouring, and chose rich silks and velvets in what he termed *"cinquecento"* shades, wine reds, Madonna blues, greens like the verdant backgrounds of a Perugino, or the olive orchards of Fiesole.

Jewels and trinkets of all sorts he heaped on her—a gold bracelet set with rubies, a ring with seven sapphires, a diamond brooch shaped like a lover's knot with a turquoise in the middle, a pair of paste buckles—these she treasured most—from the shoes of Marie Antoinette. When she protested, "But we shall have nothing left at all if you spend so much on me," he replied: "Jewels are always an investment. We can sell them if we need the cash."

Although utterly possessive, it pleased him to see in fashionable restaurants the admiring glances of other men directed at his wife. She was never beautiful, but love and its fulfilment had ripened her, the immature curves of her young body had devel-

oped, and she was exquisitely gowned. She did justice to her
clothes and David's choice of them, for she carried herself well.
He was as attentive and whole-hearted in his adoration as any
bride could wish, and if it chanced that his eyes strayed from hers
to other women's, his glances were merely, as he said, "the appreciation of one who loves all beauty—in the abstract."

"I am not beautiful enough for you, I know," flashed Charlotte, upon whom his flowery speeches had not always a desirable
effect. "I am not painted to the skies, nor do I go about half-
naked."

"Too bad that the exigencies of modesty forbid it, for wholly
so," he drawled, "you are incomparable."

She laughed, wrinkling her nose at him, not shocked. Nothing
shocked her now, for she was wise. She was experienced, no
longer a timorous virgin unversed in the ways of man, but the
equal in knowledge, if not in wickedness, of courtesans. To her
husband she gave all he asked, without reserve. She was his pride,
his own creation. "A Tanagra figurine moulded from country
clay"—or so he might have put it.

Appreciation of her charms was such a novelty that she was
inclined to overlook, or did not perhaps observe, the tinge of
patronage in his attitude. He would occasionally remind her of
his lost fortune. "Do you realise that your damned red hair has
cost me five thousand a year? If you had not been *rousse,* had
you been black or brown or even blonde, I doubt if I'd have married you." Such remarks caused trouble, as they were bound to
do. He knew just too well how to set her blazing. Quarrels between these two were not infrequent. A word, an errant glance
at some *cocotte,* his spoken admiration of the ankles of a cham-
bermaid, his tales of other women and his conquests—in the past
—which, sadistically, he would retail for her benefit—or some disagreement on a point of taste would start her off. He prided him-

self on his knowledge of art, and it annoyed him if she expressed an opinion contrary to his upon a subject of which she, professedly, knew nothing. The work of Manet, for example, she admired, but Degas, she declared, was vulgar: "Great fat women dressed as ballet dancers, and all out of proportion—just look at their legs!"

David found this observation inexcusable. To describe such grace, such technique, brushwork, line, as vulgar—depicted obviously a vulgar mind. They were viewing pictures at the Salon when she let fall her criticism, and at his soft-toned reply, she rounded on him, flashing: "You mean to say *I'm* vulgar!"

"As you choose to think." His shoulders moved in a faint shrug. "One can train the eye but not the soul of the Philistine."

"Affected nonsense!" Charlotte snapped. "You, of course, know everything. No one else has any right to speak. *I* am an ignoramus. An oaf! A clod! And you are such an *art*ist"—she rolled the word at him with the greatest scorn—"that I wonder how you manage to breathe the same air as a Philistine—or me!"

"Or I," he corrected gently. "You should pay more attention to your grammar, particularly when you raise your voice beyond its normal tone. Do you usually indulge in public brawls?"

"Only when I'm publicly insulted," hissed Charlotte, and upon his arm which she was holding in a very wifely fashion, she inflicted a most unwifely pinch. "And if you dislike my ways so much," she added through her teeth, "you had better go your own—without me."

They were both, of course, ridiculous, but no more than other lovers through the ages since the first pair in Paradise have been, who for love must tease and torture till the nerves of each are raw, till for pity and in weariness they must come close again. But with every repetition, however trivial, a little of love's bloom is worn away; so softly, imperceptibly it melts, they scarcely know that it is fading until it vanishes beyond recall and leaves them empty.

She was the weaker in the battle of two wills. Not for want of strength on her part, but because she was too fond. She knew his faults, knew that his arrogance, his self-complacency, his affectations, were an ingrained armour of defence against hostility. She had learned to know this and to understand it; knew, too, that for all his nonsense he was hers. He loved her with that possessiveness which was as racial as his pride. He was in turns overwhelmingly affectionate and moody as the devil. Her temper was as fiery as her hair and over in a second. His endured. He was more child than man, and for that, being childless, she loved him more. It was a sorrow to them both that she had not conceived. He took her to a dozen doctors; none could find the cause. There was no reason for it. "Just fate, perhaps," he said, "or penalty."

"Why? For marrying me? You regret it! You would rather have had a fat comfortable Jewess for a wife who would have given you ten sons. I am sorry to be such a disappointment!"

He was woman enough to sense the woman's chagrin at her failure, and his answer was all tenderness and reassurance. "You know that you are everything to me. It is better this way, perhaps, for a child might have come between us. I'd have been jealous of your son. I understand that it is worse for you, my darling, for I have my music."

But he was not and never would be, she soon discovered, more than a gifted amateur. He had not worked sufficiently to achieve that perfection of technique which might have won him recognition. He was erratic, often lazy. For months he would practise assiduously until she learned to dread the sound, then for months again would not take up his fiddle except to improvise, or play by ear some *Leitmotif* from an opera. He was restless always, would not stay long in any place. The year they lived in Paris was a record. From there they went to Rome, to Florence, Vienna and Bayreuth—where they took furnished apartments, since funds were getting low, and where he for a while joined the orchestra at the Opera House as third violin, for which he was paid the sum of fifty marks a week.

That time at Bayreuth was a great experience for Charlotte. She attended parties where lager beer in amazing quantities was drunk by students, in flowing ties with sword cuts on their faces, who made eyes at her, and where plump flaxen-haired young women sat on the floor and trilled like angels with their mouths full of *Leberwurst*. She was introduced to singers and musicians with names of world repute. She attracted some attention. David had insisted that her hair should now be worn parted in the centre and loose-flowing, cut level with her shoulders in the Renaissance style. The effect was much admired. A Viennese baron who had spent two years in the studios of Paris, asked to paint her. And a bony, dark-haired woman from Berlin who wore corduroy trousers like a man and wrote poetry, made feverish avowals of affection. And it almost came to swords between David and a tenor who had sent a bunch of crimson roses to Charlotte, addressed 'Lorelei,' enclosing a hidden *billet-doux*—with invitation.

It took a whole week of scenes during which time she and her husband parted for ever nearly every night, to induce him to accept her word of honour that her suitor had received no encouragement to warrant an illicit declaration.

They left for London shortly after that. David had tired of the Continent. So had she. The novelty of nomadic life was over. It would be a happy change to have stability, a home. That wish was not immediately forthcoming. Since the cessation of David's allowance from his sisters, they had been and still were incredibly hard up. Charlotte, who had been in receipt of an income from Sabrina sufficient for her own personal needs, was too proud to give any intimation of the change in their affairs. They were forced at last to realise it, most unkindly, when after three years of that haphazard marriage, they were lodged in two rooms of a back street in Bloomsbury.

It went harder with David than with her. He was in tears, when, newly arrived from Paris on their first evening in these new quarters, the absurd young couple found themselves with barely ten pounds in the bank to last three months.

"I cannot *live* in ugliness!" groaned David. "Blue cabbage roses on the walls—this horsehair—and this smell. My God! This smell. . . ."

"Why not go to your sisters and tell them that we've spent all our money?" suggested Charlotte. "And ask them to come and see you." She too disliked the smell—a blending of stale food, moth-balls, cats, and air that had never been refreshed by open windows. "I am sure if your family could see this horrid place —or smell it," she added with a shudder, "—they would never let us go on staying here, simply because we can't afford any better. Or why not approach Ferdinand? After all he is the owner of Cheam Royal and your father's eldest son, and even if he is a little queer, you've always said that he's good-natured. He might probably like to have us live with him at Cheam. I'm sure he must be lonely there with only servants to look after him, poor Ferdinand."

"A Mendoza never begs," said David grandly. "Nor takes advantage of an unfortunate brother's state of mind to cadge off him. I am surprised at your want of pride."

"Well! I'm sure," retorted Charlotte, rattled, "it wasn't I who made the fuss about the smell. I was only trying to offer a solution to our present difficulties which you seem to find so galling. And I can't stand these complaints."

David sighed. "I am resigned. You'll hear no more of them. I will get some incense and burn pastilles day and night in those silver candlesticks we bought in Florence. Would the good lady of the house object, do you think, if we took down those window curtains? and repapered the walls? After all—if it is going to be our home—"

"My poor precious!" Charlotte stroked his hair. He was sitting on the hearthrug with his head against her knees. "It is all my fault. I should never have let you spend so much when you had so little. I should not have let you marry me. You're only a baby, in spite of all your talk. Who would have believed that money— or the want of it—could be so dreadfully important?"

"I know. What are we going to do?" He twisted his head to gaze up at her with dark, wet, tragic eyes. "I think I shall *die* in this atmosphere. I can't breathe. The air is like a blanket that has been soaked in the sweat of millions of dead bodies."

"David! Don't!"

"And there are almost certain to be verminous horrors crawling on the walls—inside the cabbage roses. Even your hair looks faded here. It's turning pink."

She sat up briskly. "I've an idea! What about my jewels? You said that we could sell them if we were really poor, and now we are. You know that you've insured my ring and bracelet for five hundred pounds—"

"What I insured them for and what they are worth are two very different things—alas!" said David. "Do you hate me for bringing you to this hovel, little lover?" And before she could answer him: "You look like the Blessed Damozel leaning out from the gold bar of— Why don't you rage at me? Why are you kind? I don't deserve you should be kind." He rose and began to pace the floor, gesticulating. "What a weakling you have married! A knock-kneed snivelling swine who cannot even earn an honest penny—a low-down pimp, who drags his wife down with him to the gutter—"

"Let us go out and get some dinner," Charlotte interrupted. "I don't somehow fancy food in this house—not after what you said about the horrors. I shall go imagining things now, although it looks clean enough," she added with an anxious glance around.

"How vile I am!" He came to her to take her in his arms. "I disgust you—I revolt you—as this room revolts me. Let us leave it. Let us die together—now—tonight. Let us take exquisite slow poison that will make us sleep, or cut open our veins and bleed gently away in each other's arms—a very popular form of death, that was, by the way, with the Romans. I would watch your pure white body turn whiter, then turn green. I would fasten my lips to the spot where the red drops oozed, and with my last breath I would drink your life's blood"—his eyes rolled upwards and stayed fixed, his jaw dropped, his voice sank to a sepulchral whisper—"till I died."

"*Don't*, David!" shrieked Charlotte. "You look awful!"

His face relaxed into a mischievous grin.

"Did I do it well? Do you think I could act? Shall I go on the stage? I'd earn a fortune on the stage—a good-looking chap like me. I'd make a capital Hamlet." He strutted to the mirror and postured there before it, repeating with exaggerated gestures:

"Yet I,
A dull and muddy-mettled rascal, peak,
Like John-a-dreams, unpregnant of my cause,
And can say nothing . . .
. . . Am I a coward?
Who calls me villain? . . .

. . . .

Remorseless, treacherous, lecherous, kindless villain!
O, vengeance!
Why, what an ass am I! This is most brave,
That I, the son of a dear father—"

"Are we or are we not going out tonight?" his wife enquired.
"I want my dinner."

"And you shall have it." He plunged his hand into his pocket,
took out a sovereign case, opened it and sadly shook his head.
"One—only one! However, it will give us a square meal. And
tomorrow I will call upon Arthur Sullivan. My father used to
know him very well—I'm sure he will do what he can for me. I
see in today's *Morning Post* that he and Gilbert are rehearsing a
new opera at the Savoy. I might get taken on in the orchestra. I
should not at all object to playing Sullivan's music. It is good
music—of its kind. It will earn me at least three pounds a week.
After all, money," said David, staring at himself in the glass and
adjusting his tie, which during his recitative had become twisted,
"money is merely a matter of comparison. Three pounds is now,
to us, a fortune. We shall be rich—with love in our hearts, a roof
over our heads, food in our mouths— Yes! By Jove!" he spun
round. "I think I could do with some food, myself. Run along
and get your bonnet, and we will dine at Verrey's and crack a
bottle on the strength of my last remaining sovereign to—
'Patience'!"

II

On the 31st of January, 1885, Sabrina drove to Hampstead to
visit Stephen Marriott, who was recovering from an attack of
bronchitis. To be sure a drive to Hampstead was not a singular
occurrence, beyond the fact that Sabrina had not been outside the
house for over a month. A bad spell of frost had been followed

by several days of fog, and she, troubled with lumbago and a little cough, had been advised by her nephew George not to venture out until the weather should improve. She must take things easily, he said, and not go gadding about.

"Which means he thinks I am an old woman," she told Agnes, promoted during these last few years from housemaid to the position of personal attendant. "But I am *not* an old woman. I am not yet twenty. I've lived my threescore years and ten, and started all over again."

Agnes never failed to play up to that little joke as though she had never heard it before.

"Yes, mum, and you'll soon have your comin' of age. You're a wonder, you are, mum, really."

But, wonder or no, Agnes was the least put about that her mistress should suddenly take it into her head to go driving up to Hampstead, particularly when Dr. Marriott's orders only the last time he called were: "I don't want you to wrap her up in cotton wool, but she must be taught to remember that she's close on ninety, not nineteen. She should have at least one day a week in bed. And she's not to go out while this cold weather lasts, not even in the carriage. She can have all the exercise she needs getting up and down these stairs—and she shouldn't do much of that either. Give her light, nourishing food but don't let her over-eat."

Agnes obeyed these instructions to the letter, although to keep Sabrina in bed one day a week was no easy thing to do. After several arguments between maid and mistress in which Sabrina declared she would not be treated like a mummy, a compromise was effected.

"Half a day, then," Sabrina agreed. "On Mondays I'll come down for one o'clock luncheon; and I'll go without my breakfast on bed days. I can never enjoy my food in bed."

"And she does enjoy her food, bless her!" So Agnes told the cook. "Eats every scrap that's set before her, and twice as much —if she could get the chance. We'll have her with us another good ten years or more, I shouldn't be surprised."

That thought was in the mind of Agnes as she conducted Sabrina on that January afternoon to the brougham, with the final warning: "I don't feel it right, mum, that you're going. You don't want to get a chill just when you're set up so nicely and rid of your cough and all. I don't know what Dr. Marriott'll say to me for letting you go."

"I don't care what Dr. Marriott says to you, Agnes, nor what he says to me for that matter," stated Sabrina, firmly. "I've been kept a prisoner quite long enough—with all these faddy notions. And I don't need a foot-muff, thank you. It is quite warm today."

"Oh, yes, mum, you must have your foot-muff," demurred Agnes, and she placed Sabrina's feet in the foot-muff, and then stepped back to allow Frederick to arrange the rug and readjust the window.

"There is no need to put it up, Frederick. You can put it down again at least six inches," his mistress bade him. "I like the fresh air."

"But, madam, your first day out—"

"Yes, mum. I shouldn't really, not your first day out—"

"Goodness me!" exclaimed Sabrina. "Was ever woman so governed by her servants? Do as I tell you, Frederick. Six inches, if you please. Thank you. And now to Mrs. Marriott's, at Hampstead."

Such a fuss they made about her, these good souls, as though she were ready to fall to pieces any minute—which I have no intention of doing, Sabrina told herself, on such a lovely day as this. And through the six inches of open window she sniffed the lovely day, smiling a little at the pleasure of this treat after being

cooped up in the house so long. Quite a change to wear her out-
door clothes. Her sealskin dolman had new sleeves since she had
last worn it. Agnes had pointed out to her that the old sleeves
were getting rubbed and had sent it to the furrier's for renovation. The new fur matched very well. She was almost too warm
in her sealskin. It was one of those mild winter afternoons that
seem to have been left over from the autumn: still and heavy
with a red sun hanging in a haze, and in the air the softness of
near spring.

The outsides of some houses were already being painted. And
if, please God, said Sabrina, I am spared for one more spring, I'll
have *my* house repainted, and new curtains to my bed. And she
thought about those curtains: white dimity would be a change,
cool-looking and clean. And she would have the settee in the
drawing-room re-covered. She must remember to give the order
to Shoolbred's without delay, for it took a long while to reproduce that pattern. It would have to be specially designed. No
shop in London had stocked that cherry pattern for the last forty
years.

And thinking of that cherry pattern reminded her of fruit, and
how she would like to take some up to Stephen. Peaches. Grapes.

Leaning precariously forward she tapped with the gold knob
of her stick on the small glass pane let into the padded leather
back of the opposite seat. The horses pulled up. Frederick came
down from the box.

"Tell John to stop at the first good fruiterer's we pass. Is this
Baker Street?"

"Yes, madam. We've just passed a fruit shop, madam, a little
further along on the other side."

"You can take me there. I'll walk to it."

"But—madam—"

"I will walk to it, Frederick."

"Very good, madam."

On Frederick's arm she crossed the road. What a noise—the hurry and the flurry! Those great rumbling omnibuses and the poor horses—so hard-worked, poor patient things, and dragging such heavy loads. Full—inside and out.

"They should have *four* horses, not two," she said.

"Yes, madam."

And the way these hansoms dashed about, it was a wonder more people were not run over; but the policemen were so good the way they controlled the traffic, and she smiled her thanks to the burly young constable whose outstretched arm barred the passage of a yellow omnibus, a milk-dray, and one of Her Majesty's mail vans, to allow a very old lady to cross a crowded road.

"How kind they are! I can remember when there were no policemen in London, Frederick."

"Indeed, madam? That must be a long way back."

"It was. We called them watchmen in those days, but they didn't do much watching. There were most shocking crimes. Gentlemen would be knocked down and robbed in the streets— and sometimes killed. Garrotting, they used to call it—or did that come later? I forget. The first policemen were called Peelers, after Sir John Peel. . . . Have you ever heard of the Peelers, Frederick?"

"No, madam. I can't say as I 'ave."

"They used to wear top hats and long coats, something like yours."

"Must have looked a bit rum, madam, for a policeman."

"Do you think you look a bit rum?"

"Well, madam, I shouldn't 'ardly like to say that."

"You needn't walk so slowly, Frederick. I can go a good deal faster than this. Isn't the Regent's Park somewhere near here?"

"Yes, madam, at the fur end of Baker Street. We'll be passing it presently."

"I remember when that Park was first opened to the public by George the Fourth. I've outlived three Kings, Frederick, and seen the coronation of the Queen."

"You'll be seein' her jubilee next, madam."

"Yes. You never know. But two years hence is a long— Is this the shop? It looks very nice. I don't see any peaches."

Peaches, however, were procured, and purple grapes, and ripe green figs, and a pineapple, all becomingly arranged in a wicker basket with a blue ribbon bow on the handle. And with these, and Frederick, she returned to the brougham, feeling all the better for that walk.

"Tell John to drive once round the Regent's Park before going up to Hampstead."

"Yes, madam. Beg pardon, madam, but Agnes said to be back before five if possible because of the evening hair. It's three o'clock now, madam, we shan't 'ardly do it as it is."

She looked at him steadily until his ears turned red. He was young and new to his duties. He must be taught his place.

"Is Agnes," she said sternly, "giving you your orders, or am I? . . . The Regent's Park, Frederick."

"Ver-very good, madam."

Clare was not at home when she arrived, three-quarters of an hour later, at the house in Admiral's Grove. She found Stephen in an armchair by the fire in the morning-room, with a shawl over his shoulders, a rug over his knees, and a bottle of medicine at his elbow. His face, in contrast to the bushy white whiskers that tufted his hollowed cheeks, had a yellowish tinge. Thin strands of white hair clung damply to his forehead, which shone with a faint dew. His spidery hands, on which the gnarled veins stood out like string, lay apathetically along the leather arms of his chair. His head drooped, nodding, but as the door opened to announce Sabrina, he lifted it enquiringly; then, recognising her, his face lit up, and he made an ineffectual attempt to rise.

"No, no! Sit down." She gave him a keen glance. "How are you, Stephen? You don't look up to much. I have brought you some fruit."

"I am much obliged. How very kind! Thank you—thank you. If you will put it there—where I can see it. You will excuse my not getting up? This is my first day downstairs. I have been laid low these last three weeks in my bedroom. Clare has gone out. You are looking very well, Sabrina."

"I *am* well, thank God." Loosening her sealskin, and ignoring the more comfortable sofa, she placed herself in a high-backed chair. "You have had a nasty bout, I hear."

"Yes, but I am a good deal better—although I can't smoke yet. My taste is gone. I had to have a hospital nurse, you know," Stephen announced impressively.

"I didn't know. You must have been ill."

"Eh?"

His illness, Sabrina observed with some concern, had not improved his hearing. She repeated her remark.

"I was. She left today. I'm glad. A starchy, domineering woman. Very plain. Had a moustache"—his rheumy eyes twinkled. "They ought to shave when they get as bad as that. Clare's gone out."

"So you said."

"She'll be sorry to have missed you. She's gone shopping with Diana. Her elder girl is being married in a fortnight."

"Yes, and I've had an invitation to the wedding. The young couple called to see me—very attentive of them. A nice young man, he seemed."

"Think so? A barber's block, I call him. He's in the Blues. All la-dee-da and not an ounce of sense. Plenty o' money. Some relation of the Coutts'. They brought me that thing"—Stephen pointed a skinny finger at a queer-looking object reposing on a centre table.

"Is it a musical box?" asked Sabrina, staring.

"Something like. It's one of those—those phonographs. I'll show you how it goes. It's a—it's a wonderful invention."

Another attempt to rise brought him to his feet. The rug slipped from his knees and the shawl from his shoulders.

"Now, Stephen, pray don't overdo it—on your first day down. You've dropped your shawl."

Unheedful of this reminder, Stephen shuffled to the table. The exertion brought on a fit of coughing. Sabrina watched him with an anxious eye.

When he had recovered: "I am not quite sure how it works," he muttered. "The nurse understood it. I think you put this here, and turn this there—and then—"

Sabrina waited. How very old he looked! As old as herself or older, and he only seventy-six! She felt a sense of mild superiority.

"That's the style!" Stephen announced gleefully. "Now just you listen—"

There was a grating, whirring sound, very unpleasant, and then a deep metallic voice, unlike any ever heard, uttered incomprehensibly the words "Edison-Bell Record," followed by the rasping notes as of a hurdy-gurdy playing an air from *The Mikado*.

She recognised it as one that David often played for her upon his fiddle.

"Amazing!" she exclaimed. "Quite amazing! What will they be inventing next, I wonder. All these new ideas. What is the name of that piece, Stephen? I have heard it before."

Stephen did not reply. Stooping shakily he picked up his shawl and rug, and returning to his chair wrapped himself up again.

"My knees get cold," he explained. "Do yours?"

"No. I can't say they do. I expect I wear more clothes than you. What is the name of that piece, Stephen?"

"Eh? 'The Flowers that Bloom in the Spring-tra-la—' " He essayed a wheezy humming and stopped to clear his throat. "Have you seen the What-is-it?—*The Mikado?*"

Sabrina shook her head.

"I don't go to the play very much nowadays."

"You should. Makes a change. We go occasionally. Clare likes it. We saw the—*The Mikado* just before I caught this infernal— I think it was going out at night did it if you ask me. These Gilbert and Sullivan operas y' know—very good entertainment— capital!"

"So I believe. Charlotte's husband has been associated with—"

"Why don't that girl bring tea?" Stephen interrupted testily, glancing at the door. "You'll take a cup of tea?"

"Now, don't you worry about me, Stephen. I expect she's getting it. Did you know that Charlotte's husband"—Sabrina raised her voice—"plays in the band at the Savoy Theatre?"

"Who?"

"Charlotte's husband."

"What about him?"

"He plays the violin at the Savoy Theatre."

Stephen nodded. "Very."

Sabrina gave it up.

"Has Anthony changed his tune at all?" was Stephen's next enquiry.

"How do you mean?"

"Does he ever see his daughter now?"

"I've not heard so. I don't suppose he ever will. He's hard.

Although he's my own nephew I say it"—and saying it Sabrina
pursed her lips and straightened her back and repeated resolutely
—"hard and unforgiving. She might have starved for all he
cared."

"Is she still married to that Jew feller?"

"Of course. She has taken a post—I meant to tell you—"

What Sabrina meant to tell him was not immediately forthcoming, for at that moment the maid arrived with tea and
muffins for Sabrina, and rusks and egg and milk for him.

"Doctor's orders." Stephen lifted the tumbler that contained
the egg and milk and gazed upon it with disgust. "What stuff
they give you! Sickly!"

"Is George your doctor?" asked Sabrina while, again conscious of a faint superiority, she poured herself a cup of strong,
black tea.

"Eh? No, he don't attend any of his own family. Not medical
etiquette, he says. He's writing a book."

"A book?"

"Not a novel. A treatise. Some long-winded thing. He's clever,
mind you. He'll make his mark."

"I am sure he will. Everyone speaks most highly of him." She
helped herself to a muffin, thinking: Indigestible but I'll chance
it. Poor Stephen! Rusks!

"Well, he's doing better than if he'd gone in with his father,"
said Stephen, gloomily. "I shall die a poor man, Sabrina."

"Oh, come! You've enough for your needs."

"That, maybe. But I should have liked to have seen a son of
mine succeed me. The worst day's work I ever did was when I
sunk my fortune in a bubble. I never recovered my losses—I've
been a salaried servant for over twenty years. And I retired on
a pittance. Well, there it is!" Lugubriously he sipped his egg and
milk. "Marriotts' don't exist today except as a name. You know

that Batchelors' have bought the whole concern for tuppence?"

Sabrina looked at him and thought, he grows forgetful. Every time I see him he tells me this. It's on his mind, poor dear. And she said, cheerfully: "Talking of Batchelors'—did you know that Charlotte—"

"The girls and George between them supplement my income," Stephen interposed. "A nice thing, eh? To be beholden to your children." He rubbed his nose, which tickled. "I can't be bothered. I've lived my life. I might have lived more wisely. I should have married you"—his filmed old eyes sought furtively for hers. "It's your own fault," he offered tremulously, "that I didn't."

Over Sabrina's face a faint flush spread and faded, leaving it paler, more like worn ivory than before; her heart set up a painful fluttering, as though some captive bird had been imprisoned there beating with tired wings against the bars until it dropped. . . . Indigestion! That muffin and this tea—so much too strong. And with a hand that shook a little, she added hot water to the cup, and said between sips, hardily, "You've had a good wife, Stephen."

He nodded, blinking. "Best in the world. She likes her own way—now and then."

"We all do."

Silence fell. Sabrina's eyes strayed to the mantelpiece, where the first photograph—daguerreotype, they used to call them— stood, of Clare. A pretty young thing, with corkscrew curls and a bodice sloping from the shoulders—a charming fashion, that had always been. A pity to have changed it.

"She's gone out," Stephen mumbled vaguely, and his eyes, too, were on that photograph. "She's gone shoppin' with the girls. What were you saying about Charlotte? Clare won't have her here. She sides with Anthony."

"I am very sorry to see it," Sabrina said determinedly. "I don't believe in interfering with other people's lives. Charlotte and her husband are, in my opinion, admirably suited. She is not every young man's fancy, I admit, but she certainly is his, and they're comfortably off now—he with his playing. I think it greatly to his credit that—"

"I expect you help 'em out," said Stephen.

"And why shouldn't I? We can't take it with us. Not that they need much from me—for apart from what David earns, as I was about to tell you when the maid came— Did you know that Charlotte"—Sabrina pitched her voice to a louder key—"Charlotte has taken a post as publisher's reader with that firm you mentioned—Batchelors'?"

Stephen looked up. "Batchelors'? A post? What post?"

"As reader," repeated Sabrina calmly. "She takes a great interest in her work."

"Work!" His face expressed a startled disbelief. "What's she reading? Children's books?"

"No." With a private little smile Sabrina looked down into her cup. "Political economy."

"Polit— God bless me!" Stephen's mouth fell open. He was not quite sure if he had heard aright. Sabrina's next words assured him that he had.

"Charlotte showed me a report that she has written—and very well written, too—advising the publication of some book or other on the subject; but I confess that it was quite beyond me. However, *she* seems to understand it."

"Understand! What can she understand?" retorted Stephen, flustered. "Have Batchelors' gone daft? What made 'em take her? I never heard of it. *I'm* not consulted. A woman reading for Marriotts'! 'Pon my soul!"

"Not Marriotts', Stephen. Batchelors'."

"It's all one and the same. They bought us up and they use

my name, even if they don't use me. Well! There it is! I knew how it would be when I gave in. They're tryin' to run it on the cheap with a staff of women in the educational department and a kindergarten reading for their fiction list. Political ec—" The word caught him in the throat and set him coughing. His face went dusky red.

Sabrina was alarmed.

"Come now, Stephen! There is no necessity to get in a state about it. I would never have mentioned it had I thought— And I think I ought to leave you now. You've talked quite long enough." And she rose, conscious of a slight shakiness at her knees.

Stephen spluttered, and shook his head, dabbing at his lips with a silk handkerchief.

"Ah! I knew how it would be," he murmured, and lapsed into gloomy meditation.

"My dear Aunt! I am so sorry I was out."

Clare was in the room. She brought with her the cooling freshness of a breeze. Her face under the *chic* little velvet bonnet glowed with the flush of health. Her hair not grey, but just a shade too black, was blacker than her fur-trimmed velvet mantle. Her daughters would have it that their Mamma 'touched up.' But the colour in her cheeks was her own, a bright enough one for her sixty-odd years, and just now enhanced by her walk.

"How remarkably well you look, my dear!" Sabrina told her, kissing that smooth, ripe cheek. "And younger than ever!"

"Walking keeps me young, Aunt. We have no carriage, so I am forced to use my feet. I came home by bus from Baker Street and walked all the way from the terminus. Diana had not the time to drive me as far as Hampstead, as she had to pay some calls—but as a rule I must say my girls are very good—one or other of them lends me her carriage whenever I wish—although now that I have learned to do without so much"—Clare gave a sigh, and changed it to a laugh—"I want so very little. It is good of you, Aunt, to come all this way to see us."

"She's brought me some fruit," said Stephen pointing. "Look!"

"Delicious! How very kind! But you shouldn't— How are you feeling, Stephen? Not too tired?"

"Not tired at all. I have been most pleasantly entertained."

"You have not finished your egg and milk, I see."

"Don't like it."

"But it is good for you."

"Did you think to bring in an evening paper?" quavered her husband, frowning.

"I am sorry, I forgot. Hasn't she cleared the tea-things away yet?" Clare went to the bell and pulled it.

Sabrina fumbled with the fastening of her furs. "I am afraid, Clare my dear, it is How do you do—and Good-bye. I must be going."

"Oh, no—not so soon. I have hardly had a word with you." Turning her back on her husband, Clare dropped her voice. "I didn't want him to see a paper. He has been so worked up over this Khartoum affair—I thought the latest news would only upset him more. General Gordon has been brutally killed— shot dead by Mahdi's troops—isn't it too shocking? I bought the *Pall Mall Gazette* and read it in the bus. There are placards everywhere—the description of it is too—" Clare shuddered, and moving towards the bell she gave it another pull. "Lazy creature! I shall really have to give her notice."

For a second Sabrina's eyes were closed, the room seemed to be receding in a mist. Killed! Shot dead. . . . How terrible! But war was always terrible. And good men were always killed. . . . His wife!

"Had he a wife?" she uttered thinly.

"I am not sure. I know he had a sister—"

"What is all this whispering?" demanded Stephen, pettishly. "What are you talking about? Me?" His glance, suspicious and afraid, roved from his wife to Sabrina and back again. "The doctor's been tellin' you something about me!"

"Nothing about you." Clare went to him and smoothed his limp white hair. "We were talking of something much more interesting."

"What?" He was only half convinced.

"The wedding," Clare said blandly. "Now drink up your egg and milk."

Obediently Stephen drank it up.

"Good-bye, Stephen, I wish you better," said Sabrina. She felt very tired, suddenly, and over her heart a pain.

III

The same year that saw the death of General Gordon, Charlotte and David were living in a Chelsea cul-de-sac at the back of King's Road. The house—a little larger than a cottage—boasted a grassplot in the front and a narrow strip of garden at the back; but its chief attraction, in which it differed from its neighbours, was its isolation from the immediate vicinity of adjoining houses: it stood wholly detached between two studios, one of which was untenanted, the other the residence of a Miss Millicent Dix.

Charlotte fell in love with the little house at sight. It might, she said, have been transplanted straight from Italy. It had a faded peacock-green door, a sundial on the grassplot; its brick walls had been painted pink, and a yew tree stood sentinel at its gates. Its owner, a sculptor, had gone to live in Florence, and it was to let on a three years' lease. David needed no persuasion to leave the lodging-house in Bloomsbury which had been their

home since they had come to live in London, and the first pre-
liminaries over they lost no time in moving in. With the major
portion of a cheque presented by Sabrina—"to start them off,"
she said—he went and bought a triptych, after Taddeo Gaddi.
Very long after, it is feared, but David was contented and Charlotte, who implicitly believed in his judgment of the arts, no less.
To be sure there was little enough left with which to buy the
furniture when the price of the triptych had been paid, but they
made shift with "bargains" picked up in secondhand shops and,
from want of funds rather than from choice, achieved a monastic
severity due to lack of overcrowding, enhanced by walls that
David insisted must be white—this a protest against a surfeit of
cabbage roses.

Charlotte made the curtains, not discreditably for her, when
one considers that she couldn't sew a stitch. David chose the
colours—terra-cotta, olive-green, and every shade of yellow—and
their united efforts satisfied them both. They were enchanted
with their cottage and named it Yew Tree House. Sabrina gave
them bed linen, blankets, table glass, the cutlery, a dinner service,
and ordered to be sent from Buszards' a hamper twice a week.
"For goodness knows what they will eat," she confided to her
Agnes, "if Mrs. Mendoza does the marketing, poor child."

Mrs. Mendoza, despite the advent of a Mrs. Teagle who came
in by the day, did attempt to do the marketing. Her methods, it
appears, were more original than thrifty, for it is known that on
one occasion she returned without the groceries but with a pot
of caviare, the price of which had cost a week of dinners—and
another time she substituted passion fruit for Brussels sprouts,
and bade an astonished Mrs. Teagle to serve it as dessert.

"What a couple!" confided Mrs. Teagle to Miss Dix's Jane next
door. "Mad as 'atters, both on 'em. I don't know which is worse—
'er nor 'im. 'Er bringin' 'ome what she calls passion fruit! 'This

is the fruit,' she says, 'wot caused all that trouble in a Garden. I
could no more resist that fruit, Mrs. Teagle,' she says, 'nor what
Eve could. So give it to the master served with cream and see if
'e'll go yieldin' to temptation.' Jokin' like, yer know—but she
paid a shillin' each for 'em, she said. And as for passion fruit—
why, laugh! I thought I should 'a' died! They weren't nothin'
more'n a couple of pommygranites which you can buy fer two a
penny off a barrer. She knows no more'n a babe unborn 'ow to
go round the shops. Artists!" Mrs. Teagle's eyes rolled heaven-
wards. "Save me from artists, I says. After the last I did for in
Edith Grove, I says, never again, I says. The game's not worth
the candle. Paint! The smell o' that there paint's enough to make
yer reach yer 'eart out."

"I believe you," murmured the sympathetic Jane. "I ought ter
know. I 'ave it 'ere enough." Her Miss Dix dabbled in paint.
"But I didn't know as them two o' yours went in for paintin'."

"Only the walls and the furniture and my kitchen table and
the dustbin," said Mrs. Teagle bitterly, "which 'e's gone and
painted green if you please—and the door o' the outside W.C., and
that 'e's painted pink. 'Quite Eyetalian, Mrs. Teagle,' 'e says to me.
Eyetalian!" repeated Mrs. Teagle with commendable restraint.
"Yes! and when 'e's not messin' up my kitchen 'e's layin' in bed
till dinner-time or else playin' that dratted fiddle till I tell you I
could scream. Don't you ever 'ear it?"

Miss Dix's Jane, it seemed, had heard it.

Miss Dix had heard it, too.

She called upon the couple as soon as they were settled in, to
compliment David on his playing, to admire the decorations, to
know if there was any little thing that she could do to help.

She found David in his shirt sleeves arranging books upon
green-painted shelves, and Charlotte on a ladder in an overall,
hammering nails in the wall to hang the triptych. That, too, was

much admired. In fact, Miss Dix was greatly pleased with everything she saw, including Charlotte.

David hated her at sight, but Charlotte pronounced her most intelligent and pleasant, and it was not long before Miss Dix and she became the closest friends.

Miss Dix was tall, polygonal and forty, and of independent means. Her hair, an uncompromising rusty brown, was dressed in a bunch of braids, and strained tightly back from a high, dome-shaped forehead. She had a long thin beakish nose, a chin that ever so slightly receded, and her eyes, which were her best feature, a clear thick-lashed hazel-brown, were half obscured by spectacles. She wore tailored clothes of navy serge, or drab, frogged and braided in military fashion, with mannish linen collars, and she actually smoked cigarettes. Her voice was deep and resonant, and she had a disconcerting habit of repeating the same sentences in different words, which rendered everything she said somewhat overemphatic and involved.

For this lady Charlotte evinced the greatest admiration. There seemed no end to her accomplishments and exploits. She had travelled all over Europe. She had been to Russia, Scandinavia, Turkey, Greece—unhusbanded, alone. Brave, incredible adventure! Moreover, she had been one of the first undergraduates to enter Girton and had in 1881 enterprisingly returned there to take a postgraduate course when the Tripos examinations were thrown open to women. She was a member of the National Society for Women's Suffrage, for which she wrote pamphlets, attended meetings and occasionally addressed them. By way of relaxation she painted—not masterpieces but still-lifes—in oils.

It was due to the influence of Miss Dix that Charlotte obtained the post alluded to by Sabrina—that of reader to the publishing firm of Batchelors'. Miss Dix, it seemed, was related by distant cousinship to one of the partners, a Mr. Reginald Boles; and she had herself recently vacated the post of reader to the firm. "That is to say," she told Charlotte, "I was not a permanent member of the staff. I received no specified salary, but I was paid for my advice per manuscript. So much a manuscript. A guinea or so—not more, but I found the occupation both pleasant and instructive. A particularly delightful hobby for an enterprising young woman like yourself. A young woman of independent spirit such as you must surely find the monotony of a household so small as yours a little irksome. It is not as though you had a family to cater for. I should think you must often find the limitations of daily married life somewhat monotonous. Disintegrating. There is so little scope—you find?"

Charlotte agreed that she *did* find but very little scope, now she came to think of it—in her daily life. There was really nothing at all for her to do.

"Yes, undoubtedly you need an outlet," Miss Dix said. "With your husband absent in the evenings—and practising his violin all day—you should certainly have some interest to occupy your mind. An active mind like yours needs occupation—otherwise you will get into a groove. There is nothing so destructive as monotony."

"I hope," Charlotte said politely, "that my husband's practising does not annoy you. I am accustomed to it now, but at first it used to drive me dotty."

"No. I can't say that it affects me so drastically as that," Miss Dix allowed. "But I can understand your desire to get away occasionally from the ties of a home. The exigencies demanded by marriage, not excluding the incessant scraping of a violin practising exercises—the most irritating sound in the world, to my thinking—must be particularly irksome. I can safely say that I have never regretted my single state. I am not one of those women whose lives are one perpetual apology for their spinsterhood.

No," said Miss Dix emphatically, "I can most honestly assert that there is much to be said in favour of the life of an unmarried woman. Take myself for instance—unhampered, free, a bird of passage—I can let this place at a moment's notice and flit," said Miss Dix, taking a cigarette from a case which she carried in her pocket and lighting it and smoking while she talked with an ease and self-assurance that bespoke her independence and knowledge of the world. "I can flit—anywhere to any place—at any time without asking leave of anyone alive. And that's a good deal to be thankful for. Better far, I say," Miss Dix concluded with jocular audacity, "be one's own mistress than a man's."

As a result of this and similar conversations, Charlotte, some time later, approached this new, surprising friend with the suggestion that she should apply to the firm of Batchelors' for the post already vacated by Miss Dix.

She, professing herself delighted with Charlotte's enterprise, wrote a letter there and then to Mr. Boles.

And thus it came about that in due course a bulky manuscript arrived at Yew Tree House—in four volumes translated from the Dutch, that same *magnum opus* on political economy previously mentioned by Sabrina.

It was something of a blow to Charlotte when, notwithstanding the carefully worded report that she prepared after a laborious but conscientious reading of this tome (which it is confessed she found not only extremely dull but almost incomprehensible), she received a chilly communication from the secretary of Mr. Boles to the effect that the manuscript had been sent to Mrs. Mendoza in error, having been intended for a Mr. Carl Mendessa, the similarity of names having no doubt been responsible for the mistake, and would Mrs. Mendoza kindly return the copy by early post.

"Whatever you do, send your own report with it," was Miss Dix's advice. "Let them see how intelligently you have attacked so difficult a subject." Miss Dix confessed that she herself had been the least surprised that Batchelors' should have entrusted Charlotte with a book of this description; but knowing, as she further explained, that the judgment of at least three readers must be passed on any one manuscript, she surmised that Charlotte's report would be used in conjunction with others. Nevertheless, Miss Dix considered it, she said, a feather in Charlotte's cap to have written a report on so vast and specialised a subject as political economy. But if Charlotte would like to delve more deeply into the question of economics, Miss Dix would, with the greatest pleasure, instruct her to the best of her ability. To this purpose she suggested a course of reading at the British Museum. They could visit the reading room three days a week. Miss Dix already had a ticket of admission. Charlotte must have one, too. Had Charlotte ever visited the reading room?

No, Charlotte had never visited the reading room, but it was not long before she did.

These activities, in which he had no part, were the cause of much dissension between Charlotte's husband and herself. His dislike of Miss Dix increased as her influence obtruded. His grievance was not perhaps entirely unjustified. Until the appearance of Miss Dix upon the matrimonial horizon, his wife's interests and attention had been focussed solely on himself. Now, both interests and attention were divided, and he resented the invasion of his stronghold, which threatened not only the security of married life, but his life's whole readjustment.

Slowly, surely, everywhere, in every grade of society, spread the wide-flung tentacles of feminine emancipation. Each year brought in some further demonstration of women's efforts to establish a more just and reasonable attitude to their demands. The Married Women's Property Act of 1882 had a marked effect upon those who hitherto had rigidly opposed it, and the unceasing question of Women's Rights must be regarded no longer as a time-worn jest, but as a future menace. David's hostility to the movement, with which under Miss Dix's guidance she was to become more and more involved, was to Charlotte's thinking not only unreasonable but absurd. That he, so generally sympathetic to reform of any sort, should not see eye to eye with her in this, created a mutual tension heightened by continued disagreements, and at last came the inevitable climax.

It began, as do all such quarrels, over something unimportant, trivial, some careless remark of his or hers, long afterwards forgotten while bitter memory endures.

They were at luncheon when the argument arose, and in return for some biting sarcasm of his she replied with rising warmth to this effect:

"I am surprised that *you* who are so anxious always to be in the swim of things should take the same sort of attitude one might expect from my father. Narrow—pig-headed—and stupid. You—who follow the French impressionists and rave about their daubs—you, who uphold Wagner—call him the greatest musical genius of the century, when half the world is saying that he's a charlatan and experimentalist and so on—and yet when *I* dare to express *my* opinion on something *I* happen to be interested in—and when for the first time in history women are beginning to assert themselves as individual entities instead of dressed-up mammals—you deride us."

"Mammals!" David's brows lifted. "With what delicacy and eloquence you express yourself. Is Miss Dix responsible for this marked increase in your vocabulary?"

"Yes—you can sneer and jeer," retorted Charlotte, flushing, "and throw as much mud at us as you like. We don't care. None of us care. We know you're only jealous—you men—jealous of your tottering position in the universe. You've been gods too long, and now perhaps it's time you realised that we have *our* place in the universe and just as good a place as yours. Male and female created He them—equally—*equally!* Yes! He gave us brains as well as bodies, and the will to use them even though it has taken centuries to learn the way. But now that we've begun," stated Charlotte, darkly, "we shall go on. As time will show!"

David's upper lip curled sideways. "How ably you quote! Do you get this platform cant from your familiar? I suppose you believe every word that's told you by that bitch-faced cow next door."

"Be quiet!" Her ready fire flared on the instant to his kindling. "I won't have it—do you hear? I won't have you abuse her —nor use such disgusting language in my presence."

"Good honest language," David drawled. "The sort of language that is used by man to man. So you, who claim equality of sex, should not—according to your argument—resent it. But if I have offended"—he rose from the table to make her a mock bow—"I most humbly do apologise—and stand corrected."

"Very clever!" flashed his wife. "But your airs and graces don't impress me in the least. And I can't sit here arguing all day. I'm going out."

"And where are you going, if it is permitted to ask?"

"To a meeting."

"What meeting?"

"A meeting," Charlotte said, as cool as he, "of the N.S.W.S."

"Meaning?"

"You know as well as I do what it means."

"You flatter me"—he spread his hands. "I don't."

"Then find out," said Charlotte, making for the door.

"And does your hermaphroditic friend go with you?" he queried suavely.

"If by that remark—which I assure you is not witty—you mean Millicent—well then, she does. She has offered me a ticket to hear Mrs. Pankhurst speak at the St. James's Hall. And if you want to know who *she* is—read the papers!"

With that she turned to leave the room; but her exit was intercepted by a swift movement from him. With one hand he held the door knob; the other grabbed her wrist.

"You are not going to that meeting," he said quietly. "I forbid it."

She frowned. "Don't be absurd. Let go! You're hurting me."

He held her all the tighter, smiling still; but beneath the lowered lids his eyes were burning.

She struggled. "This is ridiculous! You'll make me late. Millicent is coming for me presently, and I have to change my dress. David! Stop this—let me be! You can't keep me here by force."

"Can't I?" He dropped his hand from her wrist to seize her in his arms. "Can't I?" he repeated viciously, as he fastened his mouth to hers and crushed her lips against her teeth with his kisses. "We'll see," he breathed, "whether I can keep you here— or not."

Palpitating and enraged, she beat with clenched fists against his chest; but the more she struggled the closer did he hold, his legs and thighs riveted to hers and every muscle rigid. Her breasts were bruised with the fierce pressure of his body, his fingers strayed and delicately touched: her sex stirred and answered, she resisted—and relaxed. But even as he felt the first tremor of her yielding and the melting softness of her mouth beneath his own, he laughed and—suddenly—he let her go.

"Brute force," she panted, as furious with herself for that momentary weakness as with him for having roused it. "Brute force always is and always has been man's answer to woman. It carries no weight with me—I can assure you."

He looked at her remotely for a moment, then flung open the door.

"Go along then," he said roughly. "Go to your meeting, but don't expect to find me here when you come back. Go on! Get out!"

Her eyes widened. Never had he used that tone to her before. He had teased her, could be bitterly ironic, supercilious, cold as ice, but never actually so rude. Amazement silenced her—though not for long.

"Why all this?" she demanded. "Why are you so peculiar? You're behaving like a navvy. You can't talk to me like that. Do you seriously think that you can prevent my going to this meeting or doing anything else I wish to do—by threats? Such silliness!" she added scornfully.

"Possibly it is. But I am just a little tired"—his eyes met hers in open challenge—"of your neglect of me and of my home. Please"—his hand waved aside her attempt to interrupt—"let me speak. You have said enough. It's my turn now. You *do* neglect my home. You have never made the least effort to learn the rudiments of housekeeping. You leave everything to that hired slut, who rooks you right and left. I don't ask or expect you to be a *Hausfrau* or a drudge, but I *do* expect a certain amount of supervision and attention to me and my merely—material—desires. To all others you respond delightfully."

"Thank you. And if you have quite finished," replied Charlotte, ominously calm, "I presume that I can go."

"I have not quite finished, but you're at liberty to go. No— wait." His hand restrained her. "I have just this to say. That I strongly object to your friendship with that woman. Yes—you shall go in a minute. Keep still. I know what I'm talking about, and you don't. You think you have some knowledge of the world, but you have none. You're a child. A baby. A fool! This woman is exerting an abnormal and unhealthy influence over you, and I intend to put a stop to it before further harm is done."

Charlotte stared at him.

"David! How nonsensical! What *can* you mean?"

"Never mind what I mean. You listen to what I say. If that woman enters my house again when I am in it—I shall turn her out. You can go now to your meeting—if you wish. But not with *my* permission."

Outrageous and insufferable presumption! Charlotte held her breath while she gathered all her forces to the rally, and with unprecedented violence the deluge broke upon them. . . .

It was the worst of all their quarrels. She hot, he cold, and both in torment from the pain of it, their love aching in their hearts, even while they vowed that life together was unbearable. They must end it. They must part.

"For," said David loudly, "there are limits to what a man can stand. I have stood too much—too patiently—from you. I have suffered your temper and your tantrums and your insults long enough. You're utterly impossible, and I'm sick of you and of these scenes. I tell you—they destroy me."

"I see!" Charlotte's fists clenched at her sides, her knuckles and her nostrils whitened. "I suppose then this is your way of telling me that there's some other woman. You're so weak—any unscrupulous wretch could lead *you* astray—any fool who'll sit and flatter you and kotow to your conceit. Who do I know whom you may be meeting every night at that theatre after the performance? And *how* do I know—it's more than likely you're deceiving me—" But even as she flung at him the accusation she knew herself at fault, for whatever his, he had never been unfaithful, nor given her a moment's cause to doubt him or mistrust. Yet, knowing this, for the life of her she could not hold her tongue, but let it rush her headlong to disaster. "Yes! And if you've found another woman," she cried passionately, "then *go* to her. You're welcome. There's no law in the land to force you to live with me whom you detest. Go! And I'll thank God for it. If you're so sick of me, then I am too—sick! Sick of your sneers, your colossal egoism—your bombastic Jewish pride—"

Then, when the pale line of his lips warned her she had harried him too far, she retracted, faltering: "Yes—well—you—you make me say these things. I don't mean half of them—David!"

Too late.

He put aside her outstretched hand, and gave her back no word, no look, but turned and left her there.

She heard the front door slam as he went out. It may have slammed more loudly for the silence in that empty room, or it may have been the wind. . . . It was not like him to bang a door in temper.

She stood, reflecting, very white and still. With all her heart she wished she had not said—what she had said. What *had* she said? What had she done?

Afraid, and filled with self-reproach, longing only for his arms and his forgiveness, for exquisite reunion and calm after this storm, she went slowly to her room. But she sought no refuge there in tears. Such was not her way. She could never weep for consolation.

To Miss Dix she sent a note.

She was laid low with the most terrible neuralgia and was so truly sorry that she could not attend the meeting that afternoon, if her dear Millicent would please excuse her.

Which brought Miss Dix to the doorstep and Mrs. Teagle to the door.

"Yes, miss, she's lyin' down. No, I'm afraid you can't see 'er. She give me orders that she's not to be disturbed on no account."

"But—it's too provoking! I have her ticket for the meeting here —it will be wasted!" cried Miss Dix. "She might have told me sooner."

Mrs. Teagle surveyed her with a flaccid eye. She shared her master's disapproval of Miss Dix.

"I'm sorry, miss, but them's 'er orders."

"Is it usual for Mrs. Mendoza to indulge in these inconveniently sudden attacks?" Miss Dix enquired sternly.

"I couldn't say, I'm sure." Mrs. Teagle's gaze, still flaccid, wandered to the lowering sky and rested on a dark and heavy cloud. "It's this shockin' weather brought it on, I shouldn't be surprised."

And in Miss Dix's face she shut the door.

Charlotte from above had heard the altercation, the click of the front gate, and Millicent's receding footsteps. Lying on her bed, wretched and remorseful, she found that the fiction of a headache was now fact. Her temples throbbed, her mind was in a tumult. As the afternoon advanced, the wind rose higher. It came screaming round the little house, which shivered in the blast as though some giant hand had struck it. The room darkened, filled with shadows, and was cold.

She rose and went downstairs to find that Mrs. Teagle had laid the supper ready and had gone. Then she remembered that it was Friday and Mrs. Teagle's half-day out, which meant cold mutton, and David loathed cold mutton, but it was doubtful if he would be back in time to eat it. He was due at the theatre by eight o'clock; therefore he must be home by six-thirty at the latest; and in the mood in which he'd left the house, he would almost certainly not be back for supper, so she must wait for him

till midnight, and then perhaps another scene. . . . These scenes!
He was right—they were destructive. Why, she wondered, loving
as they loved, must they so persecute each other? She sank down
on the hearthrug, covering her face, and groaned within her heart
that she was bad, was wicked—she *had* neglected him of late, she
had been so eager, interested in all these new ideas—in lectures,
meetings, Millicent, and then the reading of that manuscript
which, admittedly, had taken up some time. But he had not objected, he had *his* work. He was composing a sonata—if he ever
finished it, poor love! How wrong and shameful of her to have
taunted him about another woman! There was no other woman
—she was as sure of that as she could be of anything. She had
never meant to say it, but he had exasperated her past all control
with his cutting cynicism, his smile, his sneering looks. And then,
as always, when her wretched temper flared, it was as though she
were possessed of demons, who diabolically put words into her
mouth. She would lose him, certainly, unless she kept a guard
upon her tongue. . . . But in future I'll be different, I swear I
will, she promised. I'll give him right in everything and please
him all I can. He certainly had been very difficult today, adopting
that authoritative manner, forbidding Millicent the house and
talking all that nonsense about her influence. He was jealous of
the friendship—and racially possessive: 'Thou shalt have no other
gods but me!'

Well—she would even give in over Millicent rather than endure a repetition of these blood-curdling rows. Words! Meaningless, foolish words that drained love of all love's sweetness, and
dignity, and grace. Words uttered in a stranger's voice—one of
many selves who inhabited the Ego. There is no Ego, Charlotte
mused, no *one* person in oneself. I am a hundred different persons
each claiming to be Me. If there could only be some unity, some
singleness of purpose, instead of being swayed by every idiot voice

that screams and babbles in one's mind and deafens the true voice
of the soul. Soul! Another word. What is the soul? Describe it.
We live in words, and in imagination. Through words we create
false images, and destroy all that is real. We make our own destruction. God save me, Charlotte said, from mine. . . .

A coal dropped in the grate. The fire was burning low. She
knelt to mend it. The windows shook and rattled in the wind.
The rain rapped with furious fingers at the panes. What a night!
And David out in it. He would not be coming now to eat cold
mutton. It was past seven already. So she must have patience and
wait for him till twelve. . . . What if he did not come back at all
tonight? The thought, sharp and stinging, brought her, frightened, to her feet. She had driven him away, he had left her in a
rage, and there was no knowing, in that state, what he might do.
Suppose he should go drinking with his colleagues at the theatre
—or worse—in the arms of some loose woman? Having been so
wickedly accused, he might—out of revenge—

By this time she had worked herself into a fever. She could not
now endure the empty house. She would go next door to Millicent to hear about the meeting, to tell about this trouble. No!
Not to tell a word. For that would be disloyal. But for company
at least she would go and talk to Millicent.

She went out into the passage, and found hanging on the hall-
stand David's ulster. He had gone without it in this rain, would
be soaked through to the skin—would catch his death. . . . Was
there no end to all the worry? She flung the coat round her
shoulders and opened the front door.

The yew tree was creaking in the gale like an old woman with
rheumatics.

No light in Millicent's window, and the studio in darkness.
She too had not returned, was dining probably, with friends.

Charlotte went back into the house. She could eat no supper, so she cleared the table, put the cold mutton in the larder, found there some jellied broth, and placed it in a saucepan to simmer on the hob. He should have a plate of good hot soup before he went to bed, and she would build up the fire, and put his slippers out to warm.

All this she did, and then found it was only eight o'clock, and the house so still and lonely—more still, more lonely, for the howling night outside.

She could stand the emptiness, the loneliness, and her own heart's dread, no longer. She would go to the Savoy, there to wait at the stage door, and so waylay him. They would then come home together, and all would be well. And she would take his ulster with her—as a good excuse for going.

Hastily donning her hat and cloak, she hurried out. It was too windy to put up an umbrella. Her hat, skewered to her hair by several long pins, was torn—as she turned the corner—from her head. She ran after it, clutching David's ulster, the umbrella, her trailing skirt, slipped in her stride and tumbled in the gutter. The hat curvetted gaily out of reach, and came to rest under the wheels of a cab, whence it was rescued by an urchin who grinned as he handed her the battered trophy:

"There y' are, miss! It'll do to scare the birds."

She gave him sixpence for his pains, and a grin as wide and impish as his own.

She must have looked a pretty sight when she arrived at the stage door, her cloak and skirt all mud-stained from her fall, and on her wind-blown hair that shapeless hat.

The doorkeeper, to whom she was no stranger, addressed her with the easy familiarity of his kind. "Bin 'avin' a free fight, missis? Why's your husband off tonight? Is 'e ill?"

"Ill?" She stared at him in quick alarm. "What do you mean? Hasn't he come in?"

"Not as fur as I know. I ain't marked 'im off in my book, an' I bin on duty 'ere since seven."

"Unless—perhaps"—she swallowed a choking in her throat— "unless he came in earlier."

" 'E ain't in, my dear. I know because Mr. Cellier sent up to arsk me at the end o' the first act. They've 'ad to put the third violin on for 'im—but that ain't so bad as once when I remember in *Patience* the 'arp was off—and they couldn't substitoot a second 'arp for *'im,* 'cause there weren't one!"

"I wonder," said Charlotte vaguely, "if you would mind taking charge of his ulster. I brought it for him in case—he might be in presently, do you think?"

" 'E might," the doorkeeper winked. "The ghost walks ternight." And at her startled look: "Friday. Pay-night," he explained. "It's easy ter see *you* ain't bin on the boards. Why don't you go round to the front and wait for 'im? You can stand at the back o' the pit."

"No. I don't think I—he would hardly be in as late as this." She pulled open the swing door. "But if he should come, will you please tell him that I brought his ulster, and that I—that I've gone home."

"Right y' are, missis. I'll 'ang it up 'ere. You'll find 'im round at the Bodega, I shouldn't wonder. And don't be too 'ard on 'im," he called after her, "if 'e's slipped the rope for once. G'night!"

She walked up the alley that led to the Strand, feeling dazed and frightened. If not at the theatre, then where was he? Should she go in front and wait till the end of the performance, on the chance that he might call for his salary? And where and what was the Bodega? A public house? How could *she* go into a public house? Besides—David would never go drinking in a public house. Or would he? There was no knowing. . . .

She found that she was walking in the wrong direction towards Waterloo Bridge, and paused, uncertain, on the pavement, bewildered by the noise and traffic, the glare of gaslights, jostled by passers-by, one hand to her leaping hat, the other holding her cumbersome long skirt. A hansom pulled up at the curb, the cabman jerked his head enquiringly, she nodded and got in fumbling in her pocket for her purse. A nice thing if she had not enough money!

But she found a half-sovereign and gave the address to a bleary eye that peered down at her from a trapdoor in the roof. The doors swung together, the horse sprang forward—he was fresh, the evening young, and the cabby well pleased with his fare, which would take him to Chelsea and back again in time to pick up the theatre exodus. He turned down Buckingham Street, heading for the Embankment.

She leaned forward, hands folded in her lap, watching the furtive gleam of lights on the far side of the river. From the low-lying southern bank rose the slender necks of factory chimneys, smoke-girded campaniles, lost in the sullen dark. The new moon, drifting white and thin through rags of scurrying cloud, lay mirrored in the water, a drowned ghost of itself. A gull's scream pierced the blackness. She thought she saw the flight and swirl of wings.

Along Millbank, where some new buildings were in process of construction, a crowd loitered round a giant hoarding that had fallen sheer across the road.

The cab slowed down, the door in the roof reopened, the cabby's eye appeared. "This gale's done a bit o' damage, lidy. I shouldn't like to 'a' bin under that!"

"No, I'm sure," said Charlotte.

The trapdoor closed. The cabman flicked his whip. She heard

him whistling "Not for Joe," and Big Ben chime the quarter.

The house was all in darkness when ten minutes later she let herself in with her latch-key; the sitting-room as she had left it, David's slippers on the fender, the fire red and low. She shovelled on more coal, and hurried to the kitchen. The broth she had put to simmer was steaming in its pot. She placed the saucepan to one side to be heated up again when he should come.

Eleven o'clock. He would—he *must*—be in by twelve.

She took off her damp boots and sat down to wait for him, ears strained for every footstep. But she heard no sound; the street was quiet, too quiet, deathly still.

The wind had dropped as though wearied of its rage, but the rain had come again to tap its dreary tune upon the pane.

It must have been past midnight when she heard the click of the front gate, and ran, bright-eyed and eager in her stockinged feet, to open the door to him—at last.

Not David, but a policeman stood there on the step. The rain-drops glistened on his beard, and streamed from his oilskin cape.

He told her what he had to say with rough kindliness, but curtly. Such messages were no novelty to him.

There had been an accident. The wind—a hoarding had been blown down—in the wind—at Millbank. . . .

She could not breathe, she could not think, but hideously she could see—had seen—that fallen hoarding.

As one locally anaesthetised who can feel no pain but yet is conscious of the surgeon's knife, she heard him out.

He could get no answer to his knock when he had called earlier —just before ten o'clock. Her husband had been brought to the hospital—about eight. They had found an envelope in his pocket with his name and address. His skull, they said, was fractured. She must come at once if she wished to be in time. . . .

She found him in a long white ward whose wakeful occupants

from their pillows watched with incurious, dulled eyes as she passed by, unseeing, to a screened bed at the end.

He lay with closed lids, carven, still, the twin crescents of his lashes shadowing his cheeks, a bandage round his head, and on his face an unfamiliar majestic immobility. Older, he looked, and beautiful, and strange. . . .

She knelt beside him, she called his name. She fastened her lips to his that could not feel. . . . He breathed, but could not hear.

To the grave-faced doctor, to the pitying nurse: "Let him *see* me!" she cried, in her frozen anguish, wildly. "Let him speak to me! He must not go without a word. . . . One word!"

But to that despairing cry those sealed lips gave no answer; no tremor crossed that rigid face where even as she spoke a slow, gentle pallor spread and deepened to the parting breath, as dawn deepens to the day.

BOOK FOUR

GILLIAN ROSE
(called 'Jill')
Born 1890   *Died* 1934

Chapter One

I

From Sabrina Burnaby to her great-nephew Prior J. Wrotham

"100 CURZON STREET
"24th May 1887

"MY DEAR PRIOR,

"I was delighted to have your letter and to hear that you have been chosen among eleven other boys to play Cricket for Eton. I am sure that is a great Honour and I congratulate you, but I hope, my dear, that you do not neglect your Work for your Play.

"I understand from Charlotte that you will be allowed to come home from school to see the Jubilee. I hope, D. V., to see it, too, for I saw her Coronation fifty years ago. Your father tells me he has taken window seats in Whitehall for the occasion and invites me to join the family Party, which will not, I am sorry to say, include your Uncle Stephen who is very poorly, and is not allowed to leave his room. It would be pretty of you, my dear, to write a little letter to him and your Aunt Clare. Old people appreciate these small attentions, and I am sure they would both be glad to hear from you.

"I am keeping very well, I am happy to say, and it is a great boon for me to have Charlotte living here, she is so full of vitality and so thoughtful and kind, and always busy which I am thankful to see, as it keeps her mind off her sorrow. I do not think she has yet recovered from that terrible shock of two years ago, although she has been very brave. She is at present occupied with a working girls' Settlement in the East End, and that fills a good deal of her time.

"Last week we had a meeting here of the Women's Suffrage Society as I think it is called, in which she is interested. She asked my permission to lend the Drawing-room and I stayed up for a little while to hear the speeches. A Mrs. Fawcett, a highly intelligent woman, was the principal speaker, and Charlotte also made a speech. It was most interesting. I did not, however, stay for the end.

"Your Father tells me that you have not changed your mind about your future, and that you are still as determined as ever to go into the Army. I have had a long talk with him, and do really think that he will allow you to go to Sandhurst when you leave Eton, as your mind seems set on it. I see his point, my dear boy, in opposing your desire, for naturally he is anxious that you should succeed him as Head of the Publishing house first started by your Grandfather and Great-grandfather. On the other hand, as I pointed out to him, your maternal Grandfather, Colonel Paxton, came of a long line of soldiers, and was himself a distinguished Officer, so that you will still be maintaining the family Tradition on your mother's side. Perhaps my sympathies are more biassed in your favour, in that I too—as you know—was a soldier's wife, and have been a soldier's widow for more than seventy years.

"You will doubtless be hearing from your Father shortly announcing a pleasant Surprise which I am sure he would prefer to tell you himself, but which as an inveterate old Gossip I find it hard to refrain from announcing to you now.

"And now my dear boy, will you please let me know what you would like for your seventeenth Birthday which is drawing near

—your last Birthday at Eton, so it must be something very special. Charlotte tells me you would like a pair of Boxing-gloves, and of course if that is your choice, you shall have it, although I do not like to think of you fighting other boys and being hurt and knocked about, even in play. I remember that your dear Grand-father taught *me* according to School Regulations how to use *my* fists when he was home for his holidays! Does that surprise you? They did not use Boxing-gloves in his time, but fought with bare knuckles. When you next come to see me, remind me to show you some of your Grandfather's letters written from Eton. They may interest you.

"Now I must close as Agnes is waiting to take me to bed. Good-night, my dear, and God bless you, and bring you all your heart's desire. With fondest love from

"Your affectionate Great-aunt & Godmother,

"Sabrina H. Burnaby."

*Extracts from a letter from Anthony Wrotham
to his son Prior J. Wrotham*

". . . I may have been too optimistic in hoping for University honours from you—a hope, which, judging by this last year's school reports here before me while I write—could never by any wildest bounds of the imagination have been fulfilled. Any dis-tinction you might have gained at Oxford would have begun and ended—as far as I can see—with a cricket bat.

"You will of course need a coach when you leave Eton. You will never, otherwise, scrape through even so elementary an examina-tion as the entry for Sandhurst. To this purpose, therefore, I am already in negotiation with a Rev. Mr. Farthing at whose house in Lowestoft you will take a holiday course beginning the first week in August.

"I am sorry to deprive you of the promised trip to Scotland, but I have now in view other plans for myself this summer.

"I am coming down next Sunday to see you, and will bring with me a lady whose acquaintance I am anxious you should make. I may as well tell you now what will shortly be publicly announced, that I intend to marry again.

"You have already decided your own career in direct opposition to the future I have planned for you—a career which will of necessity take you far away from me, abroad, India, the Malay—Heaven knows where. Your sister was a stranger to me for seven years, and even though I offered her a home and my ready pardon for the incalculable folly of that marriage for which she paid so sad a price, she chooses to live apart from me rather than under my roof.

"In these circumstances, therefore, I cannot but feel that, deprived as I am of the companionship of my son and daughter, I am entitled to a substitute, who by virtue of her youth and charm will lighten my declining years and fill that gap in my life which has for so long been empty.

"I trust that you will conduct yourself in as gracious a manner as possible when you meet Mrs. Montgomery, my future wife, and I have not the smallest doubt but that you will be delighted with my choice.

"I send herewith an advance copy of our Royal Jubilee production 'From Churchyard to Soho' (with preface by myself) giving a history of the firm's activities from its commencement in 1820 until the present day. I have found my Aunt Sabrina's reminiscences of great value, particularly certain letters (carefully abridged) which she has permitted me to publish written by my father to her, during his incarceration at Manchester—when he was recovering from injuries sustained in the Peterloo Riots.

Although I must confess that his revolutionary views do not re-dound to his credit, they emphasise the striking contrast between those days of violence and upheaval, and the imperial solidity of our own. . . ."

And in that golden decade between Victoria's two jubilees and Salisbury's two ministries, a triumphant epoch reached its culmination. It was an era of creative interest, new thought, new hope, new action; of emotional experiment on the one hand, and unexampled progress and development on the other. All strata of society were embued with a staggering sense of freedom. The cage door of convention was burst open, and Respectability re-treated—fingers to shocked ears—before the echo of the century's mad swan-song: 'Ta-ra-ra-boom-de-ay!'

The backwash of aestheticism left over from the eighties was caught up in an exotic spume of *fin-de-siècle* verse and song and colour, that completely drowned the anaemic dialectics of the previous ten years.

Dorian Gray appeared, and *The Green Carnation;* minor poets budded to bloom within the pages of the *Yellow Book* and the *Savoy;* Alfred Harmsworth offered journalism's tribute to popular sensation and produced the *Daily Mail* for a ha'penny. Gaslight was extinguished in the glare of electricity; the safety bicycle arrived, and the first telephone. The music-halls, theatres, and restaurants responded to the cry for 'madder music, stronger wine.' The Englishman dined out—his house had ceased to be his castle; no longer did he take his pleasures sadly.

But in the midst of change and movement, that aged matriarch whose homely, white-haired presence in its widow's weeds em-bodied for her subjects the undying spirit of imperialism, re-mained changeless and unmoved.

Anthony's second wife, Edith, whom he married in August,

'87, was the widow of a captain in the Queen's Own Rifles who had been killed in the Gordon Relief Expedition.

Nearly thirty years his junior, a vivacious sprightly blonde, she was the very antithesis of the gentle creature she succeeded.

"I am sure," my sister wrote to me shortly after the marriage, "that in her, Papa has met his match. She will stand no nonsense. She realises what our poor sweet mother never realised, that Papa is nothing but a spoiled child, and cannot even at his most serious, be taken seriously.

"I must say that I think he is happier now than he has ever been, if his change of front from sour to saccharine can be taken as criterion. Poor Papa! I am sure that in his own peculiar way he loves us both. I shall never forget how when David died he made the first advance and approached me with overtures of peace—which must have cost him agonies of pride. I always feel with Papa, as with many other people, myself included, that his mind is twisted up in knots, which if unravelled would reveal an entirely different nature to the one presented to the world (or to ourselves if we could only know ourselves). If only by some process of dissection—as for instance a chemist who can define the composition of certain matters and divide those that are harmful from those that are good—if as I say, there were some process by which the machinery of human nature could be similarly divided, one would find that not only are we none of us what we seem to be, but that we are suffering from some deep-seated *malaise,* that can only be cured by the uprooting of the cause. Does all this sound exhaustingly involved? I have lately been reading Kant, and the mental acrobatics to which in consequence my brain has been submitted, must be my excuse for metaphysical discussion! Do you remember when last holidays you discovered his 'Critique of Pure Reason' in the library, how excited you were to find our grandfather's pencilled comments scrawled all over the margins—dated 1812? He must have been about your age. Did you ever finish it?

"To return to our muttons (or should one more gallantly say lamb?), I personally find our 'Edie' quite delightful. She is so utterly ingenuous and completely lacking in guile, for all her absurd little affectations—which really I do not think are affectations at all, but are as part and parcel of herself as her frills, her banjo, her chitter-chatter and her love-birds—to which, surprisingly, Papa takes no exception. He permits her a free hand in all the renovations. When you come home for the Christmas holidays you will find some startling changes. The drawing-room ceiling has been redecorated in a Leightonian design of cupids scattering roses at the feet of a stout Venus, while heads of seraphim beam along the cornice, and Della Robbia plaques, manufactured, I fear, in Birmingham, are festooned along the walls. New upholstery and curtains in salmon pink and olive green replace those chosen by our mother, and in every corner stands a Japanese vase containing pampas grass, bulrushes, and flowers in and out of season, while every cushion sports a ribbon-bow. The ante-room has been transformed into a boudoir in powder blue and yellow, with fancy goods and ornaments and novelties enough to re-stock the Lowther Arcade!

"Papa periodically issues a formal invitation—in the nature of a royal command—that I shall live at Wroth—(he strongly disapproves of my interest in the N.S.W.S.,) but I firmly insist that while Aunt Sab lives I shall remain with her here. She would be very lonely now if I were to leave her, and for how much longer can we hope to have her with us? . . ."

How long indeed? She had outlived her generation; she had outlived Stephen Marriott, who died in '88, the year that Laurence,

Anthony's younger son, was born. And she lived to see the birth of yet another of Wroth's women, Gillian Rose (called 'Jill'), in 1890.

II

I think that neither of my father's children by his first wife ever held the same place in his affections as those two of his later years by Edith—known as 'Edie.' She introduced abbreviations to all our names at Wroth. She captured all our hearts. She was as artless as her babies, gay and laughter-loving, plump. Her hair, gold-tinted, *too* gold-tinted if the truth be known, curled absurdly round her over-powdered little face. It was a source of never-ending wonder to us—and all the family—to see the way she led our father, as Charlotte put it, 'on a string.' His preposterous dignity, his stilted airs, were lost on her. She called him 'To-to.'

Charlotte was 'Charlie'—I was 'Pete.' Laurence, her first-born, became 'Larry' from the month. She adored her babies and her husband, and I think she adored us, but she was very given to superlatives. We never knew her age. She told us when she married she was thirty, but she might equally well have been eighteen or forty-five. She wore ridiculous childish clothes, and was so adorned with fal-lals, charms, necklaces and bangles that she seemed to tinkle every time she moved.

She had not been married three months before she found Wroth much too slow—'a mausoleum,' so she said, 'in winter'—and established herself and Anthony, who offered no demur, in Queen Anne Mansions, one of the first blocks of modern flats in London.

Wroth was deserted except during the summer months, when, after her babies were born, she entertained week-end visitors, who may or may not have met with Anthony's approval. They certainly met with mine.

Lawn tennis was just then becoming popular. Two tennis courts had been recently constructed—and the grounds echoed with maidenly shrieks and the swish of petticoats, for even in those progressive nineties, ladies did not prance about in shorts to pat a ball across a net, but wore garden-party frocks or, the most venturesome perhaps, a long and stiff-starched piqué skirt with shirt-blouse and linen collar.

In the evenings there would be impromptu dances in the hall, and Edie would play the banjo and sing "The Gay Tomtit" sitting cross-legged on a settee like a Turk, while all the visitors—in particular the gentlemen—applauded, and Anthony would retire to his study in a state, reserving for Monday morning, when the guests had all departed, his opinion of his wife's behaviour.

Was it necessary—he wished to know—to adopt these unbecoming postures when displaying her talent for musical comedy as expressed by the twanging of an instrument imported from the cotton fields of Alabama?

To which she would retort, "How *too* utterly obscure! *Must* you be so elephantine?" and at his shocked raised eyebrows would scream with laughter and tell him: "To-to! You'll make me die! You're so solemn! Why are you so solemn? What a cross-patch—what a face! Pete"—to me—"isn't he a cross-patch? Did *you* think my attitude so unbecoming? Did I show my ankles? How frightful! Oh, dear! We're not amused!" And with her finger to her lips she would tiptoe from the room, leaving me to face the music—*basso-profundo*.

She was in greatest favour with Sabrina, and nothing gave the old lady more pleasure than to go driving with Edie in the Park to hear the latest gossip, and of the gay doings down at Wroth. Two new bathrooms had been recently installed, and incandescent light—Anthony had rejected the idea of electricity. "However," Edie said, "one must go slowly. One thing at a time. He is only just beginning to accept my banjo." And Sabrina laughed until she cried when she was told how Prior and Edie, at the Christmas party held at Wroth for the village children, had dressed up as nigger minstrels, and blacked their faces, so that even Anthony had not recognised his wife and son. "But when he did," said Edie plaintively, "he raised the roof."

"Oh, my!" Sabrina wiped her eyes. "What a shock to the poor man! Did you wear trousers?"

"Well, no—but for two pins I would have. I had a red and white striped—very short—cotton skirt, and Prior wore white ducks, and played the bones, and I the 'jo. A young friend of his from Sandhurst who was spending Christmas with us, played the tambourine. The children loved it. Next Christmas Day we shall repeat the performance. And you, Auntie, must be there to see it."

"If I'm spared," Sabrina said. "And why should I not, indeed? I'm only twenty-five."

The old joke still endured, and there were times when she really did believe that the best part of a century lay before and not behind her; times when the past became the present, and she was still young John Burnaby's young wife. I stayed with her at Curzon Street on several occasions when up from Sandhurst, and it was then that I slowly pieced together her life story and Charlotte's, and more perhaps of Clare's and her own part in it than she may have realised.

When I went to say good-bye to her before I left for India, she handed me as a farewell gift those most precious letters of her husband's written on the field of Waterloo. "From a soldier to a soldier," she told me with her lovely crooked smile, that seemed always to hold the mellowed radiance of sunlight on worn stone.

"Keep them safe, and treasure them. They may be of interest to you and those that follow you, my dear. I would so much rather you have them, than that when I go they should be lost—or thrown away. I had thought to write instructions in my will that they should be buried with me, but that, I think, is selfish. They are of historical value, now, you see. An eyewitness's account. I know them all by heart—and he is so always with me that I don't need his written word."

For to her the days passed softly as the nights in dreams, so impregnated with the past that the present lay suspended between two worlds, and time stood by, unhurried, hushed and waiting, as the hush of a still winter waits for spring.

And yet there was so much of interest to bind her close to life: Anthony's amusing, gay young Edie, and the dear babies— who would have thought that Anthony would start another family at his age? Although he was no age at all, only just sixty. And apart from Anthony and his wife, there were Charlotte's friends, so bright and entertaining, and all so up to date, yet glad enough, seemingly, to take a cup of tea with an old fogy like herself. One who visited at Curzon Street from time to time was a lady doctor from the staff of the London School of Medicine, and another, a Miss Dix, who gave lectures, and wore odd, tailored, gentlemanly clothes, and smoked cigarettes—"Do you mind, Mrs. Burnaby?"

"Not I, my dear! I've seen worse than that in my time. I've seen a lady taking snuff—we weren't so particular."

And then sometimes there would be meetings in the drawing-room with the young women getting up to speak on this incessant suffrage, and what a business that was to be sure! Making all this fuss demanding equal rights with men. In Sabrina's day there was never such a question raised. Women took their rights for granted. "Which was more than balanced in *our* favour," she told Charlotte. "We didn't ask to stand for Parliament, or vote, but we had our say in Parliamentary matters just the same. Why, it was the women of my day who *made* the politicians, who could put them into office or out of it—by crooking a little finger. There were at least six lady patronesses of Almack's Club —and how my dear Jess ever got herself elected, I never knew. I expect Sir Rodney Perch—they were the closest friends—pulled a string or two. Yes, it was most select. Many of the nobility of England were excluded, and I remember Jess telling me a story how one night the Duke of Wellington himself was turned away because he arrived a few minutes late—none were allowed admission after eleven o'clock. And that was by order of the lady patronesses—*not* the gentlemen. Lady Jersey ruled the roost at Almack's. She introduced to London the quadrille. She brought it over here from France—before the waltz. It was not until our Queen came to the throne that women began to follow her example and pay more attention to their homes and their own husbands than to other women's! And so soon as they did *that*— men gained the upper hand. I'm not so sure that they're the better for it."

She would often talk in this strain, her memory as clear as it had always been, offering advice where it was needed, bound up in the lives of others and interested in all the family's affairs as retailed by Clare, who called regularly once a week with flowers —very charming and attentive, always busy. Clare was a great-grandmother now, and there was further talk of weddings. Elizabeth's elder boy was marrying in June. Poor Stephen had not lived to see the marriage of his grandson. That was sad—if death could be called sad. . . . And George—how proud they were of George, who had been recently appointed Physician-in-Ordinary to a very Royal Person. . . . And then there were letters from young Prior in India each month, for he never missed a

mail. Yes, life was full of compensations for so much that one
had lost. God was very good—if God, as Miss Jeans (how long
ago!) had taught her to believe, existed. Her dear Prior had been
so very sceptical and now, when he and all those dear ones from
the past lived with her, hand in hand, one was often in a puzzle
as to what was, and what was not, or would be—hereafter.

Charlotte only recently had asked her: "You, Aunt, who are
so wise, and have seen so much, and should know all that life can
teach us—do you believe in God, or is He, too, a myth? Science
accounts for the Creator in such a cold hard way. I long to feel
the truth of something warmer."

"And—do I believe?" she answered quietly. "I wish I knew! I
wish I knew how much is truth and how much the longing for
it. Your grandfather was a sceptic—almost, I fear, an atheist—and
the talks we used to have together sometimes instilled doubts in
me; and yet—he lived according to his lights, which were more
Christian than many Christians I have known. God the Father,
God the Son—friendship, fraternity—that was his password. But
God—as we are taught to know and fear Him—who can say?
Not all those who go to church are godly. Each builds his own
God—in himself, I think. To try always to be good—so far as
one can in a world of trouble—and to be kindly, and charitable
towards others, and tolerant, seems to me as fair a creed as any.
I say my prayers to God; I say them every night and morning,
and I like to think that I am heard—although your dear grand-
father used to say that prayer was a sign of weakness.

"But the longer that I live—and so far beyond my time—the
more I seem to see a wisdom and a plan in everything: in flowers,
in the seasons as they come and go, just as life comes and goes.
So that I often think—that if each year a crocus blooms again—
how can it be possible that the human soul should fade out of
existence and out of His care who made us in His Image? This,

my dear, may sound old-womanish sentiment to you who hold
such advanced views on all sorts of subjects; but, to me, it's common sense."

She recalled that talk with Charlotte when on a certain mild
February afternoon she lay dozing on her couch by the fire in
the room where she had seen the first waltz danced. Agnes had
made her comfortable with cushions at her head and a hot water-
bottle at her toes, and left her there to take her customary nap
before tea-time. And it may be that, as she lay drowsing in that
timeless void which for the very old passes their time away, the
cloud of memories that clustered round her pressed too heavily,
and brought a pain about her heart.

She may have thought of many things, of love, and youth, and
beauty; of a rose-shaded mask; of a boy's laughter, and a woman's tears. Of those dead, and of those living who had filled the
long years so richly. Of Clare, of Charlotte, of the lad in India
named for those two whom most in all her life she'd loved. Of a
pair of tiny socks, knitted by herself and reposing in the top
drawer of the bureau, to be presented that very afternoon when
Edie should arrive, who had promised to bring the six-months-
old baby Jill to see her.

That would be soon and she must be ready to receive them.
She hoped the room was not too close and airless for the baby.
Why was it that these good souls, her servants, never would
allow her enough air? Air was life. . . . That window must be
opened wider.

Rising from her sofa, she crossed the room, not very steadily
for always, when she stood upright after lying down, she felt a
little giddy with a sound as of a buzzing in her ears. She hoped
she was not going deaf—old people did sometimes, but she had
not bothered to tell George, for the less one talked about one's
ailments the better. So she went over to the window and reso-

lutely lifted the lower sash, which was rather stiff and needed quite a lot of strength to raise it up—she must remember to tell Frederick to see to it. And what a rumpus there would be—she chuckled to herself—if Frederick should come in at that moment and catch her opening the window! Now it was done, and the buzzing in her ears was silent. She thought the air smelled sweet of lime-blossom and new-mown hay—a strange delicious smell for London. . . . A slight breeze stirred the silvery white hair that framed her ivory pallor in which the features were a little blurred, a little indistinct as the shadows of an old, old painting; but those eyes beneath their wrinkled lids held a clear, startling brilliance.

And looking down upon that quiet street where so often and in secret she had crept from this same house to meet her John, it may be that some trick of light, some fancy took her, and it was as if she saw him standing as he had always stood beside a shining water with the sunlight on his face. She may have thought she heard him call, "I'm here, my Dawn. . . ."

But when she looked again the street was empty.

She went back to her sofa, and lay there with closed eyes, her hands across her breast, her frail finger-tips just touching the Mechlin at her bodice where her heart was busy with an eager, fierce excitement. . . . Soon she was drowsy and must sleep.

And while she slept her head sank lower, and she smiled in her dreams and did not stir when Agnes came to call her.

Nor did she wake.

III

Jill was in her cradle when I went with my regiment to India. She was five when I returned at the time of the Jameson Raid, which most sorry business at one stroke destroyed Rhodes' life-

long policy of conciliation with the Dutch and brought to a head
the simmering antagonism against the British that for nearly
thirty years had prevailed throughout the Transvaal. More too
than that. It set the red-herring of German sympathy with Kruger
trailing across Europe to bring the first warning savour of more
sinister events to an age of peace and harmony.

Then came the reconquest of the Sudan, Kitchener at Khartoum and I sent home from Omdurman, shot by a Dervish
sniper—on six months' leave to Wroth.

Jill was about eight then, and Larry rising ten, in his first term
at a prep school down at Hastings.

Their father had little enough to say in the matter of their up-
bringing. Edie in her own way saw to that. He, at seventy, was
too old to be bothered with the racket of children round him—
keep them out of sight and quiet when he was down at Wroth,
was all he asked. So Edie petted and spoiled them to her heart's
content and theirs, and the irascible old man who was their
father hardly counted in their youthful scheme of things more
than did their brother Pete or Charlotte.

Larry said that Charlie was 'a little bit off the top'—and Jill,
who agreed with him in most things, thought the same. Charlie
wore awful hideous old clothes, and her red untidy hair, streaked
yellowish grey in patches, was bundled up all anyhow behind.
She would visit Wroth to stay perhaps one night and then not
come again for months, and just when they had forgotten her
existence she would turn up, always in a hurry and never empty-
handed. But the presents that she brought them were invariably
by some mischance just what they *didn't* want, though they
thanked her very kindly all the same.

The time that poor old Annie died was Jill's first clear memory
of her big brother Pete.

And Annie's death was Jill's first sorrow.

Annie, it seemed, had been Pete's and Charlie's Nannie, too, which was surprising, for who could have believed her all that old—or that a grown-up brother with a moustache could have ever had a Nannie! "Do you mind as dreadfully as me," she asked him, "about Annie?" He minded perhaps *more* dreadfully, he said, because he'd known her so much longer than Jill had; which was comforting, for no grief can be unbearable when shared. But when Mum told her a French governess had come to take old Annie's place, Jill cried herself into a fever, and had to go to bed and have the glass thing in her mouth and castor oil —which her mother said was milk, but Jill knew better. And it was Pete who held her nose to help her not to taste it. . . .

Poor Jill and her cauldron of emotions! Too highly strung, she soon outgrew her small reserve of strength, lost weight and was a continuous source of worry to the over-anxious Edie. They could never let her know beforehand if she were invited to a party—any treat. The least excitement and up would go her temperature. Five Christmas days of her first ten years were spent in bed with a high fever.

A too tall child, hands, wrists, and ankles, the curve of narrowed chin, expressed that subtle delicacy of drawing which gave to the small face what Charlotte called its 'Leonardo' look. The eyes, fawn-dark and wistful, were set wide apart under faintly surprised eyebrows, and her sparrow-brown hair with its silken sheen hung uncurling, straight as rain. Anthony always said she was no Wrotham, but the image of his mother, Mary Kell. And Edie thought it such a shame that Larry should be golden-haired and pink and white, *too* beautiful—such loveliness was wasted on a boy—while Jill, poor angel, wasn't even pretty, so *mouse-*coloured and plain. And though she conscientiously endeavoured not to give more love to one than to the other, Larry stayed the favourite and Jill an also ran.

She in her ardent fashion—there were no half-measures where Jill's affections were concerned—worshipped Larry. He was her God, her whole existence—for a time. He lorded it over her, and she followed where he led—into every sort of mischief, as that other pair a hundred years before them.

The nineteenth century closed stormily, on both sides of the Atlantic. First the Spanish American War of '98, which by reason of the instinctive friendliness of Great Britain in the midst of European antagonism, cemented the relations based on mutual good-will that have endured through greater crises. Then followed a year later the Boer War, and 1900 dawned in gloom, with news of siege and of disaster.

The Queen, notwithstanding her great age, and the unceasing anxiety occasioned by the war and its reverses, devoted herself heart and soul to the nation's struggle. With that same simple conscientiousness that throughout her reign had marked her personality, she endeavoured to communicate her own distress and sympathy to the multitudes who suffered. No matter whether it were manifested in gifts of chocolates to the Tommies, or, defying her rheumatics and the fears of her advisers, in paying a personal visit to Ireland as a tribute to the loyalty of Irish recruits, the indomitable spirit never wavered.

She, who had witnessed her country's millions pass from misery and bondage to strength, freedom, justice; who had watched her dominions spread and grow in prestige and in power, handing to posterity a heritage of human affairs, of statesmanship, and intellectual progress unequalled in the history of the world—through girlhood, motherhood, widowhood, had unswervingly fulfilled the promise of Victoria the child, "I *will* be good."

Other sovereigns have been more loved, none have been more venerated; and with the war whose end she was not destined to

see, Imperialism reached its climax in a fervour of patriotic sentiment for that frail aged figure in its widow's cap, who since the
day when she stepped from the schoolroom to the throne had
consecrated her long life to faith and duty.

But we out there in the midst of it knew little of the stir the
war had made at home. I gleaned my news chiefly from Charlotte's letters, though Jill's also played a part. From her I understand that:

"Mafferking night was lovly I got out on the roof to see the
bomfires on Cheam Hill. Madamaselle was waxey. . . ."

We have reason to believe so, although one must admit we see
Jill's point. To be sent to bed at bedtime in the ordinary way
when the siege of Mafeking was over and everyone so glad, was
a mug's game, Jill decided, of which Larry would have strongly
disapproved.

More than ever on that night of nights did she long for Larry,
but he was at his school and inaccessible. And of course Mam'-
zelle being French (and pro-Boer, more than likely) *would* make
you go to bed in the ordinary way, instead of letting you stay up
till twelve o'clock. Or even ten. Or even nine. . . . And not even
half-past eight.

Jill guessed why Mam'zelle was being beastly. It was on account
of the dead frog found yesterday by the lily pond. And supposing
she had put it on Mam'zelle's plate, it was done only out of kindness, thinking that, being French, Mam'zelle might fancy it for
tea. For, as everybody knew, the French ate frogs. There was no
need for Mam'zelle to scream herself into ten fits and to rush
away to her bedroom to be sick. Nor to threaten to go writing to
Jill's father—who for better—or for worse—was not at Wroth just
then, but with Jill's mother at the flat in London.

So Jill lay in bed and fumed and burned, and listened to the sounds of cheering in the distance. All the villagers were out, and the lanes guttural and rowdy with their voices; while in the dark blue sky above the trees a pinkish glow appeared, which must certainly be bonfires—and she not allowed to see them; not even from her window which looked out on to the stables, and had no view of anything at all.

Then came the inspiration.

There was a ladder on the top floor that led on to the roof, propped against the skylight. She and Larry used it often to play pirates, but although Larry had suggested that they ought to go *some* time, they had not yet ventured out on to the roof. The occasion now demanded not to wait upon the order of the doing, but to do. . . .

It was an easy run.

In her red flannel dressing-gown, but slipperless, she sped upstairs, along the attic corridor, and nimbly up the ladder. The skylight was half open, she had only to push the iron rod a little farther out, and then it was wide enough to wriggle herself through.

Immediately outside and a jump of three feet from the skylight window was a kind of platform, just big enough to stand on before the roof began to slope. You need not fear to slide down if you stood upright on that, it was as safe as walking on the ground—and in fact safer, for on the ground you did not always look where you were going.

So there she stood and saw the fireworks shooting up from Cheam. Long green shining ones, and gleaming silver showers, and pink ones, and purple ones—and best of all a Royal Crown of gold and diamonds blazing in the middle of the sky, that had turned black as the blackest kind of pansy. And under all this loveliness the beacon flared and blossomed like a huge great chrysanthemum in flames.

Jill's hands were cold, her forehead hot, she hugged herself and shivered in a rapture of emotion that gave her pins and needles in her spine.

Her sin would not have found her out if it had not been for old Baxter, who looked up from the stableyard and saw her.

"What in the name of mischief are you doin' there, Miss Jill? God A'mighty! Do you want to break your neck?"

There was really no necessity to answer. What business was it anyway of Baxter's if she *did* break her neck?

She could see him far below her in his shirt-sleeves; she could see the top of his bald head with its fringe of greyish hair, his face, looking up, a blob of yellow in the dimness, and behind him, the light from a lantern on the ground streaming through his leather-breeched bowlegs. The stable door where Ebony slept was open, he had just been in to bed her down—and there was Jill high up on the roof. They could shout till they were silly.

So, it seems, could she.

"I'm the King of the Castle—get down, you dirty *Ras*cal. Hi! Baxter—Baxter—*Bax-ter!* You can't catch me! I'm on the roof—you can't catch me—I'm on the roof—you can't *catch me*—"

And so on.

Silence reigned. Baxter had disappeared. The stable door was shut, the last rocket dead, and the bonfire had dwindled, its fiery petals falling, burning scarlet, burning lower, burning dark . . .

And it was over.

Into Jill's eyes the tears sprang up, and dribbled down her cheeks.

"I'm the King of the Castle," she chanted dolefully. "Get down, you dirty—"

"Jeel! Jeel! *Mon Dieu! Qu'est-ce-que vous faîtes là-haut? Descendez de suite—ou vous allez tomber et vous tuer! Descendez—je vous repète.*"

Baxter, the sneak! Baxter had told Mam'zelle, who had sent him to fetch Jill down. He was climbing up the ladder while Mam'zelle danced about below and wrung her hands, and screamed, her mouth a great round O of fright, wide open. She did look funny, and Jill, peering through the skylight window, shook with laughter, while the tears dried on her cheeks.

"Mais il ne faut pas fâcher vous-même, Mam'zelle, je ne tomberais pas parceque ce ledge est très wide. Venez ici et voir pour vous-même. Il est perfectly safe, vraiment."

"Quelle impertinence! Comment osez-vous me désobéir de la sorte! Vous êtes tout-à-fait impossible—je vais écrire à votre père—vilaine petite!"

"Mais, Mam'zelle, j'ai seulement voulu voir le bonfire. Il n'y a pas anything wrong en ça, n'est-ce pas? Tout le monde est allé voir les bonfires ce soir. Peut-être vous ne savez pas que Mafeking est relievé. . . . Vous ne care-ez pas either." Jill added, *sotto voce:* "Vous n'êtes pas British. Old Smelly face."

"Come on now, enough's as good as a feast—" Baxter had reached the skylight window-ledge, an arm stretched out to grab her, his face one great broad grin. The sight of that grin roused Jill to indignation. "Come along, Miss Jill, and don't you be so naughty. Gimme your 'and. My word! *And* you're goin' to catch it when your Pa comes 'ome. You didn't 'arf give me a turn."

"Serve you jolly well right." Jill wriggled a shoulder out of his reach, and gathered her dignity and dressing-gown about her. "And I can get down alone—thank you—I got up alone, didn't I? I don't want help from a spying sneak. *Pro-Boer!*—and so is *She!"*

It is recorded with regret and with reluctance that, waving the proffered hand aside, Jill, as she climbed down the iron ladder, inexcusably stuck her tongue out to its farthest—not at the vile Baxter, but at poor, long-suffering, outraged Mademoiselle.

"So now," her letter tells me, "I am to go to bording school at Eastborn where they play reel criket with a hard ball. Father says that 3 Madamaselles in 8 months is too much of a good thing and he says I am a Dunse as I cant spell the Queens English. Is it my falt if I cant spell when I only learn this beasley French. Any how Madamaselle is going and I am glad. I hate her. Father came down with Mum but he didn't say much as I was in bed with a tempriture which I got from the roof but when I was up again he went for me like Billy O. Mum tryed to privent him but she couldnt and he was awfully waxey and boxed my ears and Mum cryed so now I am not speaking to my Father. Any how I couldnt be more misrable at school than I am at home where I am so creuelly treated. Even Mum has turned against me she says I get on her nurves and becos that old pig Madamaselle is going she is making me learn the *whole* of the subjonctifs of Vouloir et Aller *by heart* Madamaselle I mean. Charlie says you are a Captain now so I am putting Capt. P. J. Wrotham on the enveloppe I hope it gets to you safely I am asked to recite next Tuesday at the party given by the vicar at the village Hall for the widoes and orphens I am going to say the Abcent minded Beggar and go round after with the tamboreen collecting shillings.

"I am painting a picture of you on the velt shooting Bores I have put a Chinese white bandage round your head with virmillion for the blood. Kahkee is not an easy coler to make I mix raw umbar with burnt sienner and crome yellow. When it is finnished I will send it you. I cant do hands and feet as well as faces I put in the blood to make it look real. I have just finnished one of Ebony but I wont send it as it is bad horses are harder to do than people.

"Do you know goodby my Bleuebell it is a very sad one. The soldieres sing it when they march past hear. There is a training camp on the Common and Cheam Royal has been turned into a hosspittle for the wunded the old dottyman has gone to live somewere else. Will you be home soon? When you write next time will you write me a letter to myself allone and *not* inclosed in Mum and Fathers and will you adress it please *Miss Wrotham* and please let it have O.H.M.S. on it.

"With love from

"Your ever and ever and ever loving

"JILL.

"X X X X X"

And a few months later this:

"SUMMERHAYES COLLEGE
"EASTBOURNE.
"Jan. 23rd. 1901.

"DEAR DARLING PETE

"I am writing this in prep so please exscuse scrawl as I have to hurrey in case Miss Ryan catches me as we are not alowed to write letters in prep only on Sundays. Isnt it awfull about the Queen. You'll have heard the news I exspect by the time you recieve this letter. We are all frihghtfully hipped about it here. The head told us this morning at prayers and Miss Bartlett who is a bit soft cried and so did Fraulien but I dont see why she should being German. There is to be a spescial service in Chappel on the day of the funeral and we all have to wear black bands on our arms and black ties but they wont show on navy bleue. I wish we could wear real morning. All the teachers are in black today. I am in fractions this term but still bottom of my class in Arithmatic and dictatation and top in history and compasition. I have been put in the upper fith for drawing with the big girls 15 and 16 I am the youngest by 4 years. I dont like being with them they are awfully sidey. Have you met Bobs yet. I pray at prayers allways that you will not be badly wounded only a little one so that I can tell them here. There are 2 girls in the lower school whos brothers are at the front and 7 whose fathers are. Will you write me a letter that I can show to Marjorie Ward my great friend becos she allways shows me her fathers letters he is a majer. Miss Ryan is looking at me and I shall get a bad mark if I am caught writing to you. I am pritending to do my dictatation mistakes. You have to write each one 4 times it takes ages. I have had 5 bad marks this term allready if you get over 6 you have to go before the head and she jawes you.

"I am knitting you a pair of socks in sowing class we all knit things for the soldiers and I asked Miss Gee (our sowing teacher) if I could knit socks for you and she said yes but she turned the heal for me.

"Goodby my own darling Pete
"I love you *very* much
"Your ever loving Sister
"JILL.

"X X X X X X

"P.S. Wont it sound funny to say God save the *King.*"

IV

So in his sixtieth year Edward VII came into his own, and with his accession the last traces of a memorable epoch vanished. Not only she who symbolised the spirit of her age, but the ethics of that age itself had passed. Not only a new century, but a new era in history had arrived, to reconstruct the world, and revitalise a nation headed by that genial monarch, whose ineffable charm and democratic outlook was to win him—despite his all too brief reign—an unrivalled place in the affectionate remembrance of his people.

The concern occasioned by his serious illness, which postponed his coronation, detracted in some measure from the interest aroused by the resignation of Lord Salisbury, who had become almost as great an institution as Victoria. Under his nephew and successor, Arthur Balfour, leader of the Unionists, who still outwardly maintained the Salisbury policy of "isolation," those tremendous changes which under the ascendancy of Campbell-Bannerman were so profoundly to affect the future, remained thus far in abeyance.

Meanwhile, war in South Africa was over, peace signed at Vereeniging, the troops returned amid enthusiastic demonstrations, and popular interest once more focussed on the King, his much admired Queen, his lively Court—a welcome contrast to the ceremonial frigidity enforced by his autocratic mother—his frequent public appearances, his race-horses and—his motor car. He had set the fashion and society soon followed. While the carriage and pair with its cockaded coachman was still in evidence at functions, the rapidly increasing hordes of week-end visitors to the coast, or country houses, moved at petrol-driven speed, making foul the countryside with dust and smell and noise.

But at Wroth in my father's lifetime, the horse was never superseded by the motor. Not all the blandishments of Edie could move him from his detestation of these "bone-shaking monstrosities—these evil-stinking juggernauts driven by lunatics and *dung*-worms!" as he often and emphatically in a sudden fit of rage would apostrophise the dust-enveloped vehicles that roared past him on his walks and drives around that home, to which in his later years he became more and more attached.

It was Charlotte who to the immense delight of the whole family, and the horrified disgust of the master of the house, arrived at Wroth on an afternoon in January, 1905, in a sixteen-horse-power chauffeur-driven Renault, befurred to the chin, wearing motor-veil, cap and goggles and resembling, as her father put it, "nothing human."

Charlotte, since Sabrina's death, had been in possession of an ample income along with the house in Curzon Street, and though we have reason to believe that the major portion of her money went in supporting the Woman's Social and Political Union, she still retained sufficient for her own personal requirements, and not the least of them this brand-new motor car.

Edie had to bear the brunt of her husband's disapproval of that outrageous visitation, long after they had both retired for the night.

"A disgrace to her sex—a hideosity," so he denounced his daughter to his wife. But what, he asked, could you possibly expect from one so lost to all regard for the decencies of life as to go hand in hand with those female impersonators—you could scarcely call them women—who were agitating for the vote? He would *not*—declared Anthony, raising himself upon his pillow the more furiously to address the passive Edie, who, her back turned towards him, and each gold-tinted curl encased in a Hinde's curler, had resigned herself with patience to the fray— he would *not* allow one of those disgusting filthy things inside his house; so now—he said—she knew.

"It's not inside the house: it's in the courtyard," murmured Edie.

"I don't care where it is," returned her husband loudly, "but out it goes! Tomorrow! And that smirking Frenchman with it. Where is he sleeping, by the way?"

"How should I know?" retorted Edie, whose temper was beginning to show signs of wear. "With Charlie, very likely. No! No! To-to! I didn't mean it"—Edie's hand slid behind to squeeze her husband's bony knee—"but you really mustn't fuss yourself, my love-bird. You're *so* upsetting. Put the light out, won't you, and let us go to sleep."

"Sleep! How can I sleep?" Under their grizzled brows Anthony's eyes were almost starting from their sockets; his night-shirt, open at the throat, displayed a protruding Adam's apple that worked spasmodically as he swallowed. "Don't you think *I'm* upset? The things you say!"

"What things I say?" somewhat distractedly cried Edie. "I haven't said a word—for *hours!* I've listened to you shouting till I'm *sick!* You've no sense of humour, To-to—not an ounce! You're being perfectly ridiculous to work yourself into a state over Charlie and her motor. She has every right to buy a motor if she wants one. I wish to goodness *I* had her money and could buy one. Everybody's buying one from the King downwards, and if you weren't such an utterly absurd and obstinate old angel-face you'd buy one, too. Now lie down and go to sleep or you'll kill me."

Heaven alone knows how—but she could manage him. He did lie down and he did go to sleep, and in time he came to accept Charlotte's motor car and that "smirking Frenchman" as he accepted this hustling new world around him, its want of reverence, its wholesale destruction of those covenants to which throughout his life he had so rigidly adhered: solidity; background; class—and no infringement of that hard divisional line between the Upper and the Lower; the Right Man in the Right Place, and a Wrotham's place the niche he had carved for himself in the buttress of his own fortifications.

And now, under this new King—a new Democracy. Where was it leading the youth of England, this hail-fellow-well-met attitude of all grades of society, this hobnobbing with the masses, this mania for novelty, the overthrow of pre-accepted dogma and tradition as expressed by that monstrous Thing, the internal combustion engine? Where would it end? In a world-wide general combustion, in Anthony's opinion. Already they were experimenting with the heavier-than-air machine which, should it ever be perfected, would threaten British insularity. These brothers Wright—Americans—had actually flown for thirty-six miles. Flown! Literally—in the face of Providence. Everywhere, on every side, one was met with new alarming symptoms. This Education Bill, this Licensing Bill, that fellow with his monocle and orchid dressed as though for a perpetual wedding, splitting the Unionist Party with his raging, tearing campaign. "Tariff Reform and work for all." Bribery. Corruption.

But in spite of Anthony and all that he had lived by, the rolling tide swept on. It overflowed into his home, and into his house of business. Although in his seventy-fifth year, and in spite of the warning advice of his nephew George, who cautioned him against "overdoing it" and suggested it was time that he should give up work altogether and lead a retired, quiet life at Wroth, Anthony continued to hold the reins of office at the house in Soho Square.

He had recently taken into the firm young Stephen Marriott, second son of George, who from all accounts had little enough to do and still less to say in the affairs of Kell & Wrotham. And although in his home circle young Stephen may have declared the "old man's" methods "prehistoric," his fiction list full of the most "appalling drivel"—and his objection to advertisement "sheer lunacy" in the face of ghastly competition that "we" were up against—these views were never uttered in his great-uncle's presence.

But even Anthony admitted that the rise of competition was a menace that heretofore had not seriously been forced into account.

The mushroom growth of newer firms meant newer methods, cheaper output, the buying up of space in the daily papers for advertisement—as though literature were liver pills! This, the heaping of insult upon injury! It is possible that Anthony when reviling these tactics had forgotten certain passages of arms between himself and his own father in those days gone by, when he in his turn revolutionised the trade, and popularised the market.

Yet another problem even more serious than growing rivalry, was the mill-race of journalism. Man, it seemed, no longer lived by books alone. This ha'penny press, these tuppenny weeklies, these illustrated monthly rags which littered every bookstall, were harrying the old accepted standards out of place, were killing the demand for that innocuous sentimental fiction which since the time of good *East Lynne* had been issued from the house of Kell & Wrotham to delight half feminine England. But now those sugared trifles which for the last fifty years had been the firm's chief source of revenue, were losing favour. Stark realism was the order of the day. The sex-novel had replaced the love-story and *The Woman Who Did* was acclaimed by the woman who didn't. . . .

Thus, in this alien world which of his own family contained none now of his generation, Anthony for the first time in his life felt himself to be superfluous. His sister Clare had died at over eighty of a chill—the slightest chill—which she had chosen to neglect, and gone out driving in the victoria which her son George had presented to his mother when he first received his knighthood. George was doing well. Anthony estimated that his nephew George must be making fifteen thousand a year at least. He had wormed his way into Court circles—he'd not done so badly. Yes, said Anthony, and his mother went and killed herself—would go shopping in an open carriage with an east wind blowing—against all advice—to buy herself some rubbish, and was dead within a week. Well, there it was. Clare gone and he left—waiting, marking time. He'd be the next. *He'd* not see eighty. The women of his house outlived the men. But he, Anthony, had lived too long.

And with each year that passed he became more and more obsessed with the notion he was dying. He had nothing now to live for—or so he often said. His business was going to the dogs, his wife a flibbertigibbet, who should know better at her age than to go playing bridge all day and half the night. Bridge! That was her latest craze. Parties here and parties there, and week-end visitors to the house, which was no longer *his* house but hers. She ruled it. She and her children—those young devils who, when at home for holidays, behaved like hooligans—tearing about the countryside on bicycles. The boy Larry seemed less wild than Jill. He had manners, at all events, addressed his father frequently as 'sir,' showed an intelligent interest in the affairs of Kell & Wrotham, had taken a minor scholarship for Oxford, and was in fact one of those people who can invariably be relied upon to say or do the right thing at the right moment. His mother always said that Larry was *born* tactful. He was charming to everyone. From his cradle women had adored him. He was extraordinarily good-looking, six foot two, fair-haired, blue-eyed, with a first-class brain when he chose to use it—and bone-lazy.

No one understood how he managed to get that scholarship for Oxford, for as far as we know he never did a stroke of work. However, he did manage to get it, and even Anthony could find no fault with him for that.

Our father always had been more tolerant of his sons than of his daughters. The mere presence of our poor little Jill—as with

Charlotte in her time—was a source of irritation; but Charlotte still remained the sharpest thorn in the paternal flesh.

It was during the general election of 1906, which for the first time in ten years returned a Liberal majority with Campbell-Bannerman at its head, that Charlotte became a notoriety.

As one of that body of women who had organised the London Committee of the W.S.P.U., she was persistently identified with those who, for so long held in contempt and ridiculed or ignored by the Press, had come to be recognised at last as a national force, a solid mass of female agitators who uprose on all sides and in all classes, and in every city of importance, to demand the vote.

In May, 1906, the first great open-air meeting was held in Trafalgar Square, and from then onwards the anti-government policy and the heckling of Cabinet Ministers pursued its systematic course. In October of that year Charlotte, along with a number of other women, was arrested for creating a disturbance in the lobby of the House of Commons and, refusing the option of surety for good behaviour, was sentenced to six weeks' imprisonment in Holloway.

Militancy in earnest had begun.

v

Anthony and his wife were staying at Queen Anne Mansions when he read in *The Times* that announcement which blazoned forth his daughter's shame for all the world to see—the most dire calamity that ever had befallen him, his family or his good name. There is no doubt that the shock must have brought about an immediate collapse, though none was there to witness it.

The maid who came to clear away the breakfast things, to find him sitting at the table before an untouched dish of ham and eggs, reported that he seemed "all of a daze" and would not answer when she spoke to him to ask if he had finished.

"All he could do was to keep pointin' at his paper which he'd thrown on the floor. He seemed to be tryin' to speak but he couldn't get his words—his face was as white as a sheet and he looked like he was snarlin'."

It was a minor stroke. George, summoned by a telephone call from Edie, ordered him to bed for a week, and sent in a nurse to keep him there.

Anthony's one cry was that "she must be bailed out—bailed out. Pay anything to bail her out—"

And George had a face as long as his arm when he went to talk to Edie.

"I won't answer for the consequences," was his report, "if he has much more of this. On no account must he be excited or alarmed. Keep the papers from him. Lie to him. Tell him it's a mistake—a misprint—anything you like. I've given him a dose that'll soothe him down for the next twenty-four hours. And *you'd* better keep out of his way," he added sharply, for Edie was on the verge of hysterics and jumpy as a kitten, as George afterwards recounted, "twittering and giggling and crying by turns, and cuddling that preposterous Chinese lap-dog of hers—all tied up with ribbon bows."

He left her with the promise that he'd do his best to get Charlotte out of jail, and went forthwith to interview the authorities at Holloway.

An account of George's visit was duly recorded in Charlotte's letter to me, but of her own experiences during her first term of imprisonment she speaks guardedly:

". . . I was terribly upset to hear that Papa had taken this affair so violently, but one could hardly suppose that he would have taken it any other way. The Press, of course, exaggerated the whole thing. There was no disorder of the kind they intimate, no hysteria, or shrieking viragoes kicking the police. It is absolute lies. We are bound over to keep the peace for six months or take the alternative of six weeks' imprisonment, which of course is a longer sentence than the charge warrants.

"We of the second division are allowed certain privileges. As for instance, permission to write a fortnightly letter—hence this to you, my dear.

"How on earth George managed to get in to see me here, goodness alone knows. He was brought in by a wardress who stood on guard throughout the interview. Nothing as you know ever shocks or surprises George, but I think even he was a little staggered at the verminous condition of my cell! He did not hesitate to let me know that it is entirely due to my 'extremist views' as he calls them that Papa is in this state—not serious at present, although if I persist along this drastic course he says it may become so. He advises my immediate release, which could be obtained on my being bound over to keep the peace. I do not, however, intend to give an undertaking that I am already confident I shall not keep.

"We have decided for Papa's sake to let him think that I am out of jail, and have gone away from London. This to tide over another month's incarceration. I have been here now two weeks.

"You will of course be furious with me for this, my dear. I know *your* views and, while you sympathise in theory with the cause, I know you are not in favour of these insistent means to obtain our purpose. Who is? But if you want a locked door opened you must hammer till you break it down. After all—I am not the only extremist of our family. Our grandfather also suffered for justice and for right.

"Lying here at night I often think of him, and sometimes—for perhaps one becomes fanciful so long alone—I can almost believe I see him standing here against these dismal walls: I who never saw him, but who know him so well from dear Aunt Sab's description. I see him with his one eye gleaming, and that elfish grin. 'I too,' he seems to say, 'I fought—to lose.'

"But we shall fight—to win!

"Our hope lies in the new militancy, in sacrifice and service— even though it brings us here!

"I have no name now, only a number. I wear the prisoner's badge pinned to my dress—a garment of harsh brown wool marked with the broad arrow. My stockings are circular striped —not unlike those in the Tenniel drawings of Alice; and like Alice too, I grow 'curioser and curioser.'

"I seem to be living in a kind of trance and suffer no discomfort from my mattress—harder than a board—and no disgust for the food which is served to us—for surprisingly I have an appetite! Our diet consists chiefly of suet pudding.

"It is only in chapel that I really seem to come to life and feel anything at all. There we are brought in contact with our fellow prisoners. It is agonising to see the old women—some so frail and bent, so withered, so old. . . . Not for the old women, this place. I can bear it for ourselves but not for them. God knows what they have done to bring them here. They may be utterly depraved, worthless. Rotten. Then let them die. Why torture them? I can't think they are evil. Only misguided and misunderstood. . . ."

I was out in British East Africa when I received this letter, and was still there when, a year later, the news reached me by cable of our father's death.

His decline had been slow, but his end swift—of a second stroke. He died in office, in that same room where his father had died before him.

When I left England in 1906, Jill was a schoolgirl with a plait down her back and a skirt to her knees. I returned within three years to find her with her hair done up and skirts to her ankles, a graceful slip of a thing, small-boned, tall and rather lovely to my thinking, with those fawn-dark eyes of hers set wide apart in her eager little face, and a mouth that asked for trouble.

It was a time of political tension and controversy, which, culminating in the rejection of Lloyd George's Budget from the House of Lords, revived again the system—introduced by Asquith—of creating peers *en masse,* similar to that used by William IV at Grey's dictation to secure the passing of the Reform Bill. And not unparallel with that former period of agitation, ran the issues then at stake, to increase the prevailing spirit of hostility and antagonism which was to bring us step by step, and year by year, nearer to the world's Nemesis.

Nothing warned us of disaster.

The wolf-cry of a European war had been raised too often to scare the man in the street. What though Germany had four Zeppelins—what though pigs might fly? We had eight new battleships and were building super-dreadnoughts. No navy could do better, if as well.

Meantime, strikes were frequent. Unemployment stalked the streets. Social and financial crises succeeded one another like shots from a machine-gun. Riots everywhere; unrest everywhere; suffragettes everywhere—with militancy rampant.

In this atmosphere of national disturbance, of protests, challenge and revolt, Jill and her generation passed from childhood to unsuspecting adolescence—a generation doomed.

Chapter Two

I

At eighteen Jill left her school at Eastbourne and was sent to Lausanne to be 'finished.' There she became proficient in winter-sports; there, too, she learned to waltz on ice, to dance the Boston in the ballroom, to do her hair the newest way in rolls of curls at the back; to make her own *lingerie;* to speak French with a Swiss accent, to read French novels, and to paint little pictures— in water colours—from her bedroom window, of boats with brown sails on a very blue lake with very white mountains in the background.

She came home to Edie a year later with the announcement that she meant to study art.

Edie sent for Charlotte. She always sent for Charlotte or myself to arbitrate an argument with Jill.

"After all the money that I've spent on her and all those clothes I've bought—the sweetest things from Lucille's you ever saw—to go and tell me that she wants to be one of those dreadful creatures in a jibbah!" So Edie stated, somewhat incoherently, her case.

"Don't be silly, Mum. I'd loathe to wear a jibbah. All I want, Charlie," pleaded Jill, "is to be allowed to work—say three days a week—at some decent school in London. And then later on, if I'm any good, perhaps I'll go to Julian's in Paris."

"Paris!" Edie shrieked. "Do you hear her, Charlie? How can

you stand there and let that child overrule me? I won't be over-ruled by my children!" Edie beat her plump ringed hands to-gether. "I won't, I won't, I won't! I had so hoped," she added miserably, "to present her here this season. There's not a girl in London would have had a better chance."

"Chance of what?" asked Charlotte.

"Of being seen," said Edie vaguely. "Ranelagh and Ascot and Henley and that. I meant to take a house for Henley this year—just what I've always longed for—to have a pretty young thing to take about—and you could be made to look so pretty, darling, if you'd only learn to do your hair—much better looking than I ever thought you'd be. Such an ugly little girl with a great big nose—and now it's quite a nice attractive size—and only yester-day Mrs. What's-its-name said—you know, Charlie, the woman with the withered hand whose husband went off with—"

Edie stopped abruptly, glanced at Jill, approached her lips mys-teriously to Charlie's ear and whispered. Charlotte closed her eyes, patting away a yawn, and Jill said hotly, "I don't care *who* went off with who or what they said about me or my nose, but I *am* going to be allowed to paint."

"My angel! She never said a word about your nose. She was only telling me how attractive she thought you were and— Now! Don't be naughty, Jill—after all those pretty frocks I've bought you which you *never* wear. I do think you're a little bit ungrate-ful, darling. I'm sure I do my best and give you everything you want. And no man'll ever look at you if you're arty."

"Oh, Lord!" groaned Jill as she banged out of the room. "Go on, Charlie, you talk to her. I can't."

She left Charlotte to it.

Poor Edie! She who had managed Anthony when nobody else could, had nothing at all to say to Jill and Larry. She was putty in their hands. They had their way with her and with the house in Cheyne Walk, when at their advice and subsequent insistence, she was persuaded to move thence from Queen Anne's Mansions.

For "We must have a house," Jill said, "with a room big enough to dance in and a studio for me."

So to Cheyne Walk went Edie, and complained about the damp from the river and said she would not be dictated to by Jill. She *would* have her bedroom in vieux rose or heliotrope. And Jill said: "Yes, darling, your bedroom can be anything you like since no one but you will ever sleep there, but the drawing-room can't be yellow. In fact, I don't think we'll have a drawing-room at all. We'll have a sort of lounge, and no carpets, only rugs and as little furniture as possible—and a plain carpet on the stairs. No, mum, not red. You can't possibly have red. . . . Buff colour, darling. I'll show you patterns."

Jill showed her patterns, and Edie thought them frightful—"So dowdy and colourless and plain." And Larry said: "Darling, we love you very much, but your taste is ghastly. You'd much better let Jill get on with it."

So Jill got on with it, and Edie sighed for her Japanese vases and her Dresden cupids, and her cushions and her couches and her bows. But they conceded her a 'boudoir' with a satin-striped blue wall paper, and curtains of old gold, and photographs of all the family in silver frames.

Wroth had been left to me, but the children had the run of it and filled the house with young people in the summer.

When in January, 1910, I came home on leave, I found them settled in at Cheyne Walk, Jill a daily student at the Elm Grove Art School, Chelsea, and Larry down from Oxford taking his share in the management of Kell & Wrotham. He and young Stephen Marriott were of one mind as to that, and reorganised accordingly, though how, with none to teach them, except old hands with older methods, they ever came to learn the trade, was a wonder. But learn it they did and to good purpose, as time began to show.

New names were recruited to their fiction list, the staff increased, the 'die-hards,' as Larry called them, pensioned off, and new editions of past masters in slim calf-bound volumes introduced, priced modestly two shillings.

The balance sheet in the second year of Larry's entry to the firm showed a net increase of ten per cent—on the strength of which he bought himself a Napier, and with it won the touring handicap at Brooklands.

Meantime Jill went to her art school, and did her hair in a new way, parted in the middle and in plaits round her ears, and wore coloured stockings to match the flowing ties that she affected, knotted under the loose collar of her blouse.

And she enrolled herself a member of the W.S.P.U., and sold the *Women's Dreadnought* at street corners.

Edie was distracted. She complained bitterly to Charlotte: "You have no right to encourage her, letting her disgrace herself—selling that awful paper. I don't know what Pete'll say, I'm sure—he'll be disgusted. And those dreadful drawings she brings home, of naked women. Too indecent for words. *Nothing* left to the imagination."

"You don't have to learn anatomy from the imagination," Charlotte said.

"But she needn't leave them lying about for everyone to see. And I won't *have* her hobnobbing with the suffragettes!" cried Edie. "I don't care what *you* do—you can look after yourself. You've lived your life—you're independent—though goodness knows you worried your poor father into his grave with all your goings on; but I don't see why *my* child should be dragged into it—*she'll* be sent to prison next."

"If," Charlotte grinned, "she's lucky."

Edie subsided. She could not stand up to Charlie. What a crank! And such a sight she made of herself with those dreadful old clothes thrown on all anyhow, and her white untidy hair. Gone to pieces. Old. Yet not in years, for she was Edie's junior— by how much? Never mind. Yet she looks, thought Edie, staring disapprovingly at Charlotte's old felt hat, that sported by way of trimming a moulting speckled quill, she looks at least ten years older than I do.

Which was only a very slight exaggeration. Edie had grown stouter but remained seraphically young in spite of her three chins and ample bosom. Her hair was nearly—but not quite— her own, and arranged in a Royal fringe upon her forehead. Her fingers sparkled with diamonds, and she was festooned with beads. She wore a dozen charms to every bangle. She favoured for the summer a choice in 'pastel' colours—mauve or pink or blue—or pure white *Broderie Anglais* with a large bow at the back. She wore wide Leghorn beflowered hats, and hissed as she walked in a froth of glacé petticoats. Dear, kindly Edie, who tried so hard to make Charlotte take some pride in her appearance and even went so far as to present her with a box of Rimmel's powder and a pot of scarlet paste: "Rub a little in each cheek with your finger-tip, my dear—it isn't paint; pure vegetable— and it'll give you the most natural colour. I'm not telling you to make up—only to try and look presentable. There's no need to go about looking like a scarecrow even if you *are* a suffragette."

Edie had never forgiven Charlotte for turning up at young Stephen Marriott's wedding in a mackintosh.

He married in 1911, one of the Garstin girls, a great-niece of Diana's. And Laurencina's Robin is their son.

II

From 1910 to 1913 there is little of importance in Jill's life to record. The years merged one into another smoothly, pleasantly, filled with unobtrusive incidents, winter holidays in Switzerland with Larry, summer months at Wroth, dances, work.

She was undoubtedly talented, but like Larry she was lazy; and because she had more aptitude for colour than for line, she shirked drawing and went ahead at paint before she had mastered the rudiments of either.

But what she lacked in application was atoned for in other ways. She had discrimination and the gift of honest criticism, not only for the work of her associates, but for her own.

Unfortunately for Jill, she did not possess as sure a sense of values in relation to human contacts. She suffered the keenest disappointments in her friendships at that school of art in Chelsea, where among her fellow students, it seems, she was more popular with the girls than with the men. Physically she was younger than her years; at twenty she looked about sixteen. She was incurably romantic, always in and out of love, and endured a perpetual martyrdom of unrequited passion, from the moment when at sight she adored 'Gutts'—so called by the students, but more generally known as Wilfred Gutteridge, A.R.A., principal of the Elm Grove Art School. Him she loved with her whole being for the whole of her first term.

He was not much of an artist, but he knew more about paint than anyone in London; and he scattered his knowledge everywhere except on his own canvas. A slovenly giant of a man, he stood six foot three in his socks, had the grin of a schoolboy, hair as black as a boot, yellow whites to his rather goggling brown eyes, and the look—or so I judged the only time I ever saw him —of a soaker.

Not all unconscious, we presume, of the storm that he had roused in the maiden heart of Jill, he singled her out—as was his custom with attractive new young students—for particular attention in the life class, which Jill as a novice was permitted to attend two afternoons a week. For the rest she was condemned to the 'antique,' to draw the casts of hands and feet, and decapitated torsos. After a month or so of this she rebelled, took to Gutts her grievance, and demanded she should be allowed to paint.

"But you can't draw yet," Gutts said.

"I can draw better with a brush," said Jill, "than with a pencil."

"If you were to cut your hair short," Gutts told her, narrowing his eyes, "you'd come to life as a Botticelli chorister. Why don't you?"

"—don't I what?" gasped Jill.

"Cut your hair short." With outstretched thumb he described a curve in space. "You'd be even more disturbing then than you are now."

"Oh!" Jill gasped again.

Whereupon he kissed her. Put his hand under her chin, pushed her face backward, and kissed her long and skilfully upon the mouth.

It was the first time a man's lips had touched her own. Her emotion was a novelty to him.

"Why, you funny babe!"

"Don't!" Tremblingly she clung to him, clutching at his sleeve. "Don't—play with me!"

The bloodshot eyes of Gutts goggled very slightly.

"You're unbelievable! Are you going to cut your hair and let me paint you?"

So Jill cut her hair and let him paint her, and Edie said, "You see!" to Charlotte. "I knew that she'd go arty. The most shocking sight she's made of herself with that straight fringe right down to her eyebrows. Goodness knows why I ever had a daughter—they're only a perfect misery."

And Charlotte said: "I had short hair once—in Florence or Vienna—or was it Bayreuth? We were all very pre-Raphaelite in those days—"

And Larry: "I suppose you think you look like Trilby?"

And Jill: "I don't care a hang what any of you say; it's my own hair and I shall do it as I like."

She sat to Gutts on Sundays and was the talk and envy of her fellows—or rather those whose sole ambition was to be asked to sit for Gutts.

To give him his due, he did no worse to any of them than he did to Jill. Married to a shrewish wife, formerly his model, he found in drink and semi-amorous adventures with his younger and more attractive students a partial relaxation from matrimonial bondage. Jill suffered no harm from him beyond some agonies of humiliation, when she found herself relinquished for another, a superb young creature with hair redder than Charlotte's at its reddest.

To 'Ben' she turned for consolation. He, known to the world today as G. L. Benvenetti, was even at that time of his apprenticeship astonishing his young contemporaries with his post-impressionistic methods. Of Italian extraction but British-born—in Soho—he was more vehement than ever Gutts had been in every process of initiation. He laid paint on with a palette knife, and 'love on with a trowel,' as Jill to me long afterwards confided.

Heaven alone knows how far that affair progressed before her disillusion; but she emerged from it a little wiser, a little less ingenuous, and very much ashamed.

Thereafter she went warily, had 'no use,' she said, 'for men,' and became a member of the W.S.P.U.

Among the several young women brought by Jill to stay week-ends at Wroth, the most popular with all of us was Page. It seems that they were all called by their surnames irrespective of their sex—so these were to each other Page and Wrotham.

She had a face like an Aubrey Beardsley drawing, was long-limbed and black-haired, with narrow greyish eyes, high cheek-bones and a decorative mouth.

She too was a supporter of the W.S.P.U., and she and Jill were militants, but so far in theory only. The general trend at the Elm Grove School in Jill's time was anti-Suffrage. She and Page were the strongest forces there in favour of the movement, and led a small half-hearted following, who with one eye on Gutts—loud in his condemnation—ran with both hare and hounds to suit their purpose. To what extent Jill or her friend Page was gen-uinely involved, or whether this very active interest was merely a superabundance of energy and the desire for adventure, none could say. Charlotte, we have reason to believe, had her share in fanning the first sparks of their enthusiasm to conflagration.

Together they attended meetings at the house in Curzon Street, and listened in rapt silence to the exuberant verbosity of Char-lotte and of others, talked familiarly of 'Christabel' and 'Sylvia' and repeated parrot-phrases and stock arguments to all who cared to hear, concerning 'this man-made world of ours' and 'equal citizenship and living wages.' Together they walked for miles in processions, waving banners, purple, white and green; sold propa-ganda at street corners, and on one occasion, prior to a more seri-ous event, harangued for half an hour a crowd of loiterers out-side Chelsea Palace, who had come to heckle and abuse with jokes unpleasant. But not all their time was spent on matters such as these. There were other and many more distractions.

Pavlowa was at the Palace—Jill and Page went twice a week to see her, sent her anonymous bouquets—and waited with autograph albums in a queue for her arrival outside the stage door. They attended regularly the opera—in the gallery—heard *Parsifal,* the *Salome* of Strauss, *Tristan*—during which performance Jill, overcome, sat on the floor and wept. They went to all the fancy-dress 'hops' at Crosby Hall, the Chelsea Arts at Covent Garden, revels at the Botanical—Jill as a black pierrot in bell-bottomed trousers, very daring, with an emerald-green ruff the size of a cart-wheel round her neck—returning at five A.M. with six others in a taxi. They one-stepped and they bunny-hugged to the tune of "Everybody's Doing It," raved about Ethel Levey in "Hullo Ragtime," thought Gaby Deslys *too* lovely, adored Barker's Shakespeare, until the advent of the Russian Ballet, when all else was submerged in worship of Nijinsky, and Jill won a prize at the Elm's annual Sketch Club Exhibition for her "Après-midi d'un Faune," notwithstanding that it had been labelled by some unkindly wit "L'Après-midi d'un Elephant."

They managed to enjoy life, these young people of the pre-war generation. They were neither cynical nor blasé. They did not account for their emotions—or, as a side-line, other people's—in terms more suited to the privacy of a doctor's consulting room than the bar at a cocktail party—for cocktail parties were unknown. Psycho-analysis, except to a few remote students in Vienna, was unknown. Fixations were unknown, the word 'Libido' unknown—such vocabulary had not yet been invented. Young men who loved their mothers were not necessarily suffering from an Oedipus, or any other, complex; and one presumed that young unmarried girls in certain strata of society were virgins, since they did not demonstrate the fact that they were not.

But in spite of these and similar repressions, Jill and her friend Page as ardent suffragettes discussed all sorts of vital topics, besides the most important one of marriage.

There was for instance, the problem of 'the Scourge.' Charlotte had written pamphlets on the subject, which Page and Wrotham diligently handed to startled lady shoppers in Oxford Street.

Both were determined they would not marry unless 'he' were willing to undergo a pre-nuptial medical examination. And there again, the question to be considered was 'Should a married woman follow a career?' Certainly she should if she were so disposed; and only on the understanding that the man of her choice must accept and respect his wife's freedom of thought and action, would Jill contemplate taking to herself a husband. These arguments were further emphasised to Page on an afternoon in September, 1913, when, having 'done' a matinée of *The Glad Eye* in the pit, they dropped in for tea at Fuller's.

Although they were the best of friends, Page, we understand, was not nearly so communicative about her emotional state of being as was Jill. While Jill to Page confided every detail of her experimental dalliance with Gutts and Ben, Page to Jill had not so much as hinted that she was more interested in Larry than anyone else might be who was so 'pally' with his sister. True, during week-ends spent at Wroth that summer, she had painted a portrait of him in a tennis shirt thrown negligently open at the throat, and a very good portrait too; but what of that? Page was always painting portraits. She had painted Jill's portrait, and her own portrait, in a mirror—very black and white—and had even had a portrait of her father accepted for the R.A., and crowded out. But beyond the dispassionate declaration that she found Larry 'structurally good' and that she'd rather 'do his figure than his head,' Page had been noncommittal.

When, therefore, on that September afternoon in Fuller's Jill to Page propounded her views on marriage and the dangers thereby incurred, she was rather dashed to receive from Page no encouraging response. No response, in fact, at all. Page carefully selected from the dish upon the table a slice of angel cake, and answered nothing.

"For statistics have proved," said Jill, selecting in her turn a chocolate éclair, "that seventy-five per cent of the male population—over twenty-one—in Great Britain indulge in promiscuous sexual relationships; and as Christabel said last night at the meeting, the whole future of the race depends on uprooting the evil consequences of prostitution—or words to that effect. After all, if it weren't for the lascivious demands of men there wouldn't be any prostit—"

"Oh, shut up! You make me sick!" Page explosively interrupted. "You simply repeat what's told you. How can they possibly know? You can't tell me they've been round to every man over twenty-one in the British Isles in order to prove it."

And with a heightened colour in her usually pale cheeks, Page took another slice of angel-cake.

Such heresy as this rendered Jill speechless for certainly ten seconds. With horrified eyes and the chocolate éclair halted halfway to her lips, she stared at the munching Page.

"But of course they've proved it! Do you think they'd say it if they hadn't proved it? Why, the whole point of last night's meeting was to prove that *all* men, with very few exceptions, *do*—"

"You can take it from me they don't!" snapped Page. "It's all very well to bring in statistics. People always do bring in statistics when they've nothing else to fall back upon. I believe in being fair," declared Page, and the colour heightened in her cheeks. "I don't agree with the way some of them—of us, I mean," she supplemented quickly, "—draw the long bow. I mean you can't generalise. After all there are exceptions. I'm sure neither of your brothers, for instance, would— You know," she finished rather lamely.

"I don't know," replied Jill, frowning. "I'm not in the habit of enquiring into the private lives of my brothers. Prior is an old stick, anyway, absolutely pre-Flood in his attitude to women; all very nice and chivalrous, I grant you, and I'm not saying anything against chivalry—except that it tends to make you feel that you belong to another age when you were guarded behind towers and sat at your tapestry all day, while your man went out to shoot venison—or whatever it was they shot. But I don't suppose that even Prior has been entirely immune from what my sister Charlotte calls the 'mating instinct.' There's no harm in that, we know. It's promiscuity that's so rotten. I'm not saying that either of my brothers have ever been promiscuous, but I bet you anything you like that my brother Larry has some nice little chorus girl tucked away somewhere in—"

"And I bet you anything you like he hasn't!" Page contradicted hotly. "I think you're perfectly revolting, Wrotham, the way you talk. It isn't funny."

"What do you mean—it isn't funny? It's not meant to be funny. You really are being rather unintelligent about this, Page. Going off the deep end just because I said—"

"It's not what you said—it's what you inferred," Page retorted, swallowing.

"But— Good Lord!" expostulated Jill. "I never heard such rot in all my life. To hear you talk, anyone would think that you were anti. I don't propose to have an argument—but I must say I'm surprised. Come on—let's ask for the bill and go."

They asked for the bill and went, parting rather coldly outside in Regent Street.

Page jumped on a bus with a brief "So long," and Jill, with a smileless nod, walked away in the direction of Piccadilly Circus.

Although nearly six o'clock, the air was warm and summery; the amber light of an early autumn evening enriched the mellow tone of that superb crescent of Nash's, which had not yet been entirely demolished. And while her surface thoughts roamed foolishly, some remoter, more static portion of Jill's mind, and all in her that was artist, registered that lovely tone and the gold light above it, and below it the harsh contrasting streak of the scarlet motor omnibuses. She must do a sketch sometime of that curve between the Piccadilly and Swan and Edgar's—if she could get just this lighting. But what a wickedness to destroy such perfect symmetrical design with the frontage of that hideous hotel—and what in the world had made Page go off the deep end like that? The silly ass! She'd probably been listening to her people—they were all violently anti, and Page had been abroad with them for the last month, after leaving Wroth. Page was awfully weak, really; anyone could talk her round. If it hadn't been for me, reflected Jill, she'd never have been in with us at all. She's not much good in any case—can't speak, made a perfect ass of herself the only time she ever tried to. So did I for that matter. Well, anyhow I don't care if she *is* shirty, she'll have to get over it, that's all. Turning round on me like that—I bet you anything you like she's gone anti. Little swine, after all her gas about suffering for the Cause and hoping she'd get run in, so that she could go on hunger strike. I'd like to see *her* with a rubber tube shoved up against her uvula. . . . That's a jolly hat.

Jill stopped before Louise's to admire the jolly hat. So high crowns were coming in—but they won't suit me, Jill decided, I'm too wide in the face. She wondered should she grow her hair. All the Slade people had short hair now and it rather damned you. Yes, but if she *did* grow her hair, it meant altering her style, and she had a distinct style of her own. Not smart. I could never be smart—Jill decided, staring between hats at her reflection in the mirror at the back of the shop-window—I'm not the smart type. Now Page *is*. She's slick and well-drawn, but I'm a mess.

My nose is all wrong and my eyes are too wide apart and my skin looks like Thames mud. Gosh! What a mess I am! Why aren't I beautiful and exciting and black and white like Page, damn her? What on earth's the matter with her anyhow? Going off like that. You know I mightn't look so bad in that hat—it's the right colour—I wonder if it's frightfully expensive. I might go in and ask.

But Jill did not go in and ask, for in the moment that she hesitated should she or should she not—a terrific crash spun her round, in time to see the extraordinary spectacle, as of a miniature Niagara, falling in prismatic glassy waves, when the window-pane of the leather merchant's opposite curved out and over before it came hurtling in a spray of crystal splinters to the pavement.

Jill, in company with a hundred others, stood aghast and open-mouthed, while a police whistle blew twice in shrill succession, and magically from all directions policemen hurried to the spot. Then all the traffic stopped, and escaping from the surging crowd Jill dashed across the road, her heart rising to her throat with a queer sickening sensation, for she had recognised a woman in a mackintosh—and that woman was her sister Charlotte.

What followed had all the vivid unreality of nightmare. She heard feminine screams and exclamations, the jeering and booing of cab and omnibus drivers, a policeman's voice calling for order, uniformed arms barring the way. She saw blood on a man's face —he must have been hit by falling glass—and an excitable man with a beard, in the doorway of the shop, furiously gesticulating, pointing, mouthing. She saw Charlotte, her old felt hat half off her head and hanging by one pin to a lock of white dishevelled hair. She saw Charlotte's face, clay-white and very calm, with blood oozing from a cut on her chin. In her right hand she held, as though it were a sceptre, an awkward-looking instrument something like a hammer. And there she stood stock-still, an untidy shabby figure in a dun-coloured mackintosh, facing the crowd, at bay.

Suddenly, as though pulled by a wire, her head jerked up, her hat fell off. The crowd thought that a side-splitting affair. Undaunted, Charlotte lifted her voice and spoke.

"Women of England—"

Boos, jeers and hisses drowned her words. She raised a hand as though to call for silence. "Women! Hear me! There are limits to our powers of endurance—"

"You're right, there are!"

Loud laughter, grinning faces everywhere, nightmare faces, wide-open mouths, a comedy inferno. Jill closed her eyes. She could not look at Charlotte, or at those awful grinning faces.

"Women! Mothers! The Government has betrayed its trust. Today and every day your daughters—fellow-women—are being tortured in our prisons—"

"Serve 'em bloody well right!"

"Take her away. We don't want the vote—"

Above the yelling clamour, Charlotte's voice rang clear. "Will you be a traitor to your sex? This that I do is done for you and those who follow you. Man's tyranny must end—we live in a civilised world—"

"Civilised be—" A taxi-driver pushed himself to the fore. "D'you call that civilised?" he shouted, pointing to the gaping window. "*Dahn* wiv 'er, I say—and dahn wiv 'em all. Listen to me—I know what I'm sayin'. My missus is one of 'em—broken up our 'ome, she 'as—was marched off to quod with a gang of 'em last week; she don't know what she wants, but she don't want *me* no more nor our 'ome nor our kids. These — — bitches have got 'er well under; they've been an' broken up my 'ome—that's what I say. *Dahn* wiv 'em all. Every bloody one of 'em—"

He stopped abruptly, removing his cap to wipe his forehead, his face red and shining with sweat.

The crowd applauded wildly. People on the tops of omnibuses cheered. Above the din arose one feeble, unheard cry of "Shame." Jill did not know that she had spoken.

"What we cannot gain by peace," vociferated Charlotte, "must be gained by war—"

"Why can't they stop her? Why don't the police—"

"*Now* can you wonder—"

"Disgraceful!"

Jill stood wedged tightly in the heaving crowd. She could feel a man's hot breath on the back of her neck, she could smell women's perspiration—she could move neither forward nor back. The blood hammered in her temples. She felt sick. She saw a policeman's hand clamp down on Charlotte's shoulder, she saw Charlotte struggling; saw the policeman grab her round the waist and lift her bodily from the ground.

The crowd cheered again at that.

"That's the way! Treat 'em rough!"

"I've no sympathy," muttered a thin gentleman in pince-nez and a top-hat, standing just in front of Jill, "no sympathy at all. They deserve all they get. They're mad—maniacs—"

Jill was breathing deeply through her nose, her hands so tightly clenched that her nails bit into her palms. Something seemed to snap inside her head. "She's *not* mad—she's *right!* It's you and men like you who— Beast! You *beast* to say it—*beasts*—all of you—"

She dashed forward, using her fists and elbows to force her way, doubling to dive beneath the outstretched arms that made attempt to hold her back.

"You shan't take her," screamed Jill. "You shan't—"

A policeman seized her by the throat and wrist, his hand was on her mouth, she dug her teeth into it—"You're hurting me," she spluttered, "you great bully! Leave me alone—can't you? I want to know where they're *taking* her—"

"Where I'm taking you," grinned the policeman. "Come on now—since you've asked for it, and come quiet."

"Look here!" Someone thrust himself between Jill and the policeman. "You can't do that, you know. You've no right to run her in—*she* hasn't done anything."

"Now then, now then"—the policeman pushed him violently to one side. "You get out o' this or you'll get taken, too."

Jill, ceasing now to struggle, was dragged away.

She saw no more of Charlotte, for the crowd closing in blotted out all view, save that of jeering faces.

Jill found herself walked off between two policemen. Her wrist ached badly, her throat was bruised; she still had the salt acrid taste of the policeman's hand upon her lips, her eyeballs throbbed, but yet her heart exulted. This was triumph! This was life! Adventure! This was worth imprisonment—although she did not think she'd like to go on hunger strike. How sick Page would be to think she'd missed it!

. . . And that nice young man who'd tried to save her had, Jill thought, a rather interesting face.

III

As a result of that affair of September 25th, Charlotte was sentenced to three months' hard labour. Jill, charged with assaulting the police, received a two weeks' sentence in the second division. Both appeared at Bow Street and were removed immediately to Holloway.

Under Winston Churchill's new prison rule which permitted certain privileges to the suffragette prisoners, it was not compulsory for either Jill or Charlotte to be searched. Charlotte, therefore, had taken the precaution to supply herself with paper and pencils which she carried, so her diary tells us, "in a linen pocket tied round my waist, and pinned to my combinations under my corsets."

Extracts from these daily jottings, necessarily brief owing to shortage of paper, have been published by permission of my sister in John Fustian's *Ladies' Gallery*.* Although the more revolting details have been omitted in Fustian's book, we learn from the same that Charlotte went on hunger strike, and was forcibly fed over a period of three weeks, when, owing to the gravity of her condition, she was released under order of the Cat and Mouse Act.

I saw her on one occasion only, before she escaped—disguised in a black wig—to Florence, in company with a wealthy American woman, wife of an attaché at the Italian Embassy here, who was an enthusiastic sympathiser. She, for six months, sheltered Charlotte in her villa at Fiesole. I was shocked and horrified at Charlotte's appearance. She was almost unrecognisable. A hollow-eyed skeleton, with a nauseating skin eruption on her face and hands, and her hair snow-white. She greeted me with a pitiful attempt at bravado, and showed me her disguise, putting on her black wig for my benefit. I left that same evening for the Curragh, and did not see her again until the following year. Nor did she write to me. Perhaps I too forcibly expressed my own opinion of these militant tactics, and her fanatic adherence to them. However that may be, we parted that day, and did not meet again until August, 1914.

When early in the New Year I came home on week-end leave to Wroth, I found Jill there alone. She had left 'The Elm' she

* Batchelors', 1928.

told me, and had 'finished with Page.' Page, she said, was a black-leg. She had found out that Page and Larry were having an 'af-fair.' She had no use for either of them. Any friendship, whether male or female, that she had counted on in *her* life, she said, had always proved 'a wash-out.' In future she was going to concentrate all her energy on animals—not the human kind.

Her grin had the same *gamine* quality as Charlotte's at her age.

"As for instance, this"—she showed me the anatomical study of a horse—after Leonardo. "I'm making myself draw. I forced myself to do it—from a copy. And even the Elm—antediluvian though its methods of tuition are—even the Elm might cavil at a copy. However"—she put away the drawing—"anyone can slosh on paint with a palette knife, and call it art. I'm sick of this pseudo-stuff. Bad workmanship called by a big-sounding name. Post-impressionistic bunk! But it's not only my style that's changed," said Jill earnestly. "It's everything. My Ego. My Me. The old Me let me down so damnably."

I did not press her for an explanation. I knew that in due course and in her own time it would come.

And in her own time it did.

Next morning we rode through Cheam, over Cheam Hill, and down into Amersley on the other side. The day was grey and sullen, with a warning of snow in the sky, the frost-beaded turf crisp beneath our horses' feet. A spinney of young larches fringed the rounded hilltop, and between their slender stems the distance lay submerged in scarves of mist, grey upon deeper grey, veiling the valley. Everywhere winter brooded; the leaves were dead and wet under the hedges, rimed too, with frost, and barren; no sign of spring as yet, no song of bird, only that muffled quiet, the brown ploughed earth, the welcome rich relief of moist green grass, the purple dark of wood.

There was beauty in that winter's morning on Cheam Hill. I never saw it so again. A few months later tents were in the valley. Horse-lines, huts, covered all the spaces, and Cheam Royal was a hospital. Today pylons stand like the stark skeletons of robots, pointing the way we rode.

We skirted the gates of Cheam Royal, which, newly painted a bright scarlet, flaunted a yellow A.A. sign. At that time it had been recently sold by the heirs of Ferdinand Mendoza, deceased, to a private hotel syndicate, and resident visitors, for the most part retired service men or their widows, spinster ladies and their dogs, formed the standard clientèle.

"If David hadn't died, I suppose Charlie would have had that place," Jill commented as we passed the scarlet gates, "I mean—now that the poor old dotty man has gone. It was rotten luck on Charlie losing her husband like that. I suppose they were terribly in love. Was Father very beastly to her? I shouldn't be surprised if that's why she's so hot on the subject of parental control. She's awfully against all ultra-disciplinary methods, especially in education. She's all for the Montessori system. . . . Come on! I'll race you to those larches."

She raced me to the larches, and she won. She was riding a polo pony I had given her—part Arab. She was riding him astride.

"You've put on weight," Jill told me critically when I came up. "How many days a week do you hunt? I've half a mind to go back to Ireland with you. Would I have a good time? I don't suppose I should. I hate army men— Look out! It's very rabbity just here. . . . You haven't said a word about my new habit. What do you think of it?"

I told her what I thought of it, and of women who rode astride.

"Yes—well," said Jill, "you make me tired. And you're only trying to get your own back because I said you'd put on weight.

So you have. You look like the Mayor and Corporation. You only
need a gold chain. *Every*body who has any horse sense rides
astride nowadays. At least they hack astride. I don't hunt astride
because it's not so safe—although some say it is."

And presently: "You know—I think it was that time in prison
made me change." She had a disconcerting habit of pursuing her
thoughts aloud with little relevance to the immediate topic of
discussion. "I began to wonder—what was it all about? What
was I there for? What were any of us there for—suffering! As if
there wasn't enough misery in the world without *asking* for it.
An experience, certainly, but one I wouldn't be in a hurry to repeat. . . . There was an old woman used to clean my cell. One of
the other prisoners. She was frightful. She hadn't any nose. It
was all eaten away with—you know what." Jill's face screwed
up as though in pain. "That things like that can *be*. And are
allowed to be. And then you're told that God is Love. Yes—I
know—you needn't look like that. I can say what I feel, can't I?
You wait till *you* go to quod. Then you'd see. There was a tiny
little window with bars—under the ceiling, right high up. And
everything stank—the whole place stank—the lavatory stank.
There were hunger strikers in cells on either side of me. Their
screams were awful! Like a description I once read in a book—
I've forgotten the title; translated from the French—of a woman
having a baby. Just the same sort of screams. I thought it might
be Charlie, but it wasn't. She was put miles away from me. Why
does Charlie do it? Do you think it's anything to do with her
husband being killed so suddenly? They had a row or something,
hadn't they? And no time to make it up. . . . How awful! . . . I
often wonder if Charlie and the others who go in for all this self-
torture aren't trying to expiate some sort of sin. I don't know. It's
all a muddle. Life's such a *muddle*."

Jill stared between her horse's ears. The lift of her narrowed

chin was faintly arrogant, at variance with the sweet melting
curves of her lower lip. The wings of her sparrow-brown hair lay
soft against her cheek under the hard-brimmed bowler. Her thin
square shoulders opposed the virgin curves of the young breasts
that swelled beneath the boyish habit. She looked half girl, half
Ganymede.

She jerked her head round, frowning at me. "Why is there all
this fighting everywhere, this kind of negative attitude to things
and people—never anything *positive?* . . . This fuss and bother in
Ireland—any minute there may be civil war, and then all *our*
fighting, the revolt of *us* against man's tyranny . . ." She began
her parrot-talk. I told her to shut up, and surprisingly, for two
minutes, she did. Then:

"Do you remember how Walt Whitman says, 'I could turn
and live with animals, they eat and sleep and don't make me sick
discussing their duty to God'?"

I corrected the misquotation.

"Well, anyhow, that's the gist of it. And that's why I'm painting—these."

She leaned forward in the saddle till her lips touched the neck
of her little horse. "Because you—and things like you, my darling," I heard her whisper, "are the *only* things that make life
bearable."

I thought her over-young to have discovered that.

IV

Before I went back to Ireland I called to see Edie at the house
in Cheyne Walk. I found that the affair between Page and Larry
which had caused seemingly a breach between Page and Jill, had
materialised into an engagement. Larry had announced the news
to his mother that very morning. She greeted me with tears.

"I don't know what to say, I'm sure," Edie with her usual in-consequence, complained. "I want my boy to be happy, and if it's for his happiness—but is it? We know nothing about her beyond that she's one of those art-students. Of course she's stayed with us at Wroth, and we all liked her very much, but I've never met the family. I hear her father's a dentist in West Kensington. Not even West End. I'm not saying anything against dentists—I'm sure mine's a marvel—but there *is* something about teeth—" Edie paused to dab her eyes with a wisp of lacy handkerchief. "And not a word of warning. He simply walked into my room, when I was in bed, to tell me he's engaged. I don't know what your poor darling father would have said. He'd have gone mad, I think. I was only just beginning to get over the shock of Jill going to prison. What is it, Angel Face?" This is to an aged and odoriferous Pekingese that was making unpleasant sounds. "Does she want to go walkee-walkee? Does she want to be goo' girl? Open the garden door for Ching-Lu, darling, will you? She's asking to go out."

Thankfully, I opened the garden door for Ching-Lu.

"Don't you see a frightful change in me?" Edie enquired, pro-ducing from a silver chain bag a powder puff and mirror, by aid of which she tidied up her face. . . . "Oh, go along with you, flat-terer! That's all very well, but I can see for myself. I know I shall never be the same again. I'm having massage but it doesn't do a bit of good. It nearly killed me when Jill went to prison—it did really. I have to thank Charlie for that. Jill would never have *gone* to prison if it hadn't been for Charlie, and she would never have gone to that art school either. It was Charlie who persuaded me to send her there—against my better judgement. It's ruined her—that art school. I knew it would. But I was overruled. I'm weak where my children are concerned. Always have been." Edie's eyes, still childishly blue, and round as marbles, moistened again. "For all his faults I miss your father more and more with the children so difficult; and that naughty Jill—no consideration for *me* at all. They're so *selfish*. Always themselves and what *they* want—never what *I* want. Do you think I wanted to move from my lovely flat to this horrible slum? Yes, but it *is* a slum—nothing but slums at the back. And I suppose Larry and this Page— we don't even know her Christian name—Page! So ridiculous— I suppose they'll live in a studio in a mews and call it Bohemia. . . ."

Jill took Larry's engagement no less hardly than did Edie. A letter from Page announcing the news brought Jill rushing up to London in a state, and into Larry's office.

"Of all the swine!" Furiously she faced him across that desk where their father and grandfather had worked and died. *"Both* of you not to tell me! I knew, of course, that you were keen on each other, always going out together—and I was nowhere in it —wasn't wanted. But to spring this on me without a *word!* I do think, considering it was I who introduced you, that Page might have given me the hint, even if you didn't."

"If you weren't such a complete egoist," Larry drawled, "she would have. But as you're not usually interested in anything that doesn't concern yourself, she didn't see why she should."

"Oh!" Jill drew a long breath. "So that's it, is it? She's turning you against me. You've gone right away from me, lately. We're not together like we used to be. You're a *beast* to say that. I'm *not* an egoist. What a *foul* thing to say!"

Tears of indignation and self-pity sprang to her eyes. The injustice of it! She, who had suffered imprisonment, ignominy, disgrace for the Cause of Woman—to be accused of egotism—it was too much! She had lost Larry, she had lost Page—it seemed now that she had lost herself.

"If you would only consider," said Larry with a lordly smile that made her long to box his ears, "that this world was not created entirely for you and your affairs, my girl, you'd not only keep your friends—male as well as female—but you'd be a damn sight pleasanter to know."

Infamous, uncalled-for, abominable attack! Jill was silent with surprise and grievance. She knew Page had cooled off—had been cooling off for months, but to incite Larry, her own beloved Larry, to this cutting analysis, was a low-down game to play.

"If *that*," she said at last, "is what Page thinks of me, then all I can say is, the sooner she tells me so herself the better. I see it all! She was only friendly with me so that she could get *you*. Well, she's got you, and I wish you joy!"

She banged out of the room and down the passage that led to the outer office, her eyes blinded with tears. She passed through the outer office at a rush, and at the swing door that opened to the street she encountered, as she went out, a young man coming in. They collided.

"So sorry!" panted Jill.

"I am not. I am happy"—the young man removed from his head a shabby brown slouch hat—"to have this opportunity of meeting you again. I hoped—but never thought—I should. The last time we met was under cover of the police."

She recognised him then—the young man who had intervened on her behalf at the time of her arrest.

"And if," he added quickly, as Jill recovered breath, "you will only wait one moment while I deliver this" ('this' was obviously a manuscript done up in brown paper and tucked under his arm) "I will rejoin you if I may. You remember me—I hope. Perhaps you don't."

"I do," said Jill.

"Don't go," said he. "Wait half a sec. I'm coming back."

He dashed into the office.

Jill waited at the door. Her face was hot, and her heart thumped; the tears dried in her eyes like magic. She opened her bag and produced a powder puff. Surreptitiously she powdered. And in little more than 'half a sec' he was back again.

"Are you going any particular way?" he asked her. "Because my way is yours. It is now"—he glanced at his wrist-watch—"twelve-thirty-seven precisely. You wouldn't care to lunch with me, of course?"

"But—" said Jill.

"My name," he said, "is Chance. It *is* my name though I admit that it sounds doubtful. J. M. Chance. James Matthew. Your brother knows me. He has just accepted a manuscript that a dozen other publishers have refused. But that he doesn't know, and that you need not tell him. Shall we lunch at the Sa— Wait!" He plunged a hand into his pocket and drew out two half-crowns, a threepenny bit, and four coppers. "Not enough, I think, for the Savoy. I have never lunched at the Savoy. I should like to lunch at the Savoy. That experience, in view of the fact that I am about to receive a substantial cheque on account of advance royalties—is yet to come. In the meantime, shall we take a bus to Hampstead Heath and lunch at Jack Straw's Castle?"

Jill began to laugh. She stood still on the pavement of Soho Square and laughed until she very nearly cried. James Matthew Chance watched her critically.

He said: "You're inclined, I think, to be neurotic."

Jill blew her nose and powdered it again, looked up, and, blushing, told him:

"You're the most incredible person I've ever—"

"Yes, and so are you. You're utterly incredible. I knew you were incredible the moment that I saw you there in court the day that you were charged."

"You were in court!" gasped Jill.

"I was. You looked so very like a weasel."

"Like a—"

"Weasel. Shaped like a weasel. Very like a—brown one. In a trap. Thin and frightened. With little thin hands clutching at the rail of whatever it was they put you in. And I heard your name called and your address, and then I meet you coming out of Kell & Wrotham's, and it doesn't take a superhuman intelligence to deduce from a certain similarity of feature—though not of colouring—he being a blond and handsome beast and you being neither blonde nor handsome, though I hope something of a beast—"

"You're very glib, aren't you?"

"I am. It's nerves. I'm always glib when I am nervous. I shall bring the House down with my maiden speech."

"Are you then," asked Jill respectfully, "standing for Parliament?"

"Not at the moment. I wish you'd let me say—without unnecessary interruption—what I want to say, which is to this effect, that I am thankful your brother accepted my book— By the way he is your brother, I hope, and not your—"

"Brother," said Jill.

"—accepted my book before all *this,* otherwise you might have suspected some ulterior motive in my method of approach."

"As if I should!" Jill protested, turning scarlet.

"You blush! You *had* suspected me. I admit the way of an unpublished author is hard and that he will stop at no transgression, even that of ingratiatingly accosting a publisher's innocent young sister as a means to an end to see himself in print; but in this I can assure you—"

"I'm not so young," said Jill.

"I don't wish to be personal, but I should say you were four-

teen. We shall, of course, quarrel like hell, because nothing in-
furiates me more than being interrupted. You have done so six
times already in the short while I have known you—"

"I like that!" indignantly cried Jill. "It's you who won't let me
get a word in edgeways."

"You don't have to. *Ne m'importe que tu sois sage, sois belle
et sois*—nevertheless I'm very glad that my book was accepted
before I met you for the second time, because I can now force
my company upon you with an easy conscience. Do you realise
that we've been blocking up this pavement for the last fifteen
minutes? Is it not time that we moved on?" queried James Matthew Chance.

They sat side by side on top of the Hampstead bus, Jill and
James Matthew Chance. He still talked. Jill shivered in her furs,
but although he had no overcoat he appeared impervious to cold.
He wore grey flannel trousers and an old Harris tweed jacket,
and under the jacket a multi-coloured sweater, and under the
sweater a grey flannel shirt; no cuffs, no gloves. His hands—Jill
always looked at people's hands and judged accordingly—his
hands were long and mobile with faint dark hairs upon their
backs that matched the hair upon his head. This was brushed
sleekly back from a high, corrugated forehead. His grey eyes
under the forehead were set deep in, black-lashed; his mouth
blunt-cornered with a square underlip; his teeth square too, and
very white. She had no criticism to pass on his appearance, which
she found both personable and pleasing, even though his clothes
were very shabby.

"Aren't you frozen without a coat?" Jill asked him. "Would
you like to go inside?"

"You pity me. You remark I have no coat. You think I can't
afford one. Well, you're right."

"I'm sorry," said Jill, giggling.

"Granted," said he, coldly.

"Oh, dear!" Jill began to laugh again. "You make me hysterical."

"Do I? That's a good sign. Do you like me as much as I like you?"

"I don't know how much you like me."

"Enough to want to sit on the top of this bus with you for the rest of my life—or at least for the next several hours of it. Will you come with me to the first night of the new show at the Pantheon?"

"When?"

"Tonight."

"Do you mean it?"

"Would I ask you if I didn't?"

"Well, I didn't know," said Jill doubtfully, "whether—"

"I could afford it? How always right you are! I can't. But the seats are complimentary, and I go in a professional capacity—as dramatic critic to the *Daily Echo* on such occasions as my Chief is otherwise engaged."

"Oh! So you're a dramatic critic?"

"I am not a dramatic critic, but I do dramatic criticism. The two are not necessarily synonymous."

"Are you a journalist?"

"I am what is called a free-lance journalist. Would you like me to tell you all about myself? I'm dying to. You will find me a supreme egoist."

"I've just been told I'm one."

"Of course you are. All the right people are. Egotism is the fountain and the source of life."

"If that's so," said Jill frowning, "why does one take it so unkindly when one is accused of being an egoist?"

"I don't think that one does. I would take it as a compliment. The purest form of egotism is impersonal."

"But what form of egotism *is* impersonal?"

"That—or so I should imagine—which embraces the universe in relation to oneself."

"That's *colossal* egotism!"

"Exactly. Only colossal egotism *can* be impersonal—as for example the colossal egoists who wrote the Gospels. And on a plane only a degree less colossal, the chap who did the Parthenon frieze —and Michael Angelo."

"Would you say they were impersonal—and egoists?"

"Well, weren't they? To the extent that their I, their whole ego, was developed to the uttermost point of consciousness. In the case of Phidias and Michael Angelo, their consciousness did not surpass the limits of art—in the case of those others—"

"How do we know those others ever wrote the Gospels? It may all be legend."

"A legend, nevertheless, that has changed the face of the world. They, and only they, have any right to claim their ego. We— and such as we—have not. For we have no consciousness."

Here was a poser, Jill puzzled over it in silence for a minute.

"However"—he smiled down at her—"I shouldn't let it worry you. There's hope for us yet. Man's development is young—"

"But the world is old. Civilisations have come and gone—"

"Yes—and life recurs in cycles of eternal repetition. . . . Must we go on like this? I'd much rather talk about you than the riddle of the universe."

"You said you wanted to talk about yourself."

"At this moment you *are* myself."

Jill's colour heightened. I say! she thought, we're going much too fast. "And so," she said sedately, "you've had your book accepted. Is it good?"

"Not good enough. I shall write a good book one day. You don't really want to hear about my book—and neither do I. I want to hear what happened to you in prison. What did they do to you? Did you hunger-strike?"

"No, I didn't. I don't wish," said Jill, sullenly, "to be reminded of it. It was foul."

"I'm quite sure it was, but I'd like to ask you a few questions. Are you genuinely interested in Women's Rights? Do you—personally—want the vote? And why? Do you believe in militancy as a means to an end—or have you been chivied into it by those ravening old hags?"

"Ah! I thought as much!" Her glance snapped round at him. "You're anti!"

"Not at all. I'm in all probability a more sincere suffragist than you are—or ever will be. I do not, however, approve of arson, stone-throwing, window-smashing, self-flagellation—or any other form of fanaticism which is, or may be, symptomatic of over-charged sex, and the repression of the natural instincts."

"'If you want a closed door opened,'" quoted Jill, "'you must hammer till you—'"

"That sort of poppycock," he interrupted, "won't go down with me, you know, however adorable you may look while you are saying it! And we're not going to argue," he added in a hurry, "because we have to get off here. Come along." He took her arm. "We've lots more to tell each other. It's your turn now. What do you do besides taking part in suffragette riots, and getting run in by the police?"

"Well," began Jill, "I studied art for three years at the Elm Grove School, and now I'm like you a free lance."

In this manner did they talk their way from the bus stop to Jack Straw's Castle, where they lunched on hot soup, cold beef and pickles. Afterwards they walked on the Heath, still talking, and sat and watched the red sun sink behind a clump of firs, while slowly the sky crimsoned, and the bright sharp winter afternoon faded from golden rose to dusk; then one cold star came up above the fir-tops and it was evening.

"I didn't mean to spend the day with you," said Jill.

v

It was the first of many days they spent together, in London and at Wroth. Jill, who divided her time between the two, divided her life accordingly. At Wroth she worked—or thought she did—at her paintings of animals, and at the anatomy thereof. But work was now a secondary consideration in the face of more immediate demands. Jill was in love. Not besottedly or romantically in love. She and James Matthew Chance (she called him J. M. for short) had discussed Love from every angle, beginning with the Hellenic or Platonic ideal, passing through the metaphysical, as exploited by Schopenhauer, to the purely emotional as exploited by themselves, which was not, and never must be, so they unanimously agreed, all-pervading. Love, according to these two, of their time distinctly 'modern' in their approach to a subject that is always new yet older than the hills, was a necessary adjunct to their mutual existence, but by no means the whole of it. Even though they found each other unbelievably delightful, even though they were touchingly engrossed with the stupendous discovery that they 'loved,' they were far too intelligent (Jill was very partial to the word 'intelligent') to let their emotions run away with them. Oh, dear, no! He must write his books. She must paint her pictures. They must follow the paths of their respective careers, irrespective of their natural and very urgent instincts.

"You may presume," said J. M. during one of these discussions, "that the impulse which drew me so violently to you at sight is mere physical attraction. You are wrong. There is more to it than that. The human mind—or soul, if you prefer it more poetically put—has been hitherto an unknown quantity. There are certain theorists today who claim to divide this unknown quantity into two *known* quantities: the conscious and the subconscious. They claim to be able to dissect the mind—or soul—by a process of psychological analysis. Our dreams, for instance, can no longer be dismissed as the result of indigestion, but may be regarded as the expression of the unexpressed. *My* unexpressed—therefore—or subconscious mind desires you every bit as much, if not more than does my conscious."

"I see," said Jill, doubtfully.

"You don't at all. I must give you a book to read by an astounding man called Freud."

The name was new to Jill.

"These Germans," she said, "are wonderful. There's Weininger and Schopenhauer and Nietzsche—"

"This man is not a German, he's an Austrian," said James Matthew. "And a Jew."

"Ah! That accounts for it. I adore Jews."

"You do, do you? I suppose," said J. M. fiercely, "that means you've had an affair with a Jew."

"Don't be silly. I don't have affairs all over the place. You're my first real one. How unreasonable you are! I don't fly out about *your* affairs, although I'm certain you've had dozens."

"Not dozens."

"Well—half a dozen. That's what's so unjust."

J. M. frowned.

"What's unjust?"

"This one law for men and another for women. You—because you happen to be male—can know all there is to know about sex and love from the age of fifteen if you want to, so that you start life with the advantage of experience. But what experience have I? I'm still—at nearly twenty-four—a virgin."

"So I should hope!"

"There you are, you see! Why should I, at nearly twenty-four, still be a virgin—while you, at the same age and a few months younger if anything, are not?"

"Must we discuss all this? I think it a little unnecessary."

"I almost hate you when you tighten up like that. You remind me of my father. I suppose all men are—fundamentally—the same. *We* are lesser animals and must be treated as such: kept in purdah, ostracised, condemned, stoned—metaphorically speaking—for one single lapse—"

"Not," put in J. M., "among right-thinking people."

"You say not? Well then, you wouldn't mind if I—"

"Like hell I'd mind!"

Jill shook her head and sighed.

"Exactly. When it comes down to brass tacks, you're all alike. Man is jealous of his rights. Now—for the sake of argument—suppose we married."

"There's no argument about it. We're going to."

"Oh, no! Are we?" cried Jill delightedly.

"Aren't we?"

"You've not asked me."

"I ask you now."

"All right." Jill composed her face. "Go on. Begin. Propose to me properly. No one has ever proposed to me properly."

"And I've proposed to no one, either properly or improperly. . . . I love you. I want to have you. Completely, absolutely and for always. I want," whispered J. M., "to be with you; to be your husband and your man and your mate—"

Jill closed her eyes, and opened them again to gaze into his, and there they sat oblivious.

This extraordinary conversation took place in an underground teashop in Shaftesbury Avenue much frequented by members of the theatrical profession. Beneath the table J. M. gripped her knee.

"Will you marry me, young Wrotham?"

"Perhaps, one day. Not yet. I want to be sure."

"I *am* sure."

"Suppose it didn't turn out to the good?"

"Then we'd have a divorce."

"Divorce is not so easy."

"True. I'd have to knock you about and commit what is called in the newspapers, misconduct. . . . Your eyes are like a fawn's. They melt. I want to kiss your mouth."

"You can't here."

"I've only kissed as much of you as I can see. I want to kiss all of you . . . all over."

Jill caught her breath in sharply; again her eyelids closed in a delicious agony of love. "Let's go somewhere," urged J. M., "where I can kiss you."

They took a taxi and drove round Regent's Park and were madly and idyllically happy.

She was not to be so happy in all her life again as in that first half of the year 1914.

VI

Jill kept her secret firmly. None of the family guessed it. Even Larry was not told. That barb of his had struck well home. Neither he nor anybody else should again accuse her of talking too much about herself and her affairs. Even when one night at dinner Larry laconically alluded to one J. Matthew Chance, whose novel he had recently accepted to be published in the au-

tumn, and which might easily, he said, be a best seller—a bit too
pedantic, perhaps, and long-winded, but vigorous and quite well
written—Jill held her tongue, although her cheeks might have
betrayed her, if he had cared to see; but Larry had eyes only for
his Page. They were to be married in the summer; preparations
for the wedding were afloat, and Page in highest favour now
with Edie, who seemed to have forgotten that she had not always
been delighted at the thought of the engagement. Page, the most
tactful of young women, had asked Edie's advice as to the choos-
ing of her trousseau, and of the bridesmaids' dresses, and was in
Edie's estimation a paragon of virtue, beautiful to look upon and
charm personified.

To Jill, Page adopted an air of calm superiority, an elder-sis-
terly manner—although she was Jill's senior only by a year—
that Jill found extremely galling. Page was no longer interested
in art, or woman's suffrage. She had given up her painting. She
never went to private views. Matters of more urgency claimed
her time and her attention.

"You're like a hen about to lay," Jill remarked on one occasion, "all settled. I hope to God if ever I should marry that *I*
shan't get like that."

"You probably will," Page said. "People do, you know, when
they've everything they want."

"I wonder what it's like"—Jill smiled to herself—"to have
everything you want."

"Heaven," said Page.

"Yes, but it might easily be hell," retorted Jill.

She and J. M. often discussed this question of marriage. He
maintained that until he was earning an income sufficient to support her and a possible child—or children—they ought not to
'rush into it.'

She agreed—with reservations.

"You should certainly have an income, no matter how small; but I must say I hate the idea of being regarded as a parasite that has to be supported. I can support myself and we'll go fifty-fifty on the baby. We'd have enough to live on between us to get married now, today—if we wanted to. I can't believe you really want to. Do you?"

He assured her to her satisfaction that he did.

"Well, then, why not?" persisted Jill, mindful of how Page had looked when she said "Heaven."

Because he wanted to see what his book was going to do, he said. If his book were successful, he would have something other than himself to offer her, something worth while.

"What rot!" she said. The book, so far as she was concerned, was worth while—already. It didn't matter to *her* whether it were successful or not. *She* knew it was a good book. Was public opinion of his work to weigh in the balance of his life?

No, but the necessity for hard cash might. Did she think, then, that he was going to let *her* keep him? What did she think he was?

"Perhaps," said Jill thoughtfully, "we ought never to get married. Perhaps we ought to live together. We could tell the world we're married, and as a sop to social conscience I could take your name by deed poll."

"Now of course," declared J. M., "you're rushing to extremes."

"Not at all. I know perfectly well that our being married won't make any difference to my loving you, but I am a bit afraid," said Jill, still looking thoughtful, "that it may make all the difference to *your* loving *me.*"

"And why?"

"Because marriage does things to a man. Don't you remember? 'Time turns the old days to derision, our loves into corpses or wives.' Isn't that awful? Corpses or wives! Don't let it do things to you, J. M., if we get married, will you? Don't let's ever get used to one another. Let's keep it always fresh and young and lovely and surprising."

"And you don't know yet," said J. M., "how surprising I can be."

He paid frequent visits to Wroth when she was there alone, and Edie up in town. He would motor down. He had a ramshackle old saloon car—a 1906 model—and in this they would drive out to some riverside village and lunch on bread and cheese and ale at a pub. Afterwards they would sit in the car—it was not yet warm enough to sit out of doors—and he would read to her his manuscript. He was working on another. And as she listened, she criticised, and thought him fondly a great genius. He had style, form and vehemence. He was certain to succeed, and very soon they could—and would—be married.

He exercised remarkable restraint. She was his for the taking, and he made no attempt to take. Delicious, dangerous contact increased in both a heightened vitality; in him, more vigorous creative output; in her a restiveness.

So, swiftly, the winter passed and it was April. At Wroth the orchards were snowdrifts of blossom; primroses were out in woods and under hedges, and, as the spring days lengthened, the life of these young lovers narrowed to a waiting for the hours that they met. May came, with lavish outpour of full bloom, of chestnut and of lilac and golden droppings of laburnum, tall tulips in the flower beds and over all the earth the joyous green.

Early in June, Larry and Page were married and went for a walking-tour honeymoon in the Austrian Tyrol. . . . They were in Vienna on that Sunday June 28th, when the first shot was fired to murder the Archduke Franz Ferdinand and his wife, at Serajevo in Bosnia.

Even then, with the powder magazine ignited, the man-in-the-
street saw no cause for alarm. The shadow of civil war in Ireland, the failure of the conference of party leaders summoned
to Buckingham Palace by the King, were of more concern to
the British people than the troublous affairs of Central Europe
and the assassination of an Austrian Archduke.

Then followed, on July 23rd, Austria's ultimatum to Serbia,
and two days later declaration of war. The menace to the general peace of Europe could no longer be ignored. Mr. Asquith
stated that the situation was one of extreme gravity. The Kaiser
and his Council conferred at Potsdam until midnight. President
Poincaré and his Cabinet sat at the Elysée until six A.M. That
sounded grave indeed, but it would all blow over. They were
making mountains out of molehills. What had European war to
do with *us?*

But the headlines in the papers said that Russia had been mo-
bilised, and that martial law had been proclaimed in Germany.

And the man-in-the-street looked glum.

Jill and J. M. discussed the situation. Or rather he discussed it
and she listened, for naturally he must know the truth behind
these scares, being on the spot—so to speak—in Fleet Street.

J. M. said that it was obvious the whole thing, starting with
the assassination of the Archduke, was a put-up job. Germany
had been hankering for war with us for the last twenty years,
and now they were going to have it. They were going to get at
us, he said, through Belgium. We were under Treaty obligation
to defend the neutrality of Belgium, and that obligation dated
from the Franco-Prussian War of 1870, when Belgium had last
been threatened. She had seen of course the report of Sir Edward Grey's speech in today's *Telegraph?*

"We don't take the *Telegraph*," said Jill, "we take the *Times.*"

"Don't quibble. Then you should have seen it in the *Times.*

This is the situation as *I* see it," said J. M., "in a nutshell. Russia invades Austria. Austria prepares to invade Serbia, and calls on her ally—Germany—for help in accordance also with agreement—"

"Do you mean the Entente Cordiale?"

"How bright of you, my little weasel!"

"Of course! How silly of me! That's France and us. And if France calls on us—what then?"

"Then, my sweet, the deluge."

"No. J. M.! It *can't*—it *won't* happen!"

"Well," said J. M., "we will do as Mr. Asquith says. We'll wait —and see."

We waited till we could wait no longer; while those in power were straining every nerve to avert from Europe a calamity of horror unprecedented in the history of the world. We waited till the last hours of that fateful week brought the citizens of London in their thousands to the Palace gates, to know the answer to the ultimatum by which we were to stand or fall. And while we waited we shouted that we wanted war, we yelled for war, we clamoured for it. We were mad. War-mad. The fury of resentment with which we had watched the peace of Europe wantonly destroyed must at all costs be appeased—as a million graves in France today bear witness.

VII

So it came and we went to it. I saw little enough active service for I lost a leg at Mons, and after three months at a base hospital was attached to the Intelligence Department at H.Q. for the remainder of the war.

Larry joined the Oxford O.T.C., and went into training on

Salisbury Plain in September, 1914. J. M. joined the Artists' Rifles.

By the end of August, Belgian refugees arrived, and the British wounded.

My sister Charlotte with many of her fellow militants offered her services to the Government, and organised the Woman's Emergency Corps. Before the end of 1914 she wore the khaki uniform of an officer in the Women's Volunteer Reserve, and had her hair cropped short as a man's under her khaki cap.

Jill took lessons in first aid and became a V.A.D. She washed dishes, scrubbed floors, and emptied slops for fourteen hours a day. The work told on her; she ran a perpetual temperature and began to cough. Edie took her to a doctor who told her she was a 'T.B. type' and ordered her to Bournemouth for the winter. Jill refused to go. She would knock off work and take a rest, she said, but she would not go to Bournemouth.

Certainly not, when J. M. was in training down at Richmond and could see her twice a week.

And those who had said cheerfully it would be over in three months began to think it might be over in three years if we were lucky.

The price of coal went up, and the price of bread. A quart of milk cost ninepence, eggs were sixpence each. In March the Germans declared a blockade of Great Britain. In May the *Lusitania* was sunk. The posters screamed *Your King and Country Need You*. Kitchener's Army answered in its thousands. The 'Old Contemptibles' were nearly done.

Larry went out in April, 1915, and was killed at Neuve-Chapelle in May. His daughter Laurencina was born at Wroth in the same week.

The months dragged on. Horror succeeded horror, as day succeeded day. Hostile aircraft came and slaughtered our civilians.

Time was a vacuum, the world a charnel-house. What need to tell of it? Volumes have been written, and yet remain unfinished. We who know, remember. . . . But some of us forget.

VIII

In June, 1915, J. M.'s battalion was ordered to France. He had ninety-six hours leave, forty-eight of which he spent with his father, a parson in a Hampshire village; the remainder he spent with Jill.

He wired, asking her to meet his train at Waterloo. They had not seen each other since the news of Larry's death, for Jill had been at Wroth with Page when Larry's girl was born.

The train was forty minutes late. The station swarmed with khaki. Recruits were being drafted to a training camp. It might have been worse. They might have been going to France. She had not yet seen a troop train off to France. Page had asked her not to go with her to see Larry off. Page went to see him off alone. Page had been brave all through. Terribly brave. How could Page bear it so calmly? Perhaps having a baby helped. Edie was in a nursing home with a nervous breakdown. Poor Mum, who had been so hurt with Jill because she'd not worn black.

These men looked well and fit, and clean in their new uniforms. Why did they sing? Don't sing. What's there to sing for? Perhaps they won't have to go out. J. M. was going out. Don't let him go out. Let something happen not to let him go out. Make the war be over soon, can't you? Don't let him be killed. You let Larry be killed. Don't, don't, don't, God, let him be killed. . . . I can't pray, thought Jill. God doesn't hear.

> *Goodbye, Piccadilly,*
> *Farewell, Leicester Square.*

. . . Yes, well, that's all right. You don't have to go out yet. You're going into camp, under canvas. Safe.

It's a long, long way to Tipperary . . .

Don't *sing*. . . . How much longer must I wait? Make him come soon. I can't wait. God! Make him come soon. I can't. . . . Ten to twelve. How much longer must I . . .

She went up to a porter, an old bent man with a white goatee, wheeling a truck.

"I say! Can you tell me when the ten-fifty-five from—"

"Out o' the way, missie, please."

His train came in at last. A few elderly civilians got out, several men in khaki, a 'brass hat' and J. M.

"You're so *late*," said Jill.

"We were held up at Southampton by a troop train. How pale you are, my little sweet!"

His hand took hers and held it to his side. He wore the uniform of a private soldier. His face was brown as a nut. The heavy kit he carried made him appear bulky. An officer passed. J. M. jerked his hand to the salute.

"I wish you had a commission," said Jill. "It's easier out there with a commission."

"I wonder. Is it? . . . Where shall we lunch?"

"Anywhere. I don't want lunch."

"I do," said J. M.

He deposited his kit-bag and rifle in the cloakroom, and they took a taxi and drove to Jack Straw's Castle. He held her in his arms all the way, tightly, very close. She could feel the beating of his heart against her ear.

She made a pretence of eating lunch, but he ate hungrily. She pushed her plate away and set her elbows on the table and

her chin on her hands and watched his face as though she would
learn by heart each feature. She noticed things she had not seen
before, how clear and white the whites of his eyes; how his dark
hair so closely shaved to his head seemed to have bleached to a
rusty brown in contrast to the tanned skin; how the faint furrows from nose to mouth had deepened, and how on his forehead the pressure of his khaki cap had left an angry mark.

They talked, impersonally—of the war, of the air-raids, of food
rationing, of everything but Larry.

They talked of his book, which, published in the autumn of
1914, had sold barely five hundred copies. "A mistake to publish
it at all," J. M. said. "It was not a subject that would have any
appeal at a time like this. When the war's over I'll write another.
Or perhaps I won't. I've no particular desire to write again."

"But you will write again. You'll write great books," Jill said.
"All this is going to help."

"Maybe. . . . Do you mind if I have a pickled onion? But you
must have one too or I shan't be able to kiss you. I'm glad," J. M.
told her when both had eaten pickled onions, "that you were at
Wroth during last week's raid. You keep down there as much
as you can. I don't want you blown up."

She smiled bleakly.

"No, that wouldn't do at all."

"Promise me you'll chuck this V.A.D. work, darling. You're
not strong enough."

"I am. I'm awfully strong, really. Much stronger than I look."

"How are the temperatures?"

"I never take them."

"You must. You will, won't you? Promise?"

"All right." Jill moistened her lips. "What time do you leave
on Friday?"

"Two Ack Emma."

"Oh! Then it's not so long as I thought. When you said Friday I thought—"

"We'll have all today and all tomorrow," he said, not looking at her.

"Yes. . . . Where are you staying tonight?"

"At some pub or other."

Jill moistened her lips again.

"J. M.?"

"Yes, sweet?"

"Will you do something for me?"

"Anything."

"Perhaps you won't want to do this."

"If you want me to, I will. What is it?"

She spoke so softly with bent head that he had to bend his own to hear.

"Will you take me to stay with you—at some pub or other—tonight?"

He looked at her and saw her eyes, dark pools, with a star in each.

"Will you," she whispered, "J. M.?"

They went back to Waterloo, stopping *en route* at the Army and Navy Stores to buy a toothbrush, a wedding ring, and a suitcase.

"The suitcase," Jill said, "is most important of all. I *must* have a suitcase, even if there's nothing inside it. We can't arrive without any luggage for me. They'd know I wouldn't put my things in your kit-bag."

"But why buy a new one?" objected J. M. "Why not go home to Cheyne Walk and get an old one?"

"Because, silly, the servants don't know that I'm in town. I'm supposed to be at Wroth. And they'd ask questions and tell Mum.

And I'd have to lie. I don't mind lying about some things, but I don't want to lie about this . . . See?"

J. M. saw.

At Waterloo they looked up trains and discovered that one was leaving in ten minutes for a place in Surrey of which neither had ever heard. He took first-class tickets, and tipped the guard to give them a compartment to themselves.

The train halted at every station. They arrived two hours later at a village full of soldiers, and found a white inn called 'The Swan' on the edge of a green. There were only three bedrooms in the house, two already occupied, and the third, the landlord told them, was a single.

"Right. I'll sleep on the floor," said J. M.

It was a small room at the back, under the roof, with a casement window hung with ivy facing the yard, where stood a dovecote with no doves in it, and beyond the yard a meadow where two pied cows and one donkey grazed. Beyond the meadow a field of young corn swelled gently upward to a wood. In the unseen distance was heard a bugle call.

"They're under canvas somewhere near," said J. M. "The place is crowded out. I expect the married officers are in billets. We're lucky to get this room."

"Yes," said Jill.

The walls were whitewashed, the ceiling oak-beamed and low. The door, oak too, sloped at an angle. Over the narrow bed hung a text framed in straw; another hung above the washstand.

After a supper of moist cold ham and muddy coffee, they wandered through the cornfield to the little wood. The western sky was tinged with coral; frail stems of birches shone ghostly in the dusk.

"Don't let's go in," Jill said. "Woods are frightening at night. We'll sit outside—just here—and watch the moon come up."

They sat with their backs to the wood, leaning against a gate facing the shallow valley, where sprawled the grey-tented encampment. The village, a huddle of red and thatched roofs, lay to the left, and away beyond in a glory of evening gold stretched the dim outline of the hills.

They sat in silence, listening to muffled far-off sounds that emphasised the stillness: the neigh of a horse, a barking dog, the plaintive call of sheep; close behind them, the rustling and trembling of the wood.

A crescent moon shone hazily through mists of cloud; trees were black against the paling sky; there were no stars.

"Jill!" He put his hand under her chin to look through the failing light deep in her eyes. "When I come back," he said, "we will get married. But that won't make you more mine nor me more yours than we are now. This lovely thing you do for me makes me yours, heart and soul and body. You know that, don't you?"

She nodded wordlessly, turning her lips to his cheek.

He stroked her hair. "I've had a talk with my father about you. Would you like us to be married in his church?"

Again she nodded; her lips unfolded, quivering. He kissed them.

"How soft! All mine. No other man will do this to you while I'm away, will he?"

"No. Nor you—any girl—out there?"

"No, my sweet."

"There are girls out there at the base: V.A.D.'s and people—"

"There'll be no other girl. Ever."

The evening dark crept closer; low down in the west a last warm glow still lingered, dying as they watched. The moon drifted higher, silver-white; all colour turned to shadow, all shapes blurred.

Then through the tense quiet an owl hooted, startlingly near, and from the dusk-filled valley came the call of a bugle sounding the Last Post.

IX

Time crawled on, and war was still upon us. Boys who were children in 1914, were in the front line three years later. Conscription came, and those who had conscientiously objected and those who had held back, could not object or hold back any longer.

In 1918 came the great German offensive. In two days we lost 300,000 men.

Yet we rallied—how? We stayed, we strengthened, and we waited. Before the end of July our devastated divisions had been reinforced. The Americans had come—to bring fresh hope to the British and their thousands into France.

But the amazing courage and resistance with which for four years the Boche had stood the assaults of the Allied armies, could no longer be maintained. Hindenburg's line was weakening under that renewed attack, when British, Belgians, French, Americans, and the splendid troops from our Dominions joined in united forces, along the Flanders Front.

The war had taken Larry, and it took James Matthew Chance. He did not come back to marry Jill. He was killed at Festubert.

In September, 1918, Page died at Wroth of that mysterious infection called, for some unknown reason, 'Spanish flu.' Hundreds died of it at home; out there the base hospitals were full of it. Those in their fifth year of active service who had scraped through untouched, died in their beds of it. Jill, who nursed Page, took it, and recovered.

On October 4th Germany sent her peace note to President Wilson. Five weeks later, with the signing of a paper in a train, the long insufferable agony was over. The militarist spirit was subdued. "A war to end war," it was said, when for a breathing space the broken world stood still.

*   *   *

We are too near to realise the vertiginous force with which life has advanced in the process of reconstruction. The history of this new world built upon the wreckage of the old, has yet to be recorded. To the generations born during those four relentless years, the war is a name as remote as the wars of Napoleon.

To us, a memory.

Chapter Three

I

IN THE spring of the year 1934, Charlotte Mendoza, O.B.E., who had been visiting her old friend the Marchesa Berchielli at Fiesole, was on her way back to London. The crossing had been bad, and although she had stayed the night in Paris to break the journey, she was beginning to feel a trifle travel-weary. She wished now that she had come by air from Paris, much quicker and much pleasanter, and not so very much more expensive. But expense was a consideration nowadays with one's income reduced to less than half, and that Curzon Street house on her hands. There were no two ways about it. She would have to let it go. Sell it outright to the highest bidder, or convert it into flats. What a business! To say nothing of the wrench of breaking old associations. And although Prior had offered her a home at Wroth, she preferred her independence. She'd manage somehow, she always had, and she always would, for the time that she'd last out, which might or might not be much longer. I'm seventy-six, thought Charlotte, and like the whisky poster, still going strong. We *do* last out, we women of Wroth, we last longer than the men. Sabrina, ninety-five. Clare eighty-two, and I—old enough to be the grandmother of this attractive young thing opposite.

Charlotte glanced across at her vis-à-vis, who had entertained her so agreeably all the way from Dover. A doctor of medicine who, after a year's study under Freud in Vienna, was about to pursue a postgraduate course at the National Hospital for diseases of the nervous system, with a view to specialising in psychiatry. She and Charlotte had exchanged cards over a luncheon in the restaurant car, and the young woman had expressed herself as 'frightfully thrilled' to have met Charlotte. "Are you *the* Mrs. Mendoza?" 'The,' forsooth! So it seemed she was not yet forgotten by the post-war generation. It might be worth while after all to write those reminiscences for which Stephen Marriott was always clamouring. She had not thought there were any left who would care to read them. . . .

"So you're studying psychiatry," said Charlotte. (The words they use!) "What exactly does that mean?"

The girl smiled.

"More than I can tell you in the short time at our disposal, Mrs. Mendoza."

"Then," said Charlotte, briskly, "you must come and see me very soon, and tell me at your leisure. If you have any leisure. When I was your age we had leisure to spare, now we have none. Speed! Everything's speed: speed-boats; air-boats; racing-cars; news in motion; news on the air; non-stop cinemas. Soon we'll have television. The race can't go on at such high pressure. We'll crash," Charlotte stated, vigorously, "as sure as fate. You ought to know—you and your psychiatry. You come in contact with some queer specimens, I'll be bound. Hopeless neurotics, sexual perverts, megalomaniacs, and Lord knows what. The world's chock full of 'em. It wasn't so in my day. We may have been slow, but we were at least sane. Well!" Charlotte took her hat from the seat beside her and rammed it on her head. "It's a cycle. The whole of life's a cycle—of repetition—and we're at the dizziest round of it at the present moment—as Time goes. Which, according to Professor Einstein, doesn't go at all in the way we've been taught it should. But whatever the dimension, whether third, fourth, or fifth, in which we find ourselves, we will have to slow down. You mark my words! We can't go on at this pace. We'll have to stop. Man may think he can conquer the universe, but the universe'll conquer him. He's not God Almighty yet, and if he'd only remember that, he might achieve something."

"Then according to your reckoning, Mrs. Mendoza, science, progress, the mastery of the air and sea, go for nothing?"

"Yes. For this," retorted Charlotte, "to mechanise man's soul, and stultify his body. That's what progress does for you, and I who say it, know. I, who was in my way and in my time a pioneer of progress. And sometimes"—behind Charlotte's horn-rimmed glasses gleamed a twinkle—"sometimes I wonder: was it worth the pains we went through to put you, and other glorious young beasts like you, where you are—instead of where you ought to be?"

"And where"—the girl smiled again, a trifle tolerantly—"is that?"

"I'll tell you where." Charlotte leaned forward, forefinger extended to tap the girl's crossed knee. "In your own home, young lady, breeding a race of men to exterminate the congenital invertebrates who pass for such—today."

"Why, Mrs. Mendoza!" An exquisite pair of eyebrows, plucked to a meticulous pencilled line, were raised a good half-inch in protest. "That sounds like heresy to me."

Charlotte chuckled, reaching for her coat. "Heresy be damned! That's good horse sense, that is, which you as a doctor ought to know."

Which she as a doctor, did.

In the general exodus and scrimmage at Victoria they lost sight of each other, and, the formalities at the Customs barrier satisfactorily concluded, Charlotte and her luggage in charge of a friendly porter were deposited in a taxi. There, her dynamic energy exhausted, she relaxed. She felt old, and she *was* old, and she needed very badly a good strong cup of tea.

Frederick was at the door to welcome her. He had received her card from Paris by the midday post. He hoped madam had a good crossing.

"Filthy," Charlotte said.

Standing as stiffly at attention as his lumbago would permit, Frederick intimated that he was sorry to hear that. He did not wish to worry madam with domestic trifles the moment she arrived, but he felt bound to let her know that the young person he had engaged to help him in the kitchen—if madam remembered—

"Well," barked Charlotte, "what?"

"'As left, madam. I was compelled to turn her out neck and crop, so to speak. She went to a dance and came back with"—Frederick coughed behind his hand—"with what she called her boy friend, madam."

"I see," Charlotte's nose wrinkled. "But was that so very reprehensible, Frederick?"

"It's not as I've been accustomed to in this 'ouse, madam."

"There's not much left in this house that you have been accustomed to, Frederick."

"Well, madam, I've seen changes."

"Yes," said Charlotte drily. "And you'll see more before we've done. And leave that luggage alone," she ordered as, creakingly, Frederick stooped to her trunk. "Don't you *dare* go carrying it up. Why didn't you ask the taxi-man to do it?"

"Thank you, madam, I can manage."

"You can't manage. Do you want to have a heart attack? Get one of the tradesmen to help you in the morning. Here, you can carry my dressing-case. That's not heavy. And get me a cup of tea. Strong. Indian."

"Very good, madam."

With a look of obstinate resignation on his face, he, who for fifty years had served in that house under two mistresses, in better and young days as footman, and now as cook general and sole representative of the domestic staff, followed Charlotte upstairs.

After a wash and the much desired cup of tea, she sat by the fire in that room where her great-aunt Sabrina had died. Nothing was altered there; the same curtains and sofa coverings in the selfsame cherry-patterned chintz, worn threadbare now and faded; the same Aubusson carpet, thin to a shadow, but lovely in its faint, lost colour; the same white-panelled walls and the same parquet, polished by Frederick till it shone like glass.

And staring at the fire, her skirt drawn back from her knees, her sharp, pointed face still freckled in its wrinkles, topped by its thatch of rough cropped hair that had turned from flame to snow, Charlotte considered once again the problem of the house. Should she sell it outright or rent it on a lease, or keep it and convert it into service suites and occupy one of them herself, so that here one might stay—and live—and die in comfort? And at home. Yes, that's all very well, but who's going to pay for the converting? Not she, that's sure. It needs capital to convert, and *you* can't raise it, and you can't come down on Prior, either, to lend it. He has enough to do already with Jill and Laurencina on his hands. After all, it doesn't matter where you live—or die if it comes to that. Haven't you lived in two rooms before now in spite of those cabbage roses?

Charlotte smiled and sighed and took her glasses off her nose to blink with suddenly bright eyes at the fire, and put them on again a little crookedly when Frederick came to tell her: "Miss

Jill has telephoned, madam, to say she's on her way up to town and will be staying the night if convenient."

"Is it convenient? And have we anything to give her to eat?" demanded Charlotte. "She won't want a boiled egg, and that's all *I'm* going to have."

"She won't be coming to dinner, madam. She said she was going to a cocktail party, and would get something out."

"Cocktail party!" snorted Charlotte. "Very well. You'd better get her room ready."

And as Frederick withdrew she returned to her contemplation of the fire and this further problem of her sister, which in two months' holiday abroad Charlotte had deliberately shunned. To get away from all unpleasant worries had been her motive. And here she was back again with the same worries as formidable as ever. . . . Jill. And what to do with her? All this gadding about, this equivocal existence, Jill and her succession of intrigues with married men, or men hopelessly ineligible and years younger than herself—Jill and her insomnia, and those sleeping-draughts she would insist on taking, and cocktail parties, and drink, and those hangers-on of hers—what a crowd! Not an ounce of intelligence among them. All degenerates. No stamina, no stability—selfish, shiftless, useless. And Jill, poor child, for want of all she'd missed in life, fell back on such as these for substitute.

The war had played her out. She had never recovered from the loss of that young man she should have married. First Larry. Then Jill's lover, then Page, who left us Laurencina. . . . Well! The war did that and more to millions of others all the world over—and some of them went under as a result of it and some of them stayed it through. Jill was one of those who had gone under. Too highly strung—always was, and always would be. She needed some steady work or interest to occupy her mind. She had given up her art when shortly after the war she had developed that lung trouble, and had been sent to Switzerland to cure. That did her no good, brooding out there on her woes, in company with others similarly threatened. And no sooner was she over *that*, than Edie, poor soul, fell ill. Yes, Charlotte admitted, Jill had a good deal to put up with, one way and another. Circumstances were against her from the first. Edie, for five years a chronic invalid, had been a pitiable handful. Nothing organically wrong, beyond a tendency to diabetes. Just general break-up and nerves, which had resulted finally in a fatal heart attack that brought release to all concerned.

Nerves! How much today was attributed to nerves! And was it, reflected Charlotte, to be wondered at? With all this noise, this restlessness, this overcrowding, and this ceaseless rush.

Modernity.

As Charlotte had told that young doctor in the train—we were bound to crash, sooner or later. Jill was only one more victim of the post-war vortex. Yet why blame the war? Had there not been other wars? The Napoleonic wars had wrought their similar havoc. Did it not seem, reflected Charlotte, that we relived today, a parallel recurrence of conditions that existed a century ago? They of their time passed through the agony of industrial revolution, we of ours have suffered its equivalent in strikes, in conflict and confusion, no less overwhelming than the rebellious years which culminated in the first passing of the Reform Bill of 1832. But while in those earlier times events were spread over generations in the slow growth of development, we of this machine-disordered age speed from crisis to world crisis, seeking in everincreasing velocity a solution to problems that remain insoluble.

And which generation, Charlotte mused, of these last hundred years would score the deepest mark? Would that mighty matriarchal reign under which she had lived more than half her life, and which had bequeathed to this nation a heritage that not even a world war had entirely demolished, survive, when the flood of progress ebbed? Or would the whole breathless panorama of civilised life today, dissolve in a cosmic reaction against the super-flux of energy imposed upon the human brain and human faculties?

Questions such as these crossed and recrossed her mind as she sat in the darkening room, her nostrils twitching at her thoughts, her pale thin fingers folded in her lap, and some moisture from the corners of her eyes shining behind those large round spectacles, that made her look so very like a little old white owl.

An hour slipped away, and still she sat and watched the fire, seeing within its glowing heart a vision of her life, its burned-out flame and its desire; a girl, rebellious, headstrong, escaping glee-fully to love and a vagabond, gay marriage; the struggle between her purpose and her instinct; her adoring and adored young hus-band, with his elegancies and his arrogance, his swaggering buf-foonery, and the cruel sudden loss of him that wrenched from her life all sweetness, and all life's hope and joy. Would he have held her had he lived? Or would she have struggled free to walk alone—and lonely, as these long years had been? God knew how lonely!—for all their arduous achievement.

And she thought of that lonelier, longer life, whose gentle spirit she could almost sense there in that room, as though its essence lingered like the straying dead perfume from the bowl of pot-pourri in the window. She, who had lost her kingdom to regain it, not in turbulence and conflict, but in the fulfilment of her whole life's selflessness.

She and others like her, Charlotte mused, recur throughout the ages. She may come again as the mother of a race unborn, when we are all forgotten. For nothing is lost. Even though the uni-verse explodes, some whirling mass of it creates another sun. God in His mercy has made all things and creatures infinite, so that in life or after life we may receive a second chance. I had my second chance, said Charlotte nodding at the fire. I made good in my own way—if good it is—and if good it may be. My grandfather handed down to me the will to do it. And even though he failed, he aimed high. But did he fail? He and those he followed strove to temper justice with tolerance, to abolish tyranny, and the miseries that result from lack of understanding. He, and those others, lit the torch that has given to humanity some spark of loving-kindness, and yet—we had the war! There seems no sense nor reason in it.

Charlotte sighed and removed her spectacles to rub her eyes, which ached a little. She must remember to see an eye-man and get her glasses changed. She had felt a strain with these of late. I'm breaking up, she thought sardonically. My old brain is too tired to puzzle out the whys and wherefores of all these causes and effects. This, though, I believe. I may be wrong—and she glared fiercely at the fire as if to challenge there an argument—but I believe that all our actions, thoughts, desires, passions, all we live by and die for in this muddle that we call existence, passes on—to live again in some form or other. So it may be that out of suffering and chaos, and the wasted blood of youth, will arise a generation who for pity, and in courage and enlightenment, shall tread the better way.

"But I," said Charlotte, as Frederick came in to ask if she were ready for her supper, "shall *not* be here to see it."

"Beg pardon, madam?" Frederick enquired, startled.

"Nor," she said complacently, "will you."

II

The fact that Jill, who had said she was coming for a night, stayed with Charlotte at Curzon Street ten weeks, was unremarkable. She as often stayed with Charlotte as with me down here at Wroth. Both houses were equally at her disposal. But when at eighteen Laurencina came home from school to fill the place with boys and girls and their young strident voices, and the braying of the wireless, and swimming and tennis parties and dancing in the hall, Jill spent more of her time with Charlotte and less of it with us. She had no place there or anywhere, she said, and how often she had said it! Until one grew a little weary and impatient. . . .

She had her friends, if one can call them such, a curious collection who occasionally drove down to kill time on a Sunday in the summer. The men a spindle-legged and puny lot, it seemed to me, young, too young for her. Women who, like Jill and of her generation, had watched war thunder past them, and been found wanting in the aftermath—they who had also served.

She moved among them, of them but not with them. One sensed that, although outwardly she presented much the same metallic, hard appearance, fashioned to pattern, painted, dyed. She dieted to keep her figure like a boy's. Her age was a continued menace.

"I look young, don't I?" she would say to Laurencina. "I might be your elder sister."

To look young was her obsession. She took ten years off her age and swore us all to secrecy. Laurencina used to tease her. "I can blackmail you for the rest of your life. I'll get scent and gloves and stockings, all for nothing. Give me half your new bottle of Chanel, and I'll not split. But if you don't give it me, I'll tell everybody you're— What is it? Forty something? . . ."

After Edie died she made a half-hearted attempt to return to her painting, and joined an art group down in Sussex for a while; but she soon gave that up. "I'm the oldest student there," she said.

"They're all a lot of kids. And there's too much competition. Everyone's so damned competent these days. You've got to be outstanding to be anything at all. I'm not. I'm only an amateur, and an indifferent one at that."

And so she drifted, lonely and unhappy, in a sea of discontent. She had her various affairs. There was usually some man of the moment with whom she would be frenziedly engrossed. And if in these and all such interludes she found some brief respite from memory, who can blame her? In between these episodes, which of latter years occurred at longer and still longer intervals, she sought entertainment in cocktail parties, bridge, supper at the newest place with any raucous crowd that might invite her—for she could amuse them. She had developed a cynical dry humour and a caustic tongue that had given her the reputation of a wit, so that she was popular and in demand among a certain set. Accepting invitations meant returning them, and entertaining was expensive. Cocktails were expensive too, and cocktails, like cigarettes, became a habit. It was easy to drink when everybody drank, when everyone on all sides pushed a glass into your hand, so that in time and after endless rounds of parties, the craving for that glow which only came with alcohol and brought forget-fulness and freedom from the festering reminder of all that might have been—and which could never be again—became an urge, and solace. So she began to drink alone when failing company to drink with.

That was why she preferred to stay in London. In London one could always ring up 'some of the crowd' to come round in the evening to Curzon Street after Charlotte had gone off to bed. And in order to pay for the drink you and your company con-sumed, and the clothes you had to have, and treatment for the face which was beginning to look the worse for wear, you had, of course, to raise some cash. Most of her mother's jewellery went. But who wanted those comic old-fashioned rings and things when you could buy more amusing ones at Woolworth's? . . .

The life interest received by Edie under our father's will had reverted at her death to the estate—five-sixths to be divided equally between his sons and his sons' issue, and one-sixth to his daughter Jill. No portion to Charlotte, other than her mother's personal effects.

"But," Jill told her sister when, as so often was the case, the subject of her father's will recurred among her many grievances, "that doesn't matter to you. You were amply provided for by old Aunt Sabrina. And what have I? A pittance. Most of it gone west in that hellish slump. What a damned unfair will he made! Everybody says so. To go and leave practically the whole of his money to his sons when he'd already provided amply for them both before Mum died. And then to give them *her* life interest as well! It used to worry her terribly, I can tell you. She was always wondering what would happen to me in the future. Poor darling—if she knew what I'd got coming in now. A hundred a year! A lot of good that does! And Laurencina will get the whole of Larry's share as well as his interest in Kell & Wrotham's when she comes of age. Imagine it! A grand-daughter who was not even born or thought of when he made that will—while I, *his own* daughter, live on my brother's bounty. Dependent on my brother for every damn thing I possess. And supposing he hadn't been decent about it—where should I have been? On the streets, I suppose! Much my father cared. Yes, well, I can't help it. . . . I hope he's listening in from whatever place he's gone to. Your lousy old Victorians didn't care a damn about their daughters. It was always their sons. Why, it wasn't until fifty years ago that women were allowed to own property at all. All your mother's money went to Father, didn't it? Automatically. He must have been rolling. And who's got it now? His son and Laurencina, who's not even *her* grand-daughter. But most of it, I suppose, has gone down the drain in this blasted world depression—"

"We've had a war," Charlotte reminded her, "and we've had to pay for it."

"Oh, for Christ's sake! . . . Can't you forget the war?"

Charlotte looked at her.

"Can you?"

"I try to," returned Jill haggardly, and at that look on Charlotte's face she added in a fury: "It's all very well for you to sit there and pass judgment! I know I'm a failure. I know I'm weak —but you haven't had what I've had to contend with. You'd lived more than half your life when the war came. I was beginning mine. I never had a chance. I was smashed from the outset. You'd been married—"

"And lost him," Charlotte put in quietly.

"Yes, but you'd had him!" cried Jill. "Lived with him, belonged to him, been his wife. I was never my man's wife. I had one night—in his arms—untouched. He would wait, he said till we were married. . . . He never *had* me although he could have. The last night of his leave I wanted to give—all of me. I loved him. He was worth love. Men aren't worth love today. At least, not those I meet. And so—we give them, cheaply, what they ask for, and they don't value it any more than we who give it. There are no values now. We're *all* cheap. Shoddy. Rotten. . . . I used not to be rotten—"

Jill's sullen scarlet mouth loosened, pitifully. Under the thick cosmetic on her eyelashes, slow painful tears welled up, but did not fall. A sob was strangled in a laugh. "You know that thing of Duggie Byng's?

"'I'm slick Sal.
When I was a gal
I was constant and clever and clean;
I was never *de trop,*
I was pure as the snow,
But I drifted and so—you know what I mean!'"

She made an absurd contortion of her features in clever mimicry of the inimitable comedian's.

"Yes, I think," said Charlotte, gently, "I do know what you mean." And she rose from where she sat to lay a hand an instant on Jill's sleek permanent wave. Jill's hair, like all the rest of her, had been tortured into fashion. "I know," repeated Charlotte with lips that slightly quivered, "and once I felt as you felt, and suffered, my dear, as you have suffered; but I fought against it, and made the best of what was left."

Jill raised her head to look into that faded, worn old face; the spirit that peered out from behind those owl-like spectacles challenged her, unflinching.

"And what *was* left?" Jill asked in a choked voice. "What have you accomplished? You've helped to give to women freedom— but what does freedom bring? We're equal—yes! Men and women —we're *all* equal—we've been given equal rights. But what rights have I? Where are my children, and the man to give them me? What men of my age are left in this bloody world who are not already married or annexed—or else—not men at all. Hybrids. Perverts. There's a superfluity of women in England—perhaps not in other countries; I don't know. But in England there are a million or more women who've been left over. And I'm one of them."

Charlotte was silent, one rather trembly finger still stroking Jill's waved hair. Presently, clearing a thickness in her throat:

"Jill. . . . The world," she told her, "is not made for those who are left over, but for those that are to come—the generation for whom your man and all those others died—that they might live. Try to remember that, and carry on, as we've all had to carry on. We can't control fate, but we can fight it."

Jill moved her head impatiently.

"You had something to fight for. You had a cause. What cause have I?"

"There's always a cause to fight, my dear. The cause of life itself. And if you seek, perhaps you'll find."

"I have sought, and I've found nothing," Jill answered harshly. "Life's lousy. I'm lousy. And I'm getting old. I've been cheated of everything: life and hope and everything!"

"You're not the only one," retorted Charlotte, and into those brittle cheeks there flashed a sudden brightness, that gave her something of the look of a young defiant girl. "There may be, as you say, a million more. Here in our family I knew another. You never knew her, but I did. And all my life I've tried to live the better for it. She lost her husband in the Battle of Waterloo, and was a widow at nineteen. Her son, when he was born, was dead. She too lost love and hope, and everything—but she made good her losses and banked her substance in the lives of others. Not her own."

"All right. Don't preach." Jill's tone was bored, and her fawn-dark eyes so carefully made up were veiled. "One presumes that times have changed in the last hundred years or so. We ask more of life today than they did."

"And receive," said Charlotte, nodding, "a very great deal less."

III

Charlotte's house and most of its effects were put up for auction in September. She retained for her own use only so much as she might require to equip the two-roomed service suite that she had rented in a Square north of the Park, once the habitation of London's plutocrats, now the refuge of the Newer Poor.

The sale attracted some attention and was well attended, for much in that house was of value to collectors. Period stuff that had been stored in disused rooms was brought out to fall under the hammer at a price far exceeding Charlotte's calculations. Most of the family portraits had been returned to Wroth, but there still remained a youthful one of the seventh Earl of Pinkerton, in which he is depicted as a singularly ugly boy in a blue satin suit, posed in a dwarfed landscape that makes him appear a giant, and holding the bridle of a very malformed pony slightly smaller than himself.

Jess Pinkerton's bed and a set of Chippendale chairs, a Sheraton bureau, and other period pieces, were bought by a dealer for America. Lowenthal's of Bond Street had the best of what was left. All else of no appeal to modern taste and no marketable asset, was bought in job lots by smaller fry, and sold again—to fill boarding-houses and country pubs, to moulder in fusty secondhand shops, and so end the way of all things that have played their part in life and have grown weary.

On the proceeds of the joint sale of house and furniture, Charlotte bought for herself an annuity, pensioned Frederick, and presented to her sister Jill a cheque.

"Take it and go off and enjoy yourself," she told her. "Get out of London. Go abroad. Go to Italy and see some pictures. I can give you introductions to friends in Florence."

Charlotte knew, she told her, exactly what Jill needed: change of environment, change of air, of scene, of diet; to drink less and eat more, and give up sleeping-draughts. She had found an excellent remedy for insomnia, a simple, harmless remedy, far better than all your dope—prescribed by Robin Marriott, son of Stephen (managing Director of Kell & Wrotham, amalgamated now with Batchelors').

Robin was a doctor, fully qualified at twenty-three and fast following in the wake of his grandfather, at that same hospital where George in his time had carried all before him.

The remedy for sleeplessness recommended by young Robin and handed on to Jill, was—so Charlotte stated—to plug your ears with a special preparation of plastic wax. In this microphonic age, she said, it was necessary to seek repose by such means as would induce it *without* the aid of drugs. To deafen sound, but not to injure your health and your resistance by so doing.

Jill accepted gratefully the cheque, also the ear-plugs, and booked a ticket to Paris via airplane. She had never travelled by air, it would be quite a new experience; and at a cocktail party to which she was invited the day before she left, she told everyone about this new experience, and her holiday abroad.

It was the usual sort of party, given by a woman, widowed in the war, who had been three times married since. She received quite a good income from her respective alimonies and lived in a box of a house in a cul-de-sac off Knightsbridge.

In the ground floor room which might have accommodated comfortably twenty people, a crowd that must have numbered eighty were assembled. Jill saw no sign of her hostess, but many faces that she knew. Faces only, for the bodies that belonged to them were vertically hidden by other bodies that did not. Nobody sat. Several people spoke to Jill, and at the very top of their voices, for in order to be heard above the din they had to shout. All talked the same jargon—in italics—all addressed complete strangers as 'my dear' and discussed with some hilarity the latest suicide—that of a certain young man known to most of them— who had thrown himself under a train in Lancaster Gate tube station. None knew why, but many guessed, amusingly, at reasons. It was all—"most *fright*fully tragic."

"Except that one had always known he would go crackers."

"My *dear!* How *are* you? Haven't seen you for *ages*. Not since Pup's *par*ty. What are you drinking? Mine's *sep*tic." A young man with no chin and hair as light as an albino's, who looked as though he had been filleted, rested a languid, long white hand upon Jill's sleeve. "Are you going to the inquest?" he enquired. "I am. Isn't it *fright*ful? I simply can't be*lieve* it. I was at his *flat* only the night before last. I thought he seemed a bit de*pressed,* but he said it was because his doctor had put him on a diet. . . . Yes, but, my dear, he'd been knocked *off* drink. . . . What *is* this?" He held up his glass that contained an opaque yellow liquid. "Can you *bear* it? Let me get you another. What are you doing with yourself these days?"

"Flying," Jill told him, "to Paris in the morning. I've never been up before. Shall I be sick?"

"My dear! *All* the time in a brown paper bag. *I* was."

He drifted listlessly away, and somebody else gave her another drink.

Two women behind her were discussing body belts. "My dear! Mine's *too* marvellous. Yes, I *know,* but *not* if you wear the *thin*nest little thing underneath. My dear, it *does*n't—you don't *no*tice it. Rubber and milk. . . . But they *are*. . . . Charles'll tell you. Charles, aren't they made of rubber and milk?"

"Aren't what made of rubber and milk?"

". . . most bloody awful show I've ever seen."

"*Was* it? And it had such *mar*vellous notices."

"Yes. You know why?"

"Why?"

". . . And so, my dear, I simply said to him, I suppose you know that's blackmail, and he ran like a *hare*."

". . . What a *cow* the woman is!"

"Yes, but I know for a fact that his doctor had knocked him *off* drink . . ."

"But my *dear!* She has simply *ood*les of money. *She* keeps *him.*"

"Isn't he supposed to be—"

"Oh, yes, *def*initely. But that doesn't trouble *her. She's,* of course . . ."

"I say! Have you heard the latest Mae West?"

Amidst the howls of hyenic laughter that greeted the latest Mae West, somebody turned on the radio.

To Jill's imagination, stimulated by a mixture of several more drinks, the scene presented a curious distortion of perspective; and, as the noise became intensified, so the faces of the company grew featureless and blurred. The air was hot and tainted with the fumes of alcohol. Through a flimsy fog of cigarette smoke, and over and above the tangle of speech and of sound superimposed upon aerial wave-lengths, she thought she could perceive fantastic apish gestures, could hear the chattering of monkeys, loud parrot squawks, a babel of jungle voices, primeval, inarticulate, inhuman.

A man-eating woman in a coat of tiger-skin (or was it leopard?) prowled, teeth bared, glass in hand, and fingernails dipped, apparently in blood, stalking the unwary. A girl in evening dress with the face of a rakish Madonna was being led away, rather the worse for drink, accompanied by a serpentine young man in a white tie and scarcely better case. Both announced to sundry as they passed that they were "going on to Gabriel's to dine."

Of such, thought Jill confusedly, is the kingdom of Heaven. . . . And to no one in particular she said, "My dear! I'm tight."

"Yes, darling. You are."

She felt her elbow squeezed with friendly fingers, and re-focussed her eyes to find a pair that were familiar, smiling through a haze.

"My God," Jill uttered thinly, "Laurencina. What are you doing here?"

"Robin brought me. I'm staying with his people for the night. He knows the person-who's-giving-it's-son. They were up at Cambridge together. He's nice. But his mother— Gee whiz! You have to see her to believe. I say!" Laurencina clapped a hand over her mouth. "Do you think anyone heard me?"

"Shouldn't think so. They can only hear themselves. Can you snatch me a drink from that waiter?"

"No, I can't," Laurencina answered firmly. "You've had enough. Let's find Robin and go."

In that sea of gibbering faces the face of Larry's daughter swam before her, young and clear and kind, with eyes a little anxious and startlingly blue.

"You get more and more like your father," Jill said tearfully, "every time I see you. Is that a new hat?"

"No. Do let's find Robin," urged Laurencina. "It's a lousy party."

She put her arm through her aunt's, who passively submitted. Robin's figure, square and stolid, blocked the doorway. His head topped all those near him by two inches. His gaze, composed and watchful, searched the crowd.

"It's all right," said Laurencina, tugging at his sleeve. "I'm here, and so is Jill. We want to go."

"Good. Hullo, Jill!" Robin's smile had in it something that was warming, something of the flavour of old wine. At sight of it a hardness came into Jill's throat; her eyes began to water.

"This damnable stuff," she said, "that I put on my eyelashes smarts like hell."

Both regarded her with tolerant concern.

"Don't rub it," advised Laurencina. "It'll smudge. Here— let me."

She took her handkerchief and carefully removed from each eye a smear of black.

"That's better. . . . Robin, you go and get the car. We can drop Jill at her place."

Although confused, Jill was conscious of a faint surprise that they should be interested in her, or in anything she said or wished to do. They cared—or seemed to. She had observed before that these, and others of their generation, seemed to be as interested in the affairs of those around them as in their own. They listened when you spoke, and they thought before they gave you back an answer. They were abrupt, of course, and impolite, but they were decent, kind. That was the strangeness of it: they were kind.

"I suppose," said Laurencina, when Robin had gone to get the car, "that we ought to say good-bye."

"I've lost my lipstick." Jill was fumbling in her bag. She took out one of those flap-jacks and stared in its powdery mirror at her face. "Christ! What a— Lend me your lipstick."

"Haven't got one. And you don't need any more. Come on," said Laurencina.

In the very narrow hall where the company had overflowed, and the exit was congested, they were greeted by their hostess, a diminutive platinum blonde, with an old face and the body of a starved child.

She screamed at them: "But *sure*ly you're not *going!* Don't go. The crowd from the something-or-other are coming on when they've done their stuff. *Every*body's staying on for bacon and eggs—unless they're all paralytic by that time— You *mustn't* go. Stay on."

So Jill stayed on.

Those two stayed with her, until most of the guests having arrived at their various stages of inactivity, Jill was persuaded, reluctantly, to leave. Robin and Laurencina drove her back to the one-room flatlet she had rented in Queen's Gate for the week before her departure.

Both helped her undress, and put her to bed, and Robin gave her a dose which he said would prevent too bad a hangover in the morning.

It was Laurencina's suggestion that they should fetch her next day and drive her down in Robin's car to see her off at Croydon.

Weather conditions had been reported favourable; a keen wind, fitful sun and a blue sky, lightly clouded. They arrived at the airdrome with twenty minutes to spare. Jill was in high spirits, elated at the prospect of her holiday. Robin's dose, she said, had worked wonders. She had no head—to speak of—considering that poisonous mixture of drinks. She could stand a fair amount but to go and end up with Hungarian fizz—she'd never been bowled over so completely in her life—and what a pity they could not both hop over to Paris with her! She was going to have her face done at a perfectly *mar*vellous place she'd been told of in the Rue Royale. *Hell*ishly expensive, but it was worth it to be restored—as it were—from the sere. She would tell everyone she was twenty-eight. Did Laurencina think she could get away with it?

Laurencina judicially considered.

"You might—if you cut out drink and didn't make up so violently. Make-up's awfully hardening."

"Ah! But I *am* hard!" cried Jill, gaily. "What's the use of being soft? You've got to be hard these days. It's the only way to live —unless you die."

"If I thought that," Laurencina said, "then I'd damn well die and be done with it."

Jill smiled on one side of her mouth.

"Yes, but the snag is—unfortunately—that we can't die to order. Unless of course we happen to be suicidal. So far I have avoided that very obvious solution!"

"Don't talk bilge," briefly returned Laurencina.

"What else," enquired Jill with that same one-sided smile, "is there to talk?"

Robin frowned.

"It's all a phase," he said. "We're going through a phase—a process of transition. It always happens so after any great world crisis. If you read history you'll see. I'm not so sure," he added, ruminatively, "that it's a bad thing if we're forced to reconstruct. You get to a certain high-water mark in evolution, and then everything overflows, and floods you out. It's the same old story of the survival of the fittest. You have to sink or swim. We've sunk—and now we're swimming."

"And I'm flying," Jill hastily interposed, "in five minutes; so I'd better get along, or I shall miss the plane. They tell me you're not allowed on the ground, so I'll say good-bye here. It's lovely of you to have come with me—"

She kissed them both, and with lips not very steady, and eyes that were suddenly dimmed:

"Hurry up and get married, you two," she told them. "Don't wait. I—had to."

From the flat roof of the station they watched her pass under the covered gangway to take her seat.

There it rested, giant of the air, symbol of man's power, the throb of its four tremendous engines sounding the pulse and heartbeat of an apocalyptic age, man's challenge to the Cosmos.

The pigmy in the cockpit bent to the controls; the gleaming grey wings quivered like the wings of a live thing, the murmur of engines rose to a thunderous roar—

"They're taking off!" Laurencina cried excitedly. "Look! There's Jill."

She sat in the first seat behind the cockpit, her face pressed against the window between pale-coloured curtains. They saw her lips move, and her hand raised to them in a gesture that seemed to linger.

Slowly, with infinite grace the monster glided across the green, gathered speed and lifted, a man's breadth from the earth, mounted higher, ever higher . . . a silver bird in the clouds, hidden.

"Shall we?" Robin turned to look at Laurencina. She was still staring at the empty sky.

"Shall we what?"

"Do as she said—not wait."

"Well"—Laurencina's eyes, a little watery, came back to him —"I don't see that there's anything to wait for, now you're qualified."

"Quite." Robin lit two cigarettes at once and handed one to her. "That is—if Dad can be induced to stump up the needful for a practice."

"He'll jolly well have to." Laurencina slid one finger in his pocket. "I vote we feed here," she said, "I'm hungry."

They fed there, at the Aerodrome Hotel and afterwards drove back to town to pass the remainder of the afternoon very pleasantly at a cinema.

They were still too engrossed with themselves, and as an afterthought, the picture they had seen, to observe when they came out into the dusk, the announcement on the placards of the evening papers:

BRITISH AIR LINER DISASTER

FOURTEEN KILLED

EPILOGUE

(1936)

It is nearly three years since I received my sentence, and I am still here. According to young Robin I am likely to remain so, with a lengthy if indefinite reprieve. That other fellow I consulted, for all his good repute and long experience, has been mistaken. The threatened trouble has dispersed since Robin took me over as a case of kill or cure. If his success with me is criterion of his ability, then it looks as though his future may be as important as was George Marriott's past.

Charlotte lives with me, now, at Wroth, and those two live in London. That marriage seems to be successful. She has 'produced' —a son, which felicitous event is taken, to quote Laurencina, 'in her stride.' She has other things to do, she says, than run a nursery. She and Robin run a clinic down in Poplar. She manages the administrative side of it, and he gives all the hours he can spare from his rapidly increasing practice, in voluntary service to those afflicted with that same disease from which I have escaped, and in which he ultimately intends to specialise.

There have been other changes here at Wroth since I first began this story of its women.

The fourth of them is gone.

She, with her thirteen fellow passengers crashed to her death in that appalling air disaster of October, 1934. We may wonder if for her it was less a tragedy than a release. For those others, who died with her—victims of super-progress—who can say? It is not

497

for us to question the laws of accident—or destiny. One thing we
know, is certain: that the greatest of mortal man's achievements
on this plane never can, and never will, conquer the unconquerable.

But the joys and all the sorrows in the lives of lesser branches of
this vast 'family,' so called by him who has so recently passed from
us, are submerged in the grief of a nation-wide bereavement.

George the Beloved. . . .

So, throughout his Kingdom, to the uttermost ends of his Empire, runs the deep-hearted testimony of his people.

We are glad to remember, even while today we mourn him,
that less than a year ago we gave him token in that multi-
tudinous outburst of loyalty and gratitude for his twenty-five
years' faithful service. We are glad to feel he knew; and he took
to him what we rendered, not as his Royal right, but with a simple wonderment and a humility, that none of us who saw it and
who say with pride we served him, can forget.

As King we honoured him; even more as man we loved him,
but it is as the courageous ruler who shared with us years of
suffering such as no Sovereign in British history has been called
upon to face, that his memory will live again when history is
made.

GOD SAVE THE KING